ANTON REISER

BY

CARL PHILIPP MORITZ

The Hyperion Library of World Literature

ANTON REISER

A Psychological Novel

By

CARL PHILIPP MORITZ

Translated by

P. E. MATHESON

The World's Classics

HYPERION PRESS, INC.

Westport, Connecticut

Published in 1926 by Oxford University Press, London
Hyperion reprint edition 1978
Library of Congress Catalog Number 76-48443
ISBN 0-88355-582-4 (cloth ed.)
Printed in the United States of America

Library of Congress Cataloging in Publication Data
Moritz, Karl Philipp, 1757-1793.
Anton Reiser : a psychological novel.
(The Hyperion library of world literature)
Reprint of th 1926 ed. published by Oxford University Press, London, which was issued as no. 299 of The World's classics.
Includes index.
I. Title. II. Series.
PZ3.M8262An12 [PT2435.M3] 833'.6 76-48443
ISBN 0-88355-582-4

PREFACE

WHEN I was editing the reprint of Moritz's *Travels in England in 1782* (Milford, 1924), I became acquainted with Moritz's autobiography, *Anton Reiser*, which is here offered to English readers for the first time. It is remarkable not only as a psychological study, but as a document for the history of German thought and life. All who care for the education of children and young people will find in it much that is interesting and suggestive, and for the historian of literature and manners it illuminates the life of Germany at a most exciting period. It is hoped that *Anton Reiser* in its English form will give as much pleasure to the reader as it has done to the translator.

I have to thank Professor Fiedler for his great kindness in reading through my translation, which owes much to his corrections and suggestions: and Mr. Lawrence Powell for calling my attention to various books and articles on Moritz and his generation.

P. E. MATHESON.

CONTENTS

INTRODUCTION

Anton Reiser is a German classic. Its author, Carl Philipp Moritz, is known to English readers by his *Travels of a German in England in 1782*, published in 1783, and in an English translation in 1795, two years after the author's death. It has lately been republished at this Press.

Anton Reiser, in form a novel, is actually the story of the first twenty years of Moritz's own life. The Fourth Part ends, as will be seen, with the final disappointment of his hopes of a career on the stage. It was continued in a Fifth Part by his friend Carl Friedrich Klischnig (*Erinnerungen aus den zehn letzten Lebensjahren meines Freundes Anton Reiser*, Berlin, 1794), whose record has been corrected and supplemented by later research. His later life, 1776–93, may be briefly given :

After various wanderings he joined the University of Wittenberg as a student of theology, and stayed there two years. Then after trying to become a military chaplain he received a post in the *Gymnasium zum grauen Kloster* in Berlin, where he became Senior Assistant Master (Konrektor). The stimulus of the growing city, now under the influence of the *Aufklärung*, did much to encourage and confirm his powers, and he soon began to write, at first on language and psychology ; his friendship with Friedrich Gedike (1754–1803), the great humanist and an authority on Paedagogik, to whom the letters from England are addressed, illustrate his educational bent at this time: he shared fully in the humanistic movement then transforming the schools of Germany, and his *Anton Reiser* shows his intense interest in the growth of a child's mind.

The visit to England was an interlude in his Berlin life. He taught in Berlin at the *Graue Kloster* and at the *Köllnische Gymnasium* till 1786, when his eager exploring spirit found new expression in a visit to Italy, which was a turning-point in his life, for in Rome he lived in close intimacy with Goethe.[1] Goethe had help from Moritz in the prosody of his *Iphigenie*, and Moritz gained much from Goethe for his books on mythology (*Götterlehre*,[2] 1791) and aesthetics. The friendship was renewed at Weimar in 1788, when Moritz made the acquaintance of Duke Karl August, through whom he was appointed Professor der Theorie der schönen Künste und Alterthumskunde in Berlin, where he gave stimulating lectures. In spite of his friendship with Goethe and other good friends, not least the Jewish philosopher Moses Mendelssohn, he still had times of intense depression. He had had an unhappy love affair in Berlin before his Italian travel; in 1792 he married

[1] See Hume-Brown's *Life of Goethe*, p. 329, and J. Zeitler, *Goethe-Handbuch*, ii. 624 foll., a valuable appreciation of Moritz. See also Goethe's *Italienische Reise*, 1 Dec. 1786, 8 Dec. 1786, 6 Jan. 1787, 10 Jan. 1787, 18 Feb. 1787 (Weimar-Ausgabe, Band 30, pp. 227, 233, 244, 247, 274).

[2] Translated into English as *Mythological Fictions of the Greeks and Romans*, by C. F. W. Jaeger, New York, 1830.

a young girl, but the marriage was not a happy one, and lasted barely a year. He died after a short illness in 1793, to the great grief of his friends, who loved him well, and felt that he had not reached the full height of his powers. The list of his published works (more than fifty) shows the variety of his tastes and his facility in writing. All who write of him seem to regard *Anton Reiser* as his most original work, but his writings on aesthetics and language and prosody had their influence on his generation. Moritz seems never to have been happy for long : a poor physique and an inveterate habit of self-study made him liable to fits of deep melancholy,[1] which appears abundantly in the pages of *Anton Reiser*. But we cannot do him justice without reading the story of his English travels, which represent him in a happy mood, when he had recovered his balance after the storms and privations of his early life and was enjoying the sense of self-respect in a recognized position.

Moritz wrote in an age of ' Confessions ' and of sentiment : [2] he was influenced by Rousseau and Sterne, and still more by Goethe's *Sorrows of Werther*, which appeared in 1774 when he was just passing into manhood. If he had not the genius of these writers his book has the charm of a simple

[1] This summary is taken from my Introduction to Moritz's *Travels*, pp. xvi–xviii, Milford, 1924.

[2] For a characterization of the German writers of this age, as illustrating the period of self-analysis and *Weltschmerz*, see *From Goethe to Byron*, by W. Rose, M.A., Ph.D., Routledge, 1924. A chapter, pp. 91–107, is given to Moritz. See also pp. 289–301 of Erich Schmidt's *Richardson, Rousseau und Goethe*, Jena, 1875.

style, of an ingenuous and enthusiastic character, eager to be friends with the world of Nature and of men. Sensitive and impressionable, with that mixture of shyness and conceit which is common in self-conscious people, he added to the difficulties of circumstance many troubles of his own creation. His vivid imagination was a source both of joy and of acute distress. But although he tends to become sentimental, he is aware of his own weakness and has humour enough to criticize himself; above all he has the gift for making friends with people of all degrees, and is a true lover of his kind. An English reader may well think that he takes himself too seriously, but even those who cannot away with his depression and self-analysis will find something attractive in the courage and persistence with which he fought his battles for education and self-expression.[1] A quotation from a recent work which traces with insight and discrimination the history of autobiography in Germany will show the esteem in which *Anton Reiser* is held by Moritz's countrymen. 'This autobiography as soon as it appeared won attention by its wealth of psychological and social content, as well as by its crisp and luminous style, at once clear, flexible, and direct. Goethe, Schiller, Schopenhauer, and Hebbel, all paid high tribute to its merits, and within the limits which it set for itself it is certainly a permanent masterpiece of its kind.'[2] As these

[1] For an analysis of *Anton Reiser* and of Moritz's character, see Hugo Eybisch, *Anton Reiser. Untersuchungen zur Lebensgeschichte von K. Ph. Moritz und zur Kritik seiner Autobiographie*, Leipzig, 1909.

[2] *Die deutsche Selbstbiographie* von Theodor Klaiber, Stuttgart, B. Metzlersche Buchhandlung, 1921, p. 106.

words imply, the book has a wider interest than that of a personal revelation, the history of a soul. It gives a vivid picture of German life and society in the latter half of the eighteenth century. School and University, town life and government, the Stage and the Church, Catholic and Protestant, and the movements of Pietism, the roadside inn with its motley company, the formalities of a fortified city and the ceremonial of public occasions are all brought vividly before us. The literary and intellectual movements of the time come home to us in the frequent references to German and English writers, and in the record of the plays which were in possession of the stage.[1] One of the most striking features of the book is Moritz's keen interest in education. He writes with insight, sympathy, and good sense on the psychology of children, and his remarks on this subject deserve careful study. His own experiences as a boy and his life as a schoolmaster in Berlin give special value to his opinions.

Moritz's writings cover a wide field: many of them, as Herr Klaiber suggests, may have been written as 'pot-boilers' to supplement a scanty salary, but his book on German prosody and that on the mythology of the Greeks and Romans, which was the product of his visit to Rome, are said to be valuable and stimulating works. The reader of his *Travels in England* will be glad to find

[1] For the relations of Germany to England at this time, cf. Robert Elsässer, *Über die politischen Bildungsreisen der Deutschen nach England,* Heidelberg, 1917. Also: J. A. Kelly, *England and the Englishman in German Literature of the Eighteenth Century,* New York, Columbia University Press, 1921.

that he passed through his early troubles and was not spoilt by them. We find him there a man who had learnt to take the world as he found it, an eager traveller, an admirer of England and English liberty, and a passionate lover of Nature. His autobiography shows us his debt to Young and Milton, and above all Shakespeare. If he had lived longer he would have found a fresh delight in the poetry of Wordsworth, but Moritz had been dead five years when *Lyrical Ballads* appeared. His eager spirit spent itself too quickly; the hardships of his early life, his laborious work as a writer, the heavy drafts made by his emotional experience on a highly sensitive temperament, possibly too the chill he caught in Peak Cavern on his English tour, combined to weaken a constitution which was never robust, and he died at an age when many men of letters are beginning their career. Whilst I was writing this Introduction my attention was called to a touching illustration of Moritz's character: some words spoken by him in 1787 in the Protestant Cemetery at Rome at the grave of a young painter, August Kirsch. They exactly describe his own nature.[1] 'His heart was made for friendship, but was of such tender stuff that the chances of life, which would have left thousands indifferent, moved him to the depths.' There, beside the Pyramid of Caius Cestius, where a genius who shared Moritz's delight in natural beauty and in the classical world was to find rest some thirty years later, we may take leave of Carl

[1] *Jahrbuch der Sammlung-Kippenberg*, Band I, Leipzig 1921, pp. 255–67. Karl Philipp Moritz's *Leichenrede au den Maler August Kirsch.*

Philipp Moritz. 'I have lost in Moritz a good comrade', said Goethe, and Goethe's praise was not lightly given.

A word may be added on the abrupt close of *Anton Reiser*. As the story is a fragment of real life, this need not surprise us. With the final collapse of Moritz's theatrical ambitions his wanderings for the time ended, and he settled down to the routine of University life, which carried him on into the career of minister, schoolmaster, man of letters, and professor. When he wrote *Anton Reiser*, and indeed to the end of his life, he remained a 'traveller' in the material and spiritual world, but his twenty years of apprenticeship to life were over. He had learnt his lesson, and in this book he gave it to the world.

BIBLIOGRAPHICAL NOTE

PART I of *Anton Reiser* appeared in 1785, Parts II and III in 1786, and Part IV in 1790. There have been at least three reprints in the last forty years: that of L. Geiger in vol. xxiii of the *Deutsche Literatur-Denkmale*, Berlin, 1886; that of Dr. Hans Henning, with introduction and notes, Leipzig: Reclam, 1906; and that of Dr. Friedr. B. Hardt, München und Leipzig: Georg Müller, 1911, with an introduction and valuable list of Moritz's writings.

The biographical correctness of *Anton Reiser* was established in vol. v of *Euphorion*, by Oskar Ulrich who also supplied the names left blank in the original. These names have been inserted as in Dr. Hardt's edition, not because they have any special significance for the English reader, but names are more human than the blanks which discretion once dictated. Otherwise the book is translated as first published, save for the omission of one short paragraph of no importance and the addition in a few places of the names of the authors of works mentioned in the text. The brief prefaces to each part, omitted in the Reclam reprint, cannot fitly be spared, and are here translated.

I

THIS psychological romance might equally well be called a biography, as the observations in it are for the most part taken from real life. Any one who is acquainted with human affairs, and knows that what at first seemed petty and insignificant may become highly important as life goes on, will not be offended at the apparent triviality of many circumstances here related. Further, in a book, which is mainly to describe the inner history of man, no great variety of characters will be expected. The object is not to distract the imaginative faculty but to concentrate it, and to enable the soul to see clearer into its own being. The task is not an easy one, nor is it bound always to succeed : but from the pedagogic point of view it can never be lost pains to direct men's attention more to man himself and make him feel the importance of his own individual existence.

1785.

PART I

The Quietists of Pyrmont

In Pyrmont, a place famous for its mineral spring, there was living on his own estate in 1756 a nobleman who was head of a sect in Germany, known under the name of Quietists or Separatists, whose tenets were mainly drawn from the writings of Madame Guyon, a well-known enthusiast, who lived in France at the time of Fénelon, her intimate friend.

Herr v. Fleischbein, for that was his name, lived as completely secluded from all the other inhabitants of the place, and from their religious manners and customs as his house was cut off from them by a high wall which surrounded it on every side. This house formed a little republic of its own, governed by a constitution quite different from that of the countryside around it. The whole household down to the meanest servants consisted wholly of persons who made or professed to make it their sole endeavour 'to return again into their nothingness', to use Madame Guyon's phrase, to kill all passions and eradicate all individuality.

Every one was obliged to assemble once a day in a large room of the house for a sort of religious service, which had been instituted by Herr v. Fleischbein, and which consisted in all sitting round a table for half an hour with closed eyes and their heads resting on the table, waiting to hear the voice of God or the inner word. If any one heard it he made it known to the rest.

Herr v. Fleischbein also regulated the reading of his household and any one of his servants, male or female, who had a quarter of an hour of leisure was to be seen sitting and reading with an air of reflection one of Madame Guyon's works on silent prayer or the like. Everything down to the most trifling household occupations wore a serious, severe, and solemn air. In every face was to be read, so it seemed, mortification and self-denial, and in every act the effort to pass out of self and enter into nothingness.

Herr v. Fleischbein after the death of his first wife had not married again but lived with his sister Frau von P. in this retirement, in order to devote himself entirely and without interruption to the great task of spreading the doctrines of Madame Guyon. A steward called H. and a housekeeper and her daughter formed the intermediate grade in the household, and below them came the humbler servants. The household was closely united and all had unbounded respect for Herr v. Fleischbein, who really led a blameless life, though the inhabitants of the place busied themselves with the most mischievous stories about him.

Every night he got up thrice at fixed hours to pray, and he spent most of the day-time translating from the French the works of Madame Guyon, which fill many volumes; he then had them printed at his own expense and distributed them gratis to his dependants. The doctrines contained in these writings are largely concerned with what I have already mentioned: the complete mortification of all so-called self-hood or self-love, and a completely disinterested love towards God with which not an atom of self-love may mingle, if it is to remain pure ; from this arises finally a state of perfect and blessed tranquillity, which is the goal of all these efforts. As Madame Guyon devoted almost all her life to writing books, they are so surprisingly numerous that even Martin Luther can hardly have written more : among others there is a mystic interpretation of the whole Bible in some twenty volumes. This Madame Guyon had to suffer much persecution, and as her principles were considered dangerous she was put in the Bastille, where she died after ten years' imprisonment. When her head was dissected after her death, her brain was found to be almost dried up. She is still regarded by her followers as a saint of the first order, and almost worshipped as divine, and her sayings are put on the same level with those of the Bible ; for it is assumed that by her complete mortification of self she was so completely united with God that all her thoughts were necessarily divine.

Herr v. Fleischbein had become acquainted with Madame Guyon's writings on his travels in France, and the dry metaphysical extravagance which prevails in them had such a strong attraction for his habit of mind, that he devoted himself to them with the same enthusiasm with which he would probably have devoted himself in other circumstances to the loftiest stoicism, with which the doctrines of Madame Guyon, with their complete mortification of all desires, often have a striking similarity. He was accordingly revered by his followers as a saint, and they really believed that at the first glance he could see into the innermost soul of a man. Pilgrimages were made to his house from all sides, and among those who visited the house at least once a year was Anton's father. Brought up without proper education he married his first wife very early, and always led rather a wild and wandering life, during which he felt religious emotions from time to time, but paid little attention to them. Suddenly on the death of his first wife he withdrew into himself, became reflective, and, as they say, quite a changed man, and during a stay at Pyrmont became acquainted first with the steward of Herr v. Fleischbein and then through him with Herr v. Fleischbein himself. He gave him Madame Guyon's books to read one after the other, he was drawn to them, and soon became a professed follower of Herr v. Fleischbein. Notwithstanding, he took it into his head to marry again, and he made acquaintance with Anton's mother, who soon consented to marry him, which she would never have done had she foreseen the hell of misery which she was to find in the married state. She promised herself more love and regard from her husband than she had enjoyed before with her relations, but how terribly did she find herself deceived! While Madame Guyon's doctrine of complete mortification and suppression of all, even the gentle and tender passions, harmonized with the hard and insensible nature of her husband, she could never reconcile herself to these ideas, against which her heart revolted.

This was the germ of all the subsequent discord in their marriage. Her husband began to despise her religious opinions, because she would not grasp the high mysteries taught by Madame Guyon. This contempt was extended afterwards to her other opinions, and the more she felt this the more their affection as man and wife was bound to decrease, and their mutual discontent with one another to grow daily greater. Anton's mother was well read in the Bible and had a pretty clear idea of its religious system : for instance, she could talk in a very edifying way on the doctrine that faith without works is dead. She read her Bible at all hours with intense pleasure, but as soon as her husband tried to read the writings of Madame Guyon to her, she felt a sort of anxiety, probably due to the idea that she might be diverted from the true faith. So she sought to escape by whatever means she could. A further reason was that she attributed the cold and unamiable behaviour of her husband in great measure to the Guyon doctrine, which she began to curse more and more in her heart, and to curse aloud when the discord of their marriage broke out openly. Thus the domestic peace and tranquillity and welfare of a family were disturbed for years by these unhappy books, which probably neither of them could understand.

Such were the circumstances in which Anton was born, and it can be said of him with truth, that he was oppressed from his cradle. The first tones which his ear heard and his first glimmering intelligence understood were mutual curses and execrations of the indissoluble marriage tie. Though he had father and mother yet he was forsaken by both in his earliest boyhood, because he did not know which to turn to, on which to depend, for both hated one another, and yet both were equally near to him. In his earliest boyhood he never enjoyed the caresses of affectionate parents, nor the reward of their smile after some little effort. When he entered his parents' house he entered a house of discontent, anger, tears, and complaints. These first impressions were never obliterated from his mind, and they made it a place where gloomy thoughts collected, which no philosophy enabled him to expel.

As his father was on service during the Seven Years' War his mother went with him for two years to a little village. Here he had comparative freedom, and some compensation for the miseries of his childhood. The impressions of the first meadows which he saw, of the cornfield which stretched up a gentle slope crowned with green underwood, of the blue mountains and the individual shrubs and trees which cast their shadows on the green grass at its foot, and spread closer and closer as you climbed—these impressions still mingle with his pleasantest thoughts and form as it were the foundation of all the illusory pictures which his fancy paints.

But how soon these two happy years fled! Peace came, and Anton's mother went with him to the town to join her husband. The effect of the long separation was a short-lived illusion of married harmony, but the deceptive calm was soon followed by a storm which was in fearful contrast. Anton's heart melted in distress, when he had to put one of his parents in the wrong, and yet it often seemed to him as if his father, whom he merely feared; was more in the right than his mother, whom he loved. Thus his young spirit wavered to and fro between love and hate, between fear of his parents and trust in them.

When he was not yet eight years old, his mother bore a second son, on whom were concentrated the few remains of a father's and a mother's love, so that he now felt almost completely neglected, and when he was spoken of it was in a tone of depreciation and contempt which pierced his heart. How was it that the ardent longing could arise in his heart for affectionate treatment to which he had never been used, and of which therefore he could hardly form a conception ? Finally indeed this feeling was pretty well deadened ; he almost felt as if it was the natural thing to be continually rebuked, and a friendly look, which he once received, seemed something quite strange which could not be reconciled with his other impressions. He felt most intensely the need of friendship with his kind, and often when he saw a boy of his own age, his whole soul went out to him, and he would have given anything to make friends with him ; but the depressing feeling of the contempt that he suffered from his parents, and the shame he felt because of his wretched, torn, and dirty clothes kept him from venturing to address a more fortunate boy. Thus he went about almost always sad and solitary, because most boys of the neighbourhood were more neatly and respectably dressed and in better clothes and would not associate with him ; and he in his turn would not associate with those who were not because of their loose character, and also perhaps from a certain pride. So he had no one to make a companion of, no playmate of his childhood, no friend among big or little.

But in his eighth year his father began to teach him to read, and for this purpose bought him two small books, one of which contained instruction in spelling and the other a discourse against spelling. In the former Anton had to spell a good many hard biblical names—Nebuchadnezzar, Abednego, &c., which conveyed to him no shadow of an impression: this therefore was rather a slow process. But as soon as he became aware that intelligible ideas were actually expressed by the combination of letters, his eagerness to learn to read became stronger every day. After his father had given him barely a few hours instruction, to the surprise of all his relations he learnt in a few weeks for himself. To this day he remembers with intense pleasure the lively delight he then enjoyed when, with much spelling, he made out with difficulty a few lines which meant something for him. But he could not understand how it was possible that other people should read as quickly as they spoke: he despaired at that time of ever being able to achieve it. All the greater was his surprise and delight when he could do this too after a few weeks. Moreover, his success seemed to bring him some attention from his parents, still more from his relations: this he did not fail to notice, but it never became the true reason which spurred him on to diligence.

His appetite for reading was insatiable. Luckily in his spelling-book, besides verses from the Bible there were stories of good children, which he read through a hundred times, though they were not very attractive. One was the story of a six-year-old boy who at the time of persecution would not abjure Christianity, but preferred horrible torture and death with his mother as a martyr for his religion ; the other of a wicked lad, who was converted in his twentieth year and died soon after.

Then came the turn of the other little book, containing the discourse against spelling, and he read to his great surprise that it was harmful and even soul-destructive to teach children to read by spelling. In this book he also found a direction to teachers how to teach children reading, and a treatise on the production of the several sounds by the vocal organs ; dry as this seemed, he read it through from beginning to end with the greatest persistence for want of anything better.

Through reading a new world was now opened up for him once for all, in the enjoyment of which he could compensate himself in some degree for all that was unpleasant in his actual world. When nothing but noise and quarrelling and domestic discord prevailed around him or when he looked in vain for a playmate, he hurried off to his book. Thus he was driven quite early from the natural world of children into the unnatural world of imagination, where his spirit was put out of tune for a thousand joys of life which others can enjoy with a full heart.

In his eighth year he got a kind of wasting illness. He was quite given up and constantly heard himself spoken of as one regarded as dead. This he thought laughable, or rather death, as he pictured it to himself then, seemed something laughable rather than serious. His aunt, who seemed to have more affection for him than his parents, took him to a physician, and a cure of a few months restored him. He had hardly been well for a few weeks when, while walking with his parents in the fields—a pleasure all the greater for its rarity—he began to feel a pain in his left foot. This was his first walk after his recovery and was to be his last for a long time. On the third day the swelling and the inflammation in the foot had become so dangerous that they wished to amputate next day. Anton's mother sat and cried and his father gave him a halfpenny. These were the first signs of compassion he remembered his parents showing him, and they produced all the stronger impression on him from their rarity.

On the day before that fixed for the amputation a compassionate shoemaker came to Anton's mother and brought her an ointment by the use of which the swelling and inflammation were reduced in a few hours, so no amputation took place, but the trouble nevertheless lasted four years before it could be cured, during which our Anton again, often suffering inexpressible pain, was cut off from all the joys of childhood. This hurt sometimes kept him indoors for three months at a time, now healing and again breaking out afresh. Often he was obliged to whimper and moan the whole night long, and endure the most horrible pains almost every day from being bandaged. This naturally removed him still farther from the world and from commerce with his kind, and tied him still closer to reading and books. Most frequently he read while rocking his younger brother's cradle, and if he had no book then he felt as though he missed a friend: for the book had to be friend and comforter and everything to him.

In his ninth year he read all the narrative part of the Bible from beginning to end, and when one of the leading characters—Moses, Samuel, or Daniel—died, he would mourn over them for a whole day, and felt as though a friend had died, so dear to him always were the characters who had done much in the world and made themselves a name. Joab was his hero, and he was pained whenever he had to think ill of him. In particular the traits of generosity in David's story, when he spared his worst enemy though he had him in his power, moved him to tears.

Then the *Life of the Early Saints* fell into his hands, which his father prized very highly, quoting these saints as authorities on every occasion. Thus his speeches on conduct commonly began: 'Madame Guyon remarks,' or 'St. Makarius or St. Antony says'. The saints, however absurd and full of adventure their story might be, were for Anton the patterns most worthy of imitation, and for a long time he knew no higher wish than to grow like his great namesake St. Antony, and like him forsake father and mother and fly into a desert, which he hoped to find not far from the gate: and indeed he once began a journey thither, going more than a hundred paces' distance from his parents' dwelling, and perhaps would have gone farther had not the pains in his foot compelled him to go back again. At times too he actually began to prick himself with needles and torture himself in other ways, in order to grow like the saints in some degree, though he had plenty of pains besides.

While he was reading thus he had a little book given him, the proper title of which he does not remember, but which dealt with piety in the young and gave directions how to grow in piety from the sixth to the fourteenth year. The sections in this book were entitled, 'for children of six years', 'for children of seven years', and so on. Anton read the section for children of nine years, and found that there was still time to become religious, but that he was three years behind. This gave a shock to his whole being and he made a fine resolve to be converted, such as grown-up people can rarely make. From this hour he most carefully obeyed all that the book contained on prayer, obedience, patience, order, &c., and treated almost every step too quickly taken as a sin. How far I shall get, he thought, in five years if I persevere! For progress in piety was made an object of ambition in the little book, like the pleasure of being promoted at school from one class to another.

If, as was natural, he sometimes forgot himself, and jumped or ran about when he felt the pain in his foot relieved, he felt the most violent twinges of conscience and thought he had fallen several steps back again.

This little book long exercised a strong influence over his actions and thoughts: for he tried at once to practise what he read. Thus he read the evening and morning blessing for every day in the week, because the Catechism said one must read them; and he did not forget to cross himself and to say Amen! as the Catechism commanded. Otherwise he did not see much piety though he constantly heard talk of it, and his mother blessed him every evening and never forgot to make the sign of the cross over him before he went to sleep.

Herr v. Fleischbein had among other things translated the spiritual songs of Madame Guyon into German, and Anton's father, who was a bit of a musician, set tunes to them, most of which went to a quick cheerful time. If it ever happened that he came home again after a long separation, his wife let herself be persuaded to sing some of these songs to the accompaniment of his zither. This generally happened soon after the first joy of meeting, and these hours were perhaps the happiest in their married life. Anton was then most cheerful, and joined as well as he could in these songs, which were a sign of the rare event of harmony and agreement between his parents. His father, thinking him old enough, let him read these songs and made him learn some of them by heart. Indeed these hymns, in spite of their stiff translation, had such a power to move the heart, such incomparable tenderness of expression, such light and shade, and so much that was irresistibly attractive for a sensitive nature that the impression that they made on Anton's feelings has remained indelible. Often in lonely hours, when he thought himself forsaken by all the world, he comforted himself by one of these hymns of the blessed escape from self and the sweet annihilation before the source of existence. Thus, even then, his childish thoughts often bestowed on him a kind of heavenly tranquillity.

One evening his parents had been bidden to a little family festival by the landlord of the house where they lived. Anton had to look on from the window and see the neighbours' children, finely dressed, coming in, while he had to stay behind alone in the room, because his parents were ashamed of his shabby clothes. Evening came on and he began to be hungry, and his parents had not left him a morsel of bread. While he sat upstairs in his loneliness and tears, the sound of the joyous tumult floated upwards. Utterly forsaken, he felt at first a kind of bitter self-contempt, but suddenly it changed to an inexpressible feeling of sadness, for he chanced to open the songs of Madame Guyon and found one which seemed exactly to suit his condition. Such a sense of nothingness as he felt at this moment must, according to Madame Guyon's poem, be felt in order to lose oneself, like a drop in the ocean, in the abyss of eternal love. But, as his hunger began now to be irresistible, the consolations of Madame Guyon could help him no longer, and he ventured to go downstairs where his parents were feasting in a large company, opened the door a little, and begged his mother for the key of the larder and for leave to take a little bread as he was very hungry. This roused first the laughter and then the compassion of the company, not without some feeling against his parents. He was brought to the table and treated to the best dishes, which gave him quite a different kind of enjoyment from the poems of Madame Guyon. But that melancholy tearful joy still had its attraction for him, and he gave himself up to it by reading the poems of Madame Guyon whenever a desire was disappointed and something sad was impending, when for instance he knew beforehand that his foot was to be bandaged and the wound rubbed with caustic.

The second book which his father gave him to read with the poems of Madame Guyon was a book of directions for silent prayer by the same writer. The book showed how it was possible to arrive by degrees at the point of communing with God in the true sense of the word, and of hearing His voice, the true voice within, clearly in the heart. The process was, first to get free so far as possible from the senses and occupy oneself with self and one's own thoughts, or learn to meditate; but this must cease and one must forget oneself before one was capable of hearing God's voice within one.

This injunction Anton obeyed with the greatest zeal, because he was really eager to hear within him such a wonder as the voice of God. He therefore sat for half an hour at a time with closed eyes, to abstract himself from the sensual world. His father too did the same, to the great distress of his mother; but she paid no heed to Anton, because she thought him incapable of doing it for any serious purpose. Anton got so far that he thought himself pretty well withdrawn from sense and began really to converse with God, and presently on a footing of confidence. The whole day long, in his lonely walks, his work and his play, he talked with God, always with a kind of love and trust, but still as one speaks to one of his own kind, without any circumstance; and then he always felt as if God gave him this or that answer.

It happened indeed sometimes that a disappointment about some amusement or desire made him discontented. Then he would say: 'What! not grant me this trifle!' or 'You might have let this happen, if it had been at all possible!' and Anton did not scruple at times to be a little angry in his own way with God; for though he found nothing about this in Madame Guyon's writings, he thought that it was part of his familiar converse.

All these changes went on in him from his ninth to his tenth year. During this time his father took him, on account of his aching foot, to the waters of Pyrmont. What a joy it was to him to think of making the personal acquaintance of Herr v. Fleischbein, of whom his father had constantly spoken with such reverence as of a superhuman being, and how glad he was to be able to give an account there of his progress in inward godliness; his imagination painted for him a sort of temple, in which he too would be consecrated as a priest and would return as such, to the surprise of all who knew him.

So he took his first journey with his father, during which his father was rather kinder to him and devoted himself more to him than at home. Anton here saw nature in indescribable beauty. The mountains around in the distance and near at hand and the lovely valleys enchanted his spirit and melted it to tenderness, which partly sprang from expectation of the great things which were to happen to him here. His first walk with his father was to the house of Herr v. Fleischbein where his father first spoke to the steward Herr H., embraced and kissed him, and had a most friendly welcome from him.

In spite of the severe pain which Anton suffered in his foot from the journey he was beside himself with joy at entering the house of Herr v. Fleischbein. Anton remained during this day in the room of Herr H., with whom he was in the future to sup every evening. For the rest, not nearly so much notice was taken of him in the house as he had expected. He continued his exercises in silent prayer with great diligence, but they did not fail at times to take a very childish turn. Behind the house where his father lodged in Pyrmont was a great orchard ; here he happened to find a wheelbarrow and amused himself by wheeling it about the orchard. But to justify this, as he began to count it a sin, he imagined a whimsical excuse. He had read a good deal in Madame Guyon's writings and elsewhere of the Child Jesus, of whom it was said that he was everywhere, and that it is possible to hold converse with him continually and in all places. He imagined a boy somewhat smaller than himself, and as he conversed so familiarly already with God himself, why should he not do so even more with this son of his ? He trusted that he would not refuse to play with him and therefore would not object if he wished to wheel him about on the wheelbarrow. He prized it as a great piece of good fortune, to be able to wheel about so great a person and to give him pleasure in this way, and as this person was a creature of his own imagination he could do with him what he chose, and so made him find pleasure in riding for a longer or shorter time and even sometimes said, in all reverence, if he was tired of wheeling : 'I should be glad to give you a longer ride, but I cannot do it now'. Finally he regarded it as a sort of worship and no longer held it a sin to busy himself half a day with the wheelbarrow.

But now, with the consent of Herr v. Fleischbein he got hold of a book which carried him again into a new and quite different world. This was the *Acerra Philologica*. In this he read the story of Troy, of Ulysses, of Circe, of Tartarus and Elysium, and was soon familiar with all the heathen gods and goddesses. Soon afterwards, also with the consent of Herr v. Fleischbein, he was given *Telemachus* to read, perhaps because the author, Fénelon, was a familiar friend of Madame Guyon.

The *Acerra Philologica* had been an excellent preparation for reading *Telemachus*, as it had made him pretty familiar with mythology and had given him an interest in most of the heroes whom he found again in *Telemachus*. He read these books several times, one after the other, with the greatest eagerness and genuine delight, especially *Telemachus*, in which for the first time he tasted the charm of a fine artistic narrative. The passage in *Telemachus* which roused his liveliest feeling was the moving address of old Mentor to the young Telemachus, when the latter in the island of Cyprus was about to exchange virtue for vice, and his faithful Mentor, whom he had long given up for lost, suddenly reappeared, his sorrowful gaze moving him to his inmost being. This tale indeed had now more attraction for him than the Bible story and all that he had hitherto read in the *Life of the Saints* or in the writings of Madame Guyon, and as he had never been told that these were true and the others untrue, he was inclined to believe the stories of the heathen gods with all that they contained.

At the same time he could not reject what he

found in the Bible, especially as this had given him his earliest impressions. The only thing he could do then was to try to combine the different systems in his mind as well as he could, and in this way to fuse the Bible with *Telemachus*, the *Life of the Saints* with the *Acerra Philologica* and the heathen world with the Christian. The first person of the Trinity and Jupiter, Calypso and Madame Guyon, Heaven and Elysium, Hell and Tartarus, Pluto and the Devil, formed the most extraordinary combination of ideas that ever existed in the brain of man. This made such a strong impression on him that long afterwards he retained a certain reverence for the heathen deities. From the house where Anton's father lodged to the Springs and the avenue near it was a fairly long walk : nevertheless Anton dragged himself there with his painful foot and his book under his arm and sat on a bench in the avenue, and as he read gradually forgot his pain and soon found himself no longer on the bench at Pyrmont, but on some island with high castles and towers or in the midst of the wild turmoil of war. With a kind of melancholy pleasure he read how heroes fell : it pained him, but still it seemed to him they must fall.

This too had a great influence on his games as a child. A field full of rank nettles or thistles was to him so many enemies' heads, among which he many a time raged furiously, cutting down one after another with his stick. When he walked in the meadow he drew an imaginary division and made two armies of yellow or white flowers march against each other. He named the tallest after his heroes, and sometimes named one after himself.

Then he personated a sort of blind fate, and with closed eyes cut them down wherever his stick fell. Then, when he opened his eyes again, he saw the fearful destruction; here lay one hero and there another, stretched on the ground, and often with a peculiar feeling, half pleasant and half sad, he saw himself among the fallen. Then for a time he mourned for his heroes and left the fearsome battle-field. At home, not far from his parents' house, was a churchyard, in which he ruled with iron sceptre over a whole generation of flowers and plants, and let no day pass without holding a sort of review of them. When he returned home from Pyrmont he cut out paper figures of all the heroes of *Telemachus*, painted them from the engravings with helmet and breastplate, and set them up for some days in battle array, till at last he decided their fate and raged among them with cruel strokes of his knife, cut open one hero's helmet and another's skull, and saw nothing but death and destruction around him.

Even his games with cherry-stones and plum-stones all ended in death and destruction. These too must be controlled by a blind fate, as he made two sorts march against each other, and then with closed eyes made his iron hammer fall on them, to strike where it would. When he killed flies with the fly-flap he did it with a kind of solemnity, sounding the knell for each with a piece of brass which he held in his hand. It gave him the greatest pleasure to set fire to a little town he built of paper houses, and then to gaze in solemn and serious sadness on the ashes that were left.

Indeed when once, in the town where his

parents lived, a house really was on fire in the night, amid all the fright he felt a kind of secret wish that the fire might not be put out quickly. This wish was anything but mere malicious joy; it arose from a dim presentiment of great changes, migrations and revolutions, in which everything takes a new form and in which previous uniformity would come to an end. Even the thought of his own destruction was not only agreeable to him, but even caused him a kind of cheerful feeling, when in the evening, before he fell asleep, he often vividly imagined the dissolution and disintegration of his body.

Anton's three months stay at Pyrmont was in many ways of great advantage to him, for he was almost always left to himself, and had the good fortune once more for this short time to be away from his parents, as his mother stayed at home and his father had other business in Pyrmont and concerned himself little about him, though he behaved much more kindly to him here, when he saw him from time to time. Besides, there was lodging in the same house with Anton's father an Englishman, who spoke German well, and associated with Anton more than any one had done before, began to teach him English by conversation and delighted in his progress. He talked to him, went walks with him, and at last could hardly be out of his company. This was the first friend Anton had in the world, and he was sad at saying farewell to him. The Englishman when he went away pressed into his hand a silver medal, which he was to keep as a memento until he came to England, when his house would be open to him.

Fifteen years later Anton did come to England, and brought his medal with him, but the first friend of his boyhood was dead.

On one occasion Anton was called on to deny this Englishman to a stranger, who wished to see him, and to say that he was not at home: but nothing would induce him to do so, because he would not tell a lie. This was considered much to his credit, but it was just one of those cases when he wanted to seem better than he really was, for on other occasions he had made little of telling a convenient lie. His real inward conflicts, when he often sacrificed his most innocent wishes because he imagined them displeasing to God, passed unnoticed.

Meantime, the affection shown to him at Pyrmont was very encouraging and did a little to relieve his depression. Sympathy was shown him because of his foot, he had a friendly welcome in the house of von Fleischbein, who kissed him on the forehead when he met him in the street. He was not used to such greetings, and they moved him greatly. An open brow, a clear eye, and a cheerful spirit once more came back to him.

Now too he began to turn to poetry, and put what he saw and heard into verse. He had two step-brothers, who were both learning to be shoemakers at Pyrmont under a master who was also a disciple of Herr v. Fleischbein. He took his leave of them and also of the household of Herr v. Fleischbein in very affecting verses which he composed and learnt by heart.

It is true that he returned home from Pyrmont not quite in the state he had expected, but still he had in this short time become quite a different person, and his world of ideas was greatly enriched. But at home the renewed quarrels of his parents, to which the arrival of his two step-brothers probably contributed, and the interminable scolding and storming of his mother soon effaced the good impressions he had received at Pyrmont, and especially in the house of von Fleischbein, and once more he found himself in the same hateful position, which made his spirit gloomy and misanthropic.

When Anton's two step-brothers soon went away on their travels as journeymen, domestic peace was for a time restored and Anton's father sometimes read aloud to him out of *Telemachus* instead of Madame Guyon's writings, or told him some episode of ancient or modern history, with which he was really pretty familiar, for besides his music, in which he was accomplished on the practical side, he made it his special study to read instructive books, until finally the writings of Madame Guyon drove out everything else.

His talk therefore was a sort of bookish language and Anton can still remember clearly how in his seventh and eighth year he often listened very attentively to his father's talk and was surprised that he did not understand a syllable of the words ending in *-heit*, *-keit*, and *-ung*, though he could understand anything else that was said.

Anton's father too, out of his house, was a very sociable man and could converse agreeably with all sorts of people on all sorts of subjects. Perhaps the marriage would have been a happier one if his mother had not had the misfortune to regard herself often as an injured person and to enjoy the feeling, even when she was not really injured, in order to have a reason for being vexed and afflicted, and to cherish a sort of self-pity, which gave her great pleasure. Alas! she seems to have bequeathed this infirmity to her son, who now often has to fight against it in vain. Even as a child, when every one received something, and his share was assigned him without his being told that it was his, he preferred to let it alone, though he knew that it was meant for him, merely to feel the pleasure of being injured and to be able to say 'every one else has something, and I am to get nothing!' As he felt imaginary wrongs so keenly, he was bound to feel real ones even more. And certainly no one has a stronger sense of injustice than children, and to no one can injustice be done more easily: a fact which all teachers ought to take to heart every day and every hour.

Often Anton would reflect for hours, nicely weighing argument against argument, whether a punishment inflicted by his father was just or unjust.

In his eleventh year for the first time he enjoyed the inexpressible pleasure of forbidden reading. His father was a sworn enemy of all romances, and threatened to burn any book of the kind if he found it in his house. In spite of this Anton through his aunt got hold of *The Beautiful Banise*, *The Arabian Nights*, and *The Island of Felsenburg* which he read secretly and by stealth though with his mother's knowledge, in his bedroom, and devoured them with insatiable eagerness.

These were some of the happiest hours of his life. Whenever his mother came in, she merely warned him that his father might come, but did not forbid him to read the books in which she had once found enchantment herself.

The story of *The Island of Felsenburg* made a very great impression on Anton ; for a long time his thoughts were directed to nothing less than the idea of playing a great part in the world, and of drawing round him first a smaller and then a larger circle of persons of whom he should be the centre. This idea expanded till his extravagant imagination made him finally draw animals, plants, and inanimate things, in a word, everything around him, into the sphere of his existence, till he grew dizzy at the thought.

Thus it was that his imagination created most of the sorrows and joys of his life. How often on a dull day, when to his vexation and disgust he was shut up indoors, a chance sunbeam shining through the window, awakened pictures of paradise, Elysium or the island of Calypso, which enchanted him for hours ! But from his second or third year he could also remember the torments of hell which the stories of his mother and his aunt conjured up for him, sleeping or waking. Now he would see himself in a dream surrounded by friends, who suddenly looked at him with faces horribly transformed ; or again he climbed a high and gloomy staircase and a horrible figure barred his retreat, or the Devil himself appeared on the wall in the shape of a spotted cock or a black curtain. Even in the early days, when his mother lived with him in the village, every old woman inspired him with fear and horror, so continually did he hear of witches and magic ; and when the wind blew through the cottage with a peculiar moan, his mother called it, in a figure, ‘ the handless man ’, without thinking any more of it. But she would not have done so, had she known how many a fearsome hour and how many a sleepless night this ‘ handless man ’ was to give her son for years afterwards.

The last four weeks before Christmas in particular were a Purgatory for Anton, to escape which he would gladly have given up his Christmas tree covered with candles and hung with silver-covered apples and nuts. Not a day passed when some strange noise of bells or a scraping at the door or a hollow voice would not make itself heard, betokening St. Nicholas the harbinger of Christ, whom Anton seriously took for a spirit or a superhuman being; and so all through this season not a night passed when he did not awake from sleep with terror and the sweat of fear on his brow. This lasted till his eighth year, when his belief in the reality of St. Nicholas and of the Christ-child of Christmas began to waver.

His mother too gave him a childish fear of thunder-storms. His only refuge then was to clasp his hands as firmly as he could and not to unclasp them till the storm was past. This too, besides crossing himself, was his refuge and as it were his firm support, whenever he slept alone, because he thought that then neither devil nor ghost could touch him.

His mother had a peculiar expression of any one wanting to run away from a ghost, that ‘ his heels grow long ’; he felt this in the literal sense whenever he thought he saw something like a ghost in the dark. She used also to say of a dying man that 'death sits on his tongue'; this too Anton took in the literal sense and when his aunt's husband died he stood near the bed and watched his mouth very carefully to discover death, perhaps like a little black figure, on his tongue.

It was about his fifth year that he got his first idea of anything beyond his childish field of vision, when his mother was living with him in the village, and was sitting alone in the room with an old woman, their neighbour, himself and his step-brothers. The conversation fell on Anton's little sister who had died in her second year a little before, and for whom his mother remained inconsolable for over a year.

'Where can Julia be now, I wonder', she said after a long pause and then was silent. Anton looked at the window, where there was not a glimmer of light in the dismal night, and felt for the first time the wonderful limitation which made his existence at the earlier time almost as different from that of the present as being from not being. 'Where can Julia be now?' he thought, after his mother, and through his mind flashed the contrast of near and far, confined and open, present and future. No pen can describe his feeling at the moment: it came back again a thousand times, but never with the first vividness.

What a blessing is this limitation which we are always using every effort to escape! It is like a little island of happiness in a stormy sea; happy is he who can sleep securely in its bosom. No danger wakes him, no storms alarm him. But woe to him who is driven by unhappy curiosity to venture beyond those dim mountain ranges which limit his horizon for his good! He is driven to and fro by unrest and doubt on a wild and stormy sea, seeks unknown regions in the shadowy distance and his little island where he lived so securely, has lost all its charms for him.

One of Anton's happiest memories in his earliest years is of his mother wrapping him in her cloak and carrying him through storm and rain. In the little village the world looked beautiful, but beyond the blue mountains, towards which his eager gaze was always turned, the troubles which were to embitter the years of his childhood were already awaiting him.

As I have gone back in my story to recapture Anton's first feelings and ideas of the world, I must here mention two of his earliest memories, which concern his sense of wrong. He has a clear memory that in his second year, before he lived in the village with his mother, he ran from his own house to the one opposite and back again, and ran in the way of a well-dressed man, whom he pushed violently, because he wished to persuade himself and others that he was wronged, although he had an inward feeling that he himself was the offender.

This memory is remarkable because of its rarity and clearness; it is also genuine, because the incident in itself is too trifling for any one to have told him of it afterwards.

The second memory is from his fourth year, when his mother scolded him for some real naughtiness. As he was just undressing, it happened that one of his garments fell with a noise on the chair; his mother thought he had thrown it down in a temper, and punished him severely. This was the first wrong which he felt deeply and never forgot; from this time he regarded even his mother as unjust, and at every fresh punishment this incident came back to him.

I have already mentioned how he thought of death in his childhood. This lasted till his tenth year, when a neighbour visited his parents and told them how her cousin, who was a miner, had fallen down from a ladder into the pit and had crushed his head. Anton listened attentively and the crushed head made him imagine a complete cessation of thought and feeling and a kind of annihilation and blankness of his being, which filled him with fear and horror as often as he fixed his thoughts on it again. From that time onward he had a great fear of death, which caused him many a sad hour.

I must say a few words more of the earliest ideas which he formed of God and the world in about his tenth year. Whenever the sky was cloudy and the horizon narrowed, he had a sort of conscious feeling that the whole world was enclosed by a ceiling like that of the room in which he lived and if his thoughts travelled beyond this vaulted ceiling, this world seemed to him much too small, and he imagined that it must be enclosed in another world and so on *ad infinitum.* He had the same experience with his idea of God, when he wished to think of Him as the Supreme Being. One dull evening he was sitting alone at the door of his house and, thinking of this, he gazed up to the sky again and again and then looked at the earth and noticed how black and dark it was against the dull sky. Beyond the sky he imagined God, but any God, even the highest, whom his thoughts created, seemed to him too small, and he felt that He must have a greater God above Him, against whom He entirely disappeared, and so *ad infinitum.* Yet he had never read or heard anything on this subject.

What was most singular was, that his continual reflection and immersion in his own thoughts led him into an egoism which might almost have made him lose his reason. For as his dreams were in general very lively and almost seemed to border on reality, he began to fancy that he was dreaming in broad daylight, and that the people about him, with all that he saw, might be creatures of his imagination. This was an appalling thought, which made him afraid of himself whenever it occurred to him, and led him actually to try to distract his mind and set himself free from these thoughts.

After these digressions we will continue the story of Anton's life in order of time. We left him at eleven years old reading *The Beautiful Banise* and *The Island of Felsenburg.* He was now given to read Fénelon's *Conversations of the Dead* with his *Stories,* and his writing-master began to set him to write letters and compositions of his own. This was a delight which he had never felt before. He now began to make use of his reading and to introduce now and again imitations of what he had read, which won him the approval and regard of his teacher. His father played in a concert where Ramler's *Death of Jesus* was performed, and brought home a printed copy of the words. This attracted Anton so much and was so far beyond any poetry that he had hitherto read that he re-read it so often and with such delight that he almost knew it by heart. This one accidental piece of reading, so often repeated, gave his taste in poetry a form and fixity which he never lost again, just as *Telemachus* had done in prose, for in *The Beautiful Banise* and *The Island of Felsenburg*, notwithstanding the pleasure he found in them, he felt the contrast and lack of dignity in the style.

In poetical prose Carl v. Moser's *Daniel in the Lions' Den* came into his hands; this he read through several times and his father used at times to read passages from it.[1]

The season for the waters came on again and Anton's father decided to take him again to Pyrmont, but this time Anton was not to enjoy it as much as in the previous year, for his mother went with him.

By incessantly forbidding him little things and

[1] The landlady of the house, a shoemaker's wife, liked Anton to read to her out of it, because it sounded to her so 'moral': which meant to her, so elevated; and of a certain preacher, who always preached in a very bombastic tone, she said she liked him because his sermons were so 'moral'—another proof how careful we ought to be in books and talk with the people to refrain from such expressions as are not current among the people. In England even the most uneducated man knows what 'moral' means. The shoemaker's wife was in other respects a very intelligent woman, and her son, who carried on the business, a clear-headed fellow, but early led astray by excessive sensibility into religious extravagances, from which he afterwards escaped through his own force of mind and intelligent reflection. This shoemaker was always a very significant person in Anton's subsequent life.

continually scolding and punishing him out of season she gave him a distaste for all the nobler sensations he had had the year before; his feeling for praise and approval was so crushed by this that, almost against his nature, he found a sort of pleasure in associating with the dirtiest street-arabs and making common cause with them, merely because he despaired of ever winning again in Pyrmont the love and respect he had lost through his mother, who constantly talked not only to his father, whenever he came home, but also to perfect strangers, of nothing but the badness of his behaviour. The consequence was that his behaviour really began to be bad and his heart seemed to grow worse. His visits to the house of Herr v. Fleischbein were also rarer, and the time of his stay at Pyrmont went by very unpleasantly and sadly, so that he often thought with melancholy of the delights of the previous year, though this time he had less pain to bear in his foot, which began to heal again when the damaged bone was taken out.

Soon after his parents' return to Hanover Anton entered his twelfth year, which was to bring many changes: for in this year he was to be parted from his parents. But he had one great pleasure first.

On the persuasion of some acquaintances Anton's father sent him to a private Latin lesson in the Grammar School of the town, that he might in any event at least learn his declensions. To the very great regret of his mother and his relations his father absolutely refused to send him to the other lessons in the school, where religious instruction was the main subject.

Thus one of Anton's most earnest desires, to be allowed to go to a Grammar School, was partially fulfilled. On his first entrance the thick walls, dark vaulted rooms, century-old benches and worm-eaten desks, seemed to him like holy things which filled his soul with reverence. The Senior Assistant Master, a cheery little fellow, in spite of some want of gravity in his face, inspired him with profound respect by reason of his black coat and bob-wig. He treated his pupils on a fairly friendly footing: usually indeed he addressed every one in the second person (*Ihr*), but the four top boys, whom he called ' veterans ' in joke, he addressed with the complimentary third person (*Er*). Though he was very strict, Anton never had a rebuke, still less a blow from him; he therefore thought he found more justice in school than at home.

He now had to begin to learn Donatus by heart, but his accentuation was peculiar, as soon appeared when he declined ' mensa ' by heart at his second lesson. When he said ' singulariter ' and ' pluraliter ', he laid the accent on the penultimate, because in learning it by heart, the similarity of the last syllable with that of Amorites and Jebusites made him imagine that there were two people, the Singularites who said ' mensa ' and the Pluralites who said ' mensae '.

Such misunderstandings may often happen, when the teacher is content with the first words of his pupil, without penetrating into his mind.[1]

[1] At that time too Anton pronounced Latin ' ae ' like German ' ä ', a pronunciation adopted by various people recently, but for which he was laughed at then by his schoolmates and even by the Vice-Principal.

Now came learning by heart. *Amo, amem, amas, ames* was soon recited in rhythm, and within six weeks he had his *oportet* at his fingers' end, at the same time he learnt new words by heart every day, and as he never missed one he moved up the classes quickly and got nearer and nearer to the 'veterans'. How happy he was! What a splendid career Anton had before him; for the first time in his life he saw a path to fame, which he had so long wished for in vain, open before him.

At home too he spent this short time pleasantly, having to read to his parents every morning, while they drank coffee, from the *Imitation of Christ* of Thomas à Kempis, which he enjoyed doing. Then they talked about it and he was allowed sometimes to put in his word. Besides he was lucky enough not to be much at home, as he still attended the lessons of his old writing-master, whom, in spite of the many cuffs he had had from him, he loved so sincerely that he would have sacrificed everything for him. For he often had friendly and instructive talks with Anton and his schoolfellows, and as in general he seemed rather severe, this kind and friendly attitude had all the more effect, and won their hearts.

So for a few weeks Anton was doubly happy; but his happiness was soon destroyed. Lest his good fortune should make him too proud, severe humiliations were prepared for him. Though he was now educated in company with children of good standing his mother made him perform the duties of the meanest servant. He had to carry water, fetch butter and cheese from the shops, go to market like a woman with a basket on his arm, to buy eatables. I need not say how bitterly he felt it when one of his more fortunate schoolfellows passed him on such occasions with a malicious smile. But he gladly put up with this in view of the good fortune of going to a Latin school, where after four months he had risen so high, that he was able now to share the lesson of the top bench, the so-called four veterans.

It was about this time that his father took him to see a very remarkable man in Hanover, of whom he had often told him before: he was called Tischer and was a hundred and five years old. He had studied theology, and finally had been tutor to the children of a rich merchant in Hanover, in whose house he still lived, and was maintained by the present occupant, an old pupil of his, and himself now an old man. He had been deaf since his fiftieth year and any one who wanted to talk to him, had to have pen and ink in hand, and write down his thoughts, which the man answered orally in a clear and audible voice. Even in his hundred and fifth year he could read his small-type Greek Testament without spectacles and he spoke very correctly and coherently, though sometimes more slowly or loudly than necessary, because he could not hear himself. In the house he was known simply as 'the old man'. His food and what else was needed for his comfort was brought him, but otherwise no one troubled much about him.

One evening then, as Anton was sitting at his Donatus, his father took him by the hand and said: 'Come and I will take you to a man, in whom you will see united St. Antony, St. Paul, and the patriarch Abraham.' And on the way his father prepared him for what he was going to see. They entered the house. Anton's heart beat fast. They went across a long yard and climbed a little winding-stair which led them into a long dark passage, where they mounted a second stair and then went down a few steps. The passages seemed like a labyrinth. At length a little view opened up on the left, where some light from another window came through some window-panes. It was winter-time and the door was hung with cloth outside. Anton's father opened it. It was twilight; the room was large and spacious, furnished with dark hangings and in the middle at a little table strewn with books sat the old man in an arm-chair.

He came bare-headed to meet them. Age had not bowed him; he was a tall man and his appearance large and majestic. Snow-white locks adorned his temples, and an ineffable kindliness beamed from his eyes. They sat down. Anton's father wrote something for him. 'Let us pray,' began the old man after a pause, 'and include our little friend!' Thereupon he bared his head and kneeled down, with Anton's father on his right and Anton on his left.

Anton found that he was all and more than all his father had described. He imagined himself kneeling by one of the Apostles of Christ, and his heart was uplifted in great devotion when the old man stretched out his hands and began to pray with deep fervour, and continued his prayer in tones now loud now soft. His words were as the words of one, who in all his thoughts and wishes has passed beyond the grave, and who by some chance alone is left to wait a little longer than he expected on this side. All his thoughts as it were came from the other side, and as he prayed his eye and his brow seemed to light up.

They rose from prayer, and Anton in his heart now regarded the old man almost as a higher being, more than human. And when he came home in the evening, he would not join some of his school-fellows in coasting about on a little sledge, because it seemed to be profane and to spoil the sanctity of the day. His father often sent him to this old man, and he spent with him nearly all the time that he was not in school. There he made use of his library, which consisted largely of mystical books and read many of them from beginning to end. He also often gave the old man an account of his progress in Latin and of the exercises he wrote for his writing-master.

Thus Anton spent two months of extraordinary happiness. Then like a thunderclap almost at one and the same time he heard the dreadful announcement that his Latin lessons were to end with the month, and that he was to be sent to another writing-school. Tears and entreaties were of no avail, the decision was taken. Anton had a fortnight's notice that he was to leave the Latin school and his grief became greater the higher he rose in class. So to make his leaving less painful he adopted a means which one would hardly have expected in a boy of his age. Instead of trying to get higher in class, he did the opposite and either deliberately abstained from saying what he knew or used some other device to go down a place every day. The Assistant Master and his schoolfellows could not understand it and often expressed their surprise to him. Anton alone knew the reason and carried his trouble with him to school and home again. Every place he chose to go down in class cost him a thousand tears, shed secretly at home: but bitter as the medicine was that he prescribed for himself it had its effect. He had arranged so that he was bound to be bottom on the last day; but this was more than he could bear. He begged to be allowed to sit in his place again that day, and next day he would gladly take the lowest place. Every one pitied him and gave way. The next day the month was up and he did not return. How much this voluntary sacrifice cost him may be inferred from the eager efforts he had made to win his way up.

Often when the Assistant Master looked out of the window in his dressing-gown, as he went past, he thought—'If only you could open your heart to him!' but the distance between him and his master seemed far too great. Soon afterwards too, in spite of all his entreaties, he was taken away from his beloved writing-master. He had overlooked some carelessness in Anton's writing and sum-book, which roused the anger of his father. Anton most earnestly took all the blame and made vows and promises to do all in his power, but it was no good, he had to leave his faithful old master, and at the month's end begin to learn writing in the grammar school.

These two blows together were too much for Anton. He tried indeed to cling to his last support and got his former schoolfellows to tell him of each lesson set them, so that he might learn it at home and go forward with them ; but when this became impossible his virtue and goodness gave way and for a long time, from a sort of discontent and despair, he became what may be called ‘ bad ’. He got himself flogged in school out of sheer mischief, and bore the strokes with steady defiance without giving any sign, and this gave him a pleasant feeling which lingered in his memory. He fought and scuffled with street-arabs, played truant from school lessons, and tormented a dog that his parents had whenever he could. In church, where hitherto he had been a model of reverence, he chattered to his companions through the whole service.

He often felt that he was going wrong, he remembered with sadness his earlier efforts to be good, but whenever he was on the point of reforming, a sort of self-contempt and a rankling discontent overpowered his better resolutions and made him try once again to forget himself in all kinds of wild distractions.

The thought that his dearest hopes and wishes were disappointed, and that the career of honour on which he had started was for ever closed to him, rankled unceasingly without his being clearly conscious of it and drove him into all sorts of extravagance. He became a hypocrite to God and to himself and others. He read the morning and evening prayer regularly as before, but without any feeling. When he came to the old man, his former frankness was changed to dissimulation ; his pious air and the words he wrote were mere hypocrisy, in which he pretended a thirst and longing for

God, in order to keep the respect of the old man. Sometimes even he would laugh to himself as the old man read what he had written.

Then he began to deceive his father also. His father remarked one day that he had been quite a different boy three years ago when he refused to tell a lie and say ‘ not at home ’ for the Englishman.

As Anton was conscious that he had done this more from a sort of affectation than from any horror of lying, he now reflected : if this is all that is wanted to make me beloved, it will not cost me much. Thus in a short time by sheer hypocrisy which he tried to conceal from himself as hypocrisy, he succeeded so far that his father corresponded about him with Herr v. Fleischbein, and gave him news of the state of Anton's soul, in order to ask his advice.

Meanwhile, when Anton saw that the matter was taken so seriously, he became more serious too and sometimes resolved to give up his bad way of life, because he could no longer hide his hypocrisy from himself. But then he thought of the years he had neglected since the time of his previous genuine conversion, and what progress he might have made had he not done so. This made him extremely dissatisfied and sad. Besides he read a book at the old man's in which the whole process of salvation by means of repentance, faith, and religious life was described in detail with all its signs and symptoms.

Repentance must include tears, contrition, sorrow, and dissatisfaction. All this he felt. Faith involved an unwonted cheerfulness and confidence of the soul in God ; this too he could compass.

Thirdly the religious life must follow: but this was not so easy.

Anton thought that if once the will to live a good and religious life was there, one was bound to live it continuously and at every moment, in every look and movement, and even in every thought; one must never for a moment forget the will to be good. But naturally he often forgot it: his face was not always serious, nor his bearing decorous, and his thoughts wandered to earthly and secular things. And so he thought that all was over, that he had achieved practically nothing and must begin all over again. He often felt this several times an hour, and his condition was one of great distress and anxiety. He gave himself up again, but always uneasily and with a beating heart, to his former distractions. Then once more he began the work of his conversion over again and so wavered to and fro and nowhere found rest or content; meantime the most innocent pleasures of his youth were embittered and yet he never made much progress.

This continual wavering is an image of his father's way of life throughout; in his fiftieth year it was no better, yet he always hoped to find the right way that he had so long striven after in vain.

Anton had at first begun pretty well: but when he found he was no longer to learn Latin, his piety suffered a great shock. It was only a timorous constrained thing and could make no real progress.

Then he read somewhere, how useless and dangerous self-improvement was, and how one should be purely passive and let God's grace work in one.

And so he often prayed very sincerely: 'Lord, convert me and I am converted!' but all was in vain.

His father went to Pyrmont again this summer and Anton wrote to him how little progress he made in self-improvement, and that perhaps he had made a mistake, because God's grace must be everything. His mother regarded the whole letter as a piece of hypocrisy, as perhaps it partly was, and wrote below it in her own hand: 'Anton behaves like all godless boys'. Yet, as he was conscious of a real inward struggle, he was bound to feel deeply wounded at being put in the same class with all godless boys.

This depressed him so much that for a long time he wilfully lived an irregular life with other wild boys, and was confirmed in it by the scolding and the sermons, so called, of his mother; for these depressed him still more, so that at last he regarded himself as no better than a common street-boy and was all the more ready to keep company with them again.

This lasted until his father returned from Pyrmont, when all at once quite a new outlook was opened up for him. Early in the year his mother bore twins, one of whom only survived, and his godfather was a hatter in Brunswick called Lohenstein. He was one of the disciples of Herr v. Fleischbein, and through this Anton's father had known him for several years. As Anton was to be apprenticed to a master some day (for his two step-brothers had learnt their trade, and both were discontented with the handicraft they had been forced into by their father) and as the hatter Lohenstein wanted to have a lad, who at first would only lend a hand, his father thought this a splendid opening: that Anton like his two step-brothers, should be put early under the care of such a good man, who was also a disciple of Herr v. Fleischbein and should be admonished by him in the path of true religion and piety. This may have been a plan of some standing and was perhaps the reason why Anton's father had taken him from the Latin school.

Now ever since he had learnt Latin, Anton had got the idea of study firmly into his head; for he had a boundless respect for any one who had studied and wore a black coat, so that he regarded such people as almost superhuman beings. What more natural than that he should strive for what seemed to him the most desirable thing in the world?[1]

It was said that the hatter in Brunswick would take a friendly interest in Anton, that he should be treated as a child of his own and should do only light and suitable work, such as keeping accounts, running errands and the like: and further that for two years he should go to school until he was confirmed and then he could make up his mind what to do. This sounded very agreeable in Anton's ears, especially the last item of the school; for he thought that if he could only achieve this,

[1] A preacher, who lived opposite his parents' house, sometimes stood at the door in his black coat and bands, and Anton could spend an hour looking at him with the deepest respect; the buttons on his coat, the white linen which peeped out below the sleeve—were all sacred to him, and sometimes he would seriously ask, whether such a man could really be like other men.

he would not fail to distinguish himself sufficiently for ways and means to be forthcoming of themselves. He wrote himself along with his father to Lohenstein the hatter, whom he dearly loved already, and rejoiced to think of the splendid days he would spend with him.

And what a charm the thought of change of place had for him! Life in Hanover and the constant monotonous sight of the same streets and houses now became intolerable; visions of new towers, gates, ramparts, and castles rose in his mind, and one picture drove out the other. He was restless and counted the hours and minutes till his departure.[1]

At length the longed-for day arrived. Anton took leave of his mother and his two brothers, the elder of whom, Christian, might be five, and the younger, Simon, named after Lohenstein the hatter, scarcely a year old.

His father went with him and they travelled

[1] To his great vexation this was delayed by an eruption on his head, but when this was gone and his foot was completely healed, there was nothing more to stop it. All arrangements were made for his departure. His mother exhorted him every day with verses from the Bible saying how one must bend and bow oneself to go through the world, and the like, which, as he had heard it from her a thousand times already, had not the least effect. His parents fitted him out very scantily and had not some kind folk given him some clothes he would have arrived at Brunswick as a beggar. There would be nothing to say on this score if Anton's parents had not been able to do more: but, though they had an income more than sufficient for people of their class, their perpetual quarrels so disorganized their housekeeping, that they never had anything to spare for themselves and their children and yet lived miserably all the time.

half on foot, half driving, for which a cheap opportunity offered.[1]

The Migration to Brunswick.

Anton now for the first time in his life enjoyed the pleasure of a walking expedition, of which he was to have enough and to spare in the future. As they drew nearer to Brunswick, Anton became more and more eager. The tower of St. Andrew with its red dome rose majestically to the sky. Evening was coming on. In the distance he saw the sentinel walking to and fro on the high rampart. A thousand thoughts rose and faded in his mind: how would his future benefactor look, what would be his age, his walk, his features? At last he drew such a picture of him that he fell in love with him beforehand. One of the habits of his childhood had been to frame peculiar pictures and notions of persons and places suggested by the sound of their names, in which the high or low pitch of the vowels did most to determine the picture. Thus Hanover always sounded specially splendid, and he pictured it before he saw it as a town with high houses and towers, of a bright and cheerful aspect. Brunswick had long seemed to him darker and bigger, and Paris from some dim suggestion in the name, he imagined chiefly as a mass of bright whitish houses.

This is natural enough, for when one knows nothing of a thing but the name the mind strives

[1] Anton's father had agreed with some carters, who were carrying charcoal on the way to Brunswick, to give them a lift from time to time for a small sum, if they were tired.

to form an image of it even through the remotest resemblances, and for want of any other points of likeness has to take refuge in the arbitrary name, noting the sounds, hard or soft, full or thin, high or low, faint or clear, and imagines a correspondence between them and the object, which is often accidentally correct. The name Lohenstein made Anton think of a tall man, with an honest German face and an open brow. But this time his reading of names completely deceived him.

As darkness fell, Anton and his father crossed the great drawbridge and walked through the arched gates into the town. They went through many streets, past the castle and at last over a long bridge into a rather dingy street where Lohenstein the hatter lived opposite a long public building.

They stood in front of the house. It had a dark exterior and a great black door, thickly studded with nails. Above hung a sign with a hat on it and the name Lohenstein. An old woman, the housekeeper, opened the door and led them to the right into a large room, with dark painted panels, where a half-effaced representation of the five senses could be discovered with difficulty. Here the master of the house received them. A middle-aged man, rather short than tall, with a youngish but pale and melancholy face, which at rare moments assumed a forced smile : black hair, rather romantic eyes, a refinement in speech, movement and manners rarely found in working people. His speech was pure, but very slow and dragging, with words long drawn out, especially when religious things were talked of. He had an insufferably intolerant air, when he contracted his dark eyebrows over the depravity and wickedness of men, and especially of his neighbours or his own household.

When Anton first saw him he wore a green fur cap, a blue waistcoat, with a brown jerkin and black apron, his usual indoor wear, and at the first glance he felt that instead of the friend and benefactor he looked for he had found a stern master. His preconceived affection was quenched, as water quenches a spark, when the first glance of his supposed benefactor, cold and imperious, made him feel that he was to be nothing more than his apprentice.

For the few days that his father stayed with him, some consideration was shown him: but as soon as he was gone he had to work in the workshop like the other apprentice. He was employed on the meanest tasks—splitting wood, carrying water, and sweeping out the shop. In spite of his disappointment the unpleasantness was somewhat compensated by the charm of novelty, and he even found a kind of pleasure in sweeping, chopping, and water-carrying.

His imagination, which coloured everything, stood him in good stead. Often the spacious workshop with its dark walls and awesome gloom, only illuminated night and morning by the glimmer of some lamps, seemed to him a temple in which he ministered. In the morning he lit the holy quickening fire beneath the great cauldrons, which kept everything at work and active all the day long, and made many hands busy. So he regarded his duties as a kind of office, which had a certain dignity in his eyes.

Immediately behind the workshop flowed the Oker, over which was built out a projection of planks for drawing water. He regarded all this in a way as his own domain, and sometimes when he had cleaned the shop, filled the great boilers, set in masonry, and lit the fire beneath them, he could properly enjoy his work, as if he had given everything its due: his ever busy imagination quickened the inanimate things about him and made them live creatures, with which he lived and talked. Moreover the regularity which he noticed in the course of the business processes gave him a kind of agreeable sense of pleasure in being a wheel in this machine which moved so regularly, for at home he had known nothing like it. The hatter set great store by order in his house, and everything went by the clock: working, eating, and sleeping. If an exception was made, it was in regard to sleep, which had to drop out when there was night work, which happened at least once a week. Dinner was always punctually at twelve, breakfast and supper at eight morning and evening. These were the fixed points they counted on as they worked. In those days Anton's life passed thus: at work from six in the morning he counted on his breakfast, which he tasted in anticipation, and when he got it, ate it with the healthiest appetite a man can have, though it consisted of nothing but coffee-grounds with a little milk and a roll. Then he set to work again and the hope of dinner again gave new interest to the morning hours if the monotony of the work was too wearisome. In the evening he had, year in year out, a posset of strong beer: stimulus enough to sweeten the afternoon's labours. And then from supper till bed-time the thought of rest, soon to come and eagerly desired, again cast a gleam of comfort over his toilsome and disagreeable labour.

Of course he knew that next day the same cycle of life began again. But even this uniformity, wearisome as it was, was pleasantly interrupted by the hope of Sunday. When the stimulus of breakfast, dinner, and supper was not sufficient to keep the joy of life and work going, he counted the days to Sunday, which was a whole holiday, when he could leave the dark workshop for the open fields and enjoy the free and open face of nature. What charms, unknown to the higher classes, who can rest from their business when they like, has Sunday for the workman! 'That the son of thy handmaid may rejoice!' Only the workman can fully realize what a great, noble, humane meaning is embodied in this law!

If the thought of one day's rest from work was counted on for six days, it was well worth while to look forward for a third of the year to three or four festivals in succession. If ever the thought of Sunday lost its power to lighten the burden of monotony, the joy of life was quickened again by the approach of Easter, Whitsuntide, or Christmas. And when these thoughts lost their power, there was always the hope of the completion of apprenticeship and of becoming a journeyman, a hope beyond all others, which made a new and great epoch in life.

Anton's fellow-apprentice had no horizon beyond this, and certainly this made his position no worse.

It is a wise and beneficent disposal of things which gives to the laborious monotonous life of the artisan its divisions and periods, introducing a sort of rhythm or harmony, which makes it pass unnoticed without causing its possessor any feeling of weariness. But Anton's romantic ideas put him out of tune with this rhythm.

Just opposite the hatter's house was a Latin School which Anton had hoped to attend, but in vain. When he saw the boys going in and out his thoughts went sadly back to the Latin School and its Assistant Master in Hanover, and when he passed St. Martin's College and saw its grown-up students come out he would have given anything to be allowed to see the inside of this sanctuary. In his present position indeed he considered it almost impossible that he should ever be able to attend such a College, but he could not quite give up a faint glimmer of hope. Even the Choristers seemed to him beings from a higher sphere, and when he heard them sing in the streets, he could not help following them, to enjoy the sight of them and envy their brilliant lot.

When he was in the workshop with his fellow-apprentice he tried to impart to him all the scraps of knowledge which he had gained partly by his own reading, partly by the instruction he had enjoyed. He told him about Jupiter and Juno and tried to explain the difference between adjective and substantive, so as to teach him when to put a capital letter and when a small one. His companion listened attentively to him, and they often discussed moral and religious subjects. Anton's companion on such occasions was great at inventing new words to express his ideas: for instance he called following God's commands the 'fulfilness of God'. While he chiefly tried to imitate the religious phrases of Herr Lohenstein, mortification and the like, he often fell into strange confusion. When he thought that the housekeeper or any one else blackened or abused his character, he was ready to quote with special emphasis passages from the Psalms of David, which expressed no gentle sentiments towards his enemies.

Nearly all the household indeed were more or less infected with the religious enthusiasm of Herr Lohenstein, all except the journeyman. If his master talked to him too much of mortification and self-effacement, he cast on him such a withering annihilating glance that Herr Lohenstein turned away with horror and said nothing. Sometimes Herr Lohenstein could preach for hours against the whole human race, distributing blessing and damnation with a gentle gesture of the right hand. His expression then was meant to be compassionate, but intolerance and misanthropy were entrenched between his black eyebrows. He was politic enough to turn his preaching to good purpose, by warning his household to be zealous and faithful in his service, if they did not wish to burn for ever in hell fire. His people could never work hard enough for him, and he made a cross over the loaf and the butter when he went out. Anton, who perhaps could not work hard enough for him, found his dinner spoilt by a thousand repeated instructions from Herr Lohenstein how to hold his knife and fork and carry his food to his mouth, so that he often lost his appetite. At last the journeyman insisted on taking his part and he was able to eat in peace. But he did not dare to utter a sound, as his master found fault with everything he said, with his looks and his least movement: Anton could never please him, and at last was almost afraid to go into his presence, for he found fault with everything he did. His intolerance extended to every smile and every innocent outburst of pleasure, which appeared in Anton's features or movements. For in these he gave himself free outlet, knowing that he could not be contradicted.

Meanwhile the faded five senses on the black panelling of the wall had been re-varnished. The memory of the smell, which lasted some weeks, Anton ever afterwards associated with the idea of his position at the time. Whenever he smelt varnish, involuntarily all the unpleasant images of those days rose up in his mind, and conversely, when he happened to be in circumstances which had resemblance to those days, he fancied that he smelt a smell of varnish.

An accident improved Anton's position. The hatter was a hypochondriacal enthusiast; he believed in warnings, and had visions, which often roused his fear and horror. An old woman, who had lodged in the house died and appeared to him in dreams at night, so that he often woke in terror, and as he went on dreaming after he woke he fancied he still saw her shadow in a corner of the room. Anton now had to keep him company and sleep in a bed near by him. So he became in some degree necessary to his master, who became kinder to him. He often had conversations with him, asked him how he stood with God. and taught him that he must give himself wholly to God, and that then if he was fortunate enough to be elected as one of the children of God, God would himself begin and complete the work of conversion in him.

Before he went to bed Anton had to stand apart and pray in a low voice, and the prayer could not be very short or his master would ask him whether he had finished so soon, and had no more to say to God. This was a new incentive to hypocrisy and dissimulation, which were otherwise quite against his nature. Though he prayed in an undertone he tried to pronounce his words so clearly that he could be heard quite well by Lohenstein and now his whole prayer was dominated not so much by the thought of God as how he could best ingratiate himself with Herr Lohenstein by expressions of repentance, contrition, yearning for God and the like. Such was the fine result that this compulsory prayer had on Anton's heart and character.

But still Anton sometimes found a kind of secret pleasure in solitary prayer, when he knelt down in a corner of the workshop and prayed God to bring about in his soul, if it might be, even one of the great changes of which he had read and heard so much in his childhood. And so strong was the illusion of his imagination that he sometimes really had a sense of some special experience in his inmost soul : and then at once came the thought that he wanted to embody his spiritual state in a letter to his father or Herr v. Fleischbein, or describe it to Herr Lohenstein. Thus his imaginary feelings constantly served to feed his vanity, and the intense pleasure he felt arose chiefly from the thought that he could say he had felt such a divine and heavenly joy in his soul. It flattered him to think that old and grown-up people regarded his spiritual state as something important enough to trouble about. That was the reason that he so often imagined a change in his spiritual condition, so that he might complain to Herr Lohenstein that he was in a state of emptiness and drought, that he could no longer find in himself any trace of yearning for God, and then ask advice on his condition from Herr Lohenstein who gave it him with great seriousness. It even went so far that his spiritual state was discussed in correspondence with Herr v. Fleischbein, a passage in whose letter, referring to it, was shown him. It was no wonder that in this way he was encouraged to keep up his importance in his own eyes and those of others by continual imaginary changes in his spiritual state, as he was regarded as a person in whom the guidance of God was revealed in a very special way.

Now too he was given a black apron, like the other apprentice, and this circumstance, instead of making him feel humble, rather added much to his content. He now looked on himself as a person who was beginning to have a position of his own. The apron brought him into line with others like him, whereas before he was lonely and isolated. For some time the apron made him forget his inclination for study and he began to find a kind of pleasure in the other customs of the trade, which made him wish for nothing more eagerly than to be able one day to share them. He was delighted when he heard the greeting of a journeyman coming in to ask for the usual gratuity, and he could imagine no greater happiness than to come in some day as a journeyman himself, and then repeat the greeting in the prescribed words according to the custom of the trade.

Thus it is that the youthful mind always clings more to the symbol than to the reality, and little or nothing can be inferred from the early utterances of children in regard to the choice of a vocation. As soon as ever Anton had learnt to read, he found inexpressible pleasure in going to church, and his mother and aunt were overjoyed. But what drew him to church was the triumph he always enjoyed when he could look at the black-board, on which the numbers of the hymns were written, and could tell some grown-up man, who stood by him, what the number was, and when he could look up the numbers in his hymn-book as quickly or more quickly than his elders and join in the singing.

Herr Lohenstein's attachment to Anton seemed to grow stronger, the more Anton showed a desire for his spiritual guidance. He often allowed him to join in the conversations he held up to midnight with his most intimate friends, with whom it was his habit to discuss the apparitions seen by himself and others, some of them so horrible that Anton listened with hair on end.

They generally went late to bed, and when the evening had been spent in such talk Herr Lohenstein would ask Anton when he got up next morning whether he had noticed nothing in the night or heard nothing walking in the bedroom. Often too in the evening he talked to Anton alone and they read together in the writings of Tauler, John of the Cross, and such books. It seemed as though they would become lasting friends. Anton too conceived a kind of love for Herr Lohenstein, but this feeling was always mixed with a bitter taste, with a certain sense of deadening, withering influence, produced by Lohenstein's sardonic smile.

Meanwhile Anton for the time was spared the hard and menial tasks he did before. Sometimes Lohenstein took walks with him, and he even engaged a master to teach him the piano. Anton was delighted at his position and wrote a letter to his father, in which he expressed the liveliest satisfaction.

But now Anton's fortune had reached its climax in Lohenstein's house and his fall was at hand. Every one looked at him with envious eyes from the day the pianist was engaged. Intrigues were contrived like those of a petty court. He was slandered and his downfall planned. So long as Lohenstein was harsh and unjust to Anton, he enjoyed the sympathy and friendship of all the household : but as soon as it seemed as if he would make a friend and confidant of him, then enmity and distrust of him grew in proportion. And as soon as they had succeeded in reducing him to their own level and had got the piano-teacher dismissed, they no longer had any feeling against Anton, they were friends as before.

But now it was not difficult to rob him of the goodwill of one so suspicious and distrustful as

Lohenstein ; it was only necessary to repeat a few of his lively sayings, or to call Herr Lohenstein's attention on every occasion to certain real faults of carelessness and untidiness in Anton, in order to give his sentiments a different direction. This was very conscientiously done by the housekeeper and other dependants.

Meanwhile it took several months to attain this object, during which time even Anton's piano-master took pains to be converted : a good and honest man, but one who in Herr Lohenstein's opinion had not yet quite resigned himself to God and did not behave himself passively enough towards Him. This man often had to take a meal in the house, but in the end missed all by spreading too much butter on his bread. The housekeeper called Herr Lohenstein's attention to this in order to gain her object of making an end of Anton's piano-playing, that he might not be exalted above the rest of the household.

Besides, Anton had no great genius for music and consequently learnt little by his lessons. A few tunes and chorales were all he could achieve with much pains, and the piano-lesson was always disagreeable to him. Fingering too he found very difficult and the teacher always found something to criticize in the disposal of his outspread fingers.

Meanwhile he did succeed on one occasion, as David did with Saul, in driving away the evil spirit of Lohenstein by the power of music. He had committed some small fault, and as his master's fancy for him was beginning to turn into hatred he had intended in the evening to give him a severe chastisement before bedtime. Anton was aware of this, and when the hour seemed to be approaching he had the courage to play a chorale, the first he had learnt, on the piano and to sing to it. This took Herr Lohenstein by surprise: he confessed to him that he had fixed that very hour to give him a severe flogging, which he now spared him. Anton then began to remonstrate with him on the apparent decline of his friendship and affection, whereupon Lohenstein confessed to him that it was true that his affection for him was not so strong as it had been, and this must be due to Anton's spiritual deterioration, which had built a dividing wall so to speak between him and his previous love. He had put the matter before God in prayer and received this solution.

This was very sad for Anton and he asked what steps he must take to improve his spiritual condition. The answer was that the only means to save his soul was to walk his way in simplicity and commit himself to God: no further directions were vouchsafed. Herr Lohenstein did not think it proper to forestall God, who seemed to have withdrawn from Anton. The emphasis laid on the words ' walk his way in simplicity ' referred to the fact that he had for some time begun to find Anton too clever for him, he talked and reasoned too much, and generally his satisfaction with his condition made him too lively. This liveliness he regarded as the straight road to Anton's ruin: this cheerful countenance must mean that he was becoming a vicious worldly-minded man, of whom the only thing to be expected was that God would let him perish in his sins.

Had Anton better understood his own advantage, he might now have been able to put everything right by adopting a melancholy misanthropic manner and pretending anxiety and uneasiness about his soul: for then Lohenstein would have believed that God was going to draw the wandering soul to Himself. But as Lohenstein held the principle that he whom God will convert, is converted even without his own co-operation and that God chooses whom He will and rejects and hardens whom He will, in order to reveal His majesty, it seemed to him dangerous to interfere with God for any one, if it appeared that he was rejected by Him. And, to judge from Anton's lively and worldly ways, it looked to Herr Lohenstein as if it were really so with him. He thought it so important that he had corresponded about it with Herr v. Fleischbein and now he showed a passage in a letter from Herr v. Fleischbein in which he asserted that, to judge by all signs, Satan had now built his temple so firmly in Anton's heart that it could scarcely be destroyed again.

This was indeed a thunderbolt for Anton: but he examined himself and compared his present with his previous state and found it impossible to discover any difference between them; his imagination indulged in religious feelings and emotions just as often as before, and he could not convince himself that he had fallen entirely from grace and was to be rejected by God. He began to doubt the truth of Herr v. Fleischbein's oracular answer. So he lost his depression, which otherwise perhaps might have paved the way to the favour of Herr Lohenstein, whose friendship he now completely forfeited by the continuance of his cheerful air.

The first consequence was that Lohenstein removed him from his room ; he had to sleep again with the other apprentice, who began to be friendly now that he envied him no longer : the second was that he had to begin again doing the hardest and most menial jobs, and so had to remain always in the workshop and only rarely join Herr Lohenstein in the parlour. The piano-master was only retained because Lohenstein wished to complete the work of conversion he had begun in him and so bring another soul to God in place of the lost one.

Winter came on and Anton's position began really to be a hard one, he had to perform tasks which were far beyond his years and powers. Lohenstein seemed to think that as now nothing was to be done with Anton's soul, at least all possible use must be made of his body. He seemed to regard him as a tool, to be thrown away when worn out.

Frost and hard work soon made Anton's hands quite unfit for piano-playing. Almost every week he had to stay up twice at night with the other apprentice, to pull the blackened hats out of the boiling dye-vat, and then wash them immediately in the running stream of the Oker for which purpose they had first to cut an opening in the ice. This repeated transition from heat to cold made Anton's hands chap till the blood ran. But instead of this depressing him it rather increased his courage. He looked at his hands with a kind of pride, as a sort of badge of honour for his work, and as long as these hard tasks had the charm of novelty they brought him a certain satisfaction, chiefly consisting in the sense of his bodily strength : at the same time they gave him a pleasant sense of freedom which he had not known before. He felt as though he could indulge himself more after bearing the day's burden and heat like the rest. Under the heaviest burdens he experienced a kind of inward esteem which came from the exertion of his powers, and he often felt he would hardly have exchanged this for the irksome position he was in when he enjoyed the austere friendship of Lohenstein which destroyed all freedom.

Lohenstein now began to treat him with still more severity : he often had to card wool the whole day long in the bitterest cold in an unwarmed room. This was a clever device of his master to increase Anton's diligence, for if he did not want to die of cold he had to bestir himself, so far as his strength allowed, so that often in the evening his arms were almost paralysed, though hands and feet were frozen. This occupation from its constant monotony made his lot most bitter, especially if, as often happened, his imagination failed to work : on the other hand when once the quicker movement of his blood set it going, the hours often passed by unnoticed. Then he often lost himself in enchanting visions : sometimes he turned his feelings to song in recitative to tunes of his own. And when he felt specially tired of work, crushed and exhausted by his labours, he liked to lose himself in religious sentiments, of sacrifice, utter devotion and the like ; the phrase 'altar of sacrifice' appealed to him most deeply, and he wove it into all the little hymns and recitatives that he invented.

The conversations with his fellow-apprentice, August, now began to have a new charm for him, and as they were equals again, their talk became confidential. Their friendship was cemented still closer by the nights through which they often had to sit up together. But their most intimate times were when they sat together in the ‘ drying-room ’. This was a pit dug into the earth and vaulted with brick, where a man could just stand upright and two men could sit together. In this pit a great brazier was placed, and on the walls round it were hung the skins of hares treated with nitric acid, the hair of which was here softened, to be used afterwards for the finer kind of hats. Anton and August sat in front of the brazier in the steamy atmosphere of the half-subterranean pit, into which you had to crawl rather than walk ; this confinement of the place, faintly lighted by the glow of the coals, made them feel so closely united by the remote quiet and awesome character of this dark vault, that their hearts often overflowed in mutual outpourings. Here they revealed their inmost thoughts to one another and spent their happiest hours.

Lohenstein like Herr v. Fleischbein and all his followers, was a seceder, who did not hold with church and sacrament. So long as he had been friends with Anton, Anton had hardly entered a church in Brunswick. Now August took him to church on Sunday, and they went sometimes to one sometimes to another, for Anton took pleasure in hearing different preachers. Anton and August were sitting in the drying-room together one midnight and discussing different preachers, when August promised to take him next Sunday to the Brothers' Church, where he would hear a preacher who surpassed anything he could think or imagine. The preacher was called Paulmann and August told him over and over again how deeply he had often been moved and affected by his sermons. Nothing had more attraction for Anton than the sight of a public speaker, who holds the hearts of thousands in his hand. He listened attentively to what August told him. Already in his mind's eye he saw Pastor Paulmann in the pulpit and heard him preach. His only wish now was for Sunday to come.

Sunday came. Anton rose earlier than usual, attended to his duties and dressed. When the church-bells rang he had a sort of pleasant presentiment of what he would soon hear. They went to church. The streets that led there were full of a stream of people hurrying thither. Pastor Paulmann was preaching again for the first time after a long illness; that was why Anton had not been taken there by August already. When they entered they found a place facing the pulpit, but with difficulty. Every bench and all the gangways and galleries were full of people, all trying to look over one another's heads. The church was an old Gothic building with thick pillars supporting the high vaulted roof, and vast, long, arched windows of painted glass, letting only a faint light through. The church was full before the service began, and a solemn quiet reigned there. Suddenly the full-voiced organ was heard and the hymn which burst from that great congregation seemed to shake the roof. When the last verse ended, all eyes were fixed on the pulpit, and there was no less curiosity to see this idolized preacher than to hear him. At last he came forward and knelt on the lowest stair of the pulpit, before he went up. Then he rose and was presently standing before the assembled people—a man in the full strength of his years, his face pale, a gentle smile playing round his mouth and his eyes shining with heavenly devotion; even before he began his attitude as he stood there with hands quietly folded made a deep impression.

And then, as he began, what a voice! what expression! First slow and solemn, then a rapid flow: as he came to close grips with his subject the fire of eloquence began to sparkle in his eyes, to breathe from his breast, and to scatter sparks from his finger-tips. He was all movement: the expression conveyed by features, attitude, and gestures went beyond all rules of art, yet was natural, noble, and carried one away irresistibly.

There was no pause in the powerful outpouring of his feelings and thoughts; the first word was hardly spoken when the next was ready to be uttered. As one wave swallows another in the flowing tide so each fresh emotion was merged in that which followed, and yet the new emotion was but a livelier presentation of the first.

His voice was a clear tenor, which as it rose was unusually rich; it had the ring of pure metal and vibrated through every nerve. He spoke, under guidance of the Gospel, against injustice and oppression, against luxury and extravagance, and in the fiery heat of his inspiration he addressed by name the sensual luxurious town whose inhabitants were for the most part assembled in the church, laid bare their sins and crimes, reminded them of the time of war when the town was besieged and all men were in danger, when necessity made all equal and brotherly unity reigned; when the luxurious inhabitants were threatened by hunger and want and prison chains instead of the tables groaning with plenty and the bracelets and jewellery of to-day. Anton imagined himself listening to one of the prophets, chiding the people of Israel with holy zeal and rebuking Jerusalem for its sins.

Anton went home from church without saying a word to August, but wherever he was or wherever he went he thought of nothing but Pastor Paulmann. He dreamed of him by night and talked of him by day: his face, his features, his every movement were graven on Anton's mind. As he carded wool in the workshop or washed the hats he busied himself all the week with entrancing thoughts of Pastor Paulmann's sermon, and repeated to himself many times over every expression which had affected him or moved him to tears. His imagination then reproduced the majestic old church, the listening throng and the voice of the preacher, which now in his fancy sounded even more heavenly. He counted days and minutes to the next Sunday. It came, and if ever anything made an indelible impression on Anton's soul, it was the sermon he heard that day. The crowd was if possible even larger than the Sunday before. A short chant was sung before the sermon composed of the words of the Psalm: 'Lord, who shall abide in thy tabernacle? who shall dwell in thy holy hill? He that walketh uprightly and worketh righteousness and speaketh the truth in his heart. He that backbiteth not with his tongue, nor doth evil to his neighbour nor taketh up a reproach against his neighbour. In whose eyes a vile person is contemned, but he honoureth them that fear the Lord: he that sweareth to his own hurt and changeth not. He that putteth not out his money to usury, nor taketh reward against the innocent: he that doth these things, shall never be moved.'

This short and moving chant made every one thrill with expectation of what was to come. The heart was ready for great and exalted impressions, when Pastor Paulmann came forward, and with earnest solemnity in his face and a look of deep absorption, began without prayer or introduction to speak with outstretched arm: 'He that oppresseth not the widow and the orphans: he that is not conscious of secret sins: that taketh not advantage of his neighbour with wrong: whose soul is burdened by no perjury: let him lift up his hands with me to God full of confidence and prayer. "Our Father".'

Then he read from the Gospel the passage where John the Baptist is asked whether he is the Christ. 'And he confessed and denied not, and confessed I am not the Christ.' And from these words he took occasion to preach on perjury, and after he had read the words of the Gospel in a solemn subdued voice he began after a pause:

Oh, woe to thee, by sin beguiled,
Thy Lord, oh shame! denying!
How canst thou lift thy face, defiled
By perjury and lying?

Thou hast been false to Him and so
In depth of sin thou liest low,
His name profanely scorning.
When thou before Him show'st thy face
He knows thee not, so lost to grace;
Yet, if thou wilt take warning,
It may be, wretchedest of men,
That tears may quench the guilty flame
Within thy breast, now dead to shame,
So lift thy heart in hope again!
Contrition, in the length of years,
May wash thy guilt away in tears:
Thou who the path of sin didst choose,
If thou canst weep, the stain may lose,
God helping thine endeavour:
He dooms not sinners all to death,
He turns His face and pardoneth,
His promise stands for ever.

These words, spoken with frequent pauses and the most exalted feeling, produced an incredible impression. When they were ended every one breathed more freely: they wiped the sweat from their brows. Then he went on to examine the nature of perjury—to put its consequences in a more and more appalling light. The thunder rolled down on the head of the perjurer, destruction like an armed man approached him, the sinner trembled in the innermost depth of his soul, he cried 'ye mountains fall on me and ye hills cover me'! The perjurer received no mercy, he was annihilated before the wrath of the Eternal.

He was silent, as if exhausted: a panic terror seized all hearers. Anton hastily ran through all the years of his life, to see if he had ever been guilty of perjury. But then began the note of consolation: mercy and pardon were announced to the despairing sinner, if he atoned tenfold for what he had stolen from the widow and the orphan, if, his whole life long, he tried to wash away his sin with tears of repentance and other good works. Mercy was not easily vouchsafed to the criminal: it had to be won by prayer and tears. And then it seemed as though he wished to win it by his own prayer and tears, in God's sight before all the people, putting himself in the place of the contrite sinner. He appealed to the despairing: 'kneel down in dust and ashes, till your knees are sore, and say: "I have sinned against heaven and before Thee".' And so every period began with 'I have sinned against heaven and before Thee': and then followed a series of confessions: 'I have oppressed the widow and the orphan, I have robbed the weak of his only stay, the hungry of his bread,' and so through all the list of crimes. And every period closed with 'Lord, is it possible that I should find mercy?'

The whole company melted in sorrow and weeping. The refrain in each period had an incredible effect; it was as if men's feelings each time received a fresh electric shock, which raised them to the highest pitch. Even the final exhaustion, the hoarseness of the orator (it was as though he cried to God for the sins of the world) contributed to the spreading flood of emotion caused by the sermon; there was not a child who did not join in the sighing and weeping out of sympathy.

Two and a half hours had passed like minutes. Suddenly he stopped and after a pause he ended with the same verses with which he had begun. With a voice exhausted and subdued he read the General Confession, and the Absolution promised to such as repent: then he prayed for those who wished to come to the Sacrament, himself among the number, and then with uplifted hands he gave the blessing. The contrast of his lowered voice with the tone that prevailed in his sermon had a solemn and moving effect.

Anton did not leave the church: he must first see Pastor Paulmann go to the Sacrament: his every step was sacred to him. With a kind of reverence he went to the place where he knew that he had gone. What would he not have given to be able to go to the Sacrament with him? Then he saw the Pastor go home, accompanied by his son, a boy of nine. Anton would have given his whole existence to be that lucky boy. As he watched Pastor Paulmann, surrounded by people on all sides, cross the street and saw him giving friendly thanks to those who greeted him on either hand, he imagined that he saw a sort of halo round his head, as if he were a superhuman being walking among mortals. His dearest wish was to win a look from him by lifting his hat, and when he succeeded he hurried quickly home, so as to preserve this look as it were in his heart.

The next Sunday Pastor Paulmann preached on love of the brethren, and this sermon was as tender in feeling as that against perjury had been powerful: the words flowed like honey from his lips, all his movements were different, his whole being seemed altered to suit his subject. Yet there was not the least affectation. It was natural to him to merge his personality in the thoughts and emotions which his subject-matter suggested to him. In the forenoon Anton had listened with amazing weariness to the other preacher of this church: once or twice he got quite angry with him, because, just when he seemed about to say Amen, he began over again in the same tone. Now more than ever it was Anton's greatest torment to listen to a wearisome sermon like this, because he could not help making constant comparisons when once he had conceived as his highest ideal the sermon of Pastor Paulmann, which seemed to him unattainable by any one else.

When the morning sermon was over, it was Pastor Paulmann's turn to perform the consecration at the Sacrament, which Anton now heard him do for the first time. And what a venerable figure he seemed to him at that moment! He stood at the far end of the church before the high altar, and chanted the words 'Oh, thank the Lord, for He is gracious, and his mercy endureth for ever' with such a heaven-uplifting voice and such powerful expression that Anton thought himself for the moment rapt into higher regions. The whole ceremony seemed to happen behind a curtain, in the holy of holies, which his feet dared not approach. How he envied every one who could go up to the altar and receive the sacrament from the Pastor's hands! A very young woman, dressed in black, with pale cheeks and an air of heavenly devotion who went up to the altar, made an impression on Anton's heart such as he had never felt before. He never saw her again, but her image was never effaced from his memory.

His imagination now found a new field. The idea of the Sacrament occupied him at his rising and his lying down and at every moment when he was alone at his work, and the form of Pastor Paulmann hovered before his mind, with his gentle, rising voice and his eyes turned heavenwards with a light of more than earthly devotion. Sometimes too the figure of the young woman in black came back into his vision, with her pale face and her air of devout worship.

All this so inspired his imagination that he would have counted himself the happiest man under the sun if he could have gone to the Sacrament the next Sunday. He promised himself such celestial solace from the Sacrament that he shed tears of joy beforehand: at the same time he had a feeling of mild self-compassion which sweetened everything unpleasant and bitter in his lot, when he reflected that, when once he had become a journeyman, no one could rob him of this consolation. He resolved to go to the Sacrament at least once a fortnight, when once he had got to this stage, and then there blended with this desire the secret hope that perhaps this frequent attendance would finally attract the notice of Pastor Paulmann: and it was this thought above all which made these ideas so inexpressibly sweet to him. Thus even here, where perhaps it was least to be expected, vanity lay in ambush for him.

He found it impossible to believe that he would always be misunderstood and neglected as he was now. Certain romantic ideas that he had got into his head led him to think that one day some generous man, who met him in the street, would notice something remarkable in him and would take notice of him. A certain sad and melancholy air, which he assumed for this end, would, he thought, best attract attention, so he affected it more than was natural to him. Often indeed, when the face of some gentleman of quality inspired confidence, he nearly went so far as to address him and reveal his circumstances. But he was always deterred by the fear the gentleman might perhaps take him for a fool.

Sometimes too, as he went along the street, he would sing in a plaintive voice some of Madame Guyon's hymns which he had learnt by heart, hymns in which he thought he found allusions to his own lot, and then, as in romances sometimes a plaintive song sung by somebody works wonders, so he thought he might succeed in giving a new turn to his fortune by thus drawing the attention of some humane person to himself. His reverence for Pastor Paulmann was too profound for him ever to dare to address him. If he was near him, he felt a thrill as if he were near an angel. He could not imagine, or tried to rid himself of the thought, that this pastor was like other men, getting up and going to bed, and performing all natural functions like them. It was quite impossible to picture him in dressing-gown and night-cap, or he avoided the thought, as though it would have made a breach in his soul. The thought of a night-cap, especially, in connexion with Pastor Paulmann was more than he could bear, he felt it would bring discord into all his other ideas. But it happened once that Anton was standing at the church-door just as Pastor Paulmann came in and was telling the sacristan in Low German that there was a baptism afterwards. If ever Anton felt a contrast it was this: to have a man, whom he had thought of as never speaking except in the most solemn and moving tones, speak in Low German to the sacristan like the simplest workman on such a solemn thing as baptism, and that in a tone which was anything but solemn, the tone in which one might say to any one he must not forget to bring the washing-basin.

This single incident in some degree moderated Anton's idolatry for Pastor Paulmann. He worshipped him less and loved him the more. Meanwhile he had formed his ideal of happiness entirely on him. He could imagine nothing more noble or more attractive than to be able to speak publicly before the people like Pastor Paulmann and like him now and again to address the city by its name. This personal address was to him a great and moving thought, which often occupied his mind for days together: even when he went along the street to fetch beer perhaps, if he saw a couple of boys fighting, he could not help repeating the pastor's words to himself, warning the wicked city from destruction and lifting his arm to heaven to threaten it. Wherever he was, wherever he went, he delivered speeches in imagination, and when he was worked up to high passion he gave the sermon against perjury.

He lived for some time amid these pleasant fancies, which almost made him forget the wool-carding in the cold room, the icy hat-washing, and the want of sleep when he had to sit up several nights on end. Sometimes as he worked the hours flew by like minutes, when he succeeded in imagining himself in the character of a public orator.

But, either the unnatural strain on his mental faculties, or the physical effort over work which was beyond his years proved too much for him and he became dangerously ill. His nursing was not of the best. He was delirious in fever and often lay all day with no one to trouble about him.

At last his good physique won the battle, and he was restored. The illness however left behind a certain languor and depression and the humane Herr Lohenstein very nearly gave him a fatal relapse by one of his gentle admonitions. It was one evening in the twilight, when Lohenstein was taking a warm bath of herbs in a dark and distant room, when Anton had to wait on him. As he sweated in his bath and was in great tribulation, he said to Anton in a voice which pierced his marrow 'Anton, Anton, beware of hell!' and he stared into the corner.

Anton trembled at these words, a sudden shudder went through all his body. All the terrors of death fell upon him, for he had not the least doubt that at that moment Lohenstein had seen a vision, portending Anton's death, and that this had moved him to the awful cry 'Beware, beware of hell!'

Immediately afterwards Lohenstein suddenly came out of the bath and Anton had to light him to his room. He went in front of him with trembling knees, and Lohenstein looked paler than death when he left him.

If ever prayer was made to God in genuine piety and fervour, it was offered by Anton now, as soon as he was alone. He threw himself, not on his knees but on his face in a corner of the workshop, and prayed to God for his life, like a criminal on whom sentence has been passed, he prayed for a respite for conversion, if he must indeed die: for he remembered that scores of times he had run and jumped and laughed wildly in the streets, and now all the torments of hell which he would have to endure for ever in punishment weighed heavily on him. 'Beware, beware of hell' still rang in his ears, as though a spirit from the grave had called to him, and he went on praying a full hour, and would never have ceased all night, if he had found no relief from his anguish. But as one sigh of anguish after another issued from his breast, and his tears flowed at last, he felt as if God had vouchsafed to hear his prayer, God who, as at Niniveh of old, would rather have a prophet shamed than a soul destroyed. Anton had prayed away his fever, but would probably have relapsed into it, if his excited spirits had not found this escape. Thus one delusion or folly drives out another: the devils are driven out by Beelzebub. After this exhaustion Anton was refreshed by quiet sleep and rose next morning perfectly well, but the thought of death awoke with him: he fancied that at most a short respite was given him for conversion and he must make haste if he would save his soul. And he did what he could: many times a day he prayed on his knees in a corner and at last dreamed himself into such a firm conviction of God's mercy and such cheerfulness of spirit, that he often fancied himself in heaven and many a time wished he might die before he could stray from this good path.

But amid all these wanderings of his fancy it

could not but be that Nature watched her moment and came back : and then the natural love of life for life's sake awoke again in Anton's soul. Then the thought of his approaching death was indeed sad and unpleasant, and he regarded these moments as moments when he had again forfeited the divine mercy, and fell again into fresh anxiety because he found it impossible to suppress the voice of Nature within him.

And now he experienced with double force the evil consequences of the superstition which had been instilled in him from earliest childhood. Properly understood, his sufferings were those of a vivid imagination, but still they were to him real sufferings and they robbed him of the joys of his youth. He knew from his mother that it was a sure sign of death being near, when the hands do not steam in washing : so he saw himself dying whenever he washed his hands. He had heard that if a dog howls in the house with his muzzle to the ground he scents a man's death : every time he heard a dog howl it was a prophecy. Even if a hen crowed like a cock it was a sure sign that some one would soon die in the house : and here was an evil-boding hen strutting about the yard and crowing constantly in unnatural fashion like a cock. No death-knell seemed so fearful as this crowing, and this hen caused him more gloomy hours in his life than any misfortune he ever suffered. Comfort and hope of life often returned to him when the hen was silent for a day or two, but when it began again all his fair hopes and plans were suddenly ruined.

As he went about with nothing but thoughts of

death in his head, it so happened that for the first time after his illness he went again to Pastor Paulmann's church. He stood up in the pulpit and preached on death. This was a thunder-clap for Anton; for as he had learnt to apply everything to himself, following the ideas of special divine guidance, that he had imbibed, he felt the sermon on death could have been meant only for him. No criminal listening to his death-sentence could feel deeper anxiety than Anton at this sermon. Pastor Paulmann indeed added some grounds of consolation to weigh against the terrors of death, but that counted for little compared with the natural love of life, which in spite of all the fancies, which filled Anton's head, was still the feeling that predominated. He went home downcast and depressed, and for a fortnight the sermon made him melancholy, a sermon which Pastor Paulmann would probably never have delivered if he had known it would have the effect on two or three men which it had upon Anton.

Thus Anton in his thirteenth year, through the special guidance which the divine mercy through its chosen instruments had vouchsafed him had become a complete hypochondriac, of whom it could justly be said that at every moment though alive he was dead. Shamefully defrauded of the enjoyment of his youth, he was driven to madness by 'prevenient grace'.

But spring was coming on again, and Nature, which heals all, in him too began to restore what grace had ruined. Anton felt a new power of life in him: he washed, and his hands steamed again, no dogs barked any more, the hen ceased to crow, and Pastor Paulmann preached no more sermons on death.

Anton began again to go for walks alone on Sundays, and it chanced one day that, without knowing it, he came to the very gate through which he had walked in with his father a year and a half before. He could not refrain from going out and following the broad willow-planted highway that he had come by. Peculiar feelings rose in him as he went. At once his whole life came back to him, from the day when he first saw the sentinel walking to and fro on the rampart and formed all sorts of ideas of how the city would look inside and what sort of a house the Lohensteins' would be. It was as if he woke from a dream and found himself again on the spot where the dream began. All the changing scenes of his life, as he had lived it this year and a half in Brunswick, came crowding on him, and every single scene seemed to grow smaller, measured by a bigger scale, of which he was now suddenly possessed.

So powerful is the effect produced by the idea of place, with which all our other ideas are connected. The individual streets and houses, which Anton saw day after day, formed the permanent element in his ideas, with which the constantly shifting scenes of his life were connected, which gave them unity and reality, and made the distinction between waking and dreaming.

In childhood especially all other ideas are bound to be connected with ideas of place, because in themselves they are as yet too fluid and cannot yet hold together without support. That is why too in childhood it is often difficult to distinguish waking from dreaming.

. . . .

Often at waking in the morning one goes on half dreaming, and the transition to waking is gradually made as one begins to get one's bearings ; as soon as the bright shining of the window gives a fixed point everything else gradually falls into order. So it was quite natural that Anton, after he had been some weeks in the Lohensteins' house in Brunswick, still thought he was dreaming in the morning when he was really awake, because the pivot so to say, to which he had been used to attach his ideas of the day before or of his previous life, and which gave them their unity and reality, was now disturbed, because the idea of place was no longer the same.

Is it surprising then that change in surroundings often contributes so much to make us forget like a dream what we do not like to think of as real ? As years go on, especially if we have travelled much, the association of ideas with place tends to diminish. Wherever we go we see either roofs, windows, doors, pavement, churches and towers or meadows, forest, plough-land or heath. The striking differences disappear, the earth becomes everywhere the same.

When Anton walked along the street in Brunswick especially in the evening as twilight began he often suddenly felt as in a dream. This would happen to him too if he went into some street which seemed to have a distant resemblance to a street in Hanover. For a few moments his circumstances in Hanover were present again, the scenes of his life were confused with one another.

In his walks he took a special delight in hunting out places in the town where he had never been. His soul expanded then, and he felt as though he had taken a bold leap out of the narrow sphere of his existence ; everyday notions disappeared and wild and pleasant prospects, mazes of futurity were opened up for him. But he had never yet succeeded in grasping in one single complete vision his whole life in Brunswick with all its various changes. The place where he was at any time reminded him too strongly of some particular part of it, to make room for a mental picture of the whole : his ideas always revolved within a narrow circle of his existence.

In order to obtain a distinct view of his present life as a whole, it was necessary that all the threads, so to say, should be cut off which fastened his attention on what was momentary, everyday and fragmentary, and that he should be put again at the point of view, from which he regarded his life in Brunswick before it began, when it still lay before him in the twilight of the future. To this point of vision he was now transported, when he came by chance out of the Gate through which about a year and a half before he had come in along the broad willow-planted high road and had seen the sentinel walking to and fro on the rampart.

It was precisely this place, which suddenly reminding him of a thousand little things, seemed to put him exactly in the position he was in before the beginning of his present life. All that lay between inevitably came crowding into his imagination, events melting into one another like shadows or a dream. His standing on the bridge now and looking up at the high rampart, where the sentinel stood, seemed quite near to his standing and looking upwards a year and a half before. The past, all the scenes of the life that Anton had led in Brunswick, he now called up again as he had thought of them a year and a half before as still in the future, and the more than vivid presentment due to the memories of the place, made his memory for the time that had passed between become faint or disappear: at least it is hardly possible in any other way to explain the mystery of that peculiar feeling which Anton then had and which every one will remember to have had at least once in his life.

More than ten times Anton was on the point of not returning into the town, but of going straight to Hanover if the thought of hunger and cold had not deterred him. But from that day forward he had a fixed resolve not to stay any longer in Lohenstein's house, cost what it might. He therefore became more indifferent to everything, because he imagined it would not last much longer. Lohenstein himself began to become so dissatisfied with him that he wrote to Hanover to Anton's father, telling him that he might fetch his son back at any time, as nothing was to be made of him.

Nothing could have been more welcome to Anton than news that his father would fetch him home at once. In any case he concluded that he must be sent to school in Hanover before he was admitted to the sacrament, and then his intention was to distinguish himself so as to attract attention. Eagerly as he had striven before to go to Brunswick, he now hankered again for Hanover, and indulged himself once more in pleasant dreams of the future.

Notwithstanding the hard conditions he had become very fond of many things in Brunswick, so that his pleasant hopes were often tinged with sadness, and a gentle melancholy. He often stood in solitude by the Oker and looked at some little passing boat, following it as far as he could with his eyes: and then he would often have a sudden feeling as if he had taken a look into the dark future, but just when he thought he grasped the delusive vision, it suddenly disappeared.

He now took pains to enjoy once more all the regions of the city that he had so far visited on his Sunday walks, and took a sad farewell of each in turn, as if he never hoped to see them again. He heard several more sermons from Pastor Paulmann, many passages from which he has never forgotten. He was extraordinarily moved in a sermon on the sufferings of Jesus by the intensity with which Pastor Paulmann said the words: 'He looks down on his murderers in compassion, and prays and prays and prays "Father, forgive them, for they know not what they do!"'

And in a sermon on confession, given on the Gospel story of the leper, who was to show himself to the priest, the address to the hypocrites, who conscientiously observe all the outward forms of religion, but bear a malevolent heart within them, when every period began with 'you come to the confessional, you show yourselves to the priest, but he cannot see into your heart'. In this sermon too he was extraordinarily moved by an expression frequently repeated, which sounded to him like 'Ihr kommt in den Heben'. The last word, which the preacher always swallowed, so that he could not understand it, sounded like 'Heben' and this word or this sound moved him to tears as often as he thought of it. There was another phrase that often came in Pastor Paulmann's sermons—'the heights of reason', which had an equal charm for him, but this for special reasons, which it will be worth while to explain. The gallery in the church, where the organ stood and the choristers sang, always seemed to him something out of reach: he often looked up to it with longing and desired no greater happiness than for once to be allowed to look closely at the wonderful structure of the organ and all that was up there, because he could now only admire it all at a distance. This fancy was connected with another which he had brought with him from Hanover.

There too a certain tower had been an extremely attractive object: he regarded it with ecstasy morning and evening and often envied the town musicians who stood above in the gallery making music morning and evening to those below. For hours he could watch this gallery, which seemed to him from below so small that it would not reach to his knees, yet would hardly allow the musicians' heads to show over it: and the dial-plate too, which those who had been up assured him was as large as a wagon-wheel, but from below seemed to him no bigger than the wheel of a wheelbarrow. All this roused his curiosity to the utmost, so that he often went about for days with nothing but the thought and the wish to be able for once to see the gallery and the dial-plate close at hand.

Now in the tower at Hanover it was possible through the apertures above the gallery to see the bells being played; and Anton almost devoured the strange spectacle with his eyes, when he saw the great metal machine, which caused the clang that shook the whole structure, swinging up on either side, under the feet of the ringers who looked quite small as they stood high up and trod on the beams. He felt as if he had looked into the very bowels of the tower and as if the mysterious mechanism of the wonderful peal, which he had so often heard with emotion, had now revealed itself in the distance. But his curiosity was only roused the more instead of being satisfied: he had only seen one half of the bell, as it rose upwards with its huge concavity, and not its whole bulk. He had heard of the size of the bell from childhood and his imagination multiplied the image many times over, so that he had the most romantic and extravagant ideas of it.

Amid all the pains he endured in his foot, amid all the oppression from his parents under which he sighed, what was his consolation? What was the pleasantest dream of his childhood? What was his dearest desire, which often made him forget everything else? It was that he might see the dial-plate and the gallery close at hand in the tower of the New Town and the bells that hung in it. For more than a year this play of his fancy cheered the dullest hours of his life, but alas! he had to leave Hanover without his dearest wish being gratified. Yet the image of the tower in the New Town never vanished from his thoughts, it followed him to Brunswick and there often hovered before him in dreams at night as he climbed the tower up high stairs through labyrinthine windings, and stood in the gallery and touched the dial-plate on the tower with inexpressible pleasure, and then inside the tower saw close before his eyes not only the great bell but innumerable smaller ones, with other more wonderful things, until perhaps he knocked his head against the edge of the big bell which he could not look over, and so awoke.

Whenever Pastor Paulmann talked of 'the heights of reason' Anton thought with rapture of the heights of his beloved tower, with its bell and dial-plate, and then also of the organ gallery in the Brothers' Church, and then all at once his longing returned, and the phrase 'the heights of reason' made him shed tears of sadness.

The strictly theoretical part of Pastor Paulmann's sermons, which he delivered with amazing speed, was indeed lost to Anton, who found it too quick for his thoughts to follow. But he listened to him with pleasure, in the hope of hearing the exhortation; then it was that he felt as if the clouds were gathering that would presently fall in beneficent storm or gentle rain. But the day came when he went to the church with the idea of writing down Pastor Paulmann's sermon when he got home, and he felt at once, as he listened, as though light dawned in his soul. His attention had received a new direction. Hitherto he had listened with the heart, now he listened for the first time with the intellect. He no longer wanted merely to be moved by single passages but to grasp the sermon as a whole, and he began to find the theoretical part as interesting as the hortatory. The sermon dealt with love of one's neighbour: how happy men would be, if each tried to further the welfare of every one else and every one else the welfare of each individual. He never forgot this sermon with all its divisions and subdivisions; he heard it with the purpose of writing it down, and did so as soon as he got home and very much astonished August to whom he read it.

Writing down this sermon had as it were developed new faculties in his mind. For from this time his ideas began gradually to sort themselves: he learnt to reflect on a subject for himself, he tried to represent the succession of his thoughts externally, and as he could tell them to no one he expressed them in written essays, which were often strange enough. Before he had communed with God orally, now he began to correspond with Him, and wrote long prayers to Him, describing his condition. He felt himself all the more constrained to written expression, because he was cut off from all reading, for Lohenstein had long ceased to allow him any book, except a description of heaven and hell by Engelbrecht, a journeyman clothier of Winsen on the Aller, which he had given him.

There cannot be a worse braggart in the world than this Engelbrecht must have been: he had been taken for dead, and after his recovery he made his old grandmother believe that he had really been in heaven and hell: she had enlarged on his story, and so the precious book had come into being.

The fellow did not blush to assert that he had floated with Christ and the angels of God close under heaven and had taken the sun in one hand and the moon in the other and counted the stars in heaven. Notwithstanding, his comparisons were sometimes rather naïve: he compared heaven for instance to a delicious wine-soup, of which one only tastes a few drops on earth, but there could take by spoonfuls: and heavenly music surpassed that of earth as a fine concert surpasses the droning of a bag-pipe or the tootle of a night-watchman's horn. And he could not find enough to say of the honour paid him in heaven!

For want of better nourishment Anton's soul had to content itself with this poor diet: at least it served to occupy his imagination: his intellect remained neutral, he neither believed nor doubted, he only pictured it all vividly.

Meanwhile Lohenstein's anger and hatred of him frequently went as far as abuse and blows: he embittered his life most cruelly and made him do the meanest and most humiliating tasks. But nothing offended Anton more than having for the first time in his life to carry a load on his back, a pannier packed with hats, along the public street, while Lohenstein walked in front of him: he felt as if every one in the street was looking at him. Any load which he could carry in front of him or under his arm or in his hands, seemed to him honourable, and no cause for shame. But to be obliged to go bent, and bow his neck beneath the yoke like a beast of burden, while his proud master walked in front, bowed his whole spirit and made the load a thousand times heavier. He felt he must sink into the earth for weariness as well as for shame before he arrived with his burden at his destination. This destination was the arsenal, where the hats, which were regulation hats, were delivered. Anton had eagerly desired to see the inside of the arsenal which he had often passed without being able to gratify his wish, just as he had wished to see the bells and the dial on the tower in the New Town at Hanover. But now his pleasure was completely spoilt by having to see it under these conditions.

This carrying on the back weakened his spirit more than any humiliation he had suffered, and more than Lohenstein's abuse and blows. He felt as if he could not sink lower, he almost regarded himself as a despicable godforsaken creature. This was one of the cruellest situations in his life; whenever he saw an arsenal he had a lively remembrance of it, and its image ran in his mind whenever he heard the word subjugation. When anything of this sort happened, he tried to hide from every one: every cheerful sound jarred on him: he hurried to the Oker behind the house and often looked for hours with longing at the stream below. If even there he was pursued by some human voice from one of the houses near, or if he heard laughing, singing, or talking, he imagined the world was laughing him to scorn, so despised and good for nothing did he regard himself since he had bowed his neck beneath the yoke of a pannier.

He felt a kind of rapture in joining in the bitter

laughter which his gloomy fancy heard ringing over him. In one of those dreadful hours, when he burst into a wild laughter of despair over himself, his disgust at life was so strong that he began to tremble and shake on the weak plank he was standing on. His knees would support him no longer, he fell into the stream. August was his guardian angel: he had been standing behind him unnoticed for some time, and now pulled him out by the arm. Nevertheless other people had come up, the whole house was astir, and Anton was from that moment looked on as a dangerous person, to be got rid of as soon as possible. Lohenstein reported the incident to Anton's father, who came to Brunswick a fortnight later in a bad humour to fetch back to Hanover his misguided son, in whose heart, according to Herr v. Fleischbein's opinion, Satan had built an indestructible temple.

He stayed a day or two with the hatmaker, during which time Anton performed all his duties with redoubled zeal, and found peace in doing all that lay within his powers. He now in thought took leave of the work-shop, the drying-room, the wood-yard, and the Brothers' Church; the pleasantest idea he had was that, when he got home to Hanover, he would then be able to tell his mother about Pastor Paulmann.

The nearer the time of departure came, the lighter was his heart. He would now soon emerge from his narrow cramping position: the wide world opened before him. August took leave of him tenderly, Lohenstein was cold as ice. It was on a Sunday afternoon beneath a dull sky that

Anton and his father left the house of Lohenstein. He looked once more at the black door studded with large nails, and turned his back on it with satisfaction, to walk again through the Gate, outside which he had lately had such an interesting stroll. The high ramparts of the city and the tower of St. Andrew had soon vanished from sight and he could only see the snow-covered Brocken in the distance disappearing in dim twilight beneath the thickening clouds.

His father's heart was cold and reserved towards him, for he looked at him entirely with the eyes of the hat-maker and Herr v. Fleischbein as one in whose heart Satan had built his temple once for all. There was little talk by the way, they walked silently on, and Anton hardly noticed the length of the road, so pleasantly did he hold converse with his thoughts, when he should see his mother and brothers again and be able to tell them his fortunes.

At last the four handsome towers of Hanover rose to heaven, and Anton looked on the tower of the New Town, as a friend seen again after long separation, and at once his love for the bells awoke again.

So he saw himself again within the walls of Hanover and found everything new. His parents had taken a smaller and darker house in a remote street, and everything seemed so strange as he went up the steps, that he felt he could not possibly feel at home there. But if the behaviour of his father was cold and repellent, the delight with which his mother and brothers ran to meet him was loud and demonstrative: they looked at his frost-chapped hands, and for the first time he felt himself pitied again.

When he went out next day he visited all the familiar places where he had played in old days, he felt as if he had grown old and wished to revive the memories of his youth. He met a troop of his old schoolfellows and playmates, who all shook him by the hand and rejoiced at his return.

As soon as he was alone with his mother he could not fail to tell her about Pastor Paulmann. She had an unbounded respect for the clergy, and was very ready to sympathize with Anton in his feelings towards Pastor Paulmann. What blessed hours those were in which Anton was able to unbosom himself and talk to his content of the man whom he loved and respected above all men on earth! He now heard the Hanover preachers, but how different they were! Among them all he found no Paulmann except one called Schlegel, who when he was deeply moved had some resemblance to him. No preacher could win Anton's approval unless he spoke at least as fast as Pastor Paulmann: and if the preacher is viewed as orator only I am not sure whether he was wrong. A teacher must speak slowly, an orator quickly. The teacher has to enlighten the mind by degrees, the orator to penetrate the heart irresistibly: the mind must be approached slowly, the heart quickly, if any result is to be achieved. No doubt he is a bad teacher, who does not at times become an orator, and he is a bad orator who does not at times turn teacher: but when Fox speaks in the English Parliament he does it with unequalled spirit, and carries everything away in the roaring stream of his eloquence, as Pastor Paulmann did in his sermon on perjury.

One Sunday Anton heard a preacher called Marquard at the Garrison church in Hanover with the greatest aversion, because he was not in the least like Pastor Paulmann, and indeed his slow and easy speech was about the exact opposite. Anton when he came home could not help expressing to his mother a feeling of dislike towards this preacher, but what was his surprise when she told him that he was to go to this very preacher for religious instruction and confession and the sacrament, because he was her confessor and she belonged to his congregation! Anton could never have believed that he would one day come to love this man, for whom he now felt an unconquerable aversion, and that he would one day be his friend and benefactor. Meanwhile an event happened which made Anton, who was already inclined to depression, still more melancholy; his mother became dangerously ill, and for a fortnight hovered between life and death. It is impossible to describe Anton's feelings.

His existence was so closely bound up with hers that he felt that his life would end with hers. He often wept all through the night on hearing that the doctor gave up hope of her recovery: he felt that it would be impossible for him to bear the loss of his mother. This was natural enough, for he felt forsaken by every one and found himself again in her love and confidence.

Pastor Marquard came and gave his mother the sacrament; he now thought all hope was gone and was inconsolable, he prayed to God for his mother's life, and thought of King Hezekiah, who received a sign from God that his prayer was heard and his life prolonged. Anton now looked for some such sign. Perhaps the shadow on the garden wall would go back? And at last the shadow did seem to go back, for a thin cloud had passed over the sun or else his fancy put back the shadow; anyhow from that moment he took fresh hope and his mother began really to mend. So his life revived and he did everything to win his parents' affection: but with his father he had no success. Ever since he had fetched him from Brunswick he had taken a bitter irreconcilable dislike to him, which he made him feel on every occasion. Every meal was grudged him, and Anton often had literally to eat his bread with tears.

His only comfort was in his solitary walks with his two younger brothers, with whom he arranged regular expeditions on the ramparts of the city, always fixing some point to which he pretended to make a journey with them. This was his favourite occupation from earliest childhood; when he could scarcely walk he set himself a goal of this sort at the corner of the street where his parents lived, and this was the limit of his little walks. He now converted the rampart which he climbed into a mountain, the bushes through which he struggled into a forest and a hillock in the town ditch into an island, and thus within a circuit of a few hundred paces he often took journeys of many miles with his brothers, lost his path and his bearings with them in forests, climbed high crags, and visited desert islands. In a word he enacted with them as well as he could the whole ideal world of romance. At home he arranged all sorts of games with them, often rather rough ones : he besieged cities, and captured fortresses built of the books of Madame Guyon, with wild chestnuts, which he shot at them like bombs. Sometimes he preached and his brothers had to listen. The first time he had built himself a pulpit of chairs and his brothers sat on footstools in front : he became violently excited, the pulpit collapsed, he fell down and the chair he stood on struck his brothers' heads. The noise and confusion were general ; meanwhile his father came in and began to punish him pretty severely for his sermon, and then his mother came and wanted to rescue him from his father's hands, but as she was unable to do so, her anger took just the opposite direction and she began to lay on to Anton with all her might, in spite of all his prayers and entreaties. Perhaps never was a sermon so unlucky, as this sermon of Anton's, the first he gave in his life. The memory of this incident has often frightened him in dreams. Meanwhile this did not deter him from often mounting his pulpit again and reading whole written sermons with text, subject, and headings. For since he had first begun to write down Pastor Paulmann's sermons, he found it easier to arrange his thoughts, and bring them into connexion with one another. Not a Sunday passed now when he did not write down a sermon, and he soon acquired such facility that he was able to replace anything missing from memory and to reproduce at home on paper almost completely any sermon which he had heard, if he had taken notes of the chief points.

Anton was now more than fourteen, and it was necessary, if he was to be confirmed and received into the bosom of the Christian church, that he should attend for some time a school where religious instruction was given. Now there was an institution in Hanover where young people were educated to be village schoolmasters, to which was attached a free school, which served as a practising-school for the masters. The school there existed rather for the sake of the masters, than the masters for the school, but as the pupils could pay nothing, it was a refuge for the poor, who could get their children taught there for nothing, and as Anton's father had never thought of spending much on a son who was so degenerate and so fallen from divine grace, he brought him at last to this school, where the boy saw at once an entirely new career opened to him. It was a solemn sight for Anton when he saw gathered together in one class at the first morning lesson all the future teachers with their pupils, boys and girls. The inspector of this institution, who was a clergyman, had a catechism class every morning, which was to serve as a pattern to the teachers. The teachers all sat at tables, in order to take notes of the questions and answers, while the inspector walked up and down putting questions. In an afternoon lesson one or other of the teachers had to repeat with the pupils, in presence of the inspector, the catechism which he had given in the morning. Anton by this time had learnt to take notes very easily, and when the teacher repeated in the afternoon the lesson of the morning Anton had taken much better notes in his note-book as he stood in class than the teacher had done, and could answer more than he asked, which seemed to attract the notice of the inspector in a way very flattering for Anton. But, that he should not be conceited with his fortune, a humiliation awaited him almost greater than that which he felt at Brunswick when he had to carry a porter's basket for the first time.

A spelling-practice was fixed for the second lesson next morning, at which one boy had to spell a syllable alone and shout it out and the others had then to shout it with one voice after him. This clamour, which made the ears tingle, and the whole exercise, seemed to Anton sheer madness, and he was not a little ashamed, as he flattered himself that he could now read with expression, at being expected to begin to learn spelling again. Soon his turn came to shout, for it ran round the class like wild-fire: and there he sat hesitating, and at once all the fine music was put out of time. 'Go on!' said the inspector, and when he could not, he looked at him with supreme contempt and said 'stupid boy!' and put on the next boy to spell. Anton felt completely crushed at that moment, seeing himself suddenly sunk so low in the opinion of one on whom he had counted so much, and who now would no longer believe that he could spell. If in Brunswick his body had been subjugated by the load laid upon it, much more was his spirit crushed now by the weight with which the words 'stupid boy!' of the inspector fell on him.

But this time his experience was that of Themistocles, of whom it is told that when once in his youth he suffered a disgrace in public, *non fregit eum sed erexit* (it did not crush his spirit, but roused it). From the day that he was thus humbled he exerted himself ten times more than before to win the respect of his teachers, so as to put to shame, as it were, the inspector who had so misunderstood him, and to make him repent of the wrong which he had inflicted on him.

Every morning the inspector in the early hours lectured dogmatically on the system of the Lutheran church, with refutations of the Papists as well as of the Calvinists, and took as his basis Gesenius's interpretation of Luther's smaller catechism. This filled Anton's head with a good deal of useless lumber, but he learnt how to make divisions and subdivisions, and to go to work systematically.

His note-books grew bigger and bigger and in less than a year he possessed a complete system of dogma, combined with passages from the Bible to prove it, and a complete polemic against heathens, Turks, Jews, Greeks, Papists, Calvinists. He was able to talk like a book about transubstantiation in the sacrament, about the five steps of the exaltation and humiliation of Christ, about the chief doctrines of the Koran and the chief proofs of the existence of God urged against free-thinkers. And he did actually speak like a book on all these things. He had then plenty of material to preach from, and his brothers' lot was now to hear all the contents of his note-books delivered from the break-neck pulpit in the parlour. Sometimes he was invited on Sunday to a cousin's who held a gathering of apprentices :

here he had to stand at the table and deliver a formal sermon with text subject and headings before this assembly: he generally refuted the doctrine of the Papists on transubstantiation or refuted the Atheists, or enumerated with much feeling the proofs of the existence of God and set forth the doctrine of Chance in all its nakedness.

It was the practice of the Institute where Anton was taught, that the adults, who were being educated as schoolmasters, had to distribute themselves on Sunday among all the churches and take notes of the sermons, which they then submitted to the inspector. Anton now found his pleasure in taking notes of sermons doubled because he saw that in this way he shared the occupation of his teachers, and those to whom he showed the sermons showed him increasing respect and met him almost as their equal.

He finally collected a thick volume of reported sermons, which he regarded as a precious possession and two in particular were great treasures: one by Pastor Uhle, who came nearest to Pastor Paulmann in speed of delivery, given in St. Giles's church, was on the Last Judgement. Anton often delivered this to his mother with great delight: the destructive power of the elements, the crash of the universe, the trembling and shaking of the sinner, and the joyous awakening of the righteous were represented in a contrast which excited Anton's imagination in the highest degree, and this was just what he loved. He disliked cold appeals to reason. The second sermon which he prized most highly was a farewell sermon delivered by Pastor Lesemann in the Castle church, a sermon in which he was interrupted from beginning to end by tears and sobs, so much beloved was he by his congregation. The deep emotion with which this was actually delivered made an indelible impression on Anton's heart, and he could wish for no more blessed lot than to be one day allowed to give a farewell sermon like this before such a congregation, who all wept with him.

On such occasions he was in his element and found inexpressible pleasure in the melancholy feeling into which it transported him. No one perhaps has felt 'the joy of grief' more deeply than he felt it on such occasions. To be so moved in spirit by such a sermon he reckoned more precious than any other pleasure in life and he would have given up food and sleep for it.

His feeling for friendship also now found fresh food. He really loved some of his teachers and felt a longing for their society. His friendship was specially directed to a teacher called R——, who to outward appearance was a hard and rough man, but really possessed the noblest heart that can be found in a future village schoolmaster. He gave Anton a private lesson in arithmetic and writing, for which his father paid, for these were the only things which he thought it worth while for Anton to learn.

As he wrote quite correctly already, R—— soon made him write essays of his own, which received his approval. This was so flattering to Anton that at last he took courage to open his heart to him and speak to him with a frankness and freedom he had for long not been able to use to any one.

So he revealed to him his invincible bent for study and the cruelty of his father who kept him from it and wanted to make him learn nothing but a manual trade. The rough R—— seemed moved at this confidence and encouraged Anton to confide in the inspector, who might be able to help him to his object sooner than himself. This was the inspector who, when Anton did not wish to shout at the spelling lesson, had said 'stupid boy!' with a contemptuous face, which he could not yet forget, and therefore long doubted whether to reveal his bent for study to a man who had doubted his power to spell.

Meantime the respect won by Anton in the school grew daily, and he attained his desire, to be the first and attract most attention. This so fed his vanity that he often saw himself in spirit a preacher already, especially if he had on a black waistcoat and breeches: then he walked along with a dignified gait and more serious than usual.

On Saturday at the end of the week, after the hymn 'Bis hierher hat mich Gott gebracht' (So far hath God brought me) had been sung, a long prayer was read by one of the pupils. When the turn came to Anton, it was a real joy to him. He imagined himself in the pulpit, collecting his thoughts during the last verse of the hymn, and then suddenly like Pastor Paulmann with all the wealth of his eloquence bursting into an earnest prayer. His declamation then was too emotional for a schoolboy, and naturally sounded strange: so the teacher rarely let him read the prayer. Indeed in the end the teachers became jealous of him. One of them set an exercise in which one of

Hubner's Bible stories had to be told over again by the pupils in their own words. Anton dressed the story out poetically with all his fancy and delivered it with oratorical embellishment. This offended the master, who remarked that Anton should tell his story more shortly. Next time accordingly he compressed the whole story into a few words and ended in two minutes. This the master found too short and was annoyed again, and finally he did not get him to tell stories in his own words any more. In the afternoon the masters who repeated the catechism class were afraid to question him, as his notes were always fuller than theirs. The result was that he had no chance to show his capacity, which was his dearest wish, that he might attract attention.

Full of vexation at always having to sit dumb and unquestioned, he at last went with tears in his eyes to the inspector, who had often questioned him at morning lessons but seemed to have changed his mind about him. The inspector asked him what was the matter, whether one of his companions had wronged him. Anton answered that it was not his schoolfellows but his teachers who had wronged him: they neglected him now and no one asked him a question, though he knew the subject better than others. In this at least he might have justice!

The inspector tried to talk him over and excused the teachers on the ground of the number of pupils, but from that time he began to pay him more attention and questioned him at the early morning lesson more frequently.

At one lesson in the week an exercise on the

Psalms was set: every pupil had to draw lessons from them for himself, and these were written on a sheet of paper or a slate and then read aloud, which caused anguish to many. The inspector was present. Anton wrote nothing down, but when his turn came he went through the whole Psalm and gave a regular discourse or sermon on it, which lasted half an hour, so that at last the inspector said he was not to explain the Psalm, but only draw some moral lessons from it.

In this way almost a year passed, in which Anton made such extraordinary advance in his diligence and behaved so blamelessly that he completely attained his object of attracting notice, while he also drew on him the envy of his teachers.

He was now at the critical point, when he had to choose some vocation, and the severity of his father, whose object was to get rid of him soon, increased from day to day, so that the school was a sort of sure refuge from the oppression and persecution of his home.

Meanwhile his beloved teacher R—— was promoted to be a village schoolmaster and he now had no friend of his own among his masters. His friend, when he went, once more advised him to appeal to the inspector, and as it was high time in any case to take a decision he ventured one day with beating heart to ask the inspector for an interview, as he wished to talk to him of something important. The inspector took him to his room, and here Anton spoke more freely, told him his story and opened his whole heart to him. The inspector pointed out to him the difficulties and the cost of a University education, but nevertheless did not rob him of all hope, but promised to do what he could to enable him to attend a Latin school. But all this was very remote, he could not hope for anything from his parents for his support, not even board and lodging, as his father had obtained a small office eighteen miles beyond Hanover and therefore had soon to leave Hanover.

Meanwhile the inspector had talked to Councillor Götten, under whose direction the Schoolmasters' Institute was conducted, and he sent for him. The sight of this venerable old man at first discouraged Anton and his knees shook, as he stood before him; but when the old man took him kindly by the hand and talked to him quietly he began to speak frankly and to make known his desire to be a student. The Councillor thereupon made him read aloud one of Gellert's spiritual odes, to hear what sort of voice and enunciation he had, if he should ever wish to devote himself to the ministry.

Then he promised to procure him free instruction and supply him with books: this was all he could do for him. Anton was so overjoyed at this offer that his gratitude knew no bounds and he thought he had conquered all his difficulties at once, for it did not occur to him that besides free instruction and books he also needed food, lodging, and clothes. He hastened home triumphantly and announced his good luck to his parents, but his delight was very much damped when his father coldly said to him that he could not count on a penny from him if he wanted to be a student: if he was in a position to procure himself bread and clothes he had no objection to his studying. He would be leaving Hanover in a few weeks and if

Anton by then had no master to go to, he might look out for a shelter and wait at his pleasure to see whether any of the people who advised him so warmly to be a student would provide for his maintenance.

Sadly and pensively Anton now wandered about, reflecting on his fate: he clung to the idea of study even if many more difficulties stood in his way, and all sorts of plans crossed each other in his mind. He remembered that he had read that once in Greece there was a youth eager for learning who hewed wood and drew water for his maintenance, that he might be able to devote his spare time to study. He wanted to follow this example and was willing to engage himself as a day-labourer for certain hours, if he might have the rest of his time for his free use, but then he could not attend the school lessons regularly: so all his meditation and reflection only made him more melancholy and irresolute. Meantime the critical moment approached when he must make a decision. He was now to leave the school he had hitherto attended, in order to go for a time to the garrison school, because he was to be confirmed by Marquard the garrison preacher, whose preparation and catechism lessons he now began to attend, and whose notice he had attracted by his answers. But he would never have dared of his own accord to confide the troubles of his soul to this man in whom at first he could put no trust.

As no sure prospect opened up for Anton to become a student, he would probably in the end have had to resolve to learn a handicraft had not a very trivial-seeming incident given a different turn to his fortune and affected his whole future life.

II

To obviate further misdirected criticisms, such as have already been passed on this book, I find myself obliged to explain that what, for reasons which may easily be guessed, I have called a psychological romance, is properly speaking a biography, and is as nearly as possible a true and faithful presentation of a human life, down to its smallest details. Any one who is interested in such a faithful presentation will not take offence at what seems at first insignificant and unimportant, but will bear in mind that human life is a complex web in which an infinite number of tiny threads are interwoven, all of which, insignificant as they may appear, have the greatest importance in the whole structure.

A man surveying his past life is at first inclined to see in it mere aimlessness, broken threads, confusion, night and darkness; but as he fixes his gaze more closely, the darkness vanishes, the aimlessness gradually disappears, the broken threads rejoin, order appears in place of confusion and disorder, and discord is resolved into harmonious melody.

1786.

PART II

The Turning-point

The circumstance that unexpectedly gave a happier turn to Anton's fortunes was this. He was fighting in the street with two lads who came out of school with him and had teased him till he could bear it no longer. As they were struggling and pulling one another's hair, up came Pastor Marquard, and Anton's shame and confusion were great when the other boys pointed out with malicious pleasure how angry Pastor Marquard would be with him.

To think of it! I want one day to be a man respected as he is. I want every one to read this in my face, so that some one may befriend me and lift me from the dust, and yet I let myself be surprised in this position, by the man who is to confirm me, when I had an opportunity to show myself in the best light. What will he think of me? what will he take me for?

Such were the thoughts that passed through Reiser's mind and so overwhelmed him with shame, confusion, and self-contempt that he thought he must sink into the earth. But he recovered himself, his self-confidence struggled through his stifling sense of shame and gave him courage: he plucked up heart, and went straight up to Pastor Marquard and addressed him in the public street, telling him he was one of the boys who went to him for religious instruction; he must not be angry with him for fighting the other boys, it was not his usual way, they had provoked him and it should not happen again.

Pastor Marquard was much surprised to be thus addressed in the street by a boy who had just been fighting with two others: after a pause he said it was very wrong and improper to fight, but he would overlook it, if he gave it up in future. Then he asked his name and who his parents were and what school he had been to before, and dismissed him very kindly. Reiser was overjoyed and light-hearted at the thought that he had extricated himself from this dangerous situation, and his joy would have been much greater had he known that this chance incident would put an end to all his anxieties and be the foundation of his future fortunes. For at the moment Pastor Marquard had made up his mind to inquire about this young man more closely and to take him up, because he conjectured, with good reason, that if young Reiser's behaviour was not pretence, and that his face seemed to guarantee, it argued an unusual attitude of mind in a boy of his age.

The next Sunday at the afternoon lesson Pastor Marquard asked him more questions than usual, and Reiser had already in a way attained one of his wishes—to be able to speak before the assembled people in church, to speak in public—for he answered the pastor's questions on the catechism in a loud and distinct voice, in which he differed from the rest, as he gave the proper accent, while they droned their answers in the usual sing-song of schoolboys.

After the lesson Pastor Marquard beckoned him

aside and summoned him to come to him next morning. What a happy restlessness at once overmastered his thoughts, for it looked as if at last some one was going to take trouble about him, for he flattered himself that Pastor Marquard's attention had been drawn to him by his answers and he resolved to trust him and confide all his wishes to him.

When he came to Pastor Marquard next morning after an almost sleepless night, the Pastor asked him to what sort of life he thought of devoting himself, which paved the way for what he had meant to say. Anton confided his plans to him. Pastor Marquard put the difficulties before him but at the same time bade him be of good heart and gave him practical encouragement by promising to get him taught Latin by his only son, who attended the first class in the Lyceum at Hanover, and a beginning was made that very week. All the time Reiser thought the attitude and behaviour of Pastor Marquard implied that he had something more in reserve, which he would tell him in due time: in this conjecture he was confirmed by the mysterious expressions of the Garrison Church sacristan, whose lessons he still attended, and who always gave him a chair, while the others sat on benches. The sacristan, after the lesson was over, used to say to him: 'Be on your guard and remember that you are watched', 'great things are moving for you', and so on, so that Anton began to regard himself as a more important person than before and his petty vanity was fed over much and showed itself often foolishly enough in his carriage and his countenance. Many a time he came dreaming along the street with all the serious dignity of a teacher of the people, as he had done before in Brunswick, especially if he had on a black waistcoat and breeches. In walking he had taken as his pattern the carriage of a young clergyman who was then preacher at the hospital in Hanover, also Senior Assistant Master of the Lyceum, because he had a way of carrying his chin which Anton specially liked.

Rarely can any one have been happier than Anton was at that time, expecting the great things that were to happen to him. His imagination was excited to the utmost. And as the time now came near when he was to be admitted to Communion, once more the extravagant ideas about it which got into his head in Brunswick, revived, with the addition of the teaching of the Sacristan, who painted heaven and hell in so appalling a manner to those whom he helped to prepare for Communion that his hearers were often attacked by fear and terror, blended, however, with the pleasant feeling with which people generally listen to what is fearful and terrible, and then he felt the pleasure of having deeply moved his hearers, and shed tears of joy, which gave a still more solemn air to the whole scene as he stood among them in the evening in the lighted school-room.

Pastor Marquard too had weekly lessons, in which he prepared those who were to go to Communion, but what he said did not come near to the soul-moving addresses of his sacristan, although Reiser thought it better constructed and better expressed. Nothing was more flattering for Reiser than when he illustrated the idea that believers are the children of God by the illustration, that if he associated more intimately with one of his young hearers, made him come to him specially and conversed with him, he was nearer to him than the others, and in the same way the children of God were nearer to him than other men.

Now Reiser believed he was the only one of the class to whom Pastor Marquard had shown more attention than to others. This, though it flattered his vanity, soon afterwards filled him with inexpressible sadness, to think that all the rest could not share in this good fortune, which had befallen him alone, and were to be for ever it would seem excluded from close intimacy with Pastor Marquard. A sadness, which he remembered he had once felt in the earliest years of his childhood, when his aunt had bought him a toy in a shop, which he was carrying in his hand as he left the house. In front of the door sat a beggar girl of his own age in rags, who, in admiration of the lovely toy, cried out 'My God! how lovely!' Reiser might have been six or seven then: the tone of patient resignation, notwithstanding her profound admiration, with which the ragged girl said 'My God! how lovely!' pierced his heart. The poor girl had to see all these lovely things carried past her, and might not ever think of possessing one of them. She was so near, and yet as it were cut off for ever from the enjoyment of these precious things. How gladly would he have gone back and given the ragged girl his costly toy, had his aunt allowed it! Whenever he thought of it afterwards, he bitterly repented not having given it to the girl at once. It was this kind of pitiful sadness which

Reiser felt, when he thought himself honoured by the favour of Pastor Marquard to the exclusion of others, so that his schoolfellows were put so far below him without having deserved it.

Exactly the same feeling was awakened in his mind later, whenever he read in Virgil's first eclogue the words 'nec invideo' ('I envy not'). As he put himself in the place of the happy shepherd, who can sit at peace in the shadow of his tree while his friend must turn his back on house and field, he had exactly the same feeling about this man's 'I envy not' as when the ragged girl cried 'My God! how lovely!'

I have found it necessary to go back some way in Anton's life and also to anticipate in order to bring together what for my purpose is connected. I shall often do this, and from any one who has realized my object I need ask no indulgence for my apparent digressions. It can easily be seen that Anton's vanity was far too much encouraged by the circumstances which now combined to make him feel his own importance. Some small humiliation was needed and duly came. He flattered himself, not without reason, he was first among all Pastor Marquard's confirmation candidates. He sat at the top and was certain that no one else would dispute this place with him, when suddenly a young well-dressed man of his own age and of superior education attended the lessons of Pastor Marquard, and by his refined bearing as well as the special respect which Pastor Marquard paid him, threw him quite into the shade, and at once received the first place.

Reiser's pleasant dream of being the first among his comrades had now suddenly disappeared. He felt himself lowered, degraded, lumped in one class with the rest. He inquired of the Pastor's servant about his formidable rival and learnt that he was the son of a high government official and boarding with the pastor, and that he would be confirmed with the rest. The blackest envy for a long time occupied Anton's heart; the blue coat with velvet collar, which the official's son wore, his elegant bearing, and the style of his coiffure, depressed him and made him discontented, but soon arose the feeling that this was unjust and he became discontented at his own discontent. He need not have envied the poor boy, whose sun of fortune had soon set. Within a fortnight came the news that his father had been cashiered for unfaithfulness in office. Accordingly the young man's board could no longer be paid for, Pastor Marquard sent him back to his relations and Reiser retained his place at the top. He could hardly repress his delight at the consequences of this incident, and yet he reproached himself for his delight; he tried to force himself to pity, because he thought it right, and to repress his delight because he thought it wrong; yet nevertheless it got the upper hand and his only resource then was to feel that he could do nothing against fate, which had willed to make the young man unhappy. The question arises: if the young man's fate had suddenly altered again, would Reiser of his own accord have been glad to let him take his place with a smile of sympathy, or would he only have adopted this feeling with a kind of effort because he thought it right and generous? The course of his history may hereafter decide this question.

Every evening Reiser had a Latin lesson with the son of Pastor Marquard and got on so well that within a month he learnt to construe Cornelius Nepos with fair success. How delighted he was when the sacristan came in and asked what the two students were doing: and when a young minister, who had just married the pastor's eldest daughter, took the children's lesson for him one Sunday afternoon, and seemed to take more and more notice of Anton, the more he heard him answer: what an entrancing moment it was for Reiser, when he went to the pastor's house after service and the son-in-law addressed him with the greatest respect and said that as soon as he heard Anton's first answer the question occurred to him whether this might be the young man of whom he had such a good account from his father-in-law, and he was glad he was not wrong. Never in his life had Anton experienced such a feeling as this respectful treatment gave him. As he had not learnt the language of cultivated society and yet did not wish to use vulgar expressions, he used bookish language on such occasions, put together out of *Telemachus*, the Bible, and the Catechism. This often gave his answers a peculiar touch of originality, as for instance on such occasions he used to say that he had not been able to overcome the impulse to study which had irresistibly carried him away, and wished to make himself in every way worthy of the benefits shown him, and to try to pursue his life in godliness and honesty to the end.

Meanwhile Councillor Götten, to whom Reiser had applied, had arranged for him to attend the 'New Town School' without paying fees: but

Pastor Marquard said that this could not be, and that, till his confirmation, he should continue to be instructed by Marquard's son, in order that he might go straight into the Upper School in the Old Town, where the Director would look after him: owing to the jealousy between the two schools it would be better for him not to attend the New Town school first. Reiser had to tell Councillor Götten this, in order to decline the free instruction he had procured him; he was at first rather touchy and used hard words to Reiser, but finally dismissed him with the encouraging words that he would help him in some other way.

Thus Reiser's fortunes, about which no one had troubled in the past, seemed suddenly to become a matter of general interest. He heard talk of jealousy between schools on his account. Councillor Götten and Pastor Marquard seemed to be disputing which should do most for him. Pastor Marquard used the expression that he should tell Councillor Götten that arrangements had been made and would be made in the future to prepare him properly for the Upper School in the Old Town without his having first to attend the Lower School in the New Town. Arrangements then were to be made for a boy whom his own parents had not considered worth attention.

I need not say with what brilliant dreams and prospects this filled Reiser's imagination, especially as the garrison sacristan's mysterious hints and Pastor Marquard's reserve, which seemed to withhold some secret, continued. At last it came out that the Prince of Mecklenburg-Strelitz on Pastor Marquard's recommendation wished to take up young Reiser and provide . . . Reichsthaler a month for his maintenance. Thus Reiser was suddenly relieved of all anxieties for the future, his pleasant dream of a good fortune he had longed for but never hoped to achieve had become actual before he was aware and he could indulge his most agreeable fancies without any fear of disturbance by need or poverty.

His heart went out in gratitude to Providence. Not an evening passed that he did not include the Prince and Pastor Marquard in his prayers, and he often shed quiet tears of joy and gratitude, when he reflected on this happy turn of his fortunes.

Reiser's father raised no further objection to his becoming a student as soon as he heard that it was to cost him nothing: besides, as the time was drawing near when he was to take up his petty post twenty miles from Hanover, his son could not in any way be a burden. The question now was where was Reiser to live and get his meals when his parents had gone. Pastor Marquard did not seem inclined to take him into his house, and some plan had to be devised for boarding him with decent people. A bandsman, of the regiment of Prince Charles, offered to let Reiser lodge with him for nothing. A shoemaker, with whom his parents had once lodged, another bandsman, a court musician, a cook-shop-keeper and a silk-embroiderer each offered to give him free meals once a week.

This somewhat diminished Reiser's delight: he had thought that the Prince's provision would suffice for his maintenance, without his having to eat his bread at strange tables: and this feeling was not groundless, for he often found himself in a very anxious and disagreeable position, when he had literally to eat his bread in tears. Every one was eager to do him this kindness, but every one thought it gave him a right to watch his conduct and give him advice on his behaviour, advice which he then had to follow if he did not wish to anger his benefactors. Thus Reiser was dependent on people with as many different ideas as there were people who gave him free meals, and every one threatened to withdraw his help if he did not follow his advice, often the exact opposite of that of some other benefactor. One thought his hair too well dressed, another too ill dressed, one thought he went too ill clothed, another too well for one who had to live on charity, and there were countless humiliations and abasements to which his free meals exposed him, an experience to which any young man is more or less exposed, who has the misfortune to get his maintenance at school by free meals, and go from one house to another through the week for his board.

All this Reiser dimly surmised when free meals were accepted for him in the mass and no offer of any benefit was refused. There is never any want of goodwill, when people think they can help a young man to the University: they are all eagerness, every one vaguely thinking—if this man one day stands in the pulpit, it will be partly my work. So there was a regular competition about Reiser, and even the poorest wished at once to help him: thus a poor shoemaker offered to give him a meal every Sunday evening. All this was joyfully accepted for him, and his parents calculated with the bandsman and his wife how fortunate he was in having meals for every day in the week, so that the money the Prince provided could be saved up for him.

Alas! the brilliant prospect of good fortune that had presented itself to Anton's eyes clouded over again later, but the first agreeable excitement roused by the active help and sympathy of so many people in his fortunes lasted for some time. The wide domain of knowledge lay before him: his one thought the whole day long was how best to apply every hour of study, and the delight he would find in it and the amazing progress he would make and the fame and approval he would win. These pleasant thoughts were his companions when he rose and when he went to bed: he did not realize how deeply his pleasure would be embittered by the crushing humiliations of his position. If a young man is to keep his courage for diligent study he must have decent food and decent clothes. Reiser had neither. In the desire to save for him his friends let him practically starve.

His parents now left Hanover and he moved with his few possessions to the house of the bandsman Filter whose wife had befriended him from childhood. Life in this household, where there were no children, was ordered in the most methodical way possible. There was nothing, not a brush nor a pair of scissors, which had not had its definite allotted place for years. There was never a morning when coffee was not drunk at eight and prayers read at nine: every one knelt, while Frau Filter read from Benjamin Schmolk, and Reiser had to kneel with them. In the evening after nine prayers were read out of Schmolk in the same way, every one kneeling before his chair, and then they went to bed. This was the inviolable order observed by these people for some twenty years, during which they had lived in the same room : and very happy they were in it, but nothing whatever must disturb the regularity, if they were not to lose something of the inward content which largely depended on it. They had not considered this when they resolved to share the society of their room with a third person, who could not possibly fit in with their arrangements of twenty years' standing, which had become a second nature to them.

Naturally enough they soon repented of having taken on them a burden heavier than they expected. As they had only one parlour and one bedroom, Reiser had to sleep in the parlour, which now presented when they came in, an unexpected look of disorder, to which they were not accustomed, and which disturbed their contentment. Anton soon noticed this and the thought of being a burden was so vexatious and disagreeable to him that he often scarcely ventured to cough, when he saw from the looks of his benefactors that they felt him a burden. For he had to put his few things somewhere and wherever he put them they disturbed the order of the room, because every place was already assigned, and yet he found it impossible to extricate himself from this disagreeable position. All this, taken together, caused him inexpressible melancholy for hours, which he could not explain and at first set down to the novelty of his new position.

It was really nothing but the humiliating thought

of being a burden which depressed him. His life with his parents and with Lohenstein the hatter had certainly not been a merry one, but he had a sort of right to be there, because they were his parents and his employer, but here even the chair he sat on was a charity. Would that all who want to do a kindness would think this over and see if they could contrive that their well-meant resolve may never be a torment to the person they are helping! Although every one counted him fortunate, the year which Reiser spent thus was at certain hours and moments one of the most painful in his life.

Reiser might perhaps have made his position pleasanter if he had only had what in many young people is called an ingratiating manner, but for this a certain self-confidence is necessary, which he lacked from childhood; if you want to be agreeable you must think that you can make yourself agreeable. Reiser's self-confidence needed to be elicited by kindness before he could venture to make himself amiable. Whenever he noticed that people did not seem to like him, he was inclined to despair of the possibility of ever becoming the object of their affection or respect. It therefore required a great effort on his part to try to win people's notice, when he did not know how they would receive his advances.

His aunt very often prophesied to him that the want of ingratiating manners would prevent his getting on in the world. She taught him how to speak to Frau Filter and say 'Dear Frau Filter, be a mother to me, for I have no father or mother, and I will love you like a mother!' But when Reiser wanted to say something of this sort, the words seemed to stick in his throat, and if he had tried to say it, it would have come out quite awkwardly. Such tender expressions had never been elicited from him by any one's kind and considerate bearing: he had not a pliable tongue for such things. He could not follow his aunt's advice. When his heart was full, he used any expression he could find, but he had never learnt the speech of refined society; what are called ingratiating manners he would have regarded as abject flattery.

Meanwhile the time had come when Reiser was to be confirmed and publicly make his confession of faith in church, a great encouragement to his vanity: he thought of the assembled people, of himself as first among his fellow-pupils, who would attract general attention by voice, face, and gesture as he answered. The day dawned and Reiser awoke with the feeling of a Roman general before his triumph. His hair was specially dressed by his uncle, the wig-maker, and he wore a bluish coat and black small-clothes, the nearest approach to the clerical dress. But just as the triumph of the greatest general is sometimes embittered by unexpected humiliations, so it was with Reiser on this day of his honour and glory. His free meals began that day, he had the first, his midday dinner at the Garrison Church sacristan's, and the second, the evening meal at the poor shoemaker's, and though the sacristan was a man who had a most generous heart and told Reiser his whole career, how he too had entered the choir as a pupil but in his seventeenth year had exchanged the blue coat for the black, yet his wife was all envy and jealousy and every glance poisoned for Reiser the food he put in his mouth. This was not so noticeable the first day as later, but enough to make Reiser go to church with heart depressed he knew not why, and to deprive him of half the delight he had promised himself on this day.

He was now to take his oath, so to speak, to his confession of faith. With this in his mind and also remembering that his father had told him some time before how he had taken his oath of service and was anything but indifferent, yet when he went to church Reiser felt himself indifferent about the oath which he was to take. From the instruction in religion he had received he had very high conceptions of an oath, and regarded this indifference in itself as very culpable. He therefore forced himself not to be indifferent but seriously moved at this important step and was dissatisfied with himself because he did not feel it more deeply, but it was the looks of the sacristan's wife which had frightened all gentle and pleasant feelings out of his mind.

He certainly could not enjoy it properly, because there was no one who intimately shared his enjoyment, and because he reflected that that very day he had to eat at a stranger's table. However, when he came into the church and walked up to the altar and stood first in the row, it warmed his imagination, but still it did not by any means come up to what he had promised himself. And just the most solemn and important thing, the actual delivery of the confession of faith, which one had to do in the name of the rest, did not fall to his lot, though for days before he had practised the expression, tone, and gesture with which he would deliver it.

He thought that Pastor Marquard would perhaps send for him in the afternoon, but he did not, and while his companions went home to meet the tender welcome of their parents, Reiser wandered lonely and forsaken about the streets, where he met the Director of the Lyceum, who asked him whether his name was not Reiserus and when Reiser said yes, shook him by the hand in friendly fashion and said he had heard much good of him through Pastor Marquard and would soon make his better acquaintance. What an unexpected encouragement it was that this man whom he had often looked at with deep respect deigned to address him in the street and called him Reiserus ! Director Ballhorn was indeed a man made to inspire respect and affection in any one who saw him. His dress was smart but suitable, he had a fine carriage, was handsome, and wore the most cheerful face, to which he could at will give an air of great severity. He was a schoolmaster, just of the kind calculated to clear the profession of the charge of pedantry generally brought against it. How it came about that he called Reiser ' Reiserus ', heaven knows ; enough, that he did call him so, and Reiser was not a little flattered to see his name for the first time made to end in *-us* ; for he had always associated this ending with the idea of dignity and amazing learning, and already in spirit heard himself called the learned and famous Reiserus. This name, with which he was accidentally honoured by Director Ballhorn, often came into his mind afterwards, and many a time spurred him to diligence, for with the termination in *-us* the whole series of ideas awoke in his mind, of becoming a famous scholar like

Erasmus of Rotterdam and others, whose biographies he had read and seen their portraits in copper-plate engravings.

In the evening he went to the poor shoemaker, and was at least received with friendlier looks than by the sacristan's wife. Heidorn the shoemaker, for that was his benefactor's name, had read the writings of Tauler and others like them and spoke therefore a kind of literary language, tinged occasionally with a certain preaching tone. For any assertion he made he generally quoted a certain Periander: 'man must resign himself to God', says Periander: and thus everything said by shoemaker Heidorn was said by this Periander, who in fact was nothing but an allegorical person found in Bunyan's *Pilgrim's Progress* or elsewhere. But the name Periander sounded sweet in Reiser's ears; it made him think of something exalted and mysterious and he always liked to hear the shoemaker Heidorn talk of Periander.

The good Heidorn, however, had kept him too late and when he came home his host and hostess had already read their evening-prayers and could not go to bed afterwards, an event which could not have happened for years. This was why Reiser was received somewhat coldly and gloomily and had to lie down with a sad heart at the end of the day, to which he had looked forward with such eager expectation.

This week he had to make his round of meals for the first time and began on Monday with the cook-shop-keeper, where he had his meal among the other people, who paid, and no one troubled about him. This was what he liked and he always went there with a light heart. On Sunday at midday he went to the shoemaker with whom his parents had lodged and was received in the most affectionate and friendly way. The good people had known him as a little child and the shoemaker's old mother had always said 'the youngster will come to something' and now rejoiced that her prophecy seemed to be coming true. If ever Reiser lost the feeling that he was eating the bread of strangers it was at this hospitable board, where he so often afterwards forgot his troubles and went away with a cheerful face when he had arrived with a sad one. For with the shoemaker he plunged into deep philosophical discussions till the old mother said: 'Now children, stop and don't let your dinner get cold'.

What a man the shoemaker was! It might be said of him with truth, that he ought to have taught from the professor's chair those for whom he made shoes. He and Reiser in their conversations often arrived without any guidance at things which Reiser heard again in lectures on metaphysics as the profoundest wisdom, and he had often discussed them for hours with the shoemaker Schantz. For they had arrived by their own efforts at the development of ideas of space and time, of the subjective and the objective world and so on: they did not know the terminology of the schools, but helped themselves out with the language of common life as well as they could, which often came out strangely enough. In a word, Reiser in the shoemaker's company forgot all the disagreeables of his position and felt himself as it were transported into the higher spirit world and his nature uplifted because he found some one with whom he could understand and be understood and exchange thought for thought. The hours which he spent here with the friends of his childhood and his youth were certainly at that time the pleasantest in his life. This was the only place where he felt himself with confidence completely at home.

On Wednesdays he ate with his host, where the little he enjoyed, however kindly these people might mean it, was almost always so embittered that he shrank from this day almost more than from any other. For at this meal his benefactress, Frau Filter, not directly but by indirect allusions in conversation with her husband, used to review Reiser's conduct, to impress on him gratitude towards his benefactors and to drop hints of people who had learnt the habit of eating a great deal and in the end were past satisfying. Reiser, who was at that time growing fast, had indeed a very good appetite but put every morsel into his mouth trembling, when he heard such allusions. Frau Filter made these allusions not so much from greed or envy, as from her nice sense of order which was offended if any one to her notion ate too much. On such occasions she would speak of springs of mercy and wells of grace, which ceased to run if you did not draw from them in moderation.

The wife of the court musician, who gave him meals on Thursdays, though her manners were somewhat unpolished, did not annoy him half so much as Frau Filter with all her refinement. But Friday again was a bad day, for he ate with people who made him feel that they were his benefactors not by mere allusions, but quite rudely. They had known him from childhood, and they called him by his Christian name Anton, not from affection but contemptuously, though he was beginning to regard himself as a grown-up person. In fact they treated him in such a way that all through Friday he used to be sad and out of spirits, with no heart for anything, often without knowing why. The reason was that he was exposed at midday to the humiliating society of these people, whose kindness he was forced to put up with, if he was not to be regarded as unpardonably proud. On Saturday he had meals with his uncle, the wig-maker, where he paid a trifle and ate with a glad heart, and on Sunday he returned to the Sacristan.

This list of Reiser's free meals and the persons who gave them is not as unimportant as perhaps it may seem to many at first sight. It is just such apparently trivial circumstances which make up life and have the strongest influence on character. Anton's industry and daily progress depended very much on his prospect for the next day—whether he had to eat with shoemaker Schantz or Frau Filter or the Sacristan. His subsequent behaviour, which otherwise might seem in contradiction with his character, must largely be explained by his situation from day to day.

It would have been a great advantage for Reiser if Pastor Marquard had had him to meals once a week: but he gave him instead 'table-money', and so did the silk-embroiderer, and from these scanty pence Reiser had to wrest the cost of breakfast and supper every week. This was Frau Filter's arrangement, for the Prince's gift was all to be saved up for him. His breakfast then consisted of a little tea and a bit of bread and his supper of bread and butter and salt. Frau Filter told him he must rely on his dinner, while at the same time she gave him to understand that he must not overeat. Such was the arrangement of Reiser's board. For his clothes too, no money was taken from the Prince's allowance, but a coarse old red soldier's coat was bought and altered for him. In this he had to attend the public school, where even the poorest was better dressed than he, a circumstance which contributed not a little from the first to depress his spirits.

Moreover he had to fetch the bread-ration which the bandsman Filter drew, and carry it in his arms through the street, which he did if possible at twilight, but unless he was to be considered as unpardonably proud he dared not let it be seen that he was ashamed : one loaf a week was left over for him to buy for a small sum, and this had to provide his breakfast and supper.

Against all this he could not make the least protest, because Pastor Marquard put the greatest confidence in Frau Filter so far as Reiser's education and the arrangements for his living were concerned. That very week he visited the Filters and thanked them for consenting to take on them the immediate oversight of Reiser, whom he confided completely to their charge. Reiser meantime sat half sadly by the stove, though he did not want to be ungrateful for the care of Pastor Marquard, but from this moment he depended entirely on people with whom he had already spent these few days under such distressing conditions. Amid all this seeming kindness shown him he could never be happy but was always uncomfortable and embarrassed, because any sign of displeasure, even the slightest, that they showed him, was doubly vexatious when he reflected that the very spot where he lived, the shelter he enjoyed, depended merely on the kindness of such sensitive and easily offended persons as Filter and still more his wife.

However, amid all this he was cheered by the thought that next week he was to begin attending the High School. This had long been his dearest wish. He had often gazed with admiration at the great school building, with the high stone steps in front of it, as he walked across the market-place. He often stood for hours trying to see through the window what was going on inside : it chanced that he could get a glimpse of the great desk in the VIth Form class-room, and how his imagination completed the picture ! How often he dreamed of the Master's desk and of long rows of benches, where sat the lucky students of wisdom, into whose society he was soon to be received. So completely from his childhood were his pleasures provided by his own imagination, which compensated him in some degree for the real pleasures of youth, which others enjoyed in full measure.

Close by the school two long alleys led to the priests' houses, built side by side. They had such a venerable aspect that they and the school together dominated his thoughts day and night, and then the name High School, current among common folk, and the expression 'High-school boys' which he often heard, made his prospect of going there more and more significant.

The time, when this was to happen, now came and with beating heart he waited the moment when Director Ballhorn would lead him to one of these lecture-rooms of wisdom. He was examined by the Director and found fit to be put into the Vth Form. The friendliness, combined with natural dignity, with which this man first called him ' my dear Reiser ' moved him deeply and inspired complete confidence, combined with unbounded respect for the Director. What an influence a teacher has over the hearts of young people if like Director Ballhorn he can strike the right note of dignity softened by friendliness !

The Sunday after his confirmation Reiser went to Communion for the first time, and tried most conscientiously to practise the instruction he had written down and learnt by heart ; the preliminary examination by the pattern of sin and penance, then the approach to the altar with joy and trembling. He tried every means to put himself into such a state of joy and trembling, but he could not succeed and reproached himself most bitterly for the hardness of his heart. At last he began to tremble with cold and that quieted him somewhat.

He did not experience the heavenly sensation and blessed feeling which this holy food was to give him : but he put the blame for it on his own hardened heart and tormented himself about the state of indifference in which he found himself. What pained him most was that he could not properly realize his miserable state of sin, which yet was necessary for salvation. The day before he had had to make his confession in a formula learnt by heart—that he had sinned in many ways by thought word and deed, leaving the good undone and doing evil. The sins he accused himself of were chiefly sins of omission. He did not pray devoutly enough, did not love God ardently enough, did not feel gratitude towards his benefactors, and felt no tremulous joy when he went to Communion. All this distressed him, but he could not force himself to feel differently, and therefore he was very glad that Pastor Marquard gave him absolution for these misdoings. But he remained discontented with himself, for he considered religion and piety to consist mainly in watching every step he took, every smile and expression, every word that he spoke and thought that he conceived. Naturally this attention to his every act was bound to be interrupted and could not continue more than an hour in one stay: as soon as Reiser noticed his distraction he was dissatisfied with himself and finally regarded it as impossible to lead a consistently religious and pious life.

Frau Filter delivered him on the day he went to Communion a long sermon on the evil lusts and desires which were wont to spring up at his age and against which he must do battle. Luckily Reiser did not properly understand what she meant and did not dare to inquire more particularly, but only resolved that if evil desires should spring up in him, of whatever kind they might be, he would fight against them valiantly.

In his religious instruction at the Training-school he had heard all sorts of sexual sins referred to in comments on the sixth commandment and had taken notes of them, but they were names and nothing more to him and happily the inspector had painted these sins in such awful colours that Reiser shrank from picturing their enormity and did not venture even in thought to penetrate the mystery that surrounded them. His notions of man's origin were very vague and confused, though he no longer believed that children were brought by the stork. At that time his thoughts were quite pure, for a feeling of shame, which seemed natural to him, prevented his thoughts dwelling on such things or daring to talk of them to his schoolfellows and acquaintances: his religious notions of sin also helped him. It was dreadful enough that such vices, which he knew only by name, existed in the world, and he had no desire to pry into their nature.

On the Monday morning Director Ballhorn introduced him into the Vth Form of the Lyceum, where the Assistant Master and the Precentor taught. The Assistant Master was a preacher, whom Reiser had often heard, and it was he too whose bearing in his clerical dress specially pleased Reiser, who sometimes tried to imitate it with an up-and-down movement of the chin. Pastor Grupen, that was his name, was a very young man, the Precentor on the other hand was old and somewhat hypochondriacal.

The Vth Form contained boys who were nearly grown up and Reiser prided himself not a little on being a Vth Form boy (Sekundaner).

The lessons began; the Assistant Master taught theology, history, Latin composition, and the Greek Testament, the Precentor catechism, geography and Latin grammar. The lessons began at seven in the morning and lasted till ten, and in the afternoon began at one and lasted till four.

Here then Reiser had to spend a great deal of his life with twenty or thirty other young people: it was therefore a matter of some importance how these lessons were arranged.

At the beginning of every morning in the prescribed order a chapter was read from the Bible, in strict succession, however long or short it might be. After this, twice a week followed a lesson in theology according to a certain scheme of salvation, in which God's *opera ad extra* were specially distinguished from *opera ad intra*. Under the former were understood all the operations in which all three Persons of the Godhead took part—creation, redemption, &c., although they are mainly ascribed to one Person: under the latter those in which one Person was solely active and was distinguished from another, as for instance the generation of the Son by the Father, the proceeding of the Holy Ghost from the Father and the Son and so on. Reiser had heard these distinctions before at the Training School but he was delighted now to be able to give them their Latin names. The *opera ad extra* and the *opera ad intra* made the deepest impression of all his theological teaching.

The Assistant Master lectured twice a week from Holberg on universal history and the Precentor taught geography from Hübner: apart from these lessons, the whole time was spent in learning Latin, the only subject in which any one could win honour or approval, for the whole order of places was determined by success in Latin.

The method of the Precentor was to dictate every week a short essay on a number of rules out of the great Brandenburg grammar, to be translated into Latin, the expressions being chosen in such a way that the grammatical rules in question could be applied to them : so that those who had best attended to the explanation of them could do his exercise best and work his way up to a higher place. Though the German phrases collected together for the sake of the Latin sometimes sounded peculiar, the exercise was useful and excited great rivalry. Within a year Anton made so much progress that he wrote Latin without a single error, and in fact expressed himself more correctly in Latin than in German : for in Latin he knew where he had to put the accusative and dative, whereas in German he had never reflected that *mich* is accusative and *mir* dative and that it is necessary to decline and conjugate German as well as Latin. Meanwhile without knowing it he was getting hold of some general notions, which he could afterwards apply to his mother tongue. He began gradually to form clear notions of what was meant by substantive and verb, which he often confused when they were like one another, as for instance *gehn* (to go) and *das Gehen* (going). As however, errors of this kind were apt to cause mistakes in his Latin composition, he became more attentive to the subject and insensibly learnt the finer distinctions between the parts of speech and their inflexions, so that after a time he sometimes wondered how he could have made such surprising mistakes only a short time before.

The Precentor, after noting the number of mistakes in each Latin exercise with red strokes was in the habit of writing *vidi* (I have seen it) underneath. When Reiser saw this *vidi* under his first exercise he thought it was a word which he had to write himself at the end of his exercise, and that the Precentor had counted its omission as a mistake, so under his second exercise he wrote *vidi* himself, at which the Precentor and his son, who was by, laughed loud and explained what it meant. Reiser at once saw his error and could not understand how the explanation had not occurred to him, for he knew quite well what *vidi* meant. He felt like one awaking from a kind of stupid fit which had come over him, and for a few moments he was as much depressed as when the inspector at the Training College once said to him ' stupid boy ', thinking that he could not spell. Such real or apparent stupidity on certain occasions arose partly from a want of presence of mind, partly from a certain diffidence or perhaps indolence which for a time hindered the free activity of his thought.

Another important lesson was Cornelius Nepos's biographies of Greek generals, from which a chapter of the life of some general had to be repeated by heart every week. Reiser found these exercises of memory very easy, because he tried to impress on his mind not so much the words as the subject: this he always did in the evening before going to sleep, and in the morning when he woke he found the ideas far better and more clearly arranged in his memory than the evening before, as though his mind had continued to work during sleep and had completed at leisure what it had once begun, during the whole time his body was at rest. Everything that Reiser committed to memory he used to learn by heart in this way.

He now began to occupy himself with poetry, as

he had already done in childhood, when the subjects of his verse were the beauties of nature, country life and the like. For his lonely walks and the sight of the green meadows when he came out of the city gates were the only things which could inspire him with poetry. As a boy of ten he wrote a few stanzas which began

In the flowery meadows green
Heaven's goodness may be seen

which his father set to music. The poem which he now produced, was an invitation to the country, in which the words at least were not ill chosen. He gave this little poem to young Marquard through whom it came into the hands of Pastor Marquard and the Director who showed their approval, so that Reiser had almost begun to regard himself as a poet. But the Precentor showed him his mistake, going through his poem line by line and calling his attention to metrical errors as well as to faulty expression and want of connexion in thought.

This severe criticism was a great boon, for which he can never be grateful enough to the Precentor : the approval which this first product of his Muse received so undeservedly would perhaps otherwise have harmed him for his whole life.

Nevertheless the *furor poeticus* often attacked him again, and as his chief inspiration now was devotion to learning he ventured on a new poem in praise of knowledge, which began ridiculously enough

To you, fair Sciences, to you
My mind shall evermore be true.

The Precentor taught Latin verse-making and lectured on the rules of prosody, which he afterwards applied to the scansion of the *Disticha Catonis*. Reiser took great pleasure in this, for it seemed to him so scholarly to be able to scan Latin verses and to know why one syllable must be pronounced long and another short; the Precentor beat the rhythm with his hands as he scanned. To be able to watch him and join in was a real intellectual pleasure and when the Precentor finally dictated a confused multitude of Latin words which had formed verses for his pupils to rearrange them in metrical order, it was a great pleasure for Reiser, who found he could produce two regular hexameters without many errors and received an old Curtius from the Precentor as a prize.

It is true that the teaching ran in the old groove, but, notwithstanding this, in a year Reiser got so far as to be able to write Latin without grammatical mistakes and scan Latin verse properly. The simple means which produced this result was—the repetition of the old with the new, and it is a method which modern teachers should consider. However finely a lesson is expounded, if it is not constantly repeated, it gets no hold on the mind of the young. The ancients spoke a true word when they said—'Repetition is the mother of scholarship'. From ten to eleven the Assistant Master gave a private lesson on German declamation and German style, which Reiser always very much enjoyed, because he had the opportunity of distinguishing himself by his compositions and at the same time addressing an audience from the platform, which had some resemblance with preaching, always the supreme object of all his wishes.

There was one other, Iffland, who took equal pleasure in declamation. He afterwards became one of our foremost actors and most popular dramatists, and Reiser's fortunes up to a certain point were very like his. They both distinguished themselves most in declamation. Iffland excelled Reiser in lively expression of feeling, but Reiser felt more deeply. Iffland's thought was quicker and he therefore had wit and presence of mind, but no patience or persistence. Reiser therefore in every other respect soon outstripped him: he always lost when it was a question of wit and liveliness but always won, if called on to exercise sheer power of thinking. Iffland could be very much moved by a thing, but it made no lasting impression: he could grasp a thing very easily, but it generally escaped him again as quickly. He was a born actor and as a boy of twelve he could command every expression and gesture and could completely reproduce every kind of comic scene. There was not a preacher in Hanover whose sermons he had not imitated most naturally: he generally employed the interval before the Assistant Master's lesson began, in this way. Every one therefore feared him, as he had it in his power to make any one ridiculous. Yet Reiser liked him and would have been glad to see more of him, had not the difference in their circumstances stood in the way. Iffland's parents were rich and respected, Reiser was a poor boy who lived on charity, but none the less had a deadly horror of forcing himself on the rich. Meanwhile he enjoyed much more respect from his richer and better-dressed comrades than he had expected, which may have been partly due to the fact that the Prince was sending him to college, which put him in a more favourable light. For the same reason his masters showed him more attention and respect.

Though some of the members of this class were from seventeen to eighteen years old, very humiliating punishments prevailed there. The Assistant Master and the Precentor both boxed boys' ears, and for severe punishments used the whip which always lay on the desk: and those who had committed an offence often had to kneel at the desk for punishment. To Reiser the thought was intolerable that he should ever draw such a punishment on himself from men whom he profoundly loved and honoured as his teachers, and he desired nothing more eagerly than to win their love and regard. Imagine then his feelings when unawares and without any fault of his own he was called on to share the fate of some of his comrades, who were punished with a whipping by the Assistant Master for some noise they had made. 'Share and share alike', said the Assistant Master when he came to him, and he would listen to no excuse and threatened to complain of him to Pastor Marquard. The consciousness of his innocence emboldened Reiser to a defiant reply and he threatened in his turn to complain of the Assistant Master to Pastor Marquard for treating an innocent person in so degrading a fashion. Reiser spoke in the tone of injured innocence and the Assistant Master made no answer.

From this time forward all his feeling of respect and affection for the Assistant Master was scattered to the winds: and as the Assistant Master went on inflicting punishment without distinction, Reiser paid no more heed to a box on the ear or a stroke of the whip from him than if a wild animal had attacked him. And now that it made no difference whether he tried to win the esteem of this master or not, he followed his own inclination, and no longer attended as a duty, but only if the subject interested him. He often used to chatter for hours to his friend Iffland, in whose company he had sometimes to kneel at the desk. Iffland practised his wit on such occasions by comparing the desk, on which the Assistant Master leant his elbows, to the Mecklenburg arms, and himself and Reiser to the two supporters. Indeed no punishment could suppress Iffland's roguery except one in which he had to stand for an hour with his face towards the stove, so that he had no free play for his wit and no one to watch his pantomime. This was the first punishment which reduced him to tears, and he seriously tried to beg off, which he never did before. The discipline of the Assistant Master was of this kind. A boy had inadvertently put his night-cap in his pocket instead of his book, and was made to kneel for an hour with his night-cap on before the whole class, whereupon Iffland had his joke and brought quantities of cuffs on his neighbours, who sometimes could not refrain from laughing at his pantomime and his droll ideas.

What kind of effect this discipline of the Assistant Master had on the character of his subordinates, what glorious memorial he raised for himself in the hearts of his pupils, and what a crown he won thereby, may be left to his conscience. When he had distinguished himself in this heroic fashion, he would often say, 'Trust me not to go to sleep like other people', pointing, so that every one could see what he meant, at the Precentor, who in spite of his melancholy humour and some pedantic ways was a far better man than the Assistant Master. Reiser never had a blow from him, although he boxed ears freely and was liberal with the whip. He saw that Reiser was seriously trying to avoid punishment and he did not strike blindly. Under him Reiser learnt far more than under the Assistant Master because he attended out of duty, even if the subject did not interest him. And when he managed by his Latin composition to work his way up to the top of the class, it was a great encouragement to him to be praised by the Precentor and told that he must try to keep his place. Now the Precentor always gave the head boy the office of a censor or overseer of the behaviour of the rest, and as Reiser always kept his first place, he received the honourable title of *censor perpetuus* or perpetual monitor. He administered this office most conscientiously and impartially and often felt sorry to see how the boys often teased the good Precentor, who did not always take the right way of discipline, and made his life a burden to him, so that he often exclaimed in bitterness of heart, *quem dei odere, paedagogum fecere* ('whom the gods hate they make a schoolmaster'). Reiser would have given up everything for the Precentor, because he had never been unjust to him, although his behaviour to him otherwise was not always

BOOKS FROM CLOSED STACKS
Print Clearly

ND TO HUM DEPT.

.ME Frank Benner

.TE 10-4 TIME 2:10 INIT. Bg

.LL NO. M

THOR Moritz

.E Anton Reiser

) NOT ON SHELF

STACK INIT.

very friendly. Reiser was deeply moved when, in the catechism lesson, when all around was noise and uproar, the Precentor struck the book violently and said 'I am telling you God's word!' The pity was that the good man used expressions like this, which if used at the right moment are very effective, far too often, and was always quoting commonplaces like 'A boy's heart is the home of folly' and the like, so that at last the boys were so accustomed to them that no one paid any heed, and the uproar at the Precentor's lessons was continual. The Assistant Master used fewer words in his punishments and therefore secured more quiet and order.

When Reiser had been at the school for a short time, it occurred to him to join the choir, not so much to earn money as to acquire a new and honourable position of which he had always conceived a great idea from the days of his apprenticeship to the hat-maker. Here again his imagination had fair scope. It seemed to him a solemn, heavenly thing to join publicly in the songs of praise to God. The name choir had a pleasant sound: to sing God's praise in full choir was an expression which constantly echoed in his thoughts. He could hardly await the moment when he would be received into this brilliant company.

One of his comrades, who had long sung in the choir, assured him that he was so sick and tired of it, that he would sooner be quit of it to-day than to-morrow. Reiser found it impossible to believe this. He attended with great zeal the lessons in which the Precentor gave instruction in singing, and envied every one who had a better voice than he.

Not far from Hanover there is a waterfall, where by the Precentor's advice he went for an hour at a time, to shout and practise his voice: but he could never make any progress in singing, for he had not what is called a musical ear, but the theory which the Precentor included in his lesson, was all the more welcome, and he pleased the Precentor very much by the attention he gave. Reiser now felt a real affection for the Precentor and spoke highly of him to every one, and the Precentor praised him in return. It so happened that Reiser thanked him for the good account he had given of him to one of his patrons, to which the Precentor replied that Anton had given him a good testimonial too, for it had come to his ears that Reiser spoke everywhere in his praise.

Reiser would not have exchanged the joy of that moment for a great deal, so pleasant was the thought that his master now knew how much he loved him. If any one had told him at the first moment that the Precentor would one day be such friends with him, he would not have believed it: for in the first instance the Assistant Master was his man, for his smiling friendly air and unruffled forehead attracted him, while the Precentor's gloomy air and wrinkled brow alarmed him. How pleasant and friendly, he used at first to say, the Assistant Master is compared to the sullen old Precentor! but on closer acquaintance his views were soon reversed.

Reiser tried every means to secure the Precentor's respect still further. He went so far as to walk up and down a public promenade, where the Precentor used to go, with an open book in his hand, to catch the eye of his master, that he might regard him as a pattern of diligence, because he read on his walks. Although Reiser took real pleasure in the book he was reading, the pleasure of being seen in that position by the Precentor was far greater. This shews his tendency to vanity: he cared more for the appearance than the thing itself, although he did not regard this either as unimportant.

People had an amazing opinion of his diligence and were always advising him to spare his health; this was very flattering to him and he did not undeceive them, although his diligence was not as great as it might have been, if the discomfort of his position in regard to board and lodging had not often made him listless and discontented. For the unworthy treatment to which he was sometimes exposed, often deprived him of a great part of the self-respect which is a necessary condition of industry. He often went to school with a sad heart, but when he was once there he forgot his trouble, and the school lessons were really his happiest hours.

But when he returned home and many a time was made to understand by broad hints how tiresome his presence was, he would sit for hours scarcely daring to breathe: he felt the situation a horrible one, and could have made no effort, for such treatment wrung his heart. In the same way the looks of the sacristan's wife, if he had had a meal there, depressed him for some days and deprived him of courage to work. Certainly Reiser would have been happier and more contented and indeed more industrious also, if he had been allowed to buy bread and salt for himself with the money provided by the Prince, instead of having to eat his bread at strangers' boards.

He found himself once in a horribly distressing position, when the Sacristan's wife began talking at table of the bad times and the hard winter and the lack of fuel, and finally burst into tears and wondered where the bread was to come from: and when Reiser in his embarrassment let a bit of bread fall on the ground, she looked at him like a Fury, but said nothing. As Reiser could not refrain from tears at this disagreeable incident, she attacked him bluntly with reproaches for rudeness and want of manners and gave him to understand that people like that, who turned her food to poison in her mouth, were not welcome at her table. The good Sacristan, who cordially pitied Reiser, but was not master in his own house, expressed his sympathy and told him not to come again. Thus Reiser left the house shamed, humiliated, and degraded, and scarcely dared to let any one know that he had lost a day of free board. When the Sacristan met him sometimes in the street afterwards, he pressed half a gulden into his hand, to make up for the ungraciousness and avarice of his wife.

On the other hand there was a class of people who, when they gave Reiser a meal used to say every minute how glad they were to give it, and that he should make the most of it, for it was to count as a real meal, and phrases of that sort, which caused Reiser great embarrassment, so that eating was a torment instead of the pleasure it generally is. How happy he felt on the first Sunday after he had lost his board at the Sacristan's and had not yet dared to tell them at home, when he ate a penny loaf as he took a walk round the ramparts. It was lucky that he did not become servile : he might then have had more pleasure and contentment, but he would have lost all the noble pride which alone raises man above the beasts, which only care to satisfy their hunger.

The position of the meanest artisan's apprentice is more honourable than that of a young man who is dependent for his studies on charity, as soon as the charity is shown him in a humiliating way. If such a young man feels happy, he is in danger of becoming servile, and if he is not capable of becoming servile, he will fare as Reiser did : he will get sullen and misanthropic as Reiser did, for he now began to find his chief pleasure in solitude.

Once Frau Filter sent him to the Prince's house with a big parcel of linen, which was to be shown to the Prince's household for sale. To resist would have been useless, for Pastor Marquard had once for all given Frau Filter unlimited authority over Reiser, and any refusal would have been interpreted as unpardonable pride. 'It won't be a blot on your scutcheon ', she used to say. Nor could he refuse to fetch the bread which the bandsman of the regiment received, and although he did this in the twilight and chose the most out-of-the-way streets, that none of his schoolfellows might see him, one of them did once see him to his great horror, but luckily he was good-tempered enough to promise complete secrecy and stick to it, though sometimes when they quarrelled in class he threatened to divulge it.

At last a new suit was got for him from the

Prince's money, as his old red soldier's coat was worn out, but as if the object were to humiliate him, they chose a grey livery-cloth for the purpose, which again made him as conspicuous among his schoolfellows as the soldier's coat: and even so he was only allowed to wear it on solemn occasions, as for instance for an examination, or to go to Communion. But of all the humiliations he suffered what pained him mòst, and what he could never forgive Frau Filter for, was an unjust accusation, which wounded him deeply and from which he could find no proof to clear himself.

Frau Filter had adopted a little girl of three or four, the child of some relation. She planned to give her a happy surprise at Christmas by dressing a tree with candles and loading it with almonds and raisins. Reiser was alone in the room while Frau Filter went to the bedroom to fetch the child. It so happened that just as she came in, the tree, probably owing to the movement of the door, fell over, candles and all, and Reiser ran up to hold it upright, but failing to do so, drew back his hand quickly, and so it looked as if he had been busy with the tree all the time, and when Frau Filter came in was frightened and let the tree go, whereupon it fell. To Frau Filter's mind it was proved that he had wanted to steal something from the tree and so had spoilt an innocent pleasure for her and the child. She made Reiser plainly understand that she suspected him of this discreditable conduct, and he found it impossible to remove the suspicion: he had no witness, and appearances were against him. The mere thought that any one could harbour such a suspicion against him lowered him in his own eyes, and made him wish to sink into the earth or perish instantaneously. Such a condition cripples a person's morale and cannot easily be removed: he feels at such a moment reduced to nothing and would give his life to hide himself from the world. The self-confidence which is as necessary for moral activity as breathing is for bodily movement, receives such a serious shock that recovery is difficult.

When Reiser was present after this on any occasion when some trifle was missing which was supposed to have been taken, he could not help blushing and getting confused simply because he had a lively imagination of the possibility that he might be taken for the guilty person, though not openly accused: a proof how far one may go wrong in interpreting a blush or confusion in an accused person as silent confession of his guilt. The effect of repeated humiliations on a man may be that he regards himself as an object of general contempt and no longer dares to look any one in the face: in this way he may in complete innocence of heart display all the signs of a bad conscience and woe to him then, if he falls into the hands of a man who fancies himself a judge of character, and who sums him up on the first impression his looks make on him! To be reduced to the extremity of shame is perhaps one of the most distressing feelings possible. More than once in his life Reiser experienced this feeling: more than once there were moments when he felt reduced to nothing in his own eyes, when for example he had directed to him a greeting, a compliment, an invitation or the like which was not meant for him.

The shame and confusion, into which an error of this sort could plunge him, were beyond expression.

It gives one a peculiar sensation to appropriate in error a compliment intended for another. The thought that one could be so conceited is extraordinarily humiliating: and there is further the thought that one is put in a ridiculous light. In a word Reiser never had a more horrible sensation in his life than this feeling of shame to which a trifle might often reduce him. Nothing else so laid hold on his inner being, his proper self. He always felt the deepest sympathy with any one in this position. He would have done more to save a person from shame than to save him from real misfortune, for shame seemed to him the greatest misfortune that can happen to any one.

He was once calling on a merchant in Hanover, whose habit was not to look at the person he was talking to. Looking at Reiser, he invited some one else in the room to dinner, and when Reiser took the invitation as meant for him and politely declined it, the merchant with a cold look said, 'I do not mean you!' This 'I do not mean you!', coldly said, made Reiser feel ready to sink into the earth: the phrase pursued him wherever he went and made his voice broken and trembling when he had to speak to people of distinction. His pride could not overcome the blow. 'How can you imagine I should ask *you* to dinner?' So Reiser interpreted 'I do not mean you', and at that moment he felt himself so insignificant, forsaken and abject, that his face, his hands, his whole being became a burden to him, and presented the most stupid and foolish appearance, while at the same time he felt his stupid and awkward bearing more profoundly than any one else. If he had only had some one to take a real interest in his fortunes, perhaps such incidents would have wounded him less: but his fortunes were attached to the sympathy of other men by such slender threads, that when one of them was broken he feared all the rest would go, and found himself in a position where no one took any heed of him and regarded himself as a being who was entirely neglected. Shame is as violent an emotion as any, and it is surprising that its consequences are not sometimes fatal.

The fear of appearing ridiculous was at times so appalling to Reiser that he would have sacrificed everything, even his life, to avoid it. No one perhaps ever felt more strongly than he the force of *Infelix paupertas, quia ridiculos miseros facit* ('Sad is the lot of poverty because it makes the unfortunate ridiculous'), for to him to be ridiculous seemed the greatest misfortune in the world. There is indeed one kind of ridicule, which he found the least intolerable: when people laugh at something as peculiar which they have not the courage to imitate themselves, while they do not regard it with contempt. If for instance he heard people say, 'Reiser is a strange fellow, in the evening he goes round the ramparts three times in the dark, and talks to no one but himself, while he repeats the lesson of the day' he did not mind it and indeed felt it flattering to appear thus in a peculiar light. But when Iffland ridiculed his lines

> To you, fair Sciences, to you
> My mind shall evermore be true

this made him feel much ashamed and distressed and he would have given a great deal not to have written it.

When Reiser had attended the Precentor's singing lessons for a quarter, he attained the good fortune he had so earnestly longed for, of going into the choir, where he sang alto. His enjoyment of the new position lasted a few weeks, while it was fine weather. He took much pleasure in the airs and motets which he heard sung and in the friendly conversations with his schoolfellows as they wandered from one house and street to another. A choir like this is not unlike a strolling troop of actors, who in a certain measure share joy and sorrow, good and bad weather with one another, with the result that they tend to become more closely bound together.

Reiser had taken special delight in the thought of the blue cloak which was to be his distinction in future, for this had some likeness to the clerical dress. But this hope proved illusory, for Frau Filter, to economize for him, had a cloak sewn together out of two old blue aprons, in which he cut no very brilliant figure among the other choristers. The very first day Reiser noticed one chorister, who specially stood apart from the rest. One could tell at once that he came from a different part of the country, even without hearing his speech, for all his movements and gestures were quicker and more lively than those of the stiff and heavy Hanoverians. Reiser was never tired of looking at him, and when he heard him speak he could not help admiring his well-turned expressions in the dialect of Upper Saxony, while all that the

Hanoverians said seemed awkward and clumsy by comparison.

The Prefect of the Choir was a drunken senior, with whom the stranger quarrelled a great deal, and generally repaid him in very telling and biting repartees if the Prefect tried to claim any kind of authority over him. When for instance he said he had been Prefect too long to be treated with personalities by such a youngster, the stranger replied that it did not do him much credit to be so old a boy and still Prefect. This superiority in wit which enabled the stranger at once to get the better of the Prefect attracted Reiser's attention, and when he asked his name, learnt that it was Reiser and that he was born in Erfurt.

It struck Reiser as very remarkable that this young man, for whom he had such a liking, bore the same name, though from the distance of his birthplace he could not well be related. He would gladly have made his acquaintance but he did not dare to do so yet, as his namesake was in the VIth Form and he in the Vth. He was also afraid of his wit, which he did not feel ready to face, if it should be directed at him. Meantime the acquaintance came about naturally, for Philip Reiser was attracted by Anton Reiser's quiet reserved manner as Anton was by the other's lively temperament, and in spite of the difference of their characters they soon found each other out and became friends.

This Philip Reiser was a person of remarkable gifts, who had been kept down by the circumstances in which fortune had placed him. He possessed fine feeling with much wit and humour, had real musical talent and a special turn for mechanics, but he was poor and therefore exceedingly proud: he would suffer hunger, and indeed often did so, rather than accept benefits. When he had money he was free-handed and hospitable as a king: he really enjoyed what he had if he could give others a generous share of it. But he had not properly learnt to calculate income and expenditure and therefore often had to practise the great art of voluntarily giving up what he would otherwise have liked to have. Without having had any special instruction he made very good pianofortes, and so earned a considerable income, which did not help him much because of his generous nature. Besides, his head was always full of romance, and he was always desperately in love with some woman; when he fell in love he always talked like a lover from the age of chivalry. His loyalty in friendship, his eagerness to help the needy, and even his hospitality came out in this way, and were partly based on the romantic ideas which fed his imagination, though the real foundation was his kindly heart, for only in such soil can these romantic virtues spring up and take root. Even the constant study of romance will never produce such results in a selfish and shrunken character.

It is easy to see why Philip and Anton Reiser met each other halfway and on closer acquaintance seemed made for each other. Philip was almost twenty when Anton got to know him, and the extra years made him in some degree his leader and counsellor; the pity was, that in the main matter of ordering his life, he did not find a better leader and counsellor.

Meanwhile he had found the first real friend of his youth, whose society and conversation made the hours he had to spend in the choir in some degree tolerable. For now the fine weather was over, and rain, cold, and snow set in, yet the choir had none the less to sing at its appointed hours in the street. How Reiser counted the minutes, now he was frozen with cold, till the tiresome singing was over, which once had sounded like heavenly music in his ears!

Singing in the choir took away the whole of Wednesday and Saturday afternoon and all Sunday: for every Sunday morning the choristers had to be in church, to sing the 'Amen' from the gallery. On Saturday afternoon too, at the preparation for the Communion, the younger choristers had to sing a hymn with the Precentor, and one of them had to read a Psalm from the high gallery above. This was a great godsend for Reiser, he felt rewarded for all the discomforts of the choir by the chance of reading a Psalm aloud in public; he imagined himself standing like Pastor Paulmann in Brunswick, addressing the assembled people in moving tones. In other respects he soon found the choir most unpleasant. It robbed him of all the time left him for recreation, so that he could not look forward to a single day of rest in the week. His golden dreams about it disappeared and he would gladly have redeemed himself from this slavery, had it been possible, but by this time his pay as chorister had become part of his regular income, and he could not hope ever to escape from it.

The companions of his slavery were not much

better off and were equally tired of their way of life, and indeed the life of a chorister, who has to sing before people's doors for bread is a very sad one, and there are but few who do not lose their spirit over it. Most of them in the end become servile and when once that has happened, they never entirely recover.

The 'New Year singing' made a special impression on Reiser. This lasts three days on end and on account of the varying scenes which occur in it, is very like a journey of adventure. A group of choristers stand huddled close together in the street amid snow and cold, till a messenger dispatched from time to time, brings word that they are to sing in some house: they then go into the house, where they are generally invited into the parlour where an air or motet, to suit the season, is sung. Then the householder is often polite enough to entertain the choristers with wine or coffee and cakes. This reception in a warm room, after long standing in the cold, together with the refreshments offered one, were so reviving, and the variety of sights seen, perhaps twenty or more different domestic interiors in a single day, each with its family assembled, made such an agreeable impression that for the whole three days one floated in an atmosphere of enchantment and constant expectation of new scenes, which reconciled one to the hardships of the weather. The singing lasted on almost into the night, and the lighting up when evening came made the scene still more solemn. Among other places they sang at the new year in a hospital for old women, where the choristers had to sit in a circle with the old matrons and sing with folded hands *Bis hierher hat mich Gott gebracht* ('My God has led me till to-day'). At this New Year singing every one was more friendly: school order was disregarded, the VIth Form spoke to the Vth and an unusual cheerfulness possessed all hearts.

This New Year Reiser was beset by an amazing passion for writing verse. He wrote New Year's greetings in verse to his parents, his brother, Frau Filter, and who knows to whom besides, writing of silver streams winding among flowers, of gentle zephyrs and golden days, in wondrous fashion. His father took special pleasure in the silver stream, but his mother was puzzled at his phrase 'best of fathers' as he had only one father.

His reading in poetry at that time consisted of hardly anything but Lessing's Essays (*Kleine Schriften*), which Philip Reiser lent him, and which he had read so often that he almost knew them by heart. Besides it is clear that, after he joined the choir he had not much time for his own personal occupations. Nevertheless he had great plans of all sorts; the style of Cornelius Nepos was not elevated enough for him and he began to clothe the story of the generals in quite a different style, the style of the story of Daniel in the lion's den, so as to make a kind of heroic poem.

In a private lesson with the Assistant Master they read Terence's Comedies, and the thought that this author is reckoned a difficult one made him study him with greater zeal than Phaedrus or Eutropius, and translate at home every passage he read at school.

When he had thus really made great progress

in a very short time, he visited the deaf old man again, who was now much over a hundred and had been for some time childish, but now to every one's surprise recovered his complete reason a year before his death. Reiser knew his room at the end of a long dark passage, and felt a slight tremor when he heard the old man's shuffling steps from afar, but he gave him a very friendly welcome when he came in and signed to him with his hand to write something.

Reiser was overjoyed to write that he was now at a classical school and was already translating Terence, and the Greek Testament. The old man condescended to share his delight and was surprised that he could already understand Terence, which required a large vocabulary. Finally Reiser to make a complete display of his learning wrote something in Greek characters and the old man encouraged him to further diligence and bade him not forget his prayers, whereupon he knelt down and prayed with him, as he had done five years before, when Reiser first saw him.

Reiser went home much moved and resolved to turn again to God, which meant to him to think of God unceasingly : he remembered half sadly his sensations as a boy when he held conversations with God and was always waiting for some great thing to happen. These recollections had a sweet flavour of their own, for the drama which the pious imagination of believing souls enacts with the Supreme Being, whom they regard as now forsaking them and now accepting them again, while they sometimes hunger and yearn for Him and again sink into a state of dryness and emptiness of heart, is not without elevation and grandeur, and keeps the vital spirits in perpetual activity, so that even the dreams of the night are occupied with heavenly things : thus Reiser dreamt once that he was taken up into the company of the blessed, who were bathing in crystal streams, a dream which often charmed his imagination afterwards.

Reiser borrowed the writings of Madame Guyon again and remembered, as he read them, the happy days when he thought he was on the road to perfection. When nowadays his circumstances made him feel sad and out of spirits, and he did not care for reading, the Bible and the hymns of Madame Guyon were his only refuge, because of their attractive mysticism. Through their veil of enigmatic expression gleamed an unknown light which quickened his failing imagination, but he could no longer keep up the pious life or continual thinking of God. In the connexions he had now formed no one troubled about the state of his soul, and he had far too much distraction in school and choir to be able to remain faithful for a week to his inclination for unbroken meditation.

Meanwhile he paid several more visits to the old man before his death, till one day when he meant to go to him and was told that he was dead and buried ; his last words had been 'all ! all ! all !' These words Reiser remembered he had often heard from him in a kind of ecstasy in the middle of a prayer or after a pause in his talk ; it seemed sometimes as though in these words he wished to breathe out his spirit, ripe for eternity, and to put off his mortal vesture at the moment. So Reiser felt it very striking when he heard that the old man had died saying these words, and yet he felt as though he were not dead, so completely had the good old man always seemed to be living in another world ; death and eternity were almost his only thought the last times when Reiser spoke to him. This time Reiser felt almost as if the old man had only moved to another house where he meant to visit him ; and this was not at all from indifference, but because the old man's death came home to him so closely.

Meantime he had lost in the old man a friend of his youth, whose sympathy with his fortunes had often gladdened him. At many times he felt himself more forsaken than before, without knowing why. Frau Filter too was more discontented than ever with the burden of his stay, and at last, after enduring patiently for three quarters, gave him notice to leave, with the well-meant advice that he should look for another lodging.

Meanwhile the Rector of the Lyceum had gone, and the new Rector, who was chosen in his place, was a good friend of Pastor Marquard, to whom it now occurred to board Reiser with the Rector, and he called his attention beforehand to the great advantages he would enjoy if he should be fortunate enough to be taken by him into his house.

Reiser then was to go to the Rector's house! How this flattered his vanity, for, thought he, if he should be lucky enough to make himself liked by the Rector, a brilliant prospect was open to him, as the Rector now became his teacher, for at the end of the first school year he would be promoted to the VIth Form, in which only the Rector and the Director gave instruction. Really he was very much pleased that Frau Filter gave him notice, for he would never have dared to hint that he wanted to leave her: and now he could look forward to becoming an inmate of the house of the Rector, his future teacher.

But now a new fancy began to lay hold of his imagination, and one which had a great influence on his whole later life. I have already spoken of the declamation lessons instituted by the Assistant Master in the Vth Form. These had such an extraordinary attraction for Reiser and Iffland that they threw everything else into the shade, and Reiser's one desire was to have an opportunity to act a comedy with some of his schoolfellows, in order to get a hearing for his recitation. This had such an immense attraction for him that for a long time he could think of nothing else day and night and himself sketched the outline of a comedy, in which two friends were to be separated from one another and become inconsolable, and so on. He also found in Leyding's *Library*, which some one had lent him, a drama in verse, *The Hermit*, which he wanted to act with Iffland. What he wanted was to have a powerful part, in which he could speak with strong emotion and transport himself into a series of moving scenes, which he loved, but could not have in the real world, where every incident was so poor and miserable. The wish was a natural one for Reiser: he had feelings for friendship, gratitude, generosity, and noble resolution all of which lay dormant, because his outward circumstances cramped the movements of his heart. What wonder that it longed to expand in an ideal world and follow the bent of its natural feelings ? On the stage he seemed as it were to find himself again after having nearly lost himself in his real world : that is why, as days went on, his friendship with Philip Reiser became almost a stage friendship, even to the point of one being resolved to die for the other. Meantime the idea of the stage became so strong that it quite drove the desire to preach out of his mind, for on the stage his imagination had a far wider range, far more real life and interest than in the perpetual monologue of the preacher. When he ran through the scenes of a drama which he had either read or sketched in his own imagination, he was himself in succession each character that he imagined, now magnanimous, now grateful, now offended and patient, now violent and brave to meet every attack.

So the prospect of promotion to the VIth Form was very alluring, for in the Lyceum in Hanover the boys of the VIth Form enjoyed many conspicuous privileges, which few schools offer Every New Year they had a public procession with music and torches, at which they cheered the Director and the Rector. In the evening they presented the Director and the Rector in alternate years with a free-will gift, which generally amounted to more than a hundred thalers, when the boy who made the presentation delivered a short Latin speech : they were then entertained with wine and cakes and had liberty to give their master a loud resounding cheer at his house. The arrangement of the procession was generally discussed almost three months beforehand.

Every summer in the dog-days the boys of the VIth Form played comedies in public, the choice of plays and the arrangements being left to them : this occupied most of the summer. Then in January came the Queen's birthday and in May the King's, on which occasions a speech-day was arranged attended by the Prince, the Ministers, and most of the dignitaries of the town : the preparation for these occupied a great deal of time. In addition there were two public examinations every year, also accompanied by holidays. Though this meant loss of time, yet all these occasions were alluring objects for an ambitious lad, and served to enliven the interest of the school year, when it threatened to flag.

It was upon such ambitions that the wishes and hopes of the boys of the top Form in the Lyceum at Hanover centred : to be leader in the torch-light procession, or deliver the Latin speech at the presentation of the gift, or play a leading part in one of the plays performed, or to deliver a speech on the King's or the Queen's birthday. An additional attraction was the fine class-room of the VIth Form with its elegant double desk of finely polished walnut wood, and the green window-curtains : all this combined to fill Reiser's imagination afresh with alluring pictures of his future status, and to excite to the utmost his expectation of what was to come. To become a member of the VIth Form after a single year at school was a piece of luck he would hardly have dared to dream of.

Full of these hopes and prospects he travelled in the holiday week before Easter, with some carriers who were going the same way, to see his parents and announce his good fortune.

This journey, in which the road lay mainly

through forest and heath, gave an extraordinary impulse to his excited imagination: he planned heroic poems, tragedies, romances, and all kinds of things: sometimes the idea of writing his life occurred to him but the opening which he imagined was always on the lines of *Robinson Crusoe*, which he had read; ‘that he was born of poor but honest parents at Hanover in such and such a year’, and so it was to go on.

Whenever he went to his parents afterwards, whether on foot or by wagon, his imagination was always at its busiest on the journey; as soon as he lost sight of the four towers of Hanover a whole period of his past life appeared before him. The horizon of his thought expanded with the horizon of his vision. He felt himself transported from the limited circle of his existence into the great wide world, where all the wonderful events he had ever read of in romances were possible: perhaps his father or mother would suddenly come to meet him as if from afar and he would joyfully hasten to them, he fancied he heard the sound of his parents’ voice, and the first time he took this journey he really felt the purest pleasure in eager expectation to be with his parents, to whom he had such great things to announce.

When he arrived next day his parents and his two brothers welcomed him to their home in the country with heartfelt delight. They had a little garden behind the house and were so far well established, but domestic peace, as he soon saw, was still where it was before. However, he heard his father play the zither again and sing Madame Guyon’s hymns to it. They also discussed the doctrines of Madame Guyon, and Reiser, who had already constructed a kind of metaphysic of his own akin to Spinozism, was often in remarkable agreement with his father, when they talked of the 'All' of the Godhead and the 'Nothingness' of the creature as taught by Madame Guyon. They thought they understood each other and Reiser felt infinite pleasure in these conversations, for he felt it flattering that his father, who had before seemed to regard him as stupid, now conversed with him on such lofty subjects. Then they visited the Preacher and the chief people of the place, where Reiser was always drawn into conversation and acquitted himself well, because the treatment he received gave him confidence. The neighbours of his parents and any one who came there, paid attention to the son of the Registrar of Births and Deaths, whom the Prince sent to study in Hanover. The pure unalloyed pleasure which Reiser enjoyed in these days, combined with the pleasantest hopes, richly repaid all the distress and undeserved humiliations, which he had suffered for a whole year.

But no one shared so closely in his fortunes as his mother: when he went to bed in the evening she said 'God bless you' over him, and made the cross over his forehead, as she used to do, that he might sleep safely, and not an evening or a morning passed when she did not include him in her prayers, even when he was absent. Reiser parted from his parents sadly, and gloomy forebodings distressed him when he saw the towers of Hanover again.

The next day after his return he was examined by the Director for promotion, and when he had to translate something in Cicero's *de Officiis* into German, it so happened that unluckily he turned a page in the book the Director handed him so clumsily that he almost tore it in two. Such an incident was calculated to offend most deeply the feelings of the Director who in all things aimed at extreme refinement. Reiser lost heavily in his opinion by this apparent want of sensibility in feeling and manners. The Director rebuked him very bitterly for his clumsiness, so that Reiser's confidence in him, through the shame his rebuke produced, received a violent shock, from which it could never recover. The shyness which Reiser shewed thenceforward in the Director's presence, only served to lower him in his eyes still more. In a word, all the sufferings which awaited Reiser henceforward in his school years arose in great measure from the careless turning of a single page in the Director's copy of Cicero's *de Officiis*; they were mainly due to the want of regard for him on the part of the Director, whose approval, which he had valued so highly, he had flung away by turning a page too quickly.

Another trouble was that Frau Filter, though he had left her, put away his new clothes and he had to attend the first class with an old coat of Lohenstein the hatmaker which he still had, while he saw hardly any but well-dressed young people beside him in the class. The coat gave him an absurd look, as he had grown too tall for it. He was conscious of this and this contributed not a little to the shyness which he showed more than ever in this class.

The Precentor too and the Assistant Master were

vexed with him, because he had said nothing to them beforehand of his promotion, and had taken the step without their advice. He excused himself as well as he could by saying he had not thought of it. The Precentor quickly forgave him, but the Assistant Master never: he made him feel it long afterwards. He made a heavy demand on Reiser for the private lessons which he had received and which every one thought he would have given him for nothing. He made Reiser deduct this money for some years from his pay as chorister, just when he needed it most—a circumstance which depressed him very much.

He got a sitting-room and bedroom in the Rector's house, but nothing more as the Rector himself was not yet properly installed. Reiser had a blanket from his parents, and a pillow and mattress were hired for him, so as to spend as little as possible; if it turned cold at night he had to use his clothes to supplement his blanket. An old piano, which he had, served for a table, and he had a small bench from the Rector's class-room, and a small book-shelf hanging from a nail above his bed, and in his bedroom he had an old chest with a few worn-out clothes. This was all his equipment, but he felt far happier than in the greater comfort of Frau Filter's parlour.

When he was alone in his room he felt at his ease, but he was still diffident in the Rector's presence. Though he saw him in dressing-gown and nightcap, he seemed still surrounded by a halo of solemnity and dignity, which kept Reiser at a distance. He had to help him to set his library in order; in handing books to him he sometimes stood so close to him that he could hear his breathing, and then often felt some impulse of attachment, but next moment he was shy and embarrassed again. Nevertheless he was fond of the Rector, and his romantic imagination often made him wish he might be conveyed with him on to a desert island, where fortune would make them equal, so that they could converse on a friendly and intimate footing.

The Rector did everything to give Reiser courage and confidence, he had him alone to meals with him at different times and talked to him. Reiser already had plans for writing, he wanted to re-write the old *Acerra Philologica* in better style, and the Rector was kind enough to encourage him to keep up plans of this sort for the future and occupy himself with composition. When Reiser talked to the Rector on such matters he could never find the right expressions to use, which made his periods very broken, for he would rather be silent than choose the wrong word for the thought he wanted to express. The Rector helped him with much forbearance, and sometimes made him come into his room in the evening and read to him.

Reiser then often made bold to put questions to him : such as, how far a chair can be called an *individuum*, seeing that it can be divided into parts —a doubt which had occurred to him in the Rector's logic lesson and the Rector solved his doubt with great condescension, praising him the while for reflecting on such subjects ; at times too he joked with him, and if he sent him on an errand, to fetch a book or the like, he did not order him to do it but asked him. So far all went well, but there seemed to be a fatality for Reiser in turning over leaves: he had once to cut some unbound books for the Rector and did it so clumsily that he made deep gashes in the leaves with the penknife, and so nearly ruined a couple of books. The Rector was very much annoyed and reproached him bitterly as though he had damaged the leaves out of malice, to be relieved of the task, which was not at all true. The reproach wounded Reiser and did much to depress his courage, which was gradually gaining strength.

Meanwhile his spirit revived when the Rector took him with him on a short visit to a neighbouring Catholic town, to see the Festival of Corpus Christi. The Rector, the Assistant Master and the Precentor and two young clerics drove by special post in a carriage, and Reiser was given a corner in it. So he heard these respected men, who had become confidential with one another, as generally happens with a small company of travellers, joke freely with one another, and this had a remarkable effect on Reiser. Gradually the halo disappeared from their heads and for the first time he saw in them men like other men. For he had never before seen a company of clerics together, talking without constraint and putting off for a time the stiff ceremonious manner which clings to them from their profession. Only the good Precentor retained a certain stiffness of manner, and when a crowd of beggars, singing hymns, met their carriage on the road, they chaffed him about the incident, pitying him heartily because of this fearful discord which completely overpowered his ear. For the first time Reiser saw how such respected persons could chaff one another like other people. The experience was very useful to him ; hitherto he had regarded every priest as a sort of superhuman being, but now he only had to think of him as one of such a company of travellers, and he easily stripped him in imagination of the halo that surrounded him before.

Nevertheless he felt keenly what an insignificant creature he was in this company, and when accompanied by strangers and others they visited all the points of interest in the monastery and other sights of the town, he felt how it was always a matter of course that he came last in everything and yet he must regard it as a great honour. This made his behaviour in company awkward and stupid and he felt this awkwardness himself perhaps more than any one else noticed it ; for this reason during this time when he was hearing and seeing so much that was new, he was anything but happy and wished himself back in his lonely garret with his bench and the old piano, and the bookshelf that hung from the nail over his bed.

But what now began to embitter his lot more than anything else was a new and undeserved humiliation, caused by his present position, which he could not alter. When he began to attend the VIth Form, he sometimes heard a whisper behind him 'That's the Rector's Famulus', a word which Reiser associated with the meanest ideas, for he knew nothing yet of the use of the word at the University. For him it meant some one if possible lower in the scale than the servant who cleans the boots. He imagined he was looked down on by his schoolfellows with a sort of contempt : he thought of his scanty coat, which made him cut a ludicrous figure in his own eyes. In the Vth Form, in spite of his poor clothes, he had been respected by his class-mates because of the importance they attached to the fact that the Prince was educating him. In the VIth Form too this was partly known, but the notion that he was the Rector's Famulus seemed to degrade him in the eyes of all. Now in the VIth Form an immense deal depended on the place where you sat, and the upper places could only be reached by long-continued industry. Generally you could only go up one bench in half a year. The first four benches formed the Lower Form and the three back benches the Upper Form. If any one was left behind at the half-yearly promotions, it was felt as a great degradation.

Now on the third morning, while a member of the class was reading a written prayer from the lower reading desk, Reiser smiled at something his neighbour said, but when he saw that the Director noticed it, he suddenly tried to assume a grave face. And the incident of the torn book had left such an impression in his mind that this sudden change of expression had nothing fine in it but betrayed a suspicious and slavish fear, from which the Director, with a look of anger and scorn, seemed to conclude that his tone of mind was vulgar and servile. Such a look from the Director was in itself enough to arouse general attention; but when the prayer was over, he said a word or two to Reiser about his servility, which exposed him at once to the contempt of the whole class, to whom the Director's utterances were like an oracle.

Reiser after this did not trust himself to look up

at the Director, and during his lessons had to regard himself as a being entirely ignored, for the Director never put him on. A couple of lads, who came into the class after Reiser, were put above him and for some months he had to remain at the bottom. Young Rehberg, a clever fellow who afterwards distinguished himself as a painter, sat next Reiser and seemed inclined to make friends, but the glance which the Director cast on him when he spoke to Reiser quenched any spark of respect he seemed to have for him, and checked his impulse. The Director's behaviour to Reiser was the effect of his shy suspicious manner, which seemed to indicate a servile spirit; but the Director never reflected that this shy suspicious manner was itself a consequence of his first treatment of Reiser.

Reiser had now sunk in the esteem of his schoolfellows and every one made bold to win a triumph at his expense, every one wanted to practise his wit on him, and if he fought with one, there were a score of others anxious to make him the mark of their ridicule: even the valiant blows he sometimes dealt to those who went too far, which might have won fresh respect for any one else, were ridiculed. They no longer whispered 'There 's the Rector's Famulus' but as soon as he came into class in the morning they called 'There comes the Famulus' and the name was echoed from every corner. It was as if everything had combined to set upon him and make him ridiculous.

His position became a hell to him: he howled, stormed, and fell into a kind of fury, and this made new food for ridicule. At last a sort of apathy took the place of the fury of wounded pride, he ceased to see and hear what went on around him and let them do what they liked with him, so that he seemed to be a worthy object of ridicule and contempt.

It would not have been surprising if this continued treatment had at last really debased his nature ; but he felt himself at certain times still strong enough to transport himself from his real world, and this it was which kept him going. If his spirit was debased by a thousand humiliations in his real world, every romance or heroic drama that he read or thought of enabled him to exercise the noble sentiments of generosity, resolution, unselfishness, and constancy. Thus he often dreamed himself away beyond all the trouble of the earth into brighter scenes, as he sang numbed with frost in the choir, and gave his fancy play for many an hour while the melodies he heard and joined in helped to keep up the illusion. For instance, nothing seemed to him more moving or uplifting than when the prefect of the choir led off

Hylo schöne Sonne
Deiner Strahlen Wonne
In den tiefen Flor.

(' Veil, fair sun, thy blessed beams in the deep mist.') The word *Hylo* alone transported him to higher regions and always gave his imagination a wonderful lift, for he took it for some Eastern expression, which he could not understand and to which he could therefore give the exalted sense he chose ; until one day he saw the words written beneath the notes and found the words were ' Hüll, o schöne Sonne ', which the prefect sang in his Thuringian dialect as ' Hylo ', and at once the whole enchantment, which had given him so many a happy moment, disappeared. Other things which deeply moved him to hear sung were 'Du verdeckest sie in den Hütten' ('Thou hidest them in Thy tabernacle') and 'Lieg' ich nur in deiner Hut, O so schlaf ich sanft und gut' ('If O Lord, Thou dost me keep, Safe and peaceful is my sleep.')

So completely did he lull himself into the happy sensation of the protection of a Higher Being, that he forgot rain and frost and snow, and fancied himself resting at peace in the surrounding air as in a bed. But meanwhile everything outside him seemed to combine to humiliate him and bow him down.

When summer came on the Rector went away for some weeks and Reiser was left alone in his house, and spent the time agreeably, reading books out of the Rector's library, and among others came on Moses Mendelssohn's works and Lessing's *Litteraturbriefe* (Letters on Literature) from which he began to make extracts. He made a special point of extracting all bearing on the Stage, which was now the dominating idea in his mind and as it were the germ of all his future difficulties. This idea had been awakened by the recitations in the Vth Form and had gradually driven the fancy of preaching out of his head. Dialogue on the stage acquired a greater charm for him than the continuous monologue of the pulpit. Moreover, on the stage he could be everything for which he had no opportunity in the real world, and which yet he so often longed to be—generous, beneficent, noble, steadfast—raised above all that was humiliating and debasing. How he longed by a momentary illusion of imagination to realize in his own person these feelings which seemed to him so natural, yet from which he seemed for ever cut off! It was this which made the idea of the Stage so attractive to him even then. There he found himself again, with all his feelings and sensations which did not fit in with the world of reality. The Stage seemed to him a more natural and agreeable world than the real world about him. Then the summer holidays came on and the VIth Form boys, according to custom, performed various comedies. In view of the general contempt in which he was held as the Rector's Famulus, Reiser had not the least hope of receiving a part: he could not even get a ticket, to look on, from any of his companions. This depressed him more than anything he had suffered until it occurred to him to form a party of malcontents with two or three of his companions, who also had no parts, and to act a comedy on their own account in their rooms before a small number of spectators. They chose Lessing's *Philotas* for their play, and Reiser paid one of the others to give him the part of *Philotas*, which he played badly, and so played it himself.

Now he was in his element. For a whole evening long he could be generous, steadfast, and noble: the hours when he rehearsed this part and the evening when he played it were among the happiest in his life, though the theatre was only a poor room with white-washed walls and the pit an adjoining bedroom, with a blanket hung in the empty doorway to serve as curtain, and though the whole audience consisted of the master of the house, who was a potter, and his wife and apprentices, and the stage was lighted only by farthing dips stuck to the walls with wet clay.

As after-piece they gave *The Dying Socrates* from Miller's *Moral Scenes from History*, in which Reiser played only a friend of Socrates, and one of his companions called G—— the dying Socrates himself, who duly drank the cup of poison and finally died in convulsions on a bed placed in the room. It was this after-piece which embittered all Reiser's school life. The other class-mates learnt that besides their own play a comedy had been acted by those who had received no parts and they regarded this as an infringement of their rights and as an act of defiance and contempt. They tried every means to revenge themselves for this unpardonable offence as they regarded it and from that time not one of the four who had acted *Philotas* and *The Dying Socrates* could safely go in the street at night. These four were henceforward an object of hatred, contempt, and ridicule, which fell chiefly on Reiser, for the others rarely attended the school lessons. Reiser had already had nothing but contempt shown him, which, apart from the general irrational antipathy, arose chiefly from his position which was humiliating or thought to be so, from his shy manner and his short coat. With this contempt was now combined a general bitterness which tried to make the ridicule with which he was attacked as scathing as possible. And although G—— and not he had acted the part of the dying Socrates, Reiser was nicknamed the dying Socrates and the name stuck until all that generation left the school by degrees. A year before he left the school himself he had been unwell and had not left the house ; when he wanted to look on again at a comedy which the first class were acting, they let him in but looked at him with a contemptuous scornful glance and said ‘ There goes the dying Socrates ’, so that Reiser turned round sadly and went home.

In general, people show some kindly feeling and only take for their object of ridicule some one who is not very sensitive ; if they see any one is really wounded and offended, they do not persist indefinitely but love of ridicule gives place to compassion. But this was not Reiser's fortune : his figure wasted from day to day, he wandered about like a shadow, indifferent to everything, his spirit broken, he tried to live alone, but all this roused not an atom of compassion, so possessed was every one with hatred and contempt for him.

There was another besides himself, a certain T—— who was also an object of ridicule, which arose partly from a stammer, but he shook the ridicule off as a thick-skinned animal shakes off blows. When they laughed at him they excused themselves by saying that it did not hurt him, but they paid no regard to Reiser and this finally embittered him and made him a declared misanthrope. How was the spirit of emulation, industry, or devotion to scholarship to find a place in him ? He was a complete outsider, lonely and forsaken, only on the look-out for any means of secluding himself still more and withdrawing into his shell. All the work that he did alone, reading and thinking in his room, gave him pleasure, but he had no spirit or humour for the common tasks of the school-room : he seemed not to belong to it.

This was the grand fulfilment of the dreams in which he had pictured long rows of benches on which sat the students of wisdom, whom he was delighted to think of joining and with whom he hoped one day to compete for the prize!

The Rector, with whom he lived, now returned from his travels, and brought his mother with him, who set to work to put his house in order. Winter came and no one thought of heating Reiser's room; he first endured the bitterest cold and imagined that they would think of him at last, until he heard that he was to spend his daytime in the servants' room. He now began to pay no heed to externals. Despised and slighted by masters as well as schoolfellows, liked by no one because of his increasing discontent and unsociability, he gave up all idea of human society and tried to withdraw completely into himself.

He went to a second-hand bookseller and got a novel and then one comedy after another and read with a kind of fury. Any money he could spare from food he devoted to borrowing books to read and as the bookseller got to know him and lent him books without being paid in cash Reiser before he was aware had read himself deep into debt, which though it was not heavy was more than he could pay. He tried to wipe out the debt by selling his school books, which the bookseller bought of him for a song and lent him in return new books, till he fell into debt again and had to think once more of means to meet it.

Reading had now become a necessity to him, just as Orientals use opium to reduce their senses to a pleasant stupor. If he wanted a book, he would have exchanged his coat for a beggar's smock to get one. The bookseller was clever enough to trade on this passion; he gradually wheedled him out of all his books and often sold them in his presence for six times the price he had paid for them.

In these circumstances no one could be blamed for taking Reiser to be a dissipated, degenerate young man, who sold his school books instead of increasing his knowledge and making use of his teachers' instruction, who read nothing but novels and comedies and neglected his person as well, for it was natural that as he had no one in the world to please, he paid no attention to his body, and all the money that the laundress and the tailor might have got was devoted to the bookseller. For the necessity of reading took with him the place of food and drink and clothing: indeed one evening he read Gerstenberg's *Tragedy of Ugolino* after eating nothing all day long, for he had missed the hour of his free meal over his book, and the money he should have kept for supper he had spent on the hire of *Ugolino* and the purchase of a candle, by the light of which he sat up half the night in his cold room, and could appreciate the hunger scene very keenly. Still these hours which he snatched from the surrounding tumult, were his happiest: his reading intoxicated his brain, he forgot himself and the world. In this way he read in succession the twelve or fourteen volumes of the *German Theatre* which had so far appeared, and as he had read Yorick's *Sentimental Journey* two or three times with great pleasure, he borrowed from the bookseller Schummel's *Sentimental Journey through Germany*.

He had already begun to write the titles of the books he read in a special book and to append his opinion, which sometimes turned out pretty correct: on this book for instance he wrote *Exercitium extemporaneum* ('an off-hand performance') because the writer himself admitted that he had written all the miscellaneous contents of this thick volume merely in order that people might judge for what branch of writing he was best fitted. The writer of this *Sentimental Journey* afterwards made up for this 'extemporary exercise' by his *Spitzbart*. But there are few books on which Reiser more regretted to have spent time in reading than this *Sentimental Journey*. It was thus that he gradually trained himself to distinguish with success the bad and mediocre from the good.

In everything that he read however the Stage remained the dominant idea: he lived and moved in the dramatic world. He often wept as he read, and was in turn transported into violent and wild passions of anger, rage, and revenge, and then again into tender feelings of magnanimous forgiveness, triumphant benevolence, and overflowing compassion.

His whole position and his relations with the real world were so repugnant to him that he tried to shut his eyes to them. The Rector called him by his name like a servant, and once he had to ask one of his schoolfellows who was the son of a friend of the Rector's to sup with the Rector, and while he supped with the Rector, Reiser had to fetch the wine and stay in the servants' room close by the supper-room, where he could hear his schoolfellow talking to the Rector while he sat in the servants' room with the maid. The Rector gave various private lessons; and if he were unable to give one, Reiser had to go round to his schoolfellows, with whom he shared this instruction, and put them off, which increased their contempt for him.

There was good ground in his behaviour for these slights: he was unsympathetic to everything that went on outside him, and indolent and listless towards anything which drew him out of his ideal world.

No wonder that the sympathy he gave to none he received from none, he was despised, overlooked, and forgotten. But the world forgot that this very behaviour which led to his neglect, was itself the consequence of previous neglect. This neglect, which had its origin in a series of trifling circumstances, was the cause of his behaviour, his behaviour was not, as was thought, the cause of his neglect. I could wish that this thought might attract the attention of all teachers and educators and make them more cautious in judging the development of young people's character: they ought to take into account the influence of innumerable accidental circumstances and make most careful inquiry into them before venturing to pass judgement on the fate of a man who perhaps only needed an encouraging look to work a sudden change in him, because his faults of manner arose from no radical defect of character but from a peculiar chain of circumstances.

It seemed indeed to be Reiser's fate to receive favours which turned into torments. It was by favour that he lived for a year with Frau Filter, and with what pain and distress he spent the year! It was by favour that he lived with the Rector, and yet this stay which he had pictured as so delightful brought on him endless humiliations and the contempt of his schoolfellows.

Judged by appearances Reiser could not impress any one favourably, and the Rector himself told Pastor Marquard that at best he would only make a village schoolmaster. Pastor Marquard afterwards reproached Reiser with this, and this judgement of the Rector, which at that time he had not self-reliance enough to combat, depressed his spirit still more. As the Rector now seemed certain that he could make nothing of Reiser, he made use of him on all possible occasions, for all sorts of petty duties which he got him to perform in and out of the house, and Reiser was regarded exactly like a servant, although he was called a VIth Form boy.

Nevertheless he did for once enjoy the privileges of the VIth, when out of the money he received as chorister he contributed his share to the New Year's present for the Rector, and attended the torch-light procession where, by New Year's custom, music was performed and cheers were given for the Director and the Rector. Though he was the last or one of the last in order at this ceremony yet he felt it a great encouragement to find himself, in spite of his many indignities and humiliations, standing in rank and file with the rest, carrying a sword and a torch and joining in the cheers. The music, the spectators, the torch-light, the leaders with plumed hats and naked swords all inspired him with new courage, when he found himself joining in this brilliant procession. And when he stood next day with the rest of the first class and the New Year's gift to which Reiser had contributed his share, was presented to the Rector on a silver tray with a Latin address, he found himself once more filling a place in the real world with content: he no longer felt entirely excluded and rejected. But even this encouragement was embittered by the hatred and arrogance of his schoolfellows.

The Rector entertained the VIth Form, who had brought him the present, with wine and cakes. They drank his health repeatedly and finally, when the wine got into their heads, became rather noisy. Reiser drank several glasses of wine without any fear of consequences, but as he was quite unused to wine a couple of glasses turned his head, and his noble-minded companions tried to make him quite drunk, in which they succeeded, partly by cunning, partly by threats, so that Reiser talked all sorts of nonsense and had finally to be put to bed. Reiser had already sunk in the confidence and esteem of all who knew him but this incident gave the death-blow to his character. So far he had been indolent, disorderly, and idle; now he was regarded as an intemperate, vicious person because by this unseemly behaviour he had shown the greatest ingratitude in the house of his teacher who was also his benefactor.

Reiser dimly foresaw these consequences when he woke next morning and while he dressed he prepared to beg the Rector to excuse him for his conduct of the day before. He had got up his speech very carefully and among other things assured him that he would do his best to wipe out this stain on his character, to which the Rector made the not very consolatory answer that the evil consequences of this incident, if it became known, could not easily be avoided.

The Rector was quite right, for the incident was soon known and then people said : 'What ! the young man lives on charity,' even the Prince spends so much on him and when he is hospitably entertained in the house of his teacher and benefactor, who gives him shelter, he behaves like this ! What a degraded and ungrateful person ! '

Although Reiser surmised these consequences and was extremely distressed about them, yet when he entered the choir next morning and his schoolfellows laughed at his pale distracted appearance, which arose from his debauch of the day before, he felt a curious kind of pride as though his drunkenness had been an exploit, and he even made as though the after effects still lingered, in order to attract attention. For this attention, combined this time with approval rather than ridicule, flattered him. The others too looked at him as men look at one who is in the same position as they once were, for the prefect was almost always drunk. This secret pleasure, which Reiser felt when he thought he had succeeded in winning notice by his bad conduct is perhaps the most dangerous rock of shipwreck for the young who are going wrong. Meanwhile this arrogance in Reiser was very soon damped when he felt, as he did very soon, the bad consequences which the Rector had foretold. Everywhere he was met with cold and contemptuous looks ; he therefore voluntarily gave up most of his free meals one after the other, and preferred to be hungry or eat bread and salt rather than expose himself to these looks. The only house to which he still went with pleasure was that of Schantz the shoemaker, for here he was received with the same friendly looks as before and he was not made to pay there for his adverse fortune.

At that time he was far from attempting to make excuses to himself; he trusted the judgement of so many others more than he trusted his own. He often accused and reproached himself most bitterly for his indolence in study, his reading and his running into debt with the bookseller, for he was not in a position then to explain his conduct as a natural consequence of the narrow conditions in which he lived. When he was in this temper of mind, angry with himself and with his imagination heated by a tragedy which he had just read, he once wrote a despairing letter to his father, in which he accused himself as the worst of criminals, and filled the letter with innumerable dashes, so that his father did not know what to make of it and began seriously to fear for his sanity. The whole letter was at bottom a part Anton was playing. He took pleasure in painting himself, as heroes of tragedy sometimes do, in the darkest colours, and then storming in tragic eloquence against himself.

As he now had no friend in the world, not even himself, what could he strive after except to forget himself as much and as often as possible?

The secondhand bookseller therefore remained his constant refuge and without him he could hardly have borne his position: as it was he was able to make it for many an hour not only tolerable but agreeable; when, for instance, at his uncle the wig-maker's house, he could gather round him a small and by no means brilliant audience and read them with the fullness of expression and all the declamation he could command, one of his favourite tragedies such as *Emilia Galotti*, *Ugolino*, or some other mournful work such as Gessner's *Death of Abel*. He felt an indescribable delight in seeing every eye in tears, as he saw in this the proof that he had achieved his end, of moving people by what he read.

On the whole he spent the happiest hours of his life at that time either alone or in this circle at his uncle the wig-maker's, where he could exercise empire so to speak over men's minds and make himself the centre of attention. For here he had an audience; here he could read, declaim, tell stories, and teach, and he cometimes entered into discussions with the artisans who met there on very serious subjects—the nature of the soul, the origin of things, the world-spirit, and the like, with which he puzzled their wits, directing the attention of these people to things that they had never thought of in their life.

With one journeyman tailor in particular, who began to find pleasure in his speculations, he often talked for hours together, on the possibility of the origin of the world from nothing: finally they hit on the system of emanation and Spinoza's doctrine—God and the world were one. If such questions are not wrapt up in the technical terms of the Schools they are intelligible to every one and even to children.

In such conversation Reiser used to forget all his cares and all his trouble. Anything that oppressed him was far too petty to engage his attention; he felt himself transported for a time out of the encircling frame of things, which beset him on earth, and enjoyed the privileges of the spirit world: he tried to enter into philosophical conversation with any one who came across him then and to practise his intellect upon him.

Meanwhile his school lessons, in spite of the slight encouragement he received and the many humiliations he endured, were not entirely wasted. From the Director he took notes on modern history, dogmatics, and logic, and from the Rector on geography and translation of Latin authors: thus besides his reading of plays and romances he acquired some general knowledge, and without deliberate intention made some progress in Latin. All this, however, was only accidental, he missed a lesson now and then and while Livy or some other Latin author was read in class, he furtively read a novel, knowing that the Director no longer condescended to put him on.

For when he sat at lessons in school among sixty or seventy others, hardly one of whom was his friend, and to nearly all of whom he was an object of ridicule and contempt, he was bound to feel the position a very painful one, from which he felt forced to dream himself into another world where he was better off. But even this refuge was grudged him, and while he was reading a volume of the *German Theatre* before the lesson began, some one carried off the book while the Rector was coming in and laid it on his desk, and when he asked where the book came from, the answer was that Reiser was in the habit of reading it during lessons. A look of disdainful contempt directed at Reiser was the Rector's answer to this accusation. And this look cost Reiser part of the remnant of self-confidence left him, for far from making excuses to himself, be believed that he deserved this contempt and at that moment regarded himself as an abject contemptible creature quite as much as the Rector could so regard him. This incident made him sink still lower in the Rector's esteem, and his outward position got worse from day to day, and when he forgot to deliver a message which a stranger had given him to the Rector, the Rector for the first time used the severe expression that this neglect of a message entrusted to him was a piece of sheer stupidity.

This expression for a long time produced in him a sort of paralysis of spirit. This phrase and the 'stupid boy' of the inspector at the Training-School, and the 'I do not mean *you*' of the merchant he could never forget: they intertwined themselves with all his thoughts and long after robbed him of all presence of mind at moments when he most needed it.

A friend of the Rector, who stayed with him for some weeks and for whom Reiser had to go some errands, gave him and the maid a tip on leaving. Reiser had a peculiar feeling in taking the money, as though he had been stabbed, but the first sense of pain suddenly passed away when he thought of the bookseller. Everything else was immediately forgotten: he could read more than twenty books for the money; his offended pride had revolted for the last time and was conquered. From this time forward Reiser paid no attention to his person, and disregarded all externals. He took no trouble about his clothes, which grew worn and more untidy than ever. In school, in the choir, and in the street he felt a solitary among his fellows, for no one troubled about him or sympathized with him. His own outward fortunes had become so contemptible, abject, and insignificant in his eyes, that he was no longer the least interested in himself, while on the other hand he could take the liveliest interest in the fortunes of a *Miss Sara Sampson*, or a *Romeo and Juliet*, whom he often made his daily companions.

Nothing was more unbearable than to find himself, when lessons were over, and the school was emptying, among the throng of his better-dressed, cheerful, and livelier schoolfellows, none of whom now condescended to walk with him. How often at such moments he longed to be quit of the burden of his body and to be rescued by sudden death from these tormenting surroundings! When he could escape the eyes of his schoolfellows by some lane, where no one followed him, how gladly he hurried to the loneliest and remotest parts of the city, to indulge his melancholy thoughts for a while in peace!

The greatest blockhead in the school, and one universally despised, associated with him sometimes and Reiser accepted his company with joy, for after all it was the company of a human being: but when he walked with him he would often hear one or other of his schoolfellows say: *par nobile fratrum* (' a noble pair of brothers '). Thus he was classed with this real blockhead.

This, taken with the Rector's remark that he would never make more than a village schoolmaster, completely took away Reiser's self-confidence, so that he almost abandoned all belief in his own mental powers and often began seriously to believe himself the blockhead he was taken for. This thought however degenerated into a kind of general bitterness against the order of things: at such moments he cursed the world and himself, thinking himself a very contemptible being created for the ridicule of the world. The following incident may show how far the prejudice against him and the conviction of his native stupidity had gone. The Rector allowed him to attend the private lessons which he gave in his house: among others he gave an English lesson, and as Anton had no copy of the book they were reading he could not prepare at home and had to look over with some one else in class. Nevertheless in a week or two he grasped most of the rules of English pronunciation simply by listening, and when the Rector by chance once called on him to read, he read better and more smoothly than the rest who had had the book and prepared it at home. One day he heard himself being talked about in the neighbouring room: 'Reiser could not be so stupid, as he had grasped the difficult English pronunciation so soon.' But to prevent such a favourable opinion about him gaining ground, some one maintained that Reiser's father was an Englishman and therefore he remembered the English pronunciation from childhood. As the rest were quite ready to believe this, the low opinion which his schoolfellows had of Reiser was again confirmed. All this shows that the esteem in which a young man is held by his comrades is a very important element in his education and bringing up, a point to which public educational institutions have hitherto paid too little attention.

If Reiser's teachers had made a single well-directed effort towards rehabilitating him in the opinion of his fellows, it would have rescued him from his misery and converted him into an industrious and steady character. And they could easily have done it if they had tested his capacities rather more carefully and paid rather more attention to him.

The winter passed very gloomily for him. His small budget was in complete disorder; he had not ventured in his ragged clothes to fetch his monthly allowance from the Prince, he was deep in debt to the second-hand bookseller, and he had been unable to meet his other urgent necessities, washing and shoes, out of the scanty pence he received every week and his pay as a chorister, because he spent everything on the bookshop. In these circumstances he went in the Easter holidays to his parents, where he wore the sword with which he had stabbed himself as Philotas and acted the part every day to his brothers, from whom he entirely concealed his forlorn position and the contempt in which his schoolfellows held him, and did his best to find all the pleasant and creditable things he could say of himself: how the Rector had taken him as his companion on a journey, how he had learnt English from him in private lessons, how he had taken part in the torchlight procession and music, and how it all went off.

For himself too he tried so far as possible to banish everything unpleasant and depressing from his thoughts, for he wanted to appear in an advantageous and honourable light: his position should appear enviable to others, however unenviable it really was.

In this agreeable illusion he spent several days here with great pleasure, but just as he had felt light-hearted when he went out of the gates of Hanover and the four towers of the city were gradually lost to view, he felt thoroughly sick at heart when he came near to these gates again and the four towers lay below him, which seemed to him as it were four great pegs marking out the scene of his manifold sufferings.

In particular the high angular market tower with its little pointed top struck terror in him when it came into sight again; close by it was the school, and the sight of the tower at once brought to his mind the ridicule, jeering, and hissing of his schoolfellows. He used to fix his eyes on the great dial of this tower, when he went to school, to see whether he was late: the tower like the old Market Church was Gothic, built of red brick now darkened by age. It was near here that sentence of death was read out to criminals. In a word, this tower of the Market Church gathered up in Reiser's imagination everything that was capable of depressing him and reducing him to melancholy.

He could not indeed have been more melancholy than he was now, even if he had known beforehand what was to happen to him hereafter in this place during his stay. If he had had good reason for his gloomy feelings when he returned to Hanover from his parents the year before, much more had he now when one of the most dreadful crises in his life was impending. Without assuming that he had any power of divination, his depression was natural enough when one considers that his imagination rapidly reviewed his personal life, into which he was once more to be plunged, in each detail of its narrow surroundings : the school, the choir, the Rector's house. He felt that once more his life was to revolve within these narrow spheres, each confining him and choking his vital forces more than the other. How gladly at that moment would he have exchanged his whole stay in Hanover for the darkest dungeon, which would have had far less fearsome terrors for him than all these painful conditions.

Deep in these gloomy thoughts he was approaching the city gate, when a sudden thought came to him like lightning, to change his sky, and put everything in a brighter light : he remembered that he had heard at his parents' house that a company of players had come to Hanover which was to act there all the summer. This was the Ackermann company of that day, which included most of the great actors who are now scattered among all the German theatres. At this thought Reiser hurried on to the city which he now suddenly fell in love with as he had hated it before. It was still the forenoon, for he had stayed a night at a place on the way, from which he had only a few miles to walk to Hanover, and without going home he hurried at once to the Palace, where he knew that the programme and list of actors were posted up, and read that *Emilia Galotti* would be acted that evening. His heart beat with joy when he read this, at the thought of actually seeing performed on the stage with all possible illusions the very play over which he had wept so often and been shaken to the depths of his soul, but so far had only seen with the eye of imagination.

He would not have stayed away from the play that night, whatever it might have cost : but when he arrived home his bedroom had been whitewashed and some building had been going on which made it uninhabitable. This cheerless aspect of the place where he was lodged drove him more completely out of the real world of his surroundings; he longed for the moment when the play would begin.

Wherever he went, he could not conceal his delight. When he entered Frau Filter's parlour his first word was the play—she made this a reproach long afterwards, and it was the same when he came to his uncle the wig-maker, where he had to sleep for some nights in the garret, till his room in the Rector's house was made habitable again.

The following account of the cast may give some notion of the impression that must have been made on him by *Emilia Galotti*, the first play he saw while he was in this frame of mind. Emilia was played by the late Charlotte Ackermann, Orsina by her sister, and Claudia by Frau Reinike. Odoardo was played by Borchen, The Prince by Brockmann, Appiani by Reinike and Conti by Dauer. Can *Emilia Galotti* ever have been played anywhere again in such conditions ?

How powerfully this must have appealed to Reiser's mind, as he saw as it were the world of his imagination become real! Henceforward he had no other thought but of the theatre, and seemed entirely lost to all other hopes and prospects in life.

Whatever money he could scrape together he spent on the play, from which he could not stay away for a single evening, even though he had to stint his food for it. For the play's sake he often ate nothing but bread and salt the whole day, unless the Rector's old mother sent food to his room, which she sometimes did out of compassion.

And as it was now summer he enjoyed the delight of being once more alone in his room, which was more precious to him than the costliest food he could have enjoyed. The prospect of the play in the evening consoled him when he woke in the morning to a dreary day, as he now always did. For the scorn and ridicule of his schoolfellows, and the sense of his own worthlessness which they produced, and which he carried with him everywhere, lasted on and embittered his life. All that he did to escape from it merely served to dull his inward pain but not to cure it: it woke with him every morning, and while his imagination conjured up illusory pictures, yet at heart he cursed his existence. The frequent tears he shed while reading or at the theatre were shed both for his own fortunes and for those of the characters with whom he sympathized, and he found himself again in the characters of the innocent sufferers, the man discontented with himself and the world, the melancholy and the self-hater.

The oppressive heat in summer often drove him out of his room into the kitchen or the court below, where he sat on a pile of logs, and often had to hide his face when some one came in as he sat with eyes red with weeping. This was again 'the Joy of Grief', which was his portion from childhood up, even when he had to dispense with all other joys in life. So strong was this feeling that even in comedies, provided they contained some moving scenes, 'The Chase'[1] (*Die Jagd*) for instance, he cried more than he laughed. But what impression such a play must have made may again be judged from the cast: Charlotte Ackermann taking Röschen, her sister Hannchen, Fraulein Reinike the mother, while Töffel was played by Schröder, the father by Reinike, and Christel by Dauer.

If any outward circumstances, apart from Reiser's personal preferences and peculiar situation, were calculated to produce a decided taste for the drama, it was the accident which brought all these first-rate actors at that time into one company. It is easy then to conclude, how *Romeo and Juliet*, Young's *Revenge*, the opera *Clarissa*, and *Eugenie*, the plays which made the deepest impression on Reiser, must have been produced. This so completely absorbed all his thoughts, that every morning he devoured the programme, and conscientiously read every word of it: 'To begin precisely at 5.30,' and 'The performance is at the Theatre Royal', and he felt the same reverence for any distinguished actor whom he chanced to see in the street, as he had once felt for Pastor Paulmann in Brunswick.

[1] By C. F. Weisse.

Everything that belonged to the theatre he regarded as sacred and he would have given a good deal to make acquaintance with the candle-snuffer.

Two years before he had seen performances of *Hercules on Mt. Oeta*, *Count Olsbach*, and *Pamela*, in which the leading parts were played by Eckhof, Böck, Günther, Hensel, Brandes and his wife, and Fraulein Seiler, and ever since then the moving scenes from these plays haunted his memory: Günther as Hercules, Böck as Count Olsbach, and Frau Brandes as Pamela had in turn haunted his thoughts almost every day, and it was chiefly with these persons that he had pictured the plays which he read being acted, up till the arrival of the Ackermann Company.

It so happened then that, if the two sets of actors are taken together, he had now seen all the leading German actors, who are now dispersed over the whole of Germany.

Thus he formed an ideal of dramatic art, which was never satisfied afterwards, yet never gave him rest day or night, but kept him always on the move and made his life restless and fitful.

As he had seen Böck in earlier days and now saw Brockmann in the parts in which there was most weeping, they were the favourite actors in whom his thoughts chiefly centred.

But in spite of all the brilliant scenes of the stage world which hovered before his imagination, his outward circumstances grew worse from day to day. He was daily losing ground in men's esteem, was becoming less and less regular in his ways, his clothes and linen more untidy, so that at last he was loath to show himself; hence he missed school and choir as often as he could and preferred to starve rather than attend any of the free meals left him, except those of Schantz the shoemaker, where even under these adverse conditions he always had a friendly welcome and was entertained most amiably.

As the Rector at last found Reiser's incorrigible irregularity and especially his perpetual coming home late from the play more than he could bear, he gave him notice to leave. Reiser heard the announcement that he had to leave at Midsummer and meanwhile must look out for another lodging, with complete callousness and silence, and when he was alone again did not shed a tear over his fate, for he had become so indifferent to his lot, and had retained so little self-respect or pity for himself, that if his esteem and sense of pity and all the passions overflowing in his heart had not been spent on characters in the world of imagination, they would inevitably have been turned upon himself and could not fail to have destroyed his own personality.

As the Rector had given him notice he concluded for certain that Pastor Marquard would no longer trouble about him and therefore it was all over with his prospects and hopes. He spent the week or two while he was still at the Rector's in his usual way, and then went to lodge with a brushmaker, where he found the quarter he spent from Midsummer to Michaelmas the most dreadful and appalling in his whole life, and was often on the brink of despair. When he was settled there he felt himself once for all cut off from all the connexions he had taken such pains to make, and as he himself believed, cut off by his own fault. The Prince, Pastor Marquard, the Rector, all the persons on whom his future depended, were nothing to him any longer, and with this all his prospects disappeared.

What wonder that a fancy took form in him in which he sought for comfort and made it his daily companion, a fancy which saved him from utter despair. He had among other things seen the operetta '*Clarissa*, or the unknown servant-maid'[1], and no play in his present situation could have had more interest for him. The chief circumstance that roused his interest was that a young nobleman resolves to become a peasant and carries out his resolve. Reiser paid no heed to the motive which led him to this, his love for the servant, but he regarded it as a charming idea that an educated man should resolve to turn peasant, and become such a refined, polite, and well-bred peasant, that he stands out from all the rest.

In the calling which Reiser had taken up he was now of no account at all, and it seemed impossible for him to work his way up again. But he had received far more education than is needed for a peasant, as a peasant he would be raised above his class while as a young man who devotes himself to study and should have prospects he found himself far below his class. The idea of becoming a peasant then became his ruling idea and drove out everything else.

At that time a peasant's son, called M——, attended the school, to whom he had sometimes

[1] By K. D. Stegmann, 1751.

given instruction in Latin: he told him of his resolve, whereupon the other gave him a detailed description of the tasks that belong to a farm labourer, which might well have spoilt his fine dreams, had not his imagination been too strong and forcibly constructed a series of agreeable pictures.

Even in the operetta *Clarissa* a passage occurs where a peasant dissuades the young nobleman who wants to buy his farm from his purpose and finally sings a very expressive song, how the countryman is in the very midst of his best work and suddenly a storm arises

Lightnings flash,
Thunders roll,
And the peasant out of temper hurries home.

The phrase 'out of temper' was so expressed by the music that this single word might well have destroyed the whole magic of his fancy. That is the antidote to all sentimentality and exaltation: they are compatible with what is painful, or awful, with what oppresses man or rouses him to anger, but not with what puts him out of temper. But this antidote was no use to Reiser, he went about whole days a solitary figure, thinking how he could contrive to become a peasant, without taking a step to do so: he rather began to find pleasure again in these agreeable fancies. When he imagined himself a peasant he thought he was made for something better, and felt a sort of cheering compassion for himself over his fate.

So long as he was sustained by this fancy, he was only sad and depressed but not thoroughly out of temper with his lot. Even his deprivation of the necessaries of life gave him a sort of pleasure, as he almost believed that he had to pay too heavily for getting into debt and so retained the pleasant feeling of compassion for himself. But at last when he had spent three days without eating and had kept himself going with tea the whole day, hunger attacked him furiously and the whole fine structure of his fancy collapsed. He ran his head against the wall, stormed and raged and was nearly in despair when his friend Philip Reiser, whom he had so long neglected, came in to him and shared his poverty with him, which indeed was only a few pence.

Meanwhile this was only a slight palliative, for Philip Reiser was at that time not much better off than Anton Reiser, who now fell permanently into a dreadful state which bordered on despair.

As his body received less nourishment the imagination that had kept him alive became gradually exhausted and his pity for himself changed into hatred and bitterness against his own existence. Before he had taken a step to improve his position or had turned to any one with even the shadow of a request, with unparalleled obstinacy he preferred voluntarily to submit to the most fearful misery.

For several weeks he took food only once a week, when he went to Schantz the shoemaker, and fasted the other days, keeping his life going with nothing but tea and warm water, the only thing which he could get for nothing. With a kind of fearful pleasure he watched his body and his clothes falling away with equal indifference. When he went along the street and people pointed at him, and his schoolfellows ridiculed him and hissed behind his back, and street-boys made remarks on him, he clenched his teeth and inwardly joined in the scornful laughter which he heard echo behind him.

But when he came back to Schantz the shoemaker, he forgot everything again. Here he found human beings, here his heart was softened for a few moments, his mind and imagination received a new impetus as his bodily needs were satisfied, and he again got into philosophic conversation with the shoemaker, which often lasted for hours, during which Reiser began to breathe and his spirit drew breath again : then in the heat of discussion he would speak about something as cheerfully and freely as if nothing in the world had depressed him, and gave no sign of his distress.

Even at his uncle the wigmaker's, he never bemoaned himself, when he came or went away, as soon as he saw there was to be a meal : but he did make use of one device to stave off hunger. He pretended to have a dog at home, for whom he begged his uncle to give him the hardened crust of the dough in which the hair for wigs was baked, and this crust, together with the free meal of Schantz the shoemaker, and the warm water which he drank, kept him alive.

When his body had received some nourishment, he generally felt his courage revive. He had an old Virgil, which the bookseller would not buy from him, and in this he began to read the *Eclogues*. He began to learn by heart out of a weekly, *Evening Hours*, which he got Philip Reiser to lend him, and began to learn by heart a poem *The*

Atheist, which he specially liked, and some prose essays. But as soon as he began to feel the want of food again this flickering flame of courage went out, and his mental activity was paralysed. To save himself from the condition of deadly inertia he was obliged to take refuge again in childish games, which had destruction as their outcome. He collected a great number of cherry-stones and plum-stones, sat down in the garret and set them in battle order facing one another. The finest of them he distinguished from the rest by letters and figures which he painted on them in ink, and made generals of them. Then he took a hammer and closing his eyes acted the part of blind fate, letting it fall now here now there. Then, when he opened his eyes again he saw with secret pleasure the awful destruction : how here and there a hero had fallen in the midst of the inglorious multitude and there lay crushed. Then he weighed the fortunes of the two armies against one another and counted the survivors.

He occupied himself thus for half a day at a time : and his helpless childish revenge on the fate which destroyed him thus created for itself a world which he could destroy in his turn. Childish and ridiculous as this game might have seemed to any spectator, it was in fact the most awful result of utter despair ever brought about in a mortal mind by the chain of circumstances.

It will be seen from this how near Reiser was to madness at this time, and yet his state of mind became tolerable again so soon as he could take interest in his cherry-stones and plum-stones. But before he could do this, when he sat down and drew figures in ink on paper or scratched the table with his knife—there were the most fearful moments when his existence lay on him like an intolerable burden, causing him not pain and sadness but ill temper, and he tried to shake it from him with a fearful horror that came upon him.

His friendship with Philip Reiser could not help him then, because he was in much the same position. Anton and Philip Reiser were like two men wandering together in the burning desert and in danger of fainting from thirst: as they hurry forward they are not in a position to say much or to give each other mutual encouragement. But G——, who had once played the dying Socrates, still the nickname of Reiser, decided to live with him, and was indeed in the same position as Reiser, except that he had fallen into it through actual vicious living. Reiser thus found in him a worthy fellow-lodger.

Not long after, M—— the peasant's son, who was in no better circumstances, joined the other two, and thus three of perhaps the poorest men ever shut in within four walls, were living in one room together. Many a day all three of them had nothing to keep them going but boiled water and some bread. Meantime G—— and M—— still had some free meals left. G—— was a man with brains, who spoke very well, and for whom Reiser had always had much respect. At one time both of them had a spell of industry and began to read Virgil's *Eclogues* together, which gave them the purest pleasure, after they had worked through an Eclogue for themselves, each writing down a translation of it. But naturally this could not last long: as soon as each of them became alive to his position again, all courage and desire to study disappeared.

G—— and M—— were in as bad case as Reiser in regard to clothes: and so when they went out together they presented the very picture of slovenly and untidy dress, so that people pointed at them; hence when they went for a walk they tried to get out of the city by byways and narrow streets.

The three of them now led a life completely in keeping with their condition; they often stayed all day in bed, often sat together, head propped on hand, and brooded over their fate, often they parted and gave free scope, each to his own humour. Reiser reviewed his cherry-stones in the garret, M—— attacked his big loaf, which he carefully kept shut up in a box, and G—— lay on the bed hatching plans, not of the best, as afterwards appeared. There were two books Reiser read at this period at different times, as he sat on the floor among his cherry-stones: the works of the philosopher of Sans-Souci, and Pope's works in Duschen's translation. Both books he had borrowed from Schantz the shoemaker.

One day the three were walking together by the river side in a beautiful part of Hanover, where there was a small island, full of cherry-trees. To our adventurers these cherry-trees, all full of the finest cherries, were such an inviting sight that they could not resist the desire to be transported on to the island, in order to feast to their heart's content on the splendid fruit.

It so happened that a quantity of floated wood

had come down the river, which where the river narrowed between the bank and the island sometimes blocked the channel and formed a sort of bridge to the island. Under G——'s guidance, who seemed to be practised in such enterprises, a venture was attempted, which might have cost all three their lives. Where the timber had blocked the stream they pulled one piece after another from the water and carried them to a spot where the passage from bank to island seemed to be narrowest, and there they built the bridge they wanted to cross by in front of them, throwing one timber after another into the water to get a firm footing. Naturally this bridge began to sink under them, and they were pretty deep in the water before they had finished half of this dangerous crossing. However, at length, though after great danger, they landed on the island. And then a spirit of plunder and greed mastered all of them, so that each of them fell on a cherry-tree and plundered it madly. They were like men who had taken a fortress by storm; they wanted compensation and reward for the danger they had brought on themselves. When they had eaten their fill, they stuffed their pockets, handkerchiefs, neckerchiefs, hats and whatever would hold anything, full of cherries, and in the twilight made their way back over the dangerous bridge, part of which had floated away, and notwithstanding the spoils with which they were laden more by chance than by skill or caution they got back.

Reiser found himself not ill-disposed for such expeditions: he regarded it not as theft but as a raid into an enemy's country, which is considered honourable because of the courage it requires. Who knows to what adventures of this kind he would have gone on under G——'s guidance, if they had lived longer together ?

But G—— was too much of a rogue to be trusted as a leader, for he was mean enough to rob even his two fellow-lodgers and companions, Reiser and M——, carrying off a couple of books and other possessions, and selling them secretly, as afterwards appeared.

In a word this G——, with whom Reiser lived so intimately, was a thorough-paced rogue who, as he lay on his bed all day long, thought of nothing but the rogueries he wanted to carry out ; yet he could talk like a book about virtue and morality and had inspired Reiser with respect for him. For at that time he had formed a peculiar ideal of virtue, which so filled his imagination that often the very word 'virtue' moved him to tears. But his idea of virtue was far too general and vague and bore far too little relation to particular cases, to enable him ever to carry out even the sincerest resolve to be virtuous, for he never had any idea where he was to begin.

Once on a fine evening he came home from a lonely walk, and the beauty of nature had so melted his heart to tenderness that he shed many tears and silently made a vow henceforward to be for ever true to virtue, and when he had firmly taken this resolve, he felt such a heavenly pleasure over it that it seemed to him almost impossible ever to deviate from this happy resolve. With these thoughts he fell asleep : when he woke in the morning he again felt the old void in his heart, his day's outlook was so gloomy and desolate, all his outward circumstances seemed so irrevocably ruined, that an invincible disgust for life took the place of the feelings with which he went to sleep the day before. He tried to save himself from himself and made a beginning of virtue by going to the garret and destroying cherry-stones set in battle array. The proper way of beginning to practise virtue would have been to give this up and read instead an eclogue from the old Virgil which he still had, but his heroic resolve had not made him ready to face this trial; it seemed too trivial.

If one chose to test man's ideas of virtue, they would in most men resolve themselves into vague and confused ideas of this sort. At any rate one sees from this how useless it is to preach on virtue in general, without application to particular cases which may often seem trivial.

Reiser himself was often surprised to find how his sudden access of zeal for virtue could evaporate so soon and leave no trace behind; he did not reflect that self-respect, which at that time could only be based with him on the respect of others, is the foundation of virtue and that without this the finest structure of his imagination was bound soon to collapse.

During this state of things he spent any pence he could scrape together on the play, but when the company of actors went away again the middle of the summer, a meadow outside the New Gate was not only the goal of his walks but almost his perpetual resort. He established himself here sometimes the whole day long in a sunny spot, or walked along the river side and was specially delighted if in the hot midday hours he saw not a soul around him.

While he indulged his melancholy thoughts here the whole day long, his imagination was insensibly feeding on high visions, which only began gradually to develop a year later. But his disgust with life meantime became extreme and often on these walks he stood on the banks of the Leine, leaning over the rushing water, while the mysterious desire of life struggled with the sense of despair and drew back his over-hanging body with fearful force.

III

WITH the close of this Part Anton Reiser's wanderings, and with them the real romance of his life begin. This Part contains a faithful presentation of the scenes of his youth, which may perhaps serve as a lesson and a warning to those who have not yet let these priceless years slip from them. Perhaps too the story may afford some useful hints for those engaged in teaching and education: it may lead them to be more careful in the handling of their pupils and more just in their judgements on them.

PART III

In this way Reiser spent twelve dreadful weeks of his life, till Pastor Marquard at last let him know through a third person, that he would befriend him again if he would sincerely beg pardon and repent of his behaviour. This finally softened his heart, for he was tired of his own obstinacy and the long misery that it had caused. He sat down and wrote a long letter to Pastor Marquard depreciating himself with the greatest bitterness, describing himself as the most unworthy man the sun had ever shone on, and prophesying no better fate for himself than that he would one day die in the street from poverty and need. In a word the letter was couched in the most extravagant language of self-contempt and self-depreciation imaginable and yet was anything but hypocrisy. Reiser at that time regarded himself as a monster of wickedness and ingratitude, and wrote the whole letter to Pastor Marquard with all possible bitterness, never thinking to excuse himself, but rather to bring more and more accusations against himself.

Meanwhile he became aware that his passion for reading romances and seeing plays was the immediate cause of his present condition, but he had not yet enough vigour of mind to go back and discover how the reading of romances and plays had become such an imperious necessity to him: all the scorn and ignominy which from childhood up had driven him from the real into the ideal world. That was why he reproached himself more unjustly than perhaps any one else would have done, and there were many hours when he not only despised but hated and abhorred himself

Thus the confession he made to Pastor Marquard in his letter was fearful and unique so that the Pastor was amazed when he read it. Perhaps no one had ever made such a confession to him.

When Reiser had sent the letter, he only waited for the moment when Pastor Marquard would receive him, and a day was fixed to which he looked forward with strangely mixed feelings of hope and fear and resigned despair.

He had prepared himself for a very theatrical scene, but it failed completely. He intended to fall at Pastor Marquard's feet and invoke his anger. He had sketched his whole speech in imagination, and wherever he went it bore him company till the day when he was to see Pastor Marquard. Meantime a very vexatious incident occurred. His father had heard of his state and had come over to Hanover to plead for him, which was extremely disagreeable to Reiser, who thought he needed no third person to plead for him, but thought himself capable of moving Pastor Marquard's heart by the affecting speech he had got by heart.

At last came the important day when he was to speak to Pastor Marquard, and his imagination was in travail with high matters—how he would throw himself at Pastor Marquard's feet in repentance and despair, how the Pastor would be moved and bid him rise and would forgive him.

But when at last he entered the house of Pastor

Marquard and approached this long-prepared scene with trembling eagerness, while he was waiting to be called in the servant came out and told him to come in, and that his father was already with Pastor Marquard.

This news fell on him like a thunderbolt. He stood for a moment dazed: his whole plan was shipwrecked. He wanted to speak to Pastor Marquard without witnesses, for only so did he feel capable of playing the whole scene—the kneeling before Pastor Marquard and the moving and pathetic speech to him. To kneel before him in presence of a third person and especially before his father he felt impossible.

He sent the servant back with a message to say he must see Pastor Marquard alone. This was refused him, and instead of the brilliant and moving scene which he intended to enact, when he entered he had to stand like a criminal without being able to utter a word of his long-planned speech, humiliated and despised.

At that moment he was overpowered by a feeling he had never known before: he could not bear to see his father standing before Pastor Marquard as a petitioner. He would have given everything in the world if his father had been a hundred miles off. He felt himself doubly humiliated and shamed in the person of his father, and there was the further vexation that the whole scene of the kneeling had failed. All passed now in a cold, commonplace ordinary manner. Reiser stood there as undistinguished as a commonplace everyday miscreant who is reproached as he deserves. What he wanted was to paint himself as a downright miscreant and then beg for the severest penalty to be inflicted for his crime.

But perhaps no event in his life was more to his real advantage. Had the scene he had planned been a success, who knows to what he would have gone on, and what parts he would have played? Perhaps this was the turning-point of his fate, which decided whether he should be a hypocrite and a rascal or a straightforward honourable man.

The kneeling scene, though not patent hypocrisy and pretence, would at any rate have been affectation, and the transition from this to hypocrisy and pretence is very easy!

It was indeed a real benefit for Reiser that Pastor Marquard did not think any of the extravagant expressions of his letter worth attention, and so far from being moved by them, found them ridiculous and explained them as the immature offspring of an imagination excited by reading romances and plays: adding that if Reiser was really such a miscreant as he had painted himself in the letter, he would not take the least trouble about him but would abhor him as a monster.

And instead of going into explanations about pardon for the past, on condition of good behaviour in the future and so on, Pastor Marquard went on at once without sentiment to discuss Reiser's torn shoes and stockings and the debts he had incurred and how these were to be paid and his ragged clothes mended. He never gave Reiser a chance of vowing future amendment or anything solemn of that sort. His whole attitude to him, though he befriended him again, was hard and severe, but it was hard and severe treatment which roused

Reiser from his slumber and transported him from his ideal world of romance and the stage into the real world, particularly as the romantic drama he intended to play with Pastor Marquard had failed, and yet he was to be rescued from his terrible condition by no idle dream of turning peasant or the like but in actual fact.

With this crisis in his fortunes countless good resolutions and determinations sprang up in his heart: the failure of the kneeling scene was painful, but in that too he got reconciled to his fate. A new epoch of his life began.

He left the brushmaker and took lodgings with a tailor, where he had to live with the family and sleep in the garret. Frau Filter and the court musician, who lived in the same house, took him up again, and gave him a free meal once a week. Frau Filter got him to teach the little girl she had living with her, writing and the catechism, he attended the school regularly again, and new hope was entertained of him. Even the Prince sent for him and spoke to him in the presence of Pastor Marquard, who received the money for his support from the Prince and paid his debts with it.

So far all was well, and he began to work hard again, although the outward conditions were not too favourable to study: for in the tailor's room he had only his allotted place, where his piano stood, which sometimes served him as a table, and under which he had placed his whole library on a small bookshelf. When he read and worked by himself, he could not command quiet around him, and as long as winter lasted he was obliged to stay in his host's sitting-room; in summer he took his piano and books up to the garret where he slept and was alone and undisturbed.

He had not left his former lodging and his previous companions G—— and M—— more than a few weeks when a dreadful event occurred, which made him feel in a very vivid way the nearness and seriousness of the danger which had threatened him. One day G——, while singing in the choir, was arrested in the public street and put in one of the deepest dungeons of the Gate, which is assigned to the worst criminals only.

Reiser was seized with horror and trembling when he saw him carried off, and the strangest thing was that the thought that he might be regarded as an accomplice in the as yet unknown crime had the effect of producing in him signs of shame and confusion, as if he had really been an accomplice. Hence his anxiety was almost as great as if he had himself committed a crime. This was a natural consequence of the suppression of his self-confidence from his childhood up. At this time it was not strong enough to resist the judgements of others upon him. If every one had regarded him as a declared criminal, he would perhaps in the end have regarded himself as one.

At last it came out that his former fellow-lodger G—— had robbed a church, stolen lace from altar-cloths by night, and even broken locks to steal silver-rimmed chant-books which were kept in the pews.

Such then were the projects he had devised and planned as he lay on his bed, but the actual sacrilege he had committed after Reiser had left him, although he had already been guilty of various thefts. The gallows was the penalty for his crime, and the fear of a like fate came over Reiser whenever he reflected how near he had been to this fellow, and how easily he might have been led on by him from one adventure to another, as he had already made such a heroic beginning in the raid on the cherry-island. Reiser would have regarded the sacrilege at night as more heroic than mischievous, and perhaps G—— would not have found it more difficult to persuade him to join in such an adventure than in that on the cherry-island. Probably this reflection or this vague consciousness may have contributed to Reiser's confusion when G—— was spoken of. There seemed such a short step between him and the crime into which he might have been drawn, that he felt like a man who is dizzy at sight of a precipice, from which he is far enough off not to fall in, but to which he feels irresistibly drawn by his terror and thinks he is already sinking into the abyss.

When Reiser reflected how easily he might have come to share G——'s crime, it almost aroused in him a feeling of having really shared in it; from which his anxiety and confusion are easily explained.

Meanwhile G——escaped hanging: after some months in prison, his sentence was so far lightened that he was banished and forbidden the country. Reiser was unable to learn anything more of his fate. This was the last of the true 'dying Socrates', whose nickname Reiser had to bear so long, because he played not the dying Socrates himself, but only an insignificant friend who did little more than stand in a corner and weep, while the dying

Socrates was able to drink the cup of poison, to the emotion of all spectators, and display himself on his death-bed in the most brilliant light.

Reiser had for more than a year begun to keep a diary, in which he wrote all that happened to him. The diary was a peculiar one because he omitted not a single circumstance of his life and not a single occurrence of the day, however insignificant it might be. As he only noted actual events and none of the things he imagined during the day, the narrative of the events was bound to be as bald and dull and uninteresting as the events themselves. Reiser in fact always lived a double life, inward and outward, quite distinct from one another, and the diary described the outer life which was not worth recording. Reiser did not at that time yet understand the influence of the outer, real events, on the inner state of his mind; his study of himself had not yet received the right direction.

Meanwhile his diary improved as time went on, as he began to record not only events but also his intentions and resolutions, in order to see later on what he had carried out. Even at that time he laid down laws for himself, which he noted in his diary, in order to fulfil them. He also sometimes made solemn vows, for instance to get up early, to divide the hours of the day regularly, and the like.

But the strange thing was, the most solemn resolutions that he formed were generally fulfilled latest and with least energy: when it came to carrying out in detail, the fire of imagination, with which he had thought of the thing as a whole with all its pleasant consequences, had died away. On the other hand when he planned a thing casually without any show and solemnity, he often carried it out sooner and better.

His good resolutions were inexhaustible: but this made him continually dissatisfied with himself, because there were too many of them for him ever to do justice to them.

He noted as a remarkable fact in his life, and indeed it was such, that for three days he had been uninterruptedly contented with himself, for these three days were, for so long as he could remember, unique in their kind. But for these three days there was a lucky combination of circumstances, bright weather, sound health, friendly faces in those to whom he came, and so on, which made it noticeably easier for him to carry out his resolutions.

He had recourse to all sorts of means to keep himself in the path of virtue. In the first place he tried to awaken good and noble thoughts in his mind by reciting Pope's *Universal Prayer*, which he had written down in English and learnt by heart, and indeed whenever he said it he felt moved by it and quickened to good purposes and resolutions. Then he had copied a number of rules of life out of a book, and these he read at certain fixed times of the day: and he also sang very conscientiously at fixed hours every day a couple of anthems, which he found tended to encourage goodness and virtue.

If his outward circumstances had been somewhat more favourable and encouraging, with these resolutions and efforts, which are very unusual in a person of his age (he was just over sixteen) he could not have failed to become a pattern of virtue. But it was just this which always depressed him again, people's opinion of him, which he could not alter by force, and which, in spite of all his efforts to become a better man, would not quite turn again in his favour. He seemed to have ruined his reputation too much, to have deceived all men's expectation of him too far for him ever to be able to recover the respect and affection of men. In particular an undeserved suspicion had fallen on him, the suspicion of vicious living, because he had lived with such a vicious person as G——. Reiser was so far from this, that three years later when he came across an anatomical book, his eyes were opened to certain things of which he had only vague and confused notions before. But his reading at the bookshop and his frequenting of the playhouse were interpreted in the worst sense and regarded as an unpardonable offence.

Now it happened that a company of acrobats came to Hanover, and because the cost of entrance was trifling, he went one single evening to see their breakneck arts. He was seen, and because this was a kind of play, people said his old tastes had revived, and not a single evening passed when he did not visit the acrobats. 'That was where his money was going to; it was clear that nothing was to be made of him.' His voice was far too weak to be lifted against the assertion of those who would have it that they had seen him at the acrobats every evening. In a word, this single visit threw him back again farther in public esteem than all his previous industry and good behaviour had been able to bring him.

There were other things which very much depressed him. New Year came on and he was glad to think that he would again share the privileges of his position in the procession with torchlight and music, that he would go in the ranks with the rest and would no longer, as before, be one of the last in the procession.

But, in order to be able to pay for his torch and his share in the music and other expenses he waited for the distribution of the choir-money. which he had earned with bitter pains by singing in frost and rain. When he came to the Director to receive it, he found that it had occurred to the Assistant Master to claim it for the private lessons which Reiser had had from him in the VIth Form and not paid for. Reiser went to him and begged and implored him to let him have half the choir-money; but he was inexorable, and when he came to the Director, he too reproached him bitterly with having gone to the play again to see the acrobats and also with having bought bread and honey in the market in front of the school and eaten it in the street: a thing which Reiser regarded as very innocent and not degrading, but which now was interpreted as most degrading, and he was reviled by the Director as a bad lad who had no honour or shame, and with whom he would concern himself no longer.

Perhaps Reiser was never sadder and more depressed in his whole life than when he now returned home from the Director. He paid no heed to wind or snowstorm but wandered round for an hour and a half on the ramparts and in the city, giving himself up to his distress and his loud complaints.

For all his hopes were disappointed in a moment: his effort to recover the favour of the Director by his conduct: his hope to get a good share of choir-money, which was generally most considerable at the New Year, and his longing to take part next day in the procession with torches and music and publicly march in the ranks.

What pained him most was this last, and it was very natural, for by taking part in the procession he would have felt himself as it were reinstated in all the privileges of his position, with which he had been so completely put out of conceit. To be excluded from it seemed to him one of the greatest misfortunes that could happen to him. That too was the reason that he had begged the Assistant Master so earnestly to let him have half the choir-money—a request which he would otherwise never have stooped to make.

It was of no avail to rack his brain for means to get money; he could not buy a torch, and next night when his schoolfellows in glittering pomp marched along the street amid a throng of spectators, he had to sit sadly at home by his piano. He tried to console himself as well as he could, but when he heard the music in the distance, it had a peculiar effect on his spirits. He pictured to himself vividly the glitter of the torches, the throng of spectators, the tumult and his schoolfellows as the leading actors in this splendid play, and himself excluded, lonely and abandoned by all the world. This reduced him to a state of melancholy which was very like that which he felt when his parents had left him alone upstairs, while they were being entertained below by the landlord at a feast from which the merry laughter and clinking of the glasses came echoing to him above, and then too he felt equally lonely and forsaken, and comforted himself with the hymns of Madame Guyon.

Such incidents drove him again out of the world into solitude; nothing pleased him better than to sit alone at his piano and read and work by himself, and he longed for nothing so much as that summer might come quickly so that he could spend the whole day alone in the garret where his bed was.

And when this summer that he had longed for came, he enjoyed first and foremost the delight of solitary study. For some time he had been borrowing books again from the bookseller, but now his choice fell on nothing but scientific books: his reading of novels and plays had completely ceased since that dreadful period of his life.

As soon as the air began to get warm, he hastened to the garret and spent the pleasantest hours of his life in reading and study. Among other books he had borrowed from the bookseller was Gottsched's *Philosophy*, and however much the subject is watered down in it, it gave as it were the first impulse to his thinking powers: he gained from it at least an easy general view of all philosophical sciences, and thus cleared up his ideas. As soon as he became aware of this, his eagerness to survey the subject quickly increased every day. He saw that mere reading was no use, so he began to sketch out a synopsis on a series of sheets, duly subordinating details to the whole and trying thus to get a clear conception.

The mere writing down of the chief contents made the subject much more interesting, for as he kept the page in which he had noted the contents before him as he read, he gained the great advantage that he never lost sight of the whole in the details, a thing which is a main requirement in philosophical studies and is also very difficult.

All that he had not yet thought over lay before him on this chart like an unknown country and he felt a regular longing to get to know it more accurately. The outline and framework were fixed in his mind by the general survey of the whole, and he now strove to fill up one after another, the gaps, which he was only now able to feel. And what had before been merely empty names to him now gradually became clear complete conceptions, and if after that in reading or thinking he came across the name again and everything which had before been obscure and confused became luminous and clear, a pleasant feeling came over him, such as he had never felt before : for the first time he felt the joy of thinking.

His growing curiosity to get a general view of the whole quickly carried him through all difficulties of detail. His intellectual powers underwent a new creation. He felt as though the dawn of his intelligence was beginning, that day was gradually breaking, and he would never tire of looking on the refreshing light.

He almost forgot food and drink and all his surroundings, and under the pretext of illness hardly came down from his garret for six weeks. All this time he sat at his book morning and evening pen in hand, and did not rest till he had gone from beginning to end.

What prevented his zeal from slackening was, as I have said, the fact that he kept the main subject always in view, and that he never ceased the process of classifying and arranging the subject-matter in his thought as well as on paper.

Thus, though his outward circumstances had not much improved, he spent this summer not unpleasantly: at least he counted the lonely hours that he spent in the garret among the happiest in his life. From this time forward too he was less unhappy because his power of thought had begun to develop. Wherever he was, he exercised his thought instead of merely his fancy, and his thoughts concerned themselves with the highest subjects, with ideas of space and time, with the highest faculty of perception and so forth.

But even then, when he had lost himself for a time in reflection, he often felt as though suddenly his way was barred, as though a wooden wall or an impenetrable screen closed his further view once for all: he then felt as if the matter of his thought had been nothing but words. He was here beating against the impenetrable partition which makes human thought different from the thought of higher beings, against the indispensable necessity of speech, without which human thought can exercise no independent activity, and which is only a sort of artificial makeshift, by means of which we arrive at something resembling that pure thought, which we may some day perhaps attain. Speech seemed to him to stand in the way of thinking and yet he could not think without speech.

Many a time he tormented himself for hours, trying to see whether it is possible to think without words. And then the notion struck him of being as the limit of all human thinking: then everything seemed obscure and bare. Then he looked sometimes at the short duration of his own existence, and the thought or rather the non-thought of not-being overpowered his mind: he could not explain how he really was now and yet should once not have been. Thus he wandered without stay and without guide in the abysses of metaphysics. Many a time when he sang in the choir and instead of joining in his schoolfellows' conversation went away solitary, and they said behind his back, 'there goes old melancholy!' he reflected on the nature of the name and tried to get out of it what could not be expressed in words. This now took the place of the romantic dreams, with which his fancy had before enlivened so many dull hours when he sang in the choir in rain and snow on a gloomy winter's day.

He now took from the book-shop Wolff's *Metaphysics* and read it through on the system already adopted, and so when he came to Schantz the shoemaker the material for their philosophic talks was far richer than before, and they arrived independently at all the different systems propounded by philosophers ancient and modern and constantly repeated after them by innumerable people.

Meantime Director Ballhorn from whose friendship Reiser had hoped so much and had been so much disappointed, was promoted to a small town not far from Hanover as Superintendent and another Director, Schumann, had arrived in his place. Reiser, who thought of nothing but his metaphysics, was not much interested. The new Director was an old man, who possessed knowledge and much taste, and was fairly free from pedantry, a rare event in old pedagogues.

During the transition a good many school hours dropped out, which made Reiser's bad attendance less noticeable. And if ever any one made good use of non-attendance at school lessons it was he ; in a period of a couple of months he did more, and his intellect was stored with far more ideas than during all his academical years. Certainly he never heard the whole philosophical course lectured on in such detail as he then worked through it in his mind, and as to the other branches of knowledge—dogmatics, history, &c., he never heard them treated so fully at the University as he did in the parts lectured on at the school in Hanover.

In his young days he had no instruction except in arithmetic and writing, and this was now almost wholly wasted, as he had no occasion for arithmetic and his handwriting was ruined by taking notes. Now it happened that he got some practice in writing, which meant little or no gain to him, but perceptibly trained his hand. When he began to do school work again and brought exercises to the Rector, he was much surprised at the improvement in his hand and at once gave him something to copy, which had to be done in the house on the spot, so that in this way he again got access to the Rector. This encouraged him to hope he might repair his credit with the Rector but he was soon disappointed, as his father came over to Hanover and the only comfort Pastor Marquard gave him was that his son was a rascal who would come to nothing.

When his father went away he accompanied him some distance outside the City Gate and there it was that he repeated to him the comforting words of Pastor Marquard and bitterly reproached him for not acknowledging the benefits bestowed on him, and pointed to the coat he wore as an undeserved present from his benefactors. This made Reiser angry, for the coat, which was of coarse grey cloth that gave him the appearance of a servant, was already a hated object to him, and he therefore told his father that a servant's coat of that sort, which he had to wear to his distress, could arouse no great gratitude in him.

Thereupon his father, taught by Madame Guyon's writings to regard humiliation and mortification of self-conceit as sacred, fell into a rage, turned away from him quickly and cursed him on his road. Reiser was now in a state of mind he had never been in before: all he had suffered and endured from his adverse fortune, with this new fact that his father rejected and cursed him, passed in a moment through his mind. As he went back into the city he broke into blasphemy and was nearly desperate, he longed to be swallowed up by the earth and his father's curse seemed to pursue him in earnest. This again checked for a while all his good resolutions and his hitherto unbroken and voluntary industry.

Summer was drawing to a close and persistent bodily pain again began frequently to depress him : from this time he had perpetual headaches, which lasted a whole year, so that hardly a day or an hour intervened when he could feel free from this persistent pain.

The tailor, with whom he had now lived a year, gave him notice, and he moved to the house of a butcher in a remote street, where several school-fellows and a couple of common soldiers were quartered.

He was obliged here too to live in the common room, and his belongings with the piano and the bookshelf below remained as before : but instead of the garret he had a tiny room, where he slept with another chorister and in summer, when it was warm, each of them could be alone. The society of his host the butcher and the two soldiers quartered there, and two good-for-nothing choristers, could not contribute much to the education and refinement of his manners.

All gathered on winter evenings in the living room, and as he could not work amid the noise and clamour, he mixed with the rest and got what amusement he could from the people who now formed his immediate circle.

In spite of his continuous headaches he worked by himself as often as he could get a little quiet, and in this way learnt French in a few weeks, by borrowing a Latin Terence with a French translation and giving himself a lesson every day without a break. He got far enough at least to be able to understand any French book fairly well.

Meanwhile as his outward circumstances did not

mend and he was constantly oppressed by physical pain, he fell into a state in which Young's *Night Thoughts*, which he got hold of by chance at that time, was very welcome reading. He thought that he found in it all his earlier notions of the nothingness of life and the vanity of all human things. He was never tired of reading this book and almost learnt by heart the thoughts and feelings which dominate it.

The only relief for his headaches was to lie stretched on his back on the bed; he would often lie thus for whole days and read. This was the only enjoyment of life left to him, to which he clung; without it the deadly weariness would have made the wretched life he dragged on unbearable.

To withdraw at times from the noise which surrounded him, he often braved rain or snow, and at evening, when it was dark and he was sure that no one saw him, and that no one would speak to him, he took a walk on the rampart round the town, and it was on these walks that his spirit gained new courage, and the hope of working his way up out of his miserable condition sprang up again with a faint glimmer in his heart. As he looked at the lights set in the houses along the streets near the rampart and reflected that in every lighted room, often many of them in one house, a family or some other group of people or a single person was living, and that for the moment a room of this sort held within it the fortunes and the life and thoughts of a person or party; and that he too, when his walk was over, would return to a room like that, where he was confined as it were and his existence fixed to the spot: he felt a peculiar sense of humiliation, as if amid this endless mass of human fates crossing one another in confusion his own personal fate was, as it were, lost and so made petty and insignificant. But then again at times these very lights in the single rooms of the houses on the rampart, uplifted his spirit, when he drew from them a general survey, and so thought himself out of his own little cramping sphere, where he was lost among all the rest of these dwellers upon earth living unnoticed and undistinguished, and prophesied for himself a special and distinguished fortune; then, as he stepped on with quickened pace the sweet thought of it renewed his hope and courage.

Ever afterwards the sight of a series of lighted living-rooms in a strange unknown house, where he imagined a number of families, of whose life and fortunes he knew as little as they did of his own, has awakened peculiar feelings in him: the limitations of the individual life were brought vividly home to him. He realized the truth that one is only a unit among so many thousands who are and have been.

He often wished to be able to think himself wholly into the being and nature of another: when for instance he passed in the street close by some complete stranger, the thought of the man's strangeness, and of how completely the one was unaware of the name and fortune of the other, became so vivid, that he pressed as closely to the man as good manners allowed, in order to get for a moment into his atmosphere and try whether he could not penetrate the dividing-wall which parted the memories and thoughts of this stranger from his own.

One other feeling from the years of his childhood may fitly be mentioned here: he used sometimes to think in those days, supposing he had had other parents and his parents were nothing to him, but quite indifferent. That thought often made him shed childish tears: whatever his parents might be, he counted them dear beyond all others and he would not have exchanged them for the grandest and kindest. But at the same time too he had again the peculiar feeling of being lost amid the throng, and the feeling that there were innumerable parents with children besides his own, among whom they too were lost.

Whenever he was in a throng of men afterwards this sense of littleness, singleness, and absolute insignificance was awakened in him. What a quantity of material like me is here! What a mass of this human substance, out of which states and armies are built up, just as houses and towers are built of timber! Such were the thoughts which then produced a vague feeling in his mind, because he could not clothe them in words and make them clear to himself.

Once when four criminals were beheaded on the place of execution outside Hanover, he went out with the crowd and saw in the criminals only four of the crowd who were to be destroyed and cut to pieces. This seemed such a small insignificant thing, because there was still such a mass of men about him, just as if a tree were to be cut down in the forest or an ox to be felled. And when the pieces of the men's bodies after execution were wound upon the wheel and he thought how he and the men about him could be dismembered in the same way, men became to him so worthless and insignificant that his fate and everything were buried in the thought that he could be cut to pieces like an animal. So he went away home with a certain satisfaction, consuming his dough-crust on the way, for this was his terrible quarter when often for days he had nothing to live on but the dough. Food and clothing were as indifferent to him as life and death: what matter whether this or that moving lump of flesh, of which there is such a vast number, goes on in the world or not? Then he could never refrain from putting himself in the place of the executed criminals, dismembered and wound upon the wheel, and reflected, as Solomon reflected, 'Man is like the cattle, as the cattle die, so he dies.'

From this time forward when he saw an animal slaughtered he identified himself with it in thought, and as he so often had the opportunity of seeing it at the slaughterer's, for a long time his thought was centred on this—to arrive at the distinction between himself and a slaughtered animal like that. He often stood for an hour looking at a calf's head, eyes, ears, mouth, and nose—and pressing as close to it as possible, as he did with a human stranger, often with the foolish fancy that it might perhaps be possible for him to think himself gradually into the nature of the animal. His own concern was to know the difference between himself and the animal; and sometimes he forgot himself so completely as he gazed at it persistently, that for a moment he really believed that he had come to feel the nature of the creature's existence. From childhood up his thoughts were busy with the question—how would it be if he were for instance a dog or some other animal, living among men ? And as he had thought out the distinction between body and spirit he felt nothing was more important than to discover some essential difference between himself and the animal, because otherwise he could not persuade himself that the animal which was so like him in bodily structure ought not to have a spirit like himself. Where did the spirit stay when the body was destroyed and dismembered ? All the thoughts of so many thousand men, which had hitherto been parted from one another by the wall of the body in each person and were only communicated to each other by the movement of some parts of this wall, seemed after man's death to flow together into one : there was nothing to separate and sunder them any longer. He imagined to himself a man's intellect left behind and flying about in the air, and soon fluttering away.

And then the vast mass of men seemed to him to give rise to a vast formless mass of souls ; he could never see why there were just so many and no more and no less, and as the number seemed endless, the individual became at last insignificant and almost nothing. It was chiefly this insignificance, this sense of being lost in the multitude, which often made his existence a burden.

One evening he was wandering in the street, sad and gloomy ; it was already twilight but not so dark that he might not have been seen by people, the sight of whom was unbearable to him, because he thought he was an object of ridicule and scorn to them. The air was damp and cold and a mixture of rain and snow was falling and he was wet through. Suddenly the feeling arose in his mind that he could not escape from himself. This thought weighed on him like a mountain; he strove hard to rise above it, but the burden of existence seemed to weigh him down again. To think that one day and every day he must rise with himself, go to bed with himself, and at every step drag his hated self along with him!

His self-consciousness, with the sense of being worthless and rejected, was as burdensome to him as his body with its feeling of wet and cold, and he would at that moment have very gladly laid aside his body, like his wet clothes, if only a death that he desired had smiled a welcome to him from any quarter.

That he must be unalterably himself and could be no other, that he was shut up in the narrow prison of self—this gradually reduced him to a despair which led him to the bank of the river, in a part of the town where it had no railing. Here he stood half an hour, struggling between the most dreadful disgust of life, and the instinctive inexplicable desire to go on breathing, till at last he sank exhausted on a felled tree-trunk, which lay not far from the bank. Here, as if in defiance of nature, he stayed awhile and let the rain wet him through, till the feeling of feverish cold and the chattering of his teeth brought him to himself again, and he chanced to remember that he would get fresh sausage to eat that evening at his host's, the butcher, and that the room would be very warm. These purely sensual and animal ideas again revived the love of life in him, he forgot himself as a man, as he had done after the execution of the criminals, and returned home an animal in his thoughts and feelings. As animal he wished to live on, as man he felt every moment of continued existence intolerable.

But just as the world of books so often before had rescued him from his real world when it came to the worst, it so happened that just then he had borrowed Wieland's translation of Shakespeare from the book-shop, and a new world was opened up at once to his thoughts and feelings! Here was more than all he had ever thought, read, or felt. He read *Macbeth*, *Hamlet*, *Lear*, and felt his spirit irresistibly uplifted: every hour that he read Shakespeare was unspeakably precious. Wherever he was, wherever he went, he lived, thought, and dreamed Shakespeare, and his dearest wish was to communicate all that he felt in reading him: and the nearest person who had a feeling for it was his friend Philip Reiser, who lived in a remote part of the town, where he had built himself a new workshop and made pianos. He still sang in a choir, but not in the one in which Anton Reiser was. Thus circumstances had parted them for a long time, notwithstanding their earlier close friendship. But now when Anton Reiser found it impossible to enjoy Shakespeare to himself, he could find no one better to hasten to than his romantic friend. To read him a whole play from the Shakespeare volume and to note with pleasure all his feelings and comments was the greatest delight Reiser had ever enjoyed.

They devoted whole nights to this reading, when Philip Reiser played the host, made coffee at midnight and put wood in the stove. Then they both sat by a little lamp standing on a small table, and Philip Reiser bent his long neck to listen as Anton read on and the rising passion mounted with the growing interest of the action.

These Shakespeare nights are among the pleasantest memories of Reiser's life. If his mind was educated by anything it was by this reading, which completely threw into the shade all his other dramatic reading. He learnt even to rise above his outward circumstances in a higher spirit, even in his melancholy his imagination took a higher flight.

By Shakespeare he was led through the world of human passions; the narrow circle of his ideal existence was extended. He no longer lived so isolated and insignificant a life as to be lost in the multitude, for by reading Shakespeare he had shared in the feelings of thousands. After he had read Shakespeare in this spirit he was no longer an ordinary commonplace person, before long his spirit rose above all the outward circumstances that had crushed him and all the ridicule and scorn he had suffered, as the course of this story will show.

Hamlet's soliloquy directed his eyes to human life as a whole: when he felt himself tormented, oppressed, and confined he no longer thought of himself as alone: he began to regard this as the universal lot of mankind. This gave a higher note to his complaints. The reading of Young's *Night Thoughts* had already done this in some measure, but now Shakespeare took its place.

Shakespeare strengthened the weakened bond of friendship between Philip and Anton Reiser. Anton needed some one to whom he could address all his thoughts and feelings, and on whom could his choice fall rather than the man who had shared his feelings over the Shakespeare of his adoration ?

The need of communicating his thoughts and feelings led him to the idea of writing a new kind of diary, in which he wished to record not so much trivial external events as before, but the inner history of his mind, and to do this in the form of a letter to his friend. His friend was to write back, and so both were to get mutual practice in style. This practice more than anything trained Anton Reiser to be a writer : he began to feel an indescribable pleasure in being able to clothe thoughts of his own in appropriate words, to communicate to his friend. Thus a number of little essays came into being, under his hands, some of which he need not have been ashamed of even in maturer years.

The exercise was indeed one-sided, for Philip Reiser was backward with his essays, but Anton Reiser thus had some one, to whom he confided his feelings and tastes, whose approval or blame was not indifferent to him, and of whom he could think when he was writing.

One thing was strange : when he wanted to begin writing, the words 'What is my existence, what is my life ?' always came to his pen. So these words appeared on several scraps of paper he had meant to write on, but threw away when he could not get on. His vague conception of life and existence, which lay like an abyss before him, always forced its way up in his mind: he felt constrained to settle this most important point of his doubts and cares, before he fixed his thoughts on anything else. It was very natural then that these words always came to his pen involuntarily when he tried to write down his thoughts.

At length the expression worked its way through the thoughts and the first thing he succeeded in clothing in fairly suitable words was a metaphysical essay on the ego (*Ichheit*) and self-consciousness.

For now that he wished to think farther and record his thoughts, naturally nothing touched him more nearly than this, he wanted first of all to be right with himself before he went on to anything else.

He began to follow up this idea of the *individuum* which he regarded as supremely important ever since he had learnt some logic a few years before, and as he now at last came up against the highest degree of being determined on all sides and completely self-identical, he felt after some reflection as though he had escaped from himself and could only look for himself again in the series of his recollections of the past. He felt that existence depended solely on the chain of these uninterrupted memories. True existence seemed to him to be confined to the *individuum* proper, and he could think of no true *individuum* except an eternally unalterable being, comprehending everything in a single view.

At the end of his inquiries his own existence seemed to him a mere illusion, an abstract idea, a gathering up of the resemblances which each following moment in his life had with the moment vanished. Through these notions of his own limitation his notions of God were ennobled, he began through this great conception to have a sense of his own existence, which otherwise seemed to disappear from under his hands, to be torn off aimless and fragmentary. It was from these reflexions that his first written essay was composed, in the form of a letter to his friend, with whom he used often to discuss this subject and who always seemed at least to understand him.

Meantime his headaches continued, but at last he was so used to them that his condition seemed quite dangerous or unnatural, if he had a day without headaches.

His meetings with Philip Reiser became more frequent and he unexpectedly acquired a new friend. This was a son of the Precentor, Winter, one of his schoolfellows, against whose face and features he had always had a sort of antipathy and at the same time thought himself despised by him. Winter learnt from his father that Anton Reiser had written verses and as he had promised to write a birthday poem for some one he looked up Reiser and asked him to compose the poem, which he had not the will or the time to compose himself. This was the first occasion which led Reiser to bring his neglected poetry out again.

The little poem was a success. Winter visited him frequently after this and promised that he would procure him the acquaintance of a remarkable man, who lived in obscurity and was nothing more than a vinegar-distiller. Reiser was very eager for this friendship, but he had a long time to wait.

The verses which he had written for Winter with success had roused his dormant bent for poetry, but his indolence led him back to rhythmical prose, to which his ear had grown accustomed by repeated reading from Ebert's excellent translation of Young's *Night Thoughts* and now only an external occasion was wanted to give his imagination an unusual impulse.

This occasion occurred on a dull and rainy Sunday afternoon, when he was singing in the choir. He had spoken to Winter, who inquired among other things about his reading and was surprised that he always found him with a book in his hand. Reiser replied that it was the only thing left which could make up to him in some measure for the contempt to which he was so generally exposed in school and choir. This conversation with Winter which led him to reflect on his position, made him sensitive again to vivid impressions, and it so happened that V—— with whom and G—— he had played *The Dying Socrates* just then made him the object of his coarse wit and tried by all sorts of allusions to turn the ridicule of his companions on him; they presently chimed in and for nearly half an hour Reiser was the butt of their sallies of wit.

He said not a word, but felt wounded to the heart as he went away alone, and though he tried to turn his misery into contempt, he could not succeed; till at last his imagination worked him into a bitter misanthropic humour which nothing but the thought of his friend Philip Reiser could soften. As he was now dominated by the resolve to record his thoughts and feelings for his friend, this feeling at last prevailed over his vexation and misery, and he tried to clothe in words what he had felt and was still feeling, in order to present it in a more vivid form to his imagination. Thus before the singing was over, the essay which he meant to write at home was completely composed, amid all the tumult and contemptuous ridicule around him, and the pleasure of composing raised him in some measure above himself and his own trouble. As soon as he arrived home he wrote down the following words, with a peculiar mixture of feelings, pain at his condition and joy that he had succeeded in giving form in language to a lively picture of his position.

TO R.

'How sad is man's existence: and this worthless existence we make still less tolerable for one another, when we ought rather to lighten one another's burden in this desert of life by close companionship.

'Is it not enough that we are wandering in the world amid constant illusion and error, as in an enchanted land? Need monsters yell at us, aye and a malicious satyr pierce our heart with his scornful laughter?

'How desolate and sad is everything about me! And I must wander lonely and forsaken, with nothing to support or guide me!

'Ah happiness! I see a throng yonder—men like myself, wandering through this desert. "Oh, take me to you, my friends, take me to you, that

I may wander through the desert with you, and then it will turn to a green meadow!"

'They take me to them—what happiness!

'Woe's me! What do I see? Are they still men, my brothers? Alas! their masks fall from them: they are devils, and the desert turns to Hell. I fly and they howl after me with scornful laughter. "Have you deceived me then, you human masks? No mask shall deceive me again! Welcome night and solitude and blackest melancholy! Begone for ever from me all jests and laughter and boisterous joys, the masks of death!"

'So thinking I went on, and gloom and sorrow filled my heart. When suddenly a young man stood before me. His face announced a friend, his gentle eye spoke feeling: I would have escaped in haste, but he clasped my hand as a friend and I waited. He embraced me and I him, our hearts rushed together, "And round us was Elysium."'[1]

. . . .

Reiser could really have drawn no truer picture of his condition at that time: there was no exaggeration in what he said, for the people in whose near company he was living, became to him tormenting spirits, and the chief of the 'shrieking monsters' was V—— whose coarse malicious wit had deeply wounded Reiser that Sunday afternoon, for before this V—— had always professed to be his friend: at least he and the banished G—— were the only two who associated with Reiser after the performance of the play, for they alone shared his hatred and scorn of their schoolfellows. And now V——

[1] Klopstock's 'Rosenband', *O.B.G.V.* 79.

himself took the side of those who made Reiser an object of ridicule, and indeed roused ridicule by the coarse jests with which he made merry at Reiser's expense. All this combined to put him in the misanthropic humour, in which he wrote this essay. It was only the thought of Philip Reiser, and the fact that the Precentor's son, his former enemy, was beginning to be his friend, that so far softened his bitter humour that at the close of the essay he relented and gave way to gentler feelings. He had sketched several little essays of this sort in his diary, addressed to his friend, when spring returned and the usual public examination took place at the school, at which he appeared. But his heart sank when he compared himself with the rest and found himself the worst dressed; he sat like one lost, no attention was paid to him and not a single question put to him. He bore it during the morning, but when he went again in the afternoon and saw himself again lost in the throng, he could bear it no longer, he went out again before the examination began.

He hurried straight outside the City walls—it was a dull cloudy sky—and went to a little wood, which lies not far from Hanover. As soon as he was out of the bustle of the town and saw the towers of Hanover behind him, a thousand shifting sensations overpowered him. At once he saw everything from a different point of view; he felt himself transported from all the petty circumstances which confined, tormented, and oppressed him in the City of the four towers into the wide open air of Nature and he breathed more freely again. His pride and self-confidence rose, he looked back with clearer eyes at what lay behind him and saw it in one concentrated vision.

He saw the priests in their black gowns and bands mount the steps, his schoolfellows assembled and the priests distributing the prizes among them: and then how each went home, and all went its usual round, and within the town that lay behind him and from which every step carried him farther, the intermingling throng. Everything seemed to him to be interwoven as closely as the huddled mass of houses which he still saw in the distance; and then he thought of the peace of the open country, how no one noticed him or cast a malicious glance, while in the city was the noisy tumult, the rattle of carriages, which he had to avoid, the gaze of men from which he shrank. All this as his imagination painted it in miniature, awoke in him a wonderful feeling, like that of the moment between daylight and twilight, when one half of the sky is red with sunset, and the other resting in darkness.

He felt unusual power in him to lift himself above all which weighed him down, for he felt within how small a compass that noisy world was bounded, with which his cares and troubles were interwoven, and before him lay the great world.

But then the melancholy feeling returned. Where was he to find firm footing in this great empty world, where he saw himself driven out from all human relations? Where human destinies were clashing on one tiny spot of earth he [1] was nothing, nothing at all! The thought came to him that from childhood up his fate had been to

[1] Reading *er* for *es*.

be crowded out. If he wanted to look on at anything, when it was a case of putting oneself forward, every one else was quicker than he and got in front of him. He thought one day he would find an empty place where he could fit in without jostling any one, but he found none, and retired, and now was looking at the throng from a distance, as he stood lonely there. And as he stood lonely there, the thought that he could look on the throng so quietly without mingling in it, made up somewhat for the loss of what he missed seeing: alone he felt himself nobler and more distinguished than lost among the crowd. His pride, which came to the fore, overcame the vexation that he felt at first, because he could not join the crowd, it drove him back on himself and ennobled and exalted his thoughts and feelings.

So it was on his lonely walk, that dull and rainy afternoon when he escaped from the unkind glances of his assembled schoolfellows, and from the complete neglect and unbearable sense of being unnoticed which threatened him, as he hastened from the Gate of Hanover towards the lonely wood.

This solitary walk developed in him in a moment more feelings and contributed more to his spiritual education than all the lessons he had ever had in school. It was this solitary walk, which raised Reiser's self-esteem, widened his horizon, and gave him a clear idea of his own isolated existence, which for a long time was cut off from all connexions, self-centred and independent.

As he looked on human life as a whole, he learnt for the first time to distinguish what is great in life from its details. All that had vexed him seemed petty and insignificant and not worth thinking of. But now other doubts and anxieties which he had long harboured sprang up in his mind; on the origin and aim and end of his existence, which seemed wrapt in impenetrable darkness, on the whence and whither of his pilgrimage, which was made so hard for him, he knew not why. What was to come of it all?

This made him profoundly melancholy. As he walked painfully across the sand of the barren heath outside the wood, the heavens were overcast and a fine rain wetted him to the skin. When he entered the wood he cut himself a thorn stick and walked on. He came to a village and was picturing to himself the quiet peace which reigned in these country cottages, when he heard a couple, probably man and wife, quarrelling in one of the houses and a child screaming.

Everywhere then, he thought, where men live there is discomfort and dissatisfaction, and he walked on. The loneliest desert seemed to him desirable, and when even here deadly ennui oppressed him, he ended by longing for the grave, and as he could not see why all life long he had been oppressed and jostled and excluded, he at last doubted whether his life had any rational cause: his existence seemed to him a product of a dreadful blind chance. Evening came on quicker than usual, because the sky was dark and it began to rain again. When he reached home it was quite dark and he sat down by his lamp and wrote to Philip Reiser: 'Drenched with rain and stiff with cold I come back to you, and if not to you, to death, for since this afternoon the burden of life, which I see to be aimless, is intolerable. Your friendship is the support to which I cling if the desire for annihilation is not to overwhelm me irresistibly.'

And then once more the thought arose, of winning his friend's approval by the expression of his feelings. This was the new support to which his love of life clung, and as all his feelings had been so strong and vivid that afternoon, it was easy to recall them. So he began :

A Poem from the Heart.

My friend, to you I'd tell my sorrow :
If words such eloquence could borrow,
You in my pain would have a part.
'Tis not by hopeless love I'm wounded,
Not lust of gold or fame unbounded
Has wrought this havoc in my heart.

This opening referred partly to Philip Reiser's love-fancies, with which he often wearied his friend, telling him all the gradual advances he had made in the favour of his beloved, and his hopes and prospects, all limited to the attainment of his lady's favour. Anton Reiser had no feeling for love-making, for he had never thought of winning a girl's love, as it seemed impossible that one so badly dressed as he and so much the object of general contempt would ever succeed in love. For just as he considered the contempt shown him as a part of himself, so he counted his bad clothes as part of his body, which seemed to him as unattractive as his mind was estimable. In a word, the thought that he could ever be loved by a woman, seemed to him the most absurd thing in the world. For he formed so high an ideal of the heroes who were loved by women in the plays and romances he had read, that he never thought he could attain to it. So he found love-stories very tedious and most tedious of all the stories of his love-adventures which Philip Reiser told him and which he listened to many an hour out of good-nature.

Besides, these stories of his friend were very much in the style of a novel. The whole process from the first friendly introduction to the regular declaration of mutual love, with all the doubts, anxieties, and gradual advances which lay between, went their prescribed course as in a novel, and Anton Reiser had to put up with hearing at length from his friend what he had skipped or read hastily in the novels. Thus the thought that he was wounded not by hopeless love but by quite other things was the most natural opening of his poem to Philip Reiser. It was his doubts and anxieties about his miserable aimless existence that oppressed him, and he went on :

A tumult raging in my breast
Deals death and havoc without rest,
All other pains subduing.
Who gave me this enquiring mind
The depths to plumb with folly blind,
But to my own undoing ?

Unfathomed depths, which to my eyes
Bring night and sorrow, for my prize
Black Melancholy sending.
She comes on brazen throne to reign
Within my heart, and in her train
She summons grief unending.

Then followed the train : cares and sorrow

Then comes Despair, her arrows dead
Bring final ruin on my head,
'Tis death to look upon her.

Then after the picture of successive feelings, the strain sank back into one of self-pity.

Ay now, no Spring of joy is left,
Of all fair things I am bereft.

Then the train of thought rose to general reflections on life, ending again in the dreadful doubts with which the poem began :

My way is over moorland dreary,
All joy is fled, of life I'm weary,
Where all is mockery and scorn
. . . . . .
I wander, but I have no goal.
Whence come I ? Answer to my soul,
You better know, Wise Man, than I.
My life, each moment perishing,
Yet struggles on with timorous wing
Towards its goal, it knows not why.

Who gave me life ? Who set the bound
That narrowly confines me round ?
From what dark chaos am I sped ?
To what dread night descend, when Fate
Beckons me through the awful gate
And I am numbered with the dead ?

This poem flowed straight from his heart. Even the rhyme and the rhythm caused him little difficulty and he wrote it down in less than an hour. Afterwards he began to make poems, for the sake of making them, and had less success.

But the spring and summer of 1775 were spent in very poetic fashion. The pleasant Shakespeare evenings that he had spent in winter with Philip Reiser were now replaced by pleasanter morning walks.

Not far from Hanover, where the river forms an artificial waterfall, is a little coppice, as pleasant and inviting as could be found anywhere. To this spot they arranged pilgrimages before breakfast. The two walkers took their breakfast with them and when they reached the wood they plucked the moss off some tree trunks and made themselves a soft seat on which they lay, and when they had eaten their breakfast, read to one another in turn. For this purpose they specially chose Kleist's[1] poems which they almost learnt by heart on these occasions. When they came next day they searched the wood till they found their camp of the day before and made themselves at home in the wide freedom of Nature, an exhilarating feeling. Everything in this wide circuit belonged to their eyes and ears and feelings—the fresh green of the trees, the song of the birds, and the cool fragrance of morning. When they returned, Philip went to his workshop and made pianos, while Anton attended school, where he now found a new generation of schoolfellows, so that he could go there with a light heart.

There were many hours too when Anton Reiser sought his beloved solitude again, though he now had a friend, and if there was a fine afternoon he had chosen a spot by the riverside in a meadow outside Hanover, where a small clear brook ran over a pebbly bottom and fell into the passing river. This spot too, from his constant visits, had

[1] Ewald Kleist's *Der Frühling*.

become a sort of home for him amid the wide surrounding Nature. Here he felt himself at home, yet bounded by no walls of any sort, but enjoying the free untrammelled use of all that was about him. He never visited this spot without his Horace or Virgil in his pocket. Here he read 'Bandusia's fountain' and how the hurrying stream

obliquo laborat . . . trepidare rivo.

From here he watched the sunset and the lengthening shadows of the trees. By this brook he dreamed away many a happy hour of his life. And here too sometimes the Muse visited him, or rather he sought her: for now he was anxious to produce a great poem, and because he now wished to compose for the sake of composing, he did not succeed: he was readier with the wish to write a poem than with a subject to write of, and not much good generally comes of that. The thoughts were now forced or common-place; one saw that what he wrote had been meant for a poem. Nevertheless even in these bad verses his melancholy humour glimmered through: every gay or pleasant picture was covered as it were with a veil. The leaves only put on their young green to wither again: the sky was bright, only to cloud over.

Philip Reiser did not approve of these poems, yet Anton had reckoned on his approval at every rhyme on which he spent his pains: but his friend was a severe and impartial critic, who did not easily leave a dull thought, a strained rhyme, or a superfluous word uncriticized. He specially made merry over one couplet in Anton Reiser's poem :

> Alternate joy and pain in life find room
> And life itself sinks to the silent tomb.

Philip Reiser never ceased to let his humour play on this passage, which he declaimed in a comic tone. He called his friend 'my dear Hans Sachs' and paid him other compliments which were not very encouraging. Yet he did not condemn him altogether, but selected some passable passages from the poems, which he did not entirely disapprove.

Through this mutual intercourse and fruitful criticism the ties between the two friends became more closely knit, and Anton Reiser's effort, whether he wrote verse or prose, was always to win his friend's approval.

Then an incident occurred which does not seem to do much credit to Anton Reiser's heart, though it is based on human nature. The son of Pastor Marquard, who had gone to the University and returned consumptive, was given up by the doctors, after all remedies had been tried in vain, and they prophesied his death for certain in the spring ; and Reiser's first thoughts when he heard this were that he would make a poem on this incident which would bring him fame and approval and perhaps the favour of Pastor Marquard. In fact he had begun the poem a week before young Marquard died. Instead of feeling moved to write the poem because he was distressed he tried to work himself into a state of distress, in order to make a poem on the event. So on this occasion the poet's art made him actually a hypocrite. But young Marquard had latterly not interested himself much in Reiser nor taken his part against the gibes and insults of his schoolfellows, but as it sometimes happened, even joined in them. It was therefore natural enough that Reiser was more concerned about his poem than about young Marquard himself, though again he was to be blamed for pretending that he had feelings which he really had not. It is true that his mind was not quite easy; his conscience often reproached him but he quieted it by trying to persuade himself that he did really feel melancholy over the early death of young Marquard, who had been robbed in the flower of his years of all hopes and prospects in life.

As this poem was a piece of hypocrisy, it too was a failure and did not win the approval of his friend, who found something to criticize in almost every line. Even Pastor Marquard, to whom he sent the poem, took no special notice and so his purpose failed. But soon afterwards an incident occurred which was the occasion of his being inspired to poetry in a less artificial manner. It happened that at the beginning of summer a young man of nineteen, a man of considerable property and a very good friend of Philip Reiser, was drowned while bathing in the river. Philip Reiser commissioned his friend to compose a poem on this incident, the best his powers could compass; he wanted to have it printed, and even if it were not printed it would, if well done, be a valuable production.

This commission from his friend roused Anton's

ambition; he tried hard to picture the scene vividly and after weighing phrase against phrase for a day and a half and using every effort to win his friend's approval, he finally composed the following stanzas:

We feel some grief when 'neath years' heavy weight
An old man dies and sighing falls asleep,
But when swift death strikes down with sudden fate
One in the spring of life pain rankles deep.

The youth breathed lightly the glad summer air,
As from drear night the fairest morn arose:
For gentle sleep had scattered every care
And waked to Dawn on joyous ways he goes.

He hails the day, and to his eyes appear
A thousand days of joy, in courage strong
His breast no doom forebodes or danger near,
His prospect is of happy life and long.

The sun unclouded and the heavens bright
Invite him to the joys of sky and fields,
Glad Nature, rich in rapturous delight
Her splendour and her solemn glory yields.

But ah! what shadow lurks behind the gleam
With fearsome menace? Youth, no further go!
Step back! Too late, he's swept beneath the stream.
Ah God! So young! Yet Fate has laid him low.

Beneath still waves death lay for him in wait
And now the engulfing stream goes proudly on,
His friends are true, hearts bleed to see his fate,
They mourn aloud for him that's dead and gone.

Yet death has lost its sting, when hot tears flow
From tender eyes, that shine with heavenly smile,
'Twere blessedness, if one should die, to know
Such loving tears would mourn me for a while.

The last stanza referred to the fact that a beautiful young woman, a near relative of the drowned man, who had been bathing with her brother, hastened to the spot from the town on hearing the news of the unfortunate event, and did not conceal her tears in presence of the throng of people standing by the river. Anton noticed this and felt it deeply, so that he almost envied the dead man, for the tears his death called forth. Reiser had gone to the river intending to bathe, and found the young man drowned, and his companion not yet dressed again ; he saw the indifferent and uninterested spectators assemble, saw the body of the young man, whom he had known well through Philip Reiser, pulled out and every means to restore him used in vain. All this made such a lively impression on him that the poem which he composed on this incident had a certain truth of expression, which made it very different from the poem on young Marquard.

This poem then, with the exception of some harsh expressions, won Philip Reiser's approval, which encouraged Anton so much that without any special occasion he composed some essays in prose and verse to win his friend's approval. But the essays and poems which had no proper occasion, would never come out well : he tormented himself for a fortnight over a subject he had chosen, a contrast between the worldling, whose hope ends with this life, and the Christian who has a joyous prospect of life beyond the grave. This idea was a reminiscence of his reading of Young's *Night Thoughts*. The subject of his verses was indifferent to him, as he had no special occasion for writing poetry except his general desire to do so and his anxiety to win his friend's approval, and so the result of his reading the *Night Thoughts* laid hold of him, and he gave it a rational turn by making his Christian enjoy all the permitted pleasures of the worldling while he gave him in addition the advantage of a joyous prospect of eternity, so that compared with the worldling he was bound to win all round.

On this idea, a just one but too strained and artificial, was based a second poem, which did not win Philip's approval, and with which he himself, in spite of the trouble it had cost him, was never satisfied.

The Worldling and the Christian.

Once o'er the self-same flowery meadows
A Christian and a Worldling went,
Joy flowed in streams, and as they journey'd
Each with life's joys was well content.

The Worldling used his life right shrewdly,
Eternity for him was there:
Beyond the world and time his spirit
Could rise into no loftier air.

He shrewdly used the daily pleasures
That Nature furnished him for nought:
The flowery meads, the wondrous glory
That dawn of day before him wrought.

The Christian too these noble pleasures
Of earth enjoyed with cheerful heart,
Not born to gloom alone, but taking
In common joys of life his part.

But where to him was but the foretaste
Of nobler joys beyond compare,
The Worldling saw a brief existence
And then the awful end—despair.

This summer then was a summer of poetry for Anton Reiser. His reading, combined with the impression made on him by the beauty of Nature, had a wonderful influence on him: wherever his foot trod the world shone with a romantic and enchanting light. But notwithstanding his close association with Philip he was before everything fond of lonely walks. The most attractive to his romantic mind was the path along the meadow by the riverside, outside the New Gate of Hanover. The solemn hush in the meadow at midday, the tall oaks scattered here and there, standing lonely in the sunshine, and throwing their shadows on the green meadow; a little coppice, where one could hide and listen to the sound of the waterfall near by: the pleasant wood beyond the river, where he and Philip Reiser took their early morning walk: cattle at pasture in the distance, and the city with its four towers and the tree-planted rampart encircling it, like a picture in a camera obscura. All this combined to produce in him that peculiar feeling one has when one becomes vividly aware that at this moment one is here and not elsewhere, that this is our real world, the world of which we often think as something purely ideal. The thought occurs to one that when in novels we read about places the ideas we form of them always grow more wonderful the further we imagine them to be from us: and when we then think of our present surroundings, with all their details great and small as imagined by a dweller in Pekin for instance, to whom they must appear equally strange and wonderful, the part of the world in which we live assumes a glamour, which makes it look as strange and wonderful as if we had travelled that moment a thousand miles to see it. At one and the same moment we have forced on us the sense of the expansion and the limitation of our existence, and from the mixed feeling so produced arises the peculiar kind of sadness which comes over us at such times.

Reiser at that time began to reflect on such phenomena, and to ask himself how objects could make such impressions on him, but the impressions themselves were too lively for him to be able to reflect on them in cold blood, and his mental powers were not yet sufficiently strong and well-trained properly to subordinate the pictures which his imagination painted : and a further hindrance to reflection lay in a certain indolence and tendency to resign himself to easy enjoyment.

Nevertheless since the previous summer he had conceived the idea of writing an essay on love of the romantic and getting it printed in the Hanover Magazine : he constantly collected ideas for it and had plenty of opportunity to do so, as his own experience furnished them daily. But he never got the essay finished.

He could not understand at that time why the single trees scattered on the meadows with their shadows in the noonday sun made such a deep impression on him : it did not occur to him that their lonely stations with the great irregular spaces between them gave the neighbourhood that solemn majestic appearance which moved his feelings so deeply. These lonely trees gave to his own loneliness, as he walked beneath them, a touch of sanctity and dignity. Whenever he passed beneath the trees, his thoughts turned to high things, his steps grew slower, his head drooped and his whole being grew more serious and solemn: then he effaced himself in the undergrowth near by and sat in the shade of a copse, where he read or indulged pleasant fancies to the sound of the near waterfall. In this way hardly a day passed when his imagination was not fed with new pictures from the real or the ideal world.

In addition to these influences *The Sorrows of Young Werther* had appeared that year, which had some effect on all his ideas and feelings of that time—of solitude, love of Nature, patriarchal life, the conception of life as a dream and so on. At the beginning of summer he got hold of it through Philip Reiser, and from that time it formed his constant reading and was never out of his pocket. All the feelings he had had on his lonely walk that dismal afternoon, and which inspired the poem to Philip Reiser, were revived in his soul. He found here his idea of nearness and distance, on which he intended to dwell in his essay on love of the romantic. His reflections on life and existence he here found carried further. 'Who can say "this is", when everything hurries past with lightning speed?' That was the very thought which had so long made him picture his own existence as illusion, dream, and fancy.

But as for the peculiar sorrows of Werther he had no feeling for them. To sympathize in the sorrows of love cost him some effort: he had to transport himself forcibly into this situation if it was to move him. For to love and to be loved seemed to him a strange and alien thing, for he could not imagine himself as the object of a woman's love. When Werther spoke of his love, he felt very much as he did when Philip Reiser talked to him for hours of the progress he had made in the favour of his beloved. But what chiefly appealed to Reiser's feelings were the general reflections on life and existence, on the empty pageant of human efforts, on the aimless confusion on earth, the vivid descriptions of natural scenes, and the reflections on human fate and human destiny.

The passage where Werther compares life to a puppet-play, in which the figures are worked by strings and he himself joins in the playing or rather is played with in that way, and takes his neighbour by his wooden hand, and shrinks back—awoke in Reiser the remembrance of a like feeling which he had often had when he gave his hand to some one. Daily habit leads one to forget that one has a body, which is just as much subject to all laws of decay in the material world as a piece of wood which we saw or cut to pieces, and that its movements are determined by the same laws as any machine constructed by man. This destructible and material character of our body is only realized by us at certain moments, making us frightened of ourselves, as we suddenly feel that we fancied we were something which we are not, and instead are something which we fear to be. When we give another our hand and only see and touch his body without having any notion of his thoughts, the idea of our material nature is brought more vividly home than when we are contemplating our own body, which we cannot so well separate from the thoughts with which we associate it, and therefore forget it in these thoughts.

But what he felt most deeply of all was Werther's describing how his cold joyless existence near Charlotte struck him with horrible coldness. It was exactly the sensation he felt once on the road when he wanted to escape from himself and could not, and felt all at once the whole burden of his existence, with which a man must rise and go to rest every day of his life. The thought grew unbearable to him too at that moment and led him to hasten to the river, where he was fain to cast off the intolerable burden of this wretched existence—but his hour too had not yet come.[1] In a word, Reiser fancied that he recognized himself, with all his thoughts and feelings, love excepted, in Werther. 'Take the little book for your friend, if through fate or your own fault you cannot find one nearer.' These were the words he thought of, whenever he drew the book from his pocket: they seemed to fit him exactly: for he thought it was partly fate and partly his own fault that he was so forsaken in the world, and he could not converse with his friend as he could with this book. Almost every day when the weather was fine with *Werther* in his pocket he went the river-side walk in the meadow, where the single trees stood, to the little copse, where he was so much at home, and sat under a green bush, which formed a sort of bower over him (as he visited it again and again, he came to love it as much as the place by the brook), and so in fine weather he lived quite as

[1] In *Leiden des jungen Werthers,* Dec. 12, 'Meine Uhr ist noch nicht abgelaufen.'

much in the open air as at home, sometimes spending almost the whole day there, first reading *Werther* under the green bower and then Virgil or Horace by the brook. But the over frequent reading of Werther had a bad effect on both his writing and his thought, as the turns of style and even the thoughts of the writer became so familiar to him by constant repetition that he often took them for his own, and even some years later in the essays which he wrote he had to contend with reminiscences from *Werther*, an experience shared by several young writers brought up at that period.

Meanwhile, the reading of Werther, like that of Shakespeare, raised him above his circumstances. The strengthened feeling of his isolated existence, as he thought of himself as a being in whom heaven and earth are reflected as in a mirror, gave him a sense of pride in his humanity; he was no longer the insignificant abject being, that he appeared in other men's eyes. What wonder then that he clung with all his soul to the reading which, whenever he tasted it, restored him to himself?

It was precisely at this time too that the new epoch of poetry came, when Bürger, Hölty, Voss, the Stolbergs and others appeared, and their poems were first printed in the issues of the *Musenalmanach*, which then began. The current issue contained specially good poems by Bürger, Hölty, Voss, &c.

Reiser at once learnt by heart, as he read them, Bürger's *Lenore* and Hölty's *Adelstan*, and these two ballads he had mastered often stood him in good stead afterwards on his wanderings. Even at that time he would often collect about him at twilight, either in his host's house or at his uncle the wigmaker's a circle of people, to whom he recited *Lenore* or *Adelstan und Röschen*, and thus shared with the writers the pleasure of the enjoyment arising from the applause their works received, for he was so constituted that he always felt this applause as theirs, and wished them into the circle with him.

But his respect for the writers of such works as *The Sorrows of Werther* and various poems in the *Musenalmanach* began to be extravagant: he deified them in his thoughts, and would have counted it a great happiness to enjoy a sight of them. Now Hölty was then living in Hanover and a brother of his was Reiser's schoolfellow and could easily have made him acquainted with the poet. But Reiser's self-depreciation was at that time still so great that he never dared to tell Hölty's brother of his wish, and with a kind of bitter defiance denied himself this happiness so much desired and so near his reach. Meantime he sought every opportunity of conversation with Hölty's brother, and every detail that he told him of the poet he counted important. How often he envied this young man for being brother of a man whom Reiser regarded almost as a being of a higher species! He envied him his intimacy; that he could speak to him as often as he liked, and call him 'thou'. This extravagant reverence for poets and writers increased rather than diminished; he could imagine no greater happiness than some day to have access to this circle, for he did not venture to envisage such happiness except in dreams.

His walks now became more interesting; he went out with ideas gathered from reading, and returned home with new ideas drawn from observation of Nature.

He again made some attempts at poetry, but his verse revolved about general ideas, and inclined to speculation, which was always his favourite occupation. Thus, he was walking once in the meadow, where the scattered trees stood, and his thoughts rose on a sort of ladder to the notion of the infinite. Thus, his speculation was transformed into a kind of poetic inspiration, with which was blended the desire to win his friend's approval. He imagined an ideal wise man, who has as many ideas as a mortal can have and yet always feels in himself a void which can only be filled by the idea of the infinite. And thus, with some effort in expression he produced the following poem:

The Soul of the Sage.

The sage's spirit upward soaring
Far up beyond the clouds had gone,
And ardent ever in exploring
Still heavenward was pressing on.

The spirit fain would fill the measure
Of want that sick at heart he feels,
And seek afar the flying treasure
Of Truth that ever from him steals.

He builds him structures vast by thinking,
And boldly scans all heaven's host,
He flies through space with eyes unblinking
Yet ever empty feels and lost.

His soul pursues with utmost daring
Herself, which still herself doth fly,
Sounds her own being, but despairing
Finds there is nought to satisfy.

Then high above, like eagle winging
The sage beyond himself had passed:
And God, of all creation's singing
The theme, had reached by thought at last.

And now the soul, her hunger sated,
Knows what a void was hers before
And to a sea of joy translated
Enjoys God's presence ever more.

As he had now forced the idea of God into a poem he tried next to convey the idea of the world into verse. Thus, his whole poetic art was directed to general ideas: his inclination never drew him to the portrayal of the details of Nature in man and outside him. His imagination was constantly at work to clothe in poetic images the great ideas of world, God, life, existence, and so on, which he had tried to comprehend with his intellect; and these poetic images were always taken from what is great in Nature—clouds, sea, the sun, and the stars and so on.

The poem on the world was speculation rather than poetry, and was therefore a very forced composition. It began:

Man struggles up from out the dust,
With him his world doth rise;
Man also in the grave is thrust
And low his world too lies.

Philip Reiser criticized this poem severely, except one stanza, which he thought tolerable:

One piles up riches for his treasure,
Another gathers bays;
Each finds some game to suit his pleasure,
And that for ever plays.

Reiser's imagination was now at war with his intellect; it wanted to encroach on the intellect at every opportunity and clothe the most abstract ideas in images. This state of things meant pain and torture for Reiser, and it was in this state of things that he produced the poem on the world, which was neither speculation nor poetry proper but an unhappy mixture of the two.

Though rainy weather prevailed for some time, Reiser did not abandon his solitary life of poetry. He shut himself up in his bedroom, where he set to rights as well as he could an old tumbledown piano, and tuned it with great difficulty. There he sat all day long at the piano, and when he had got to know the notes learnt to sing and play to himself nearly all the airs out of *The Chase*, *The Death of Abel*, &c. In the intervals he read through Fielding's *Tom Jones* and Haller's *Poems* several times, and spent several weeks in this solitude with almost as much pleasure as when he studied philosophy in the garret at his former lodging. He knew Haller's poems almost by heart.

Here Philip Reiser visited him one afternoon and commissioned him to write a chorale, which he would set to music. This complimentary commission was so encouraging to Anton Reiser that he set to work composing as soon as he was alone, and striking a chord on the piano from time to time, in less than an hour produced the following verses:

God is the Lord. In worship kneeling
Oh Nature sing, with depth of feeling
Thy great Creator's gracious ways.

Peel forth, ye winds, to God your praises,
Praise Him ye vales and peaceful places,
Ye flowers, blossom for His praise.

Let thunder roll to do Him honour;
His praise aloud let all proclaim,
Each rocky cave and mountain height
In one great chorus all unite
To sing your great Creator's fame.

All things on earth, which now are living,
Shall grateful thanks to God be giving,
Shall praise Him loud with joyful voice.
Thus, what the God of all creation
Chose to exist, in adoration
To Him in song doth aye rejoice.

Philip Reiser set the verses to music and they were actually sung in the choir without any one knowing the writer. The new composition was much approved, and every one was specially pleased with the words. Anton Reiser was not a little flattered when he heard his own words sung by his schoolfellows, who despised him, and heard them express their approval, but he did not tell a soul that the verses were his, but preferred to enjoy to himself the quiet triumph which this unsought approval secured him. They were his thoughts which now many times over, as often as the new chorus was sung, engaged the attention of many men, singers and listeners both. If there is anything calculated to feed the vanity of one who writes verses, it is when his thoughts and utterances are thought worthy of being set to music. Every word seems in the process to be raised so to speak to a higher power, and the feeling which came to Anton Reiser when he heard his verses sung may well have been experienced by any one who has ever heard his own words sung in chorus before a considerable audience. There are living instances of the extraordinary outbursts of vanity caused in certain persons by such triumphs.

Anton Reiser's triumph did not last long: for as soon as it was known who the writer of these verses was, all sorts of faults were found with them, and some of his schoolfellows who had read Kleist's poems declared that they were taken straight from Kleist. There may well have been reminiscences of Kleist, but the closing thought of what God has chosen for existence was closely connected with Reiser's metaphysical theory, in so far as only living and thinking creatures can be regarded as possessing existence proper. Philip Reiser was satisfied with the poem, except the idea of Nature kneeling before God like a lady, which he criticized as too bold an image.

While Philip Reiser then was making pianos for a living Anton Reiser was busy making verses which Philip was to criticize. Philip had never tried to write a verse and so was not jealous of him, indeed, he sometimes gave him a subject to write on, for example his own condition, his love troubles, his rise and fall in fortune; and Reiser wrote a song to the moon long before so many sighs and love laments in *Siegwart* and innumerable poems had been addressed to her:

Dost look with pity, silent moon,
From heaven and take my part?
For, ere I whisper, thou too soon
Canst read my troubled heart.

And then, in a later stanza, referring to Reiser's condition:

Oft am I fain to rise,
Yet fall upon the morrow,
And then with trembling feel
My lot is one of sorrow.

Meantime, Anton Reiser did not neglect his school lessons, where the new Director, who though something of a pedant was also at bottom a man of taste and knowledge, arranged recitation-lessons, which stirred Reiser's ambition. But any one who wished to make a public appearance as a reciter was bound to have good clothes, which Anton lacked, for besides his coat of grey cloth, which was like a livery, he had nothing but an old overcoat, and he had not the courage to appear in either. It was his shabby clothes then which here again stood in his way and depressed his spirit.

At last this obstacle was removed as the Prince gave enough for a good coat to be procured for him. And then all his thoughts and efforts were directed to producing a poem which he would think worthy to be recited in public.

Now it was not usual for any one to compose himself the poem he meant to recite: every one copied a poem from somewhere or other, and when he recited put the copy in front of him or handed it to the Director, who followed it. But Anton had set his heart on composing the poem he meant to recite, and was at a loss to find a fit subject, his chief desire being to handle a subject which would give him good opportunity for declamation. One fine evening, full of these ideas, he was taking a walk round the rampart in bright moonlight, when he remembered a poem against atheists, which he had nearly learnt by heart a couple of years before on account of its declamatory style, but the thoughts in which he now found extremely commonplace. Meanwhile, the subject was so vividly in his mind that he took another turn round the rampart, and by the end of it had completed in his head his poem *The Atheist*.

His thoughts had followed a line of their own, quite different from the commonplace idea in the poem, which he knew by heart. He imagined the atheist as the slave of the storm wind, the thunder, the wild elements, sickness and disease, in a word as the slave of all the irrational lifeless creatures, which are stronger than he and have become his masters because he will not worship the Spirit of eternal goodness. The need to believe in a God awoke so strongly in Reiser's mind on this occasion, when his one object was to compose a poem and recite it, that he felt a kind of righteous indignation against the person who would rob him of this consolation, and kept this fire burning till his poem was finished. It began and ended with the glad conviction of the existence of a rational Cause of all things which exist and come to pass, and in spite of all irregularities and frequent harshness of expression the range of feelings expressed in it as a whole were beyond anything which Reiser had up till then been able to achieve. It will not be out of place therefore to record it, though it does not merit preservation for its own sake.

The Atheist.

There is a God. 'Tis well ! for what His grace has given
The Father of my days I owe, whose hand divine
Assigned me every joy, the pain with which I've striven
And pain to come. Courage, my heart ! do not repine !

When night's dark veil gives place to light and lovely
morning,
Sing songs of joy to God, who lovely morning made !
And when the thunder loud in hollow winds gives warning
Sing songs of joy to God, who storm and thunder made.

In Him, my heart, for aye, at morn and night take pleasure.
Praise Him, for thought of Him is blessedness to gain.
To live and think without Him is to lose the treasure
Of Heaven, and dwell in darkness and in endless pain.

Thou who dost doubt the truth that God in heaven
reigneth,
Thou fool, dispel that doubt immediate from thy breast,
Which nought for thee but Hell and constant torment
gaineth,
Believe in God and then : to Heaven thy soul 's addrest.

What ! canst and wilt thou not accept God's grace to
guide thee,
The Spirit of pure love eternal, in thy soul ?
Then feel the dismal fires of torment that betide thee,
And take the raging elements to rule thee and control.

When thunder-storms with awesome threat in heaven are
roaring,
The engulfing sea doth rage, the open grave invites,
Then, sinner, make thy prayer to these thy Gods, adoring
These whom thy madness chose ; which 'gainst thy
reason fights.

Should sickness threaten thee with fearsome tooth de-
vouring
Thy very heart, and death thy failing weakness quell
With grinning terrors, then before his overpowering
Lordship kneel down : Disease is God, adore him well.

Sink then into thy grave ; let with the dust decay
Thy soul, that chose in madness buried here to sink :
Resign thee, if thou canst, to Nothingness a prey,
Thou whom God made a creature loftily to think.

Whoso will not see God, his world is turned to hell,
Himself becomes a dream, illusion holds him fast.
Once in thy thought grasp God, and all is bright and well
And upward soars thy soul in mighty flight at last.

His whole being was moved by the feelings that succeeded one another in his mind as he composed this poem : he shrank back with horror and dread from the fearful abyss of blind chance, on the brink of which he stood, and clung with all these thoughts and feelings to the consoling idea of the existence of a benevolent Being ruling and guiding all.

As this poem too won his friend's approval he learnt it by heart and resolved to recite it the next day, when the recitation practice came. He appeared there with his new-bought coat, which looked pretty well and was the first good coat he ever wore, no insignificant circumstance to him. The new coat, which he regarded as putting him on an equality with his schoolfellows, from whom he had been so long distinguished by his shabby dress, inspired him with courage and confidence, and what was most remarkable, it seemed to win him more respect from others, who before had not troubled about him but now began to talk to him.

And as he now publicly appeared on the platform in the lecture-room, where he had so long been an object of general contempt, in front of his assembled schoolfellows, to recite the poem he had composed, for the first time his depressed spirit recovered itself, and again hopes and prospects of the future sprang up in his soul.

He had given the Director a copy of the poem to read, which the Director returned to him, without his yielding to the temptation of saying he had himself composed the poem. He was content with the inner consciousness of it; and found it agreeable when his schoolfellows asked him where the poem he had recited came from, and he then named some poet, from whom he professed to have copied it.

Reiser asked permission from the Director to be allowed to recite again the next week and when he received it, he adapted the poem to Philip Reiser, and entitled it *Melancholy*. He now made it begin

> I fain would tell my soul's deep sorrow:
> If words such eloquence could borrow,
> Speak, words, and so relieve my pain!

The last stanza

> Who gave me life? Who set the bound
> That narrowly confines me round?
> From what dark chaos am I sped,
> To what dark night descend, when Fate
> Shall guide me through the awful gate
> And I am numbered with the dead?

he recited with real pathos, expressed in voice and gesture, and after he had ceased reciting he remained standing for a moment with raised arm, which was as it were the symbol of his continued and horrible doubt.

When he got back from the Director the copy of his poem, the Director expressed his approval of the recitation, and told him that the two poems he had recited were well chosen.

It was now more than Reiser could do to resist the temptation of telling the Director that the poems were his own and so winning for his work the approval he had received for his selection. But he kept silence and waited a few days till he had in any case to go to the Director, to have a Latin essay looked over, which he and his schoolfellows had to compose every week as an exercise in style. On this occasion he handed the Director a copy of the two poems which he had recited, and told him that he was the author of them.

The Director, who had hitherto regarded him with some indifference, on hearing this clearly looked on him with more favour, and from that moment appeared to become his friend : he began to discuss the art of poetry with him and inquired about his reading, and Reiser went home with his heart rejoicing over the good reception of his poems. Next day he informed Philip Reiser of his good fortune, who sincerely rejoiced with him in the thought that he would now no longer be misunderstood, and that perhaps happier days awaited him.

It so happened that the next Monday morning Reiser came rather late to the first lesson, which was taken by the Director, who then used publicly to criticize the Latin essays without mentioning names. When he came into the room he heard the Director, who sat at his desk, reading out his poem *The Atheist* and criticizing it line by line. As soon as he came in all eyes were turned on him. Reiser could hardly believe his ears when he heard, for such public criticism was the first of its kind.

The Director blended so much praise and encouragement with his criticism, and showed on the whole so much approval of the two poems which Reiser had recited, that from that day instead of the ridicule from which he had so long suffered, he received the respect of his schoolfellows, and in this way a new epoch of his life began. His fame as a poet soon spread in the city; on all hands he received commissions to write occasional poems, and his schoolfellows all wished him to instruct them in poetry, and to learn from him the secret of writing verse. The Director had so many verses brought him that he had to stop it, and he never publicly criticized verses afterwards.

What pleased Reiser most was the notable advance which he fancied he had made in the year in the education of his taste, for a year before the poem to atheists, which he now thought very stupid, had pleased him so much that he thought it worth while to learn it by heart. But into this year many experiences had been crowded: his reading of Shakespeare, of Werther, and of many excellent poems in the *Musenalmanach*, as well as his study of the philosophy of Wolf: and further the influence of solitude and the quiet undisturbed enjoyment of Nature, which sometimes did more for his education in a single day than whole years had done before. He again began to attract notice, and those who hitherto had thought he would come to nothing began to think that perhaps he would come to something after all.

While his fortunes thus took a better turn

Reiser nevertheless retained his melancholy humour, and found peculiar satisfaction in it. Even on the day when the unexpected honour of the public criticism of his poems occurred he wandered round the city in the afternoon in melancholy solitude through the dull and rainy weather. In the evening he wanted to go to Philip Reiser to tell him his good fortune, but when he went there and found he was not at home everything seemed dead and desolate: he could not properly enjoy his good fortune in having in some measure won the respect of the people about him, because he had not been able to tell his friend.

And as he returned sadly home he pursued the idea of not finding his friend at home and of returning with sorrow-laden heart, when he wanted to confide his sorrow to him; till he conceived the dreadful thought that he had found him dead, and then in despair cursed his fate because he had lost the greatest boon in life, a faithful friend. Out of this arose the following verses, which he wrote down when he got home:

I looked to find my friend
To tell him of my trouble,
And found him not.
Then sorrowful went
With heart so heavy
Back to my cottage.

I looked to find my friend,
My joy with him to double,
And found him not.
Then sadness came o'er me
As joy came before,
I went in silence.

I looked to find my friend,
To tell him my luck,
And found him dead.
Then curs'd I my luck
And straightway I swore
So long as mine eyes can shed a tear,
To sorrow for this my only friend,
For this one friend I had, no more.

. . . .

It was about this time that, through the son of the Precentor, Winter, he made a very interesting acquaintance with the philosophic vinegar-maker, with whom his friend had wanted to make him acquainted half a year earlier, but without success. Winter then called for him one evening and Reiser was full of expectation, and on the way Winter instructed him how to behave to the vinegar-maker, not to say 'good evening' on arriving, nor 'good night' when he left. Then they went by the long Easter Street, which is full of medieval houses, through the great gateway and across a long yard to the brewery, where the vinegar-maker had his separate quarters out behind, in which the casks stood in a great shed, constantly kept warm, in rows beside one another, so that they formed long passages, where one could lose oneself. When you spoke here there was a faint echo. As no one was to be seen Winter began to call 'ubi', and a voice in the distance answered 'hic'. Thereupon they went into the brew-house proper, close to the shed where the casks stood, and the vinegar-maker in his white jacket and blue apron, with bare arms, was standing at the window writing: he would be ready in a moment, he said, and gave Winter a paper, on which were some Latin verses he had just written for him.

The vinegar-maker seemed to Reiser to be a man of about thirty : in every movement of his muscles and in his flashing eye repressed power seemed to be expressed. The very first sight of him inspired Reiser with respect, but at first the brewer seemed not to notice him and talked to Winter about some new music and other things, speaking all the time in Low German, and yet expressing himself with such clearness and dignity that the coarsest dialect in his mouth had a certain charm. The result was that when he spoke people hung on his lips with pleasure and admiration, as Reiser often found later, when the vinegar-maker discoursed wisdom among his casks.

As it was a fairly cold autumn evening the vinegar-brewer led his two guests into his spacious warm shed, where the long rows of casks stood, and set before them a kind of sweet and very palatable beer. The conversation then became general, and as the talk fell on a common acquaintance, an old man with droll and peculiar ways, the brewer began to describe his character in minute detail with a humour worthy of Sterne. After that he read a passage from *Tom Jones* with such expression and with such just and clear delivery, that Reiser had never been better entertained, and when he went away could not sufficiently express his delight at this new acquaintance.

From this time forward either in Winter's company or alone he visited the vinegar-brewer almost every evening, and as they sat on their wooden stools by the warm stove among the casks under the hanging lamp, reading *Tom Jones* or making character sketches, he was more happy and contented than he had ever been except with Philip Reiser: but in his intercourse with the vinegar-maker he always felt uplifted and strengthened, when he reflected that a man of such knowledge and capacity submitted with such patience and steadfastness to his lot, which cut him off completely from all intercourse with the more cultivated world and from all the nourishment which his spirit might have drawn from it. And the very thought that such a man lived in such retirement and obscurity made his value more striking to Reiser, as a light in the darkness seems to shine brighter than when it is lost amid a multitude of other lights.

As a vinegar-brewer Kunze, that was his name, was really a great man, as he would perhaps have been as a scholar, though not in the same degree, for without this struggle against his circumstances the lofty patient strength of his spirit would not have had the same opportunity for exercise. There probably was not any human virtue which it was possible for him to practise in his position, which he had not practised.

He always saved enough from his hard-won earnings to entertain at his evening meal from time to time some young people, to whose education he took pleasure in contributing, and he often was able to take a walk with them, when he always took pleasure in paying for their refreshment. Besides he maintained a poor family daily in this brewery, where his uncle, a broken-down old man, for whom he worked, was master.

Winter and Philip Reiser and the vinegar-maker were now Reiser's chief society, with the addition of a young man who, encouraged by Reiser's example, in spite of the poverty of his parents had also determined to be a student. The vinegar-maker tried to draw him too into his circle through Winter, in order to contribute to his education. His conversations were largely true Socratic dialogues, which he often seasoned with the subtlest ridicule of the childish folly or vanity of his young companions.

When winter approached, Reiser was encouraged by an incident which cheered him more than anything that had happened to him before. He was entrusted by the Director with the honourable task of composing a German speech for the birthday of the Queen of England; which he was to deliver on that solemn occasion, which came in January. This was the highest and most distinguished honour to which a pupil of the school could aspire, and only few achieved it: for in general the speeches on the King's and Queen's birthdays were delivered only by young noblemen. The Prince and the Minister with all the chief people of the city used to attend the ceremony, and after the speech they generally complimented the young speaker, who was regarded as the hope of the State: a sight, which often depressed Reiser when he thought he would never attain to such a distinction in his life.

And now, after being generally despised and slighted at the beginning of the year, it suddenly came about that, without any effort on his part, this encouraging duty fell to his lot, which he proceeded to discharge with the greatest zeal.

He determined to compose his German address in hexameters. Now the Director had lent him the *Litteraturbriefe*[1] (Letters on literature), and recommended him to read them carefully and in them he came across the review in which Zachariä's translation of Milton's *Paradise Lost* was criticized for its bad hexameters, and some excellent remarks were made on the structure of the hexameter, its caesura, &c. Reiser laid hold of this and took the greatest pains to give finish to his hexameters. He often produced only two or three lines in a day, and then in the evening he went to Philip Reiser and submitted his verses to his criticism. At the same time they read together all the volumes of the *Litteraturbriefe* and again resumed this winter their Shakespeare evenings.

In November Reiser had completed about half his address and took it to the Director for his criticism. He very much approved of his work, but informed him that he would not be able to deliver the address publicly, as that involved expenses which Reiser would not be able to meet. The news struck Reiser down like a thunderbolt. All the brilliant prospects with which he had flattered himself during the composition suddenly vanished in a moment and he sank back into his old insignificance. The Director tried to console him, but he went away from him with a heavy heart and the melancholy thought that he was destined to perpetual obscurity. Then he thought

[1] Lessing's *Briefe die neueste Litteratur betreffend.*

of the lines he had written for Philip Reiser, which now suited his present condition:

Oft am I fain to rise
Yet fail upon the morrow
And then with trembling feel
My lot is one of sorrow.

And when next day in the choir among other things the words were sung

Thou strivest, happiness to reach
And seest thy effort is in vain

he applied this too to himself, and again felt all at once so forlorn, contemptible and insignificant, that he did not like to tell even Philip Reiser of his new trouble, in order not to have to speak to him of his fortunes, which once more began to be hateful and to seem no longer worth the trouble of thinking about.

Meanwhile, after tormenting himself about his trouble, he thought of a means of achieving his object, which very soon occurred to him when he began to think about it: he had only to go to Pastor Marquard, who had again begun to have hopes of him, and had only to ask him to get the Prince to supply what was needed for buying new clothes and for defraying the expenses of the delivery of the address. The Pastor consented at once and promised Reiser success in advance. Thus, Reiser's anxieties were at once removed again, and he could now complete the address he had begun with a light heart, to deliver it on the Queen's birthday. But as the frost began again he could no longer stay alone up in his bedroom, but had once more to sit in the evening with the landlord's household in the living-room, where the landlord and the soldiers quartered there forced him to join the games, in which they spent the long winter evenings. Here he chiefly composed his address in the afternoon and in the evening twilight, with his head resting against the stove.

And now he had found a good remedy for his melancholy humour: whenever he found it beginning to get the better of him he went out in the evening in the heaviest rain and snow, after it was dark, and walked once round the ramparts, and as he walked on quickly he never failed to find new hopes and prospects springing up insensibly, the most brilliant of which was close at hand. In these walks round the rampart he composed the best passages in his address, and difficulties of metre which seemed insurmountable when he rested his head against the stove, easily resolved themselves here.

The rampart round Hanover had from his childhood up been the favourite scene of his pleasantest imaginations and his most romantic ideas. For here he saw the closely packed houses of the town, and the open face of the country, with gardens, fields, and meadows, close bordering on each other and yet so absolutely distinct that the contrast could never fail to make the liveliest impression on his imagination. Then, too, as he walked round the place within which most of his experiences had been enacted, a thousand dim recollections of the past rose and thronged his mind, and combined with his present position to add interest to his life, and especially in the evening the sight of the scattered lights in the rooms of the houses built close to the rampart always produced the effect I have described before. Ever since he had recited his verses he was respected by almost all his schoolfellows. This was something to which he was not at all accustomed, and was beyond his experience. He hardly believed it possible that any one could still respect him : after all that he had gone through he imagined that there must be something in his person or his expression which would perhaps make him look absurd and ridiculous as long as he lived. This sense of being esteemed heightened his self-respect and made him quite a different creature : his looks, his expression changed, his eye grew bolder, and if any one wanted to ridicule him he could look him straight in the face and put him out of countenance.

Moreover, his material position was at once completely altered. Through the influence of the Rector and of Pastor Marquard, who had now conceived the highest hopes of him, he soon had so many lessons to give that he earned a monthly income which for his present needs was fairly considerable, an unaccustomed experience with which he did not at all know how to deal properly.

None of his rich and important schoolfellows was now ashamed of associating with him or visiting him in his humble lodging. He also saw himself this year in print, as he composed various little New Year's wishes in verse for a printer, who sold such things. Although his name got no notice, and no one knew that the verses were his, yet the sight of these first printed lines from his pen gave him indescribable pleasure whenever they met his eye. And when some days before the address was delivered his name appeared on a notice in Latin, with the names of two of his schoolfellows of the highest families, publicly printed, his name appearing as Reiserus, the name the previous Director had once given him; and when he vividly recalled the interval between the two occasions when the name was given him, first orally and then in print, and all he had suffered deservedly or undeservedly—it brought tears of joy and sadness to his eyes: for a year or even half a year before he had not dared to dream of such a sudden change of fortune. This Latin notice with his name was publicly posted on the notice-board in front of the school and at the church door, so that passers by stopped to read it.

Now it was the custom that the young people who delivered speeches on such occasions should in person invite the notabilities of the city a few days before. What a change, when Reiser whom before even his schoolfellows did not deign to address in the street or to walk with him because of his shabby clothes, now with hat under arm and sword at his side paid his visit of ceremony to the Prince, and invited him to the celebration of the birthday of his sister, the Queen of England! In this business of the invitations he could show himself to the leading inhabitants of the city, and was received by them with the most encouraging demonstrations of politeness.

He had then, without thinking of it, and indeed when he had given up all hope of it, attained the most honourable dignity to which a pupil of the highest class in Hanover could attain, and which was attained by few.

This method of entrusting the young people themselves with the invitations gives them much encouragement, and is on many grounds to be recommended for imitation . . . By these invitations Reiser was for a few days introduced to a world which hitherto had been quite unknown to him: he talked freely with ministers, councillors, preachers, scholars; in a word with persons of every sort of class, whom he had only admired at a distance. All were condescending and polite, and said something pleasant and encouraging, so that Reiser's self-reliance in these few days gained more than in years before. Among others he invited the poet Hölty, but on this occasion did not get to know him well, for only a display of confidence could dispel Reiser's shyness, and Hölty was not the man for this, for he was always somewhat embarrassed at the first conversation with a stranger. Reiser took this embarrassment for contempt, and was wounded by it because he had a great regard for Hölty, and so did not venture to visit him again.

When he had done playing his distinguished part in the daytime he went in the evening to his vinegar-maker, where he found Philip Reiser and Winter and the other young man who had been encouraged to study by his example; they received him with open arms, and he told them of his visits and of the persons whose acquaintance he had made, and so shared his pleasure with them.

Frau Filter and his uncle the wig-maker, and all the people who had given him free meals, vied with one another in showing him their pleasure and sympathy. His parents, who had heard nothing of him for a long time, and had long given up their hopes of him, were delighted when they heard of this sudden favourable turn in his fortunes and received the Latin notice, in which their son's name was printed in CAPITALS.

With all this public distinction Reiser still stayed on in his old lodging, where his host, the butcher, his wife and maid, and a couple of soldiers quartered on him shared the room with him. When, in spite of this humble dwelling, one of his rich and important fellow-students visited him, he felt a secret pleasure, that without attractive quarters or other external advantages he was sought out for his own sake. This made him sometimes quite proud of his humble home.

At last came the day of his triumph, when he was to win honour and applause in public in the most conspicuous way possible for one in his position, but it awakened in him a peculiar feeling of melancholy. All his desires and efforts had been concentrated on this moment, and up to this time the attention of a large proportion of people was fastened on him, and now, when this was over, everything was to be flat, and the everyday scenes of his life were to return. This thought very often roused in Reiser the strange but sincere desire that when his address had been delivered he might fall down and die. Now it so happened that on the very day the address was delivered, the weather became extremely cold, and many were kept from coming, so that the number of the audience was rather smaller than usual, though the assembly was sufficiently distinguished. Meanwhile, everything that day seemed dead and desolate to

Reiser. Imagination had to make way for reality, and the very fact that this of which he had dreamed so long was now realized, and that there was nothing more to come, made him thoughtful and sad. He measured the whole of his future life by this standard, and saw everything as in a dream in the dim distance ; he could not focus it properly. He mounted the platform with melancholy thoughts, and while the music played, before his speech began, he was thinking of something quite different from his present triumph : he thought and felt the emptiness of life, while the pleasant idea of his actual condition at the moment only glimmered as through a dim mist before his eyes.

In order to show the progress he had made in the expression of his thoughts, it is perhaps to the purpose to give some extracts from the address which he delivered. It began :

Lo what incense smoke from joyous regions arises
Up through the ether high to the very throne of the Godhead !
These are the quiet prayers of happy peoples ascending,
Cloud and fire, for Charlotte the Queen to God the Eternal.

With resonant harping
Sound ye nations the praise of George in jubilant triumph,
Happy nations ! and hushed be my song, for my effort is idle
His high fame to extol with my verse. The adventurous eagle
Boldly mounts over rocks and clouds and mountains uprising,
Ever approaching, he dreams, his goal, yet sees not he tarries
Still on the earth he had left, snail-slow. No earthly poet
Harmonies fit shall frame to approach the music of virtues
Blent in his life, our King's, beyond imitation exalted.

For now at the height of his greatness
Stands King George in his heart revolving the good of his peoples ;
Plans it, fulfils it too, unshaken by clamour of thunder,
Stands high-set, like God's beneficent cedar, that shelters
Bird and beast in his shade, and the storm-wind spends all its fury
But on the cedar's umbrageous leaves, that curl in the tempest.
Thus secure 'mid the storms that thunder about and around him
Stands King George, when peoples are raging ; but you his people
True to your King can only weep, your countenance veiling,
Look not upon your brothers in distant kingdom rebelling
False to their King

. . . .

All true hearts to-day beat high at thought of Queen Charlotte
Pardoning him who is fain in rashness of youth to adventure
Praise of her name. But silence ! my song, for far-away thunders
Loud acclaim of her people, their Queen with clouds of sweet incense
Praising to-day and shouting as one 'Long life to Queen Charlotte !'
Shouting till forest and mountain the cry 'Long life to her !' echo.

Reiser in composing this address had formed an ideal in his mind, which really inspired him, and there was the added stimulus of his speaking in public. That thought so to speak filled the gaps where his inspiration failed or grew faint.

As, however, he really knew little or nothing of his subject he was at the pains to get hold of a number of eulogies already written on the King and Queen : these he read and constructed an ideal from them without using a single phrase from any of them, avoiding plagiarism, of which he had the greatest horror, as carefully as possible. Indeed, he was ashamed of the phrase 'forest and fortress re-echo' because once in *The Sorrows of Werther* the phrase 'forest and mountain resound' occurs. Reminiscences often escaped him, but he was ashamed when he noticed them.

On the day he gave the address he was, as I have said, more depressed than ever: everything seemed to him so dead and empty: the occasion with which his imagination had so long been occupied was past and gone.

In the afternoon he was invited with the other two who had made speeches to drink coffee with the first Burgomaster. This was an honour to which he was quite unused and he did not know how to behave: he did not recover his spirits until he had taken off his fine clothes, and went again in the evening to his vinegar-maker where he found Winter and S—— and Philip Reiser, who really rejoiced in his good fortune, and whose sympathy he valued more than all the glories of the day.

Reiser now had more lessons to give, and his income thus improved so much that he was able to hire a better lodging, and sometimes to invite some of his comrades to coffee, and to live, for a schoolboy, on quite a dignified footing. But the money he now earned seemed so much compared with his income and needs in old days that he did not in the least realize its value or the necessity of saving. Thus, his larger income made him poorer than he was before, and the effect of his good fortune became in the end the source of new misery.

But now that he had so suddenly and unexpectedly recovered the esteem of all who knew him, and of those on whom his good fortune depended, this naturally had an effect on his character, spurring him on to the noble ambition of deserving this esteem still further; he began to attend the lectures more carefully than ever, and by taking notes, to make as much of them his own as he could.

The recitation practice continued, and Reiser composed for this purpose a poem on the defects of reason, a subject which the Director had set. Reiser brought into this all the doubts which had borne him company so long.

The ideas of 'all' and 'being', as the highest ideas of human understanding, did not satisfy him: they seemed to him to be a narrow and painful limitation. The idea that with them all human thinking should come to an end! The words of the old Tischer on his death-bed came to his mind—'all, all, all!' That just where the boundary lies between the old existence and a new one he repeated so often this highest limiting notion: the wall of partition was as it were to be broken down. 'All' and 'Being' must in their turn become notions subordinate to a higher, more widely embracing notion. 'All that is' must still have beside it something which together with 'all that is' is included under something higher and more exalted. Why should our thought be the final limit? If we can say nothing beyond 'all that exists', is a higher or the highest thought not to be able to express anything beyond? The dying Tischer perhaps wished to say more when he twice repeated his 'all', but his tongue or his thoughts failed him and he died. These were the peculiar thoughts which Reiser brought into his poem on 'The Defects of Reason', which contained these words among others :

The All, that boldest flight of Reason e'er attains,
Is far from that, whereto the struggling seraph strains !

The poem ended on a very orthodox note : that one must in the end take refuge with the light of revelation :

A light which goes in front and through dark shadows guides
Illumining our way. Woe to who-e'er derides !

The Director much approved of the conclusion : but the poem as a whole he regarded as unintelligible, which was quite natural.

Once more Reiser composed a poem on *Contentment* : as it were for his own instruction or as a guiding rule for his own life ; and after he had lulled himself into a gentle tranquillity, once more black melancholy raised its head at the close : after expressing a series of quiet feelings in his poem he wound up with expressions of despair :

Yet sufferings unmeasured make
Your life a torment here below.

And if you find no saviour near,
No one to end your crying need,
See in the thunder-cloud appear,
Kind Death, and greet a friend indeed !

As he pursued a thought of this kind he often felt a kind of distressing rapture, if such there can be.

This poem was as it were a picture of all his feelings, which though they were at first tranquil and gentle had a way of ending thus. His nature had been attuned to this train of feelings by all the countless wounds and humiliations which he had suffered from youth up. Even in face of the brightest, most laughing prospect black melancholy always tended to return and cloud his vision. As soon as he began to express such thoughts he became natural and sincere. For instance he was commissioned to write a lover's complaints for some one: a situation into which he could not transport himself by any effort. As he did not believe he could ever be loved by a woman, for he held his appearance to be so far from attractive that he had given up all idea of ever pleasing, he could never put himself in the place of one who complains that he is not loved. All he knew of this state was the product of thought, he could not feel it. Nevertheless, the lover's complaints he composed were fairly successful, because he compressed into them what he knew from novels and from Philip Reiser's confidences. But, finally, he imagined the lover in a state when crushed by his sorrows he is reduced to despair, and then without any further regard for the cause of his despair he imagined the man in despair and was able to put himself in his place. So the last stanza of the lover's complaints quickly took shape in his hands:

In deepest darkness lying,
Where wanderer never came,
Where birds of death are crying,
By oak-tree's hollow frame
Distressful I'll be weeping
While stars their watch are keeping,
Till, as I ever more complain,
Day dawns again.

Sometimes even he seemed to succeed on the tender note, if it was associated with a certain gentle sadness. For instance, he composed for some one a poem of farewell to his beloved, which, after a bitter complaint at parting, ended thus :

Farewell ? for me there 's only weeping,
My heart is heavy, dim my eye,
For you Time holds glad days in keeping,
Belovèd one, goodbye ! goodbye !

And in his address on the Queen's birthday the following passage, which I did not quote before, was the one in which his feeling was truest and strongest :

She smiles and the glad are triumphant,
Even the mournful dry their eyes and cease from their weeping,
Joy enlightens their faces, they smile and greet with a blessing
This proud day whereon for their comfort was born Queen Charlotte.

In his own mind he counted himself one of the mournful whose sorrow was turned to joy, and he found more sweetness in imagining himself among the mournful than among the joyful. This was again 'the Joy of grief', to which his heart inclined from childhood.

He spent the winter pretty happily, but as his imagination had been so deeply stirred and his feelings roused to such a high pitch by so many conflicting desires and hopes, it could not but happen that he began to feel the monotony of his life. He was in his nineteenth year : he had been five years at school and did not yet know how he would get to the University. He began to feel as much cramped in Hanover as he did in the days when his journey to the hat-maker in Brunswick was impending. All his thoughts began gradually to take a wide range, and he dreamed himself into a romantic future. And when spring came suddenly a strange desire for travel, which he had never before felt so strongly, arose in him.

Bremen is fifty miles from Hanover, and the place where Reiser's parents lived was just half way: the great project, which Reiser had been cherishing for some weeks, was to sail from Bremen down the Weser to the sea, and his imagination pictured wonders from this journey.

The sight of the Weser, of ships, of a commercial city, occupied his mind waking and dreaming. He got one of his schoolfellows to give him a letter to his brother who was in the service of a merchant in Bremen and set off on foot with a ducat in his pocket. This was the first strange romantic journey which Anton Reiser took and from this time forward he began to justify his name (*Reiser* = traveller). He had furnished himself for the journey with a map of Lower Saxony, a portable ink-pot and a portable note-book of white paper, in order to be able to keep a regular journal of his travel on the way.

As soon as he had left the gates of Hanover his courage and his hopes grew with every step he took, and he was so much inspired by his journey that some nine miles from Hanover he seated himself on a hill by the road, planted his ink-pot, which was provided with a spike, in the ground and so half reclining began to write his journal. Some coaches drove past, and the people, to whom a man writing on a hill by the road-side was bound to be a strange object, leaned over to look at him. This made him feel shy at first, but he soon recovered from the unpleasant effect their staring had on him; for these people, who did not know him, he regarded himself as non-existent, he was as good as dead for them, and so he concluded the essay which he wrote in his pocket-book on the hill by the road-side with the words:

What matters what the people do
When I am in my grave?

And then he stepped on and came in the evening twilight close past the village where his parents lived, inquired for the nearest village on the road to Bremen, and as it was only a mile further went on and spent the night there.

Next day he walked on over the sandy desolate moor and asked his way from one village to another, but could not reach Bremen; he was obliged to spend the night again in a village, which was the last before Bremen, and the third day his most ardent desire was fulfilled; he came in sight of the towers of Bremen and saw actually before his eyes what his imagination had so long been busy with. He had seen no considerable town except Hanover and Brunswick, and from the very sound of its name Bremen had impressed him as remarkable; his imagination had pictured the town as dark and grey, and he was now extremely curious to see it from within, and ventured to enter the gate without a passport, and when asked who he was gave himself out as an inhabitant, and when asked more particularly, as one of the employees of the principal to whose servant he had a letter to deliver, and so was allowed to pass in. As soon as he was in the town he walked up and down the streets once or twice, and then the first thing he did was to inquire whether one of the big boats which lay in the Weser would be sailing to the river mouth, where the Hessian troops destined for America were lying at Bremerlehe, and were to sail immediately.

It happened that one of these boats was starting, and Anton for the first time went on board ship and was carried five and twenty miles beyond Bremen, where they put in and stayed the night in a village. Though the weather was stormy and rainy this voyage gave Reiser infinite pleasure. He stood on the deck, map in hand, and passed in review the places on both banks whose names he knew; he ate and drank with the sailors and went with them to the inn in the evening. From there his intention was to go on next day with another ship to the sea-coast, already in thought he saw the vast waves before him, and his imagination was excited to the utmost, when suddenly a question he had not properly considered during his journey occurred to him, whether his purse would hold out, and was horrified to find, on asking the skipper for his bill and paying it, that he had only a few pence left.

He did not venture to eat in the evening but alleged a headache and asked to be shown to bed, where all night long he planned how he might escape with honour from his inn, if his reckoning came to more than the few coppers he still had left. When he asked next morning what he had to pay, it chanced that the few coppers he had left sufficed, but he had not a farthing over, and was now seventy-six miles from Hanover, fifty-one from the place where his parents lived, and twenty-five from Bremen. He alleged that he could not go on to the sea coast because he had reflected that it would keep him too long, and so, glad that he had escaped with honour, he left the inn where he had spent the night and took the direct road back to Bremen.

His letter to the merchant's clerk in Bremen was now his only hope: apart from this, for fifty miles or so, to the home of his parents, he was destitute. He had not tasted anything when he started, and had to make up his mind to remain in this condition all day long. The way which first went along the bank of the Weser was sandy and tiring, but nevertheless he went on in good spirits till midday when the sun's heat became scorching. Hunger, thirst and weariness overcame him together with the thought that here he was, a stranger in the desolate country, penniless and destitute. He tried to collect some crumbs from his pocket, and in the process found two Bremen groats, each worth about a halfpenny. In the circumstances this was as welcome as finding a treasure; he collected all his remaining strength to press on to the next village, where for one of his groats he procured a little beer, which was quite an unexpected refreshment, for he had settled that he had to walk the twenty-five miles to Bremen without drinking. The drink of beer gave him fresh courage, as did the other groat which he still had in his pocket. Hunger asserted itself but he tried to overcome it and remained resigned. A poor journeyman artisan joined him on the road, who entered every village and begged: and Reiser found a sort of pleasure in the strange fact that this poor artisan, who perhaps might envy him as a well-dressed man, was really richer than he.

In the afternoon he reached Vegesack, and with a hungry stomach gazed at a sight he had never seen before, a number of three-masted ships which lay in the little harbour. The sight gave him inexpressible pleasure, in spite of his miserable condition, and as this condition was due to his own carelessness, he was not willing to admit to himself any sort of discontent. He reached Bremen towards evening, but before he reached the town he had to get carried across the river, for which he had to pay a Bremen groat, and it seemed to him a great piece of luck that he had kept precisely this sum, without which he could not have reached the town on which his fate depended. At last he reached the town at sunset, and as he was properly dressed and had all the appearance of a man taking a walk, stopping for a time and looking round and then going on again, they let him pass through without hindrance.

He thus found himself again within the circuit of a populous town, where no one knew him, and as he looked down sadly over the railing into the Weser he was as forlorn and lonely standing in the street as if he had been on an uninhabited desert island.

For a time he was content with this forlorn condition ; which had in it an element of romance, but when rational reflection again triumphed over imagination his first care was to make use of his letter to the merchant's clerk.

But what was his horror, when on inquiring for him at his house he learnt that he would not be back till late in the evening. He remained standing in the street not far from the man's house, darkness came on, he dared not go into an inn without money, all his romantic ideas which up to this point had relieved his condition disappeared, and the only feeling left was the cruel necessity of having to spend the night tortured with hunger and weariness in the open air, in the midst of a populous town. As he was standing in this melancholy embarrassment, looking round in every direction, a well-dressed man came towards him and asked him sympathetically whether he was a stranger. He could not bring himself to reveal his condition to him, but was determined rather in any event to spend the night in the open air, which he would have done, had not a piece of luck befallen him after so many difficulties. The merchant's clerk had torn himself away from the company he was with, to attend to some business at home, and when he heard that some one had wanted to deliver a letter from his brother and had afterwards gone for a walk near the water, he hurried off to look for the bearer of the letter, who had been described to him, and actually met Reiser whom he recognized at once, when he had given up all hope of finding a shelter for the night.

As soon as the young merchant saw his brother's handwriting he was extremely friendly and agreeable to Reiser, and offered to take him to an inn. Reiser then discovered to him his actual condition, though not without romancing. He had been induced to gamble, against his habits, and had lost all his cash : for he was ashamed to say that he had provided himself with too little money for this journey, for he thought that he would thereby lose still more in the opinion of the young man, from whom alone he could now expect help.

But then his untoward fortunes were at once altered: the clerk offered to advance him enough to free him from all want. He took him to a reputable inn where Reiser on his recommendation was admirably entertained, and spent the evening so pleasantly that he was repaid for all the troubles of the day.

A few glasses of wine, which he drank with the merchant's clerk, had such an extraordinary effect on his vital spirits after the fatigue and exhaustion of a whole day, that he entertained almost the whole company, which used to assemble there every evening, with anecdotes of Hanover and merry sallies, which were not usual with him. These won the approval of everybody in this little circle, among whom was the man who saw him standing sad and forlorn in the street, and among all the passers by was the only one to whom a stranger, standing sad and forlorn, seemed important enough to be troubled about or addressed. This gave the man an extraordinary attraction in Reiser's eyes for this readiness to address a perfect stranger, and take trouble about his condition, is exactly that universal humanity by which you can distinguish the Good Samaritan from the priest and Levite who pass by.

Reiser hardly ever spent a pleasanter evening in his life than this when he saw himself in a strange town, in a circle of perfect strangers, drawn into conversation and listened to with encouraging approval.

The merchant's clerk pressed him to stay some days longer in Bremen, showed him the sights of the town, and Reiser found in just the place where he stood lonely and forlorn in the street, so many people who were interested on his behalf, conversed with him, and went out with him, that he got a kind of attachment to these persons who showed him so much ready and kind-hearted civility, and proofs of friendship, which made it hard for him after so short a time to part with them for ever.

He dined at midday with a party of gentlemen, who treated him as a stranger with special politeness, a treatment to which he was hitherto unaccustomed. The merchant's clerk advanced him enough not only to pay his bill at the inn, but also to travel back to Hanover in comfort, which he did on foot. And as this thoughtless scheme of his now turned out so well, he unconsciously began to develop the idea of seeking his fortune in the wide world which lay open for him instead of waiting for it in the narrow circumstances that he had so far enjoyed.

He had found in a strange town a whole number of people who took notice of him, felt with him and made his stay pleasant, things he had not been used to in Hanover. He had gone through adventures, and experienced the quickest change of fortune in a short time : scarcely an hour before he had felt abandoned by every one, and immediately afterwards found himself in a circle of people who were all attentive to him and gave him a share of their conversation.

No wonder then that the thought was stirred in him to exchange the sad monotony of his previous life and condition for varied experiences of this sort, by which, in spite of all the hardships he had to bear, he felt his spirit pleasantly stirred in a way he had never felt before. Even the sadness which he felt, when the gates of the town, where yesterday he had sat sociably at the same table with a number of friendly people, disappeared from his eyes, and he had lost from his field of vision the last conspicuous traces of this place which had become so dear to him in a short time : even this sadness had a charm for him which he had never felt before. He seemed to himself a bigger man because he had taken a journey for the first time, of his own motion and without any impulse from without, to an entirely strange city and had there in a couple of days found more people who wished him well than he had been able to find in Hanover in the course of years. Wayfaring began to have a great charm for him : he imagined away his fatigue by a thousand agreeable thoughts ; when it grew dark he looked on the road winding in front of him, on which he had constantly to fix his eyes, as a faithful friend guiding him.

This idea he turned in the end to poetical use, it became an image or figure, which he linked with a thousand things. 'As a traveller holds on his way', 'faithful as the road to the traveller' and so on. He pursued this play of ideas as he went, and the monotony of the country in the surrounding darkness and so the weariness of constant lifting of his feet disappeared imperceptibly and had no effect on his temper.

It was quite dark when he came to his parents. They were surprised that he had passed close by them and travelled to Bremen before coming to them, but nevertheless they gave him a joyful welcome this time because of the many pleasant pieces of news they had received from him.

And Reiser had by this time collected so much material for mystical conversations with his father that they very often talked on into the night. Reiser attempted to give a metaphysical explanation of all the mystical ideas his father had drawn from the writings of Madame Guyon, of 'all' and 'one', of 'perfection in the one' and so on: he found the task easy, as mysticism and metaphysics coincide in so far as the former by the power of the imagination often accidentally produces what in the latter is the work of the reflective reason. Reiser's father, who had never looked for this in his son, seemed now to conceive a high idea of him and to cherish a sort of respect for him.

But even here Reiser's tendency to melancholy continually prevailed. He was standing at the door with his mother when the child of a neighbour was being carried to the grave, and the father followed with dishevelled hair and streaming eyes. 'If only they were carrying me to burial too' said Reiser's mother, who indeed had not had much joy in her life, and Reiser, who might still have expected plenty of joy in life, inwardly agreed with her as heartily as if the greatest sorrow had befallen him.

This time when he took leave of his mother and brothers on going away he felt more emotion than usual. He went on foot to Hanover, and when he saw the four towers again to which he had already returned several times under so many different circumstances, once more he was struck with the painful feeling that he was to come back from the wide world into this narrow circle of all his old relations and connexions: the familiar things there seemed to him so stale. But when he entered the Gate and found a play-bill posted up at a street-corner all at once his spirits brightened. It was a most agreeable surprise. His first walk, as it had been three years earlier, was to the Palace, where the theatre was, and a full play-bill with the actors' names was posted up. They were playing *Clavigo*, Brockmann playing Beaumarchais, Reinike Clavigo, the elder Fräulein Ackermann (the younger was already dead) played Maria, Schröder Don Carlos, Frau Reinike the sister of Maria, Schütz Buenko, and Böheim the friend of Beaumarchais. So excellent was the cast, even down to the most insignificant parts. Reiser knew all these excellent actors: is it surprising then that his expectations were at the highest pitch, to see them produce a play again, one which he had not yet read but which he knew to be by the author of *The Sorrows of Werther?*

Through this accidental circumstance, associated with his recollections of the adventures which he had had on his travels, he formed in his mind a peculiar romantic ideal, which had a very great influence on several years of his subsequent life. Theatres and travel became unconsciously the two leading ideas in his imagination, which explains the decision he came to afterwards.

He found it hard again now to miss the play a single evening, but this filled his head so full of theatrical ideas that his proper business of continual learning and teaching (for he had filled almost his whole day with teaching) began sometimes to be irksome to him, and then he made no scruple of missing one of the hours of teaching or learning, reckoning on each occasion that he was only missing one hour.

The Twins by Klinger was first put on the stage at this time, and indeed was produced with all possible skill, Brockmann playing Guelfo, Reinike the old Guelfo, Frau Reinike the mother, Fräulein Ackermann Camilla, Schröder Grimaldi, and Lambrecht the brother of Guelfo. This horrible play had an extraordinary effect on Reiser: it captured all his feelings. Guelfo thought himself oppressed from the cradle. Reiser thought the same of himself, and remembered all the wounds and humiliations to which, almost as far back as he could think, he had been constantly exposed. He forgot the Prince's son and all his connexions, and saw only himself in the oppressed Guelfo. The bitter laugh to which Guelfo gave vent in his despair gripped Reiser's innermost feelings, reminding him of all the fearful moments when he was really on the brink of despair, and gave utterance to a laugh like Guelfo's, when he regarded his own existence with scorn and loathing, and often broke with a dreadful ecstasy into loud scornful laughter.

The self-loathing which Guelfo felt when he breaks in two the mirror, in which he sees himself after the murder: his feeling that he wishes to do nothing but sleep—sleep; all this seemed so true to Reiser, so closely taken from his own soul, which was constantly in travail with dark fancies of this sort, that he thought himself completely into the part of Guelfo and lived in it for a time with all his thoughts and feelings.

While plays were thus being acted at the Royal Opera Theatre by the Schröder Company, the time of the summer holidays was approaching, when the VIth Form used to give a play in public. Reiser had no doubt that this time a part would be assigned him, as he was one of the most important members of the class ever since he delivered the address on the Queen's birthday; he therefore thought they would not do anything without him. What was his surprise then when he learnt that they had begun without him, had already settled the plays to be acted and not allotted him a part! As he now really had many friends and followers among his schoolfellows, he could not explain this exclusion, till he became aware that there was such jealousy over the parts and such a painful struggle among them to outdo one another that every one had enough to do to look after himself, and no one was called upon who did not force his way in.

Reiser often returned in memory to this scene in his life, and reflected how the whole play of human passions was developed in these childish struggles for such an insignificant thing as a part in a play acted by the VIth Form at Hanover, just as if it had been the most serious event, and how this mutual struggle, this pressure and counter-pressure were so faithful a picture of human life in little, that Reiser saw in them as it were the way prepared for all his future experiences.

The incident arose partly from the fact that the arrangement of the plays and the distribution of the parts was left entirely to the members of the VIth Form. This gave the affair a republican spirit, which left room for the development of various forces, and for the employment of cunning and craft and the formation of cabals, as happens at a Parliamentary election; for on such public occasions, if for instance a procession with music and torches had to be organized, votes were taken for the election of a leader of the procession or any other public post.

Reiser thus saw himself once more, when he least expected it, excluded from that which he longed for more than ever with all his heart and for which he had already borne so much. He tried to console himself with the thought that he was underrated, that his companions had done him injustice, but in the end this did not content him; he was specially offended that his friend Winter, who was one of the company of players, had told him nothing of it, though he knew how much Reiser desired to take part. But Winter thought he would appear in an unfavourable light if he proposed some one as a member who had attracted no one's attention but his own. He did not mean to be unkind to Reiser, and remained his friend as before, but his friendship stopped at this point: an experience which many a man perhaps has had occasion to go through in his life. It is hard to make a stand in friendship, if everything declares against your friend: we begin no longer to trust our own judgement, which seems to require some support from outside, however slight. If a thing is set in motion by one person, people are willing enough to be the second to vote for it; every one shrinks from being the first, a friendship must be a very strong one, if it is not to give way to the opposing policy.

Winter was a very straightforward man, and when Reiser asked him what was on foot among himself and his companions who were constantly meeting, at first Winter gave him plainly to understand that he did not want to tell him, until Reiser pressed him and learnt the whole story, whereupon Winter excused himself by representing the whole thing as unimportant, and as something which would hardly be carried out, and so on.

This experience which he went through for the first time with his friend Winter was one which he found only too often confirmed in later life. Iffland, whom I have already mentioned as having afterwards become a most popular playwright, was the most intellectually distinguished of the VIth Form of that time. Reiser had tried to attach himself to him some years earlier, but the inequality of their circumstances had then prevented it. Now, however, that Reiser had begun to distinguish himself, Iffland began to draw towards him of his own accord, and they often discussed their future on their walks. Iffland, too, was living entirely in the world of fancy, and had at that time conceived a very attractive picture of the pleasant life of a country parson, and had therefore resolved to study theology, and talked to Reiser constantly of the quiet domestic happiness he would enjoy in his village in the bosom of a small community which loved him. Reiser who was familiar with such plays of fancy from his own experience prophesied to him that he would never carry out this resolution to his own advantage, for if he became a pastor, he would probably become a great hypocrite; however moving his appeals, and however powerful his eloquence, he would only be playing a part. A secret feeling told Reiser that he would probably do the same himself, and that was why he could give him such good advice.

Iffland did not indeed become a pastor, but strangely enough these ideas of quiet domestic happiness, which he so often expressed to Reiser at that time, were not lost, but were realized in almost all his dramas as he could not realize them in his own life.

When, however, the players came again to Hanover all those attractive ideas of quiet happiness in a village were very soon driven out of Iffland's mind, and the ruling idea with him as with Reiser was again the theatre. Iffland was one of the leading members of the company who had combined for the production of the play, but he too had on this occasion forgotten his friend Reiser.

This neglect on the part of those whom he still counted his best friends, in a matter which lay so near his heart, was very distressing to him.

He spoke about it to Iffland, who excused himself by saying that he did not think that Reiser cared about it. And what vexed Reiser most was to hear that when they were distributing the parts he had not any enemies in the company who wanted to exclude him, but that no one had thought of him or even mentioned him.

Meanwhile, when he explained that he would like to have a share in it, there was no opposition, provided he would be content with one of the parts which were left. He had then to make up his mind to this, and in the first play, *The Deserter from Filial Love*, received the part of Peter, which he did not like very much but preferred to no part at all.

The story of these seeming trifles will not be found unimportant, when it is seen in the sequel that they had a great influence on his later life, and that the distribution of parts in the plays he acted with his schoolfellows, was a picture as it were of one part of his later life. He did not wish to push himself, and yet he was not strong enough to bear being ignored. The fact that he had now become a member of the theatrical society involved him in many expenses which exceeded his means, and reduced his income through broken engagements. He had to entertain his companions, as every one did, and the rehearsals made him miss many of the lessons he was giving. Besides, his head was now filled with dreams, he was no longer fit for continuous and serious thought or diligent study. He now framed literary projects, he wanted to write a tragedy—'The Perjurer'. In imagination he saw the play-bill posted, with his name on it, and he went up and down his room like a madman thinking out and feeling out all the shocking and fearful scenes of his tragedy. The perjurer repented of his perjury too late, and murder and incest had already followed from his crime when driven by stings of conscience he was about to repair his perjury by sacrificing all the property he had won by his perjury, and what most flattered Reiser's imagination was the thought that if he could only finish his tragedy at school, he would raise great expectations and win a great reputation. Even in his ninth year, when he went to the writing-school, he had planned with one of his companions that they should write a book together, and both flattered themselves with the thought of the reputation they would make. The boy who planned with him the book that was to contain both their life-histories was a clever fellow, who was wrecked by over-work, and died in his seventeenth year. In those days he used sometimes to act with him before the master came in and the lesson began, and always found inexpressible pleasure in this amusement, though at that time he had never seen a play, and had only a vague second-hand idea of what it was. He had a very exalted idea of what it meant to construct a book. To him a book was so sacred and important a thing, that he could hardly believe in any mortal, at least any living mortal, making one. Even long after that he felt it strange to be told that the authors of some famous books were still alive—that they ate, drank and slept like himself.

In his sixteenth year when he first read the works of Moses Mendelssohn, the name, combined with the ancient head of Homer on the title-page, produced the illusion that Moses Mendelssohn was some ancient sage, who had lived centuries ago, and whose writings had been translated into German, and he remained under this delusion till he happened to hear his father say that Mendelssohn was alive, that he was a Jew, of whom all Jews were very proud, and that Reiser's father had seen him at Pyrmont and could describe him. This produced at once a great revolution in Reiser's mind. His ideas of old and new, present and past, were strangely confused. He found it hard to get used to the idea that a man whom his imagination had so long placed in bygone centuries was still alive. He thought of such a man as a divinity moving among men: and to see such beings face to face and converse with them was his dearest wish. And now he had given expression to his thoughts in various ways, and he began to hope that he might some day produce a work, which would win him a way into that brilliant circle, and so earn the right to mix with beings whom hitherto he regarded as exalted far above him. That was the chief explanation of the passion for writing, which began to torment him day and night.

To win fame and applause had always been his dearest wish: but he did not want to wait for it, he wanted it at once, and with the natural indolence of man, wanted to reap without sowing. So the theatre precisely suited his wishes. Nowhere was immediate applause to be won as it could be here. He looked at a Brockmann or a Reinike with reverence when he saw them in the street, and could desire nothing better than to win for himself the place in other men's minds that they occupied in his. His dearest wish was, like them, to exhibit before a multitude of men, such as is rarely or never assembled, all the moving passions of rage, revenge, magnanimity, and as it were to impart his passion to every nerve of the spectator. That seemed to him a sphere of action which was unmatched for intensity of life. But he had joined the company of actors too late to get a part that he cared for, and he was exceedingly annoyed. Meanwhile, he was cheered by getting a second part, for he received the compensation of writing a prologue for *The*

Deserter, which was to be printed with the *dramatis personae.*

They were now only waiting for the departure of the regular players, for the VIth Form had obtained leave to act in the great Royal Opera House, so that the performance would be more brilliant than it had ever been before. The whole production was left to the young people, and as Reiser was now one of the company he took part in all the discussions and debates. He had never been used to this and it seemed quite strange, he felt as if it were not quite proper that he should be considered. Though there was now no external reason for it he still loved solitude, and his pleasantest hours were those when he walked some way outside the Gate to a windmill, standing in a romantic region of alternating hill and valley: then he would get a cup of milk and sit in an arbour in the garden reading or writing in his note-book. This had been his favourite walk some years before and he had often gone there with Philip Reiser.

When *The Sorrows of Werther* appeared and he read the charming descriptions of Wahlheim he thought at once of the windmill and of the many hours he had enjoyed in solitude there. Then outside the New Gate there was a tiny wood artificially laid out, with so many winding serpentine paths that when you wandered in it, it seemed six times as large as it really was. On every side it had a view on to green meadows, where beyond the single tall trees beneath which Reiser loved to walk, and behind the shrubs where he had so often hidden, was to be seen the gleam of the river, with whose banks he had become familiar by his frequent walks, at so many stages of his fortunes. Often as he sat on a bench at the edge of the wood, and looked out into the open, all the past scenes of his life, the troubles and the cares which had borne him company on many a hot summer's day rose up before him again, and thinking of them he fell into a gentle melancholy, to which it was pleasant to give way. Away in the distance he could see the bridge over the brook by which he had sat so many hours, reading and writing poetry. As the wood was so near the town, he would often walk out there in the moonlight and sometimes would play the part of Siegwart, though he had not read *Siegwart*, which did not appear till a year later.

Here, the year before this, when he was nineteen, he had kept his birthday one raw September evening, and vowed most solemnly to himself to make better use of his life in future than in the past.

On these lonely walks he composed his prologue, which began, like his address, with the words 'Welch' ein ', for he had fallen in love with the soft sound of these words, which seemed to him to contain a wealth of ideas and to fit in with what followed. He could think of no words which gave a fuller sound, and so he began his prelude with *Welch' eine Göttin*:

What Goddess this, with rapture takes
The man of feeling ?
With pity scenes she oft awakes
That captivate his eager eyes
While melancholy thoughts arise
With gladness in his heart.
'Tis heaven-born Fancy's magic art;
She carries him by flowery ways
Down to the peaceful vale below
Where cottage folk, god-given friends,
She to his eyes doth show, &c.

This prologue was printed with the list of *dramatis personae* as a little book, and on the title-page 'written by Reiser, spoken by Iffland'. Reiser thus saw himself in print again, and what was more, was commissioned by his companions to invite the Prince to the play, which he did with his sword at his side in the gala-clothes he had worn when he gave the birthday-address.

The nobility and the dignitaries of the city too were invited by the young men in person and Reiser again had the opportunity, as on the birthday occasion, to see close at hand some people of the great world whom he had only admired at a distance: he saw that the Ministers, Counts, and Nobles to whom he now talked face to face, were not strikingly different beings, but that they, like the common people, often had something peculiar and even comical in their expressions, which made the halo round them disappear, as soon as you heard them speak and conversed with them at close quarters.

Brilliant as Reiser's position seemed, when he paraded thus in the streets, and paid his respects in the leading houses, yet this position could, rightly understood, only be called a 'brilliant wretchedness',[1] for as his outgoings far exceeded his income his circumstances were growing more difficult and his position more precarious every day. Besides, he was oppressed by his monotonous life, and saw no prospect of a decent life at the University, and now he had so set his heart on that immediate applause which an actor can win, that his thoughts constantly turned rather to the Stage than to the University.

[1] Goethe's *Werther*, Dec. 24, 1771.

That period was the most brilliant in the history of the German Stage, and it was not surprising that many young people were excited by it to think of adopting a career so brilliant as that of the stage. The theatrical world in Hanover at that time shared in this movement. It had seen the united artistic efforts of the most distinguished actors—a Brockmann, a Reinike, a Schröder, and witnessed their triumphs, and it was indeed no ignoble idea, to emulate their success. Moreover, it did not require three years preliminary study at the University to attain this end. Reiser, too, had the irresistible desire to travel, which had possessed him ever since his adventurous pilgrimage to Bremen, and the thought of transporting himself out of all his previous associations, in which at the best he had been only half successful, and seeking his fortune in the wide world began gradually to dominate him. But so far it was only a mere play of fancy, he had not yet resolved to put his idea into action.

Meanwhile, his father visited him in Hanover, and he was able for the first time to entertain him in his own room, which was very well furnished, and had a handsome wall-paper. He proceeded to describe his position to his father in the most attractive and advantageous light, and represented the performance of the play as a means of again attracting attention to himself, both by the printed prologue and his personal invitation to the Prince. He would thus, as on the occasion of the birthday speech, display himself in the most favourable light.

Reiser's father on this occasion gave expression

to a true and important thought; that such events as the birthday speech, when a man has opportunity to display himself to advantage, were to be looked on as a victory which must be followed up, because few such occur in life.

Reiser accompanied his father on his return an hour's walk outside the City-Gate, and it chanced that they stood still, so Reiser remembered afterwards, just at the spot where his father had once cursed him. They had been discussing the most weighty and exalted subjects, on the borderland of mysticism and metaphysics, and now Reiser's father made a compact with his son that henceforward they would both in common devote themselves to the attainment of that great purpose—union with the highest thinking Being. Thereupon he laid his hands on his son's head and gave him his blessing on the very spot where he had once cursed him.

Reiser then returned home in very good humour, which lasted until his imagination was once more roused by the distribution of the parts in the other plays which were to be performed besides *The Deserter*. Once more the ambitions which had been lulled to sleep by quiet reflection were awakened. The plays were *Clavigo*, *The Punctual Man* (*Der Mann nach der Uhr*) and *The Page* (*Der Edelknabe*). He had been content to take a minor part in *The Deserter*, and now counted on having at least the part of Clavigo. While all his desires were concentrated on the Stage, this part in particular made the strongest appeal to him: and it was given not to him, but to another, who obviously played it worse than Reiser would have done.

Reiser's vexation was so great that it plunged him into a kind of real melancholy. If any one should think this improbable or unnatural he should consider that this was the crisis when Reiser's supreme desire was to be fulfilled or disappointed—the desire to exhibit his talents in public before the assembled inhabitants of his own city, and to be able to show how deeply he felt what he said, and what power he had in voice and expression to give utterance to what he felt so deeply. To awake in the breast of thousands the emotions that Reinike, when playing Clavigo, had awaked in him, was for him a thought so great, proud and uplifting, that perhaps no one ever felt so strongly about any part in a tragedy. This would have fulfilled beyond expectation the desire he had conceived five years before. The audience was distinguished and numerous beyond precedent. The theatre, which held several thousand people, was so full that no room was left, and among the spectators was the Prince with all the nobility, the clergy and scholars and artists of the city. In his position he could not wish for anything better than to display his powers in public with all the strength of emotion and experience, which hitherto he had had to keep to himself, before an audience like that, especially in a city which if not his native city, was that in which he had been brought up and had suffered such vicissitudes of fortune.

But from *The Dying Socrates* onwards the genius of the stage seemed to frown on him. He tried every argument and entreaty to get the part of Clavigo, but his rival prevailed. The blow struck him on his most vulnerable side, in the most sensitive part of his nature, and it embittered everything. No one who might have resigned the part of Clavigo to him would have lost so much as he did by not getting it. The trouble which darkened his life for the moment spread like a mist over all the rest of his existence: once more he sought solitude where he could, and began to neglect his outer man.

Meanwhile Philip Reiser was making pianos in his room, and took no part in all these humours. Anton Reiser had rarely come to him since his association with the actors, but now, when his desire was disappointed, he renewed his visits and indulged his melancholy in his company, without telling him the real reason of it, for he was not willing to confess even to himself that his depression arose from his not receiving the part of Clavigo: he wanted to persuade himself that it was a consequence of his view of human life in general. Meanwhile from the time that he failed to get the part of Clavigo his life in Hanover became distasteful, and he began to be restless. He felt that he must fulfil his long-cherished desire, wherever it might be; he must realize somewhere all that his persistent play-reading and long-continued devotion to the theatre had matured in his mind.

When *Clavigo* was rehearsed, he had hidden himself in one of the boxes, and while Iffland raged as Beaumarchais on the stage, Reiser lying on the floor of the box, raged against himself, and his madness went so far that he cut his face with some bits of glass that lay on the floor, and tore his hair. For at that moment the whole scene came before his eyes—the lighted theatre, the eyes of countless spectators fixed on him alone, and himself before all these searching glances expressing the inmost resources of his being, working on the feeling of every spectator through his own emotions; and now he was to be a cipher, lost amid the multitude as a mere spectator, as he now was, while a blockhead who played Clavigo attracted all the attention which should have been given to him, the man of deeper feeling. After all the previous experiences he had gone through the part of Clavigo had become as it were the object of his life; under the pressure of a multitude of circumstances his life had become completely dominated by his imagination, which now claimed to exercise its rights over it. The strain on his nerves was too great and he broke down.

When this dreadful rehearsal was over, Reiser found himself again quite alone, without a friend or any one to care for him: yet he wanted to confide his trouble to some one and went to Iffland, who from that moment became a closer friend than ever before, for he felt the same need which drove Reiser to him. Iffland's imagination too was strained to the utmost and the attraction of the Stage had become overpowering; he wanted some one to whom he could confide his desires and his distress.

His father and elder brother had feared with good reason that his leaning toward the Stage might be encouraged and become irresistible through the applause that his acting had won, and they had therefore forbidden him to take any further part in the dramatic performances: he made all kinds of objections and was at that moment engaged in negotiations with his father. He confided to Reiser his resolve to devote himself to the Stage, as he had earlier talked to him of his resolve to become a village preacher.

The parts which Iffland had played were the Deserter in *The Deserter from Filial Love* and the Jew in *The Diamond*, which was played as an after-piece to *The Deserter*. He had played the Jew in so masterly a manner that he afterwards made his début in that part before Eckhof and so began his career on the stage. As he had shown his talent for comedy in the Jew, he showed what he could do in tragedy as Beaumarchais, and in this part his acting was so moving that one seemed to see and hear Brockmann himself; and now the pleasure of appearing publicly in this part was to be thwarted. He compelled Reiser to spend the night with him and they lost themselves in entrancing dreams of the blessedness enjoyed by the acting profession, until they both fell asleep.

They were now almost inseparable, and were together day and night. One warm but dull morning as they were walking outside the Gate, Iffland said it would be good weather for running away. The weather seemed just suited for travel: the sky lay close over the earth, all objects seemed obscure, as if forcing attention solely on the road to be traversed. Both were so much moved by the idea that they very nearly acted on it, but Iffland wanted to act his Beaumarchais again in Hanover if possible, so they returned to the city. Though Iffland begged hard for Reiser he could not get him the part of Clavigo. Instead, the man who played Clavigo resigned to him the part of the Prince in *The Page* and in *The Punctual Man* that of Master Blasius. Reiser was melancholy because he was not to play Clavigo, and Iffland that he was not to play any more, but both tried to persuade themselves that they were discontented with life, and one night loaded two pistols, with which they whiled away nearly a whole night, declaiming 'To be or not to be'. Indeed Reiser's disgust with life went so far that he did not stir when Iffland pointed the loaded pistol at him and put his finger on the trigger, while Reiser did the same to him.

But next day he went to see Philip Reiser, and had a more serious scene. He had had a sleepless night, his hollow eyes were heavy and stupid, discontent sat on his brow, his will-power had gone. He said 'Good-day!' to Philip Reiser and then stood like a block. Philip Reiser who had often seen him demoralized but never so much as this, and who now began to fear that it was all over with him, seriously offered to shoot him sooner than see him become, as he was doing, an abandoned and wicked person. Philip Reiser's ideas were as romantic and extravagant as Anton's, and he was not to be trifled with. Anton Reiser then declined the offer and assured him that he would recover from his present demoralized condition.

Meantime his position began to be more precarious than ever. The expenses entailed by his taking part in the production of the play, which far exceeded his income, and his neglect of the lessons he was giving plunged him deeper and deeper in debt and he soon began to feel the want of the barest necessaries of life, as he had not learnt the art of living on credit. The dresses he had to provide for the part of the prince in *The Page* cost more than all his usual outgoings for a month, and yet even so he did not achieve his aim, which was to appear in a striking tragic part, which had always been his ambition.

Of the three pieces acted in one evening *Clavigo* was the first, *The Punctual Man* the second, and *The Page* came last. While *Clavigo* was being acted Reiser was in the dressing-room close to the stage and did his best to dull his senses and stop his ears. Every sound he heard from the stage was a stab in his heart: for the finest palace that his imagination had built in years of work was now shattered and he had to look on without being able to interfere in the least. He tried to console himself with the two parts he had still to play, and to fix his attention on them but it was in vain. While the part of Clavigo was actually being played by another before such a throng of spectators he felt like a man who sees all his possessions burning in the flames without hope of rescue. Up till the last day he had hoped to obtain this part, cost what it might, but now it was all over.

And when all was over and *Clavigo* played to the end, he felt somewhat easier: but a sting was still left in his breast. His playing of Master Blasius, in *The Punctual Man*, in which Iffland played the title part, was generally applauded, but this was not the applause he wanted. He wanted, not to stir men to laughter, but to move their deepest feelings. The prince in *The Page* was a fine character, but all too gentle, and in one sense the whole performance went wrong. For when *Clavigo* and *The Punctual Man* were over, most of the audience went away, as it was very late, and barely a third remained to see *The Page*. This and the torturing thought of Clavigo which he could not suppress, made him act the prince very carelessly and with far less success than he might have done, and so when all was over he went home sad and discontented. But all the time he was thinking how to satisfy his desire some day and appear in a violent and moving part, cost what it might. That this was denied him on the first occasion only made his desire the stronger: and how could he have surer hope of fulfilling his wish than by making acting, which he loved with all his heart, his main business in life? The thought, then, of devoting himself to the theatre, instead of being repressed, acquired still greater hold over him. But as every one tries to find the most urgent motives for doing what he wishes, in order as it were to justify his behaviour in his own eyes, Reiser tried to persuade himself that the payment of the petty debts he had been led to incur was so impossible and the exposure of them so disagreeable that he thought he must leave Hanover for this reason alone. But his real motives were, the irresistible impulse to change his condition, and the desire to make a public appearance in some way or other as soon as possible, in order to win fame and applause. For this purpose the Stage was bound to seem the obvious means, as there it is not counted for vanity when a man wishes to display himself to advantage as often as possible, but the hunger for applause is so to say privileged.

Meanwhile his petty debts began to harass him, and he suffered besides several humiliations which made him feel further stay in Hanover distasteful. One of them consisted in this, that a young nobleman, whom he was teaching, and with whom he used often to have some conversation in his room after the lesson, took leave of him without waiting for Reiser himself to take leave. Very likely he really thought that Reiser was on the point of going and so anticipated his farewell a little, but his action struck Reiser as so strange and shocking that it completely upset him, so that when he left the house he stood still for a while and let his arms fall. This premature 'I have the honour to take leave of you' was suddenly associated in his mind with the 'stupid boy!' of the inspector at the training-school, the 'I don't mean you' of the merchant, the 'par nobile fratrum' of the VIth Form, and 'what stupidity!' of the Rector. He felt himself for some moments a nonentity, all his resources were paralysed. The thought of having been *de trop* even for a minute weighed on him like a mountain; he would have liked to rid himself at that moment of an existence which was so burdensome to an outsider.

He went out of the City-Gate to the grave-yard, where the son of Pastor Marquard was buried, and wept the bitterest tears of depression and discontent at his grave. He saw everything now in a sad and melancholy light; the whole future looked gloomy: he would fain have mingled with the dust under his feet, and all this only because of this premature farewell. The words left a sting which he tried in vain to get rid of, though he did not confess this to himself but tried to explain his depression and discontent by general considerations on the emptiness of human life and the vanity of things. It is true that these thoughts found a place, but they would only have occupied his intellect and not moved his feelings but for that controlling idea. At bottom it was the feeling of humanity oppressed by social conditions which laid hold of him and made life hateful. Necessity made him teach a young nobleman, who paid him for it and when the lesson was over could politely show him the door when he chose. What crime had he committed before birth, that he had not become a person, about whom a number of other men were bound to be attentive and concerned? Why was he assigned the part of the worker and another of the paymaster? If his circumstances had made him happy and content, he would have seen purpose and order everywhere; now all seemed contradiction, disorder, and confusion.

As he went home he was dunned by one of his creditors and as he walked gloomily along with bowed head he heard one youth say to another 'There goes Master Blasius!' This so enraged him that he boxed the youth's ears in the street; and the youth shouted abuse after him till he reached his lodging.

From that day forward the sight of the streets of Hanover was a torment to Reiser, and he especially loathed the street where the young man had shouted after him; he avoided going through it, when he could, and when he was obliged to go he felt as if the houses would fall on him. Wherever he went he fancied he heard the jeering mob or an impatient creditor.

These humiliations had followed one another so closely that he was unable to struggle out of the sense of oppression, which made his place of residence henceforward hateful to him. The thought of leaving Hanover and trying his fortune in the wide world was henceforward a fixed resolve, but he confided it only to Philip Reiser. The latter was at that time very much occupied with his own affairs, being engaged in a love romance again, so that he gave all his mind to pleasing his lady love. Anton Reiser's fortunes then interested him less than they would have done at another time. Though Anton was perhaps about to leave Hanover for ever in a few days, his friend talked to him of all the details of his love-affair, as though Anton could await its issue. This vexed him at times but Philip Reiser was his closest confidant and he had no one else to whom he could unbosom himself.

As he was to seek his fortune in the wide world and had to choose some place in the wide world as the goal of his wanderings, he chose Weimar, where at that time the Seiler Company, now under the direction of Eckhof, was said to be. It was here that he wished to try to carry into action his resolve to go on the Stage. While he was occupied with these thoughts, he suffered one more humiliation, which confirmed him in his resolve. One afternoon he was walking with a number of his companions, who belonged to the dramatic society, in a public garden outside the city. It may be that his thoughts gave him a strange distracted appearance which marked him out from his companions; and before he was aware of it, his companions all at once begun to make fun of him again so that he found it impossible to utter a word in answer to all they said. As their wit had free play there was no end to their jokes, and as several officers were near by, listening to the conversation, Reiser could bear it no longer: he slipped from the table, paid his reckoning and rushed off as quickly as he could, and as soon as he was alone, broke out into loud curses against himself and his fate. He ridiculed himself, because he thought himself born for ridicule and scorn.

How was it that he seemed as it were branded on the forehead for the scorn of the world? What was there ridiculous in him, which nothing could get rid of? which now, even when his schoolfellows respected him, exposed him to their laughter? The inexcusable behaviour of his parents in repressing him as a child had so completely crippled his nature that he had never yet recovered his spirit. It had become impossible for him to regard any one as his equal. Every one seemed to him in some way more important and significant in the world than himself, and so demonstrations of friendship seemed condescension. As he thought he might be despised he was despised, and he often took for contempt what any one with more self-respect would never have taken for it. That seems to be how character works on character; when a character meets with no character to resist it, it encroaches and destroys like a river when the dam gives way. The more self-assertive nature irresistibly overwhelms the less assertive by mockery, despising or stamping it as ridiculous. To be made ridiculous is a kind of annihilation, and to make a man ridiculous is a kind of murder of self-confidence. On the other hand to be hated by all is, in comparison, a thing to desire. Thus universal hatred would not destroy self-reliance, but give it new strength to live for centuries and gnash defiance at the world that hates. But to have no friend 'and not even to have an enemy' is the true hell, which sums up in itself all the tortures which the sense of nonentity inflicts on a thinking being. This torture Reiser felt whenever for want of self-respect he found himself a fit object of ridicule and scorn: his only pleasure then was in solitude, to break out into scornful laughter against himself, as if to complete what others had begun.

> If those around more perfect men and stronger
> Destroy me by their gibes each day and hour,
> Why listen then to pity any longer,
> And weeping basely cower ?

When he escaped from the scornful circle of his schoolfellows, he wandered about in the lonely country, and went farther and farther from the city, but without any definite aim. He went across country till it was dark, then struck a broad road, leading to a village which he saw in front of him. The sky grew overcast and threatened rain, ravens began to croak and two flying overhead seemed to bear him company, till he came to the small narrow churchyard of the village, enclosed by irregularly heaped stones, which formed a sort of wall. The church had a tiny spire, roofed with shingle and had only a tiny window in each of its thick walls, through which the light came slanting in. The door was half buried in the earth and so low that it looked as if you could only get in by stooping. The church was small and unpretending and the churchyard was equally tiny, with the mounds of its graves crowded together and overgrown with tall nettles. The horizon was dark; in the dim twilight the sky seemed to hang close overhead, and one's sight was confined to the small space visible around. The tiny village and church and churchyard made a strange impression on Reiser. The end of all things seemed to come to a point here: the close and narrow coffin was the conclusion, with nothing beyond. The coffin-lid was the dividing wall which prevented each mortal's further vision. The picture filled Reiser with loathing: the thought of this conclusion, this cessation into narrowness growing ever more narrow, with nothing behind or beyond it, drove him with fearful force from this tiny churchyard and chased him through the dark night, as if he were fain to escape the coffin which threatened to confine him. The village and its churchyard were an object of terror so long as he saw them behind him. A strange horror had come on him in the churchyard: the desire he had often felt, seemed to be granted, the grave seemed to claim its prey and to open its abyss behind him as he fled. Not till he reached another village was he at peace again.

What made the thought of death so terrible to

him in the churchyard was the idea of littleness, which, dominating all else, gave him a fearful sense of void which was at last unbearable. Littleness borders on passing away and annihilation. It is the idea of littleness which produces pain, a sense of void and sadness: the grave is the narrow house, the coffin is a dwelling, silent, cool, and small. Littleness gives a sense of void, and this causes sadness. Sadness is the beginning of annihilation, infinite emptiness is annihilation. Reiser in the tiny churchyard felt the terrors of annihilation. The transition from being to not-being presented itself so vividly and with such force and certainty, that his whole existence hung by a thread, which threatened to break at any moment.

All at once all sense of weariness with life disappeared: he tried to fill his mind again with a wealth of ideas, to save himself as it were from total nothingness, and as he chanced upon the high road to Nienburg, where his parents lived, and the whole region was familiar, he resolved to walk on through the night and surprise his parents again with an unexpected visit. He was already four miles from Hanover and had therefore about twenty more to go.

But the thought that he could not confide his resolve to his parents and would have to take leave of them with a heavy heart, made him abandon this plan, especially as it began to rain heavily towards midnight. He turned then once more towards the city, walking across country through the corn in the rain and dark. It was a warm summer night, and on this misanthropic evening walk the rain and darkness were most welcome companions: he had a sense of largeness and freedom, with Nature all about him. Nothing oppressed or confined him; here he was at home in every spot, when he chose to lie down and was exposed to no mortal eye. At last he felt it happiness to walk at random through the high corn, unfettered, with no goal to which he was bound to aim his steps. In this peace of midnight he felt as free as the deer in the forest, the wide earth was his bed, all Nature his domain.

So he walked on through the night, till day dawned, and when he was able gradually to distinguish objects again, he thought he was still about two miles from Hanover, but all at once found himself close by a large graveyard wall, which he had never noticed there before. He summoned all his powers of mind, and tried to find his bearings, but in vain, he could not bring this long graveyard wall into relation with other objects, it remained a phantom, which really made him doubt whether he was awake or dreaming. He rubbed his eyes, the long wall was there still, and besides, his strange night walk and the absence of the usual pause by which the impressions of day and night are normally separated, had confused his imagination. He actually began to fear for his reason, and perhaps was really on the border of madness, when he once more saw the four towers of Hanover again through the mist and knew where he was. The morning twilight had deceived him and made him take this region close to the city for another two miles away which was very like it. The large graveyard with a little chapel in the middle was the regular graveyard close to Hanover and Reiser at once recognized all the surroundings. He woke as from a dream.

If there is anything which can bring one near to distraction, it is perhaps our ideas of space and time more than anything, for all our other ideas are bound to pivot on them. This day did not seem a new day to Reiser because the operations of his perceptive faculty had not been interrupted between that and the preceding day. He went into the market, it was early morning, and the streets were silent as death. The house, the room where he lived, everything seemed strange and peculiar. His night walk had produced a change in his whole system of thought: he no longer felt at home in his lodging, and his ideas of place wavered to and fro in his brain. He was in a dream all day long, yet the memory of his walk was agreeable. The croaking of the two ravens flying over his head, the tiny churchyard, the cornfields he walked through, were all focused in one picture by his imagination and grouped themselves dimly as a beautiful night-piece, which often afterwards in lonely hours delighted his fancy.

But henceforward his stay in Hanover was if possible more distasteful, and the spirit of wandering had mastered him, as it had several of the young men who had taken part in the acting. One called Timaeus, who before was a very quiet, industrious and regular person, told Reiser in confidence of his discontent with the profession of theology, for which he was destined, and discussed with him the blessings of the actors' profession, declaiming against the unjust prejudices which still depreciated this honourable calling.

This conversation took place on a walk to a little village outside Hanover, and they were so engrossed in their conversation that they were overtaken by night and were obliged to stay in the village. This unusual stay in a strange place put more romantic ideas in their heads; they felt as if they were already on an adventure, sharing good and bad fortune. The bold purpose of these two adventurers, to rise above the prejudices of the world and follow their inclinations, or as they called it their vocation, was not unfulfilled. Reiser made the first move, and Timaeus soon followed him, but was happily brought back again.

Meanwhile Reiser, before he carried out his purpose, took one more night walk with Iffland, who came with another of the acting company to see him at eleven and invited him to walk to Deister, a mountain twelve miles from Hanover. Reiser, to whom such night walks began to be habitual, at once agreed: it was a warm moonlit summer's night. The conversation on the way was all poetical, sometimes sincere, sometimes affected, as it chanced. As they passed through a village the fresh scent of hay met them. Indeed this walk was one of the pleasantest that can be imagined, so that it seemed designed by chance to excite Reiser's imagination still farther and make the passion for wandering that had been kindled in him completely overmaster his reason.

Before day-break the three adventurers reached a village which lay close to the foot of the mountain; there they went to an inn and slept some hours.

But when they got up next morning all the beautiful pictures of the magic lantern had vanished; bald reality with all its inevitable disagreeables confronted them again. They sat facing one another for an hour and yawned. If anything could have cured Reiser of his fancy, it would have been this morning after such a night. They now did not care to climb the mountain, they felt flat and tired, they took the nearest way back to Hanover. They found it rather oppressive because of the burning sun, but they began to extemporize rhymes by the way, and so somewhat relieved the monotony of the walk.

Reiser nevertheless remained fully determined to travel, whatever his fortune might be; and he preferred anything that might happen to him to the monotony and to the half and half happiness of life in Hanover. All his thoughts ranged wide afield. Besides he saw no means of paying his debts, without confiding them again to Herr Marquard, whose friendship and respect he felt sure he would then lose. The various humiliations too that he had recently had to bear were still fresh in his memory and made him hate the neighbourhood of Hanover and his stay there.

He managed to represent his position to his only confidant, Philip Reiser, as so miserable that he at last approved of his decision to leave Hanover, and gave him directions how to go, having himself walked from Erfurt to Hanover. From Erfurt Reiser intended to go to Weimar, in order to be received as a member of the Seiler or rather the Eckhof company of actors. And, if he succeeded, he meant from Weimar to pay his debts in Hanover and try to recover his good name, by a resurrection, so to speak, in Weimar after his civil death in Hanover. This last was one of the pleasantest ideas that he entertained. He brought Philip Reiser his few books and papers and gave them him to take care of: he had pawned some of his clothes to meet the expense of the play, and the rest of his things he gave to his landlord to cover his rent. He told him that his father had fallen very ill and that he was going away for a week to see him, if any one should ask after him.

And now all was so far in order except the ready money for undertaking a journey of more than a hundred and sixty miles. This consisted, after all his efforts to scrape money together, of a single ducat, with which he had the courage to start on his journey, though Philip Reiser represented to him the recklessness of his enterprise. But Philip could give him no help, for the very good reason that he generally had no money and just now had none at all.

Anton Reiser then could literally say that he carried with him all he had. The good suit, in which he had given the address on the Queen's birthday, together with an overcoat, formed his entire wardrobe: he wore a gilt dress-sword by his side and shoes and silk stockings. A clean dress shirt, with an extra pair of silk stockings, a duodecimo copy of Homer's *Odyssey* with the Latin version, and the Latin notice of the declamation on the Queen's birthday, with his name in print—were all he carried in his bag.

It was on a Sunday in the middle of winter that

he spent the morning with Philip Reiser making himself ready for his journey, in order to begin his travels in the afternoon, and as the days were beginning to lengthen, to walk twelve miles to the nearest town on his tour. It was a bright sunny day: people were walking in the streets in their Sunday best and some of them outside the City Gates, to return to their homes in the evening. On this day Reiser was to leave Hanover for ever; it gave him a strange feeling, which was neither pain nor sorrow, but a kind of stupor. He shed no tears on leaving, and was as cold and unmoved as if he had travelled through a strange town, on which he must now turn his back in order to go on farther. Even his farewell to Philip Reiser was cold rather than affectionate. Philip Reiser was very busy with a new cockade on his hat, and in the last hour that they spent together talked of the love-affair that he was engaged in, as if Reiser could have awaited its development. In a word the whole conversation was as if they would meet again the next day and all would go on as before. But what vexed Anton Reiser most of all was the thought that his friend could be so completely taken up at the moment of farewell with the cockade on his hat. The cockade long after hovered before his eyes and embittered his memory whenever he thought of it. The parting from Hanover and his only friend was made much easier by this incident. Nevertheless Philip Reiser meant well by him: it was only that on this occasion petty vanity and the infatuation of a lover got the better of his friendly sympathy, and the cockade, which would perhaps please his fair lady, had become very important in his eyes, though Anton Reiser took no interest in it.

'So cold, so unmoved to knock at the brazen gate of death.'

These words from *The Sorrows of Werther* had run in Anton Reiser's head all the morning, and when Philip Reiser was about to open the great gate, which was the very point where they parted (for to avoid rousing suspicion that he knew Anton Reiser was going away he was purposely not to accompany him) he paused inside for a moment, looked fixedly at Philip Reiser, and at that moment he felt as if he were knocking 'so cold and unmoved at the brazen gate of death'. He gave his hand to Philip Reiser, who could not say a word, drew the gate to, and hastened round the nearest corner, that the friend from whom he had now parted might not gaze after him. Then he crossed the rampart quickly to St. Giles's Gate and took another look sideways at his former home in the Rector's house, which he could see from the rampart. It was two o'clock in the afternoon and the bell was ringing for church. He quickened his steps as he came nearer the Gate; he felt again as if the grave were opening wide behind him. But when he had left behind him the town, with its ramparts and their green vegetation, and as he looked back on the houses crowded closer and closer together, his heart felt lighter and lighter, until at last the four towers, which hitherto had marked the scene of all his troubles and vexations, disappeared from view

IV

This Fourth Part of Anton Reiser's biography deals, like the earlier Parts, with the important question, how far a young man is capable of choosing his own vocation.

It contains a faithful description of the various self-deceptions into which a man without experience fell through mistaking his vocation for poetry and the stage.

This Part also contains some hints which may have use and significance for teachers as well as for young people, who have the character to examine themselves and see what are the signs which distinguish a true vocation for art from a false one.

This narrative shows that a mistaken bent for art, based only on inclination without a true vocation, may become as powerful and produce the same phenomena, as are found in the true artistic genius, which is ready to endure everything and sacrifice everything to attain its end.

The earlier Parts of this story show clearly that Reiser's irresistible passion for the stage was simply a result of the circumstances of his life. From childhood up he found himself thrust out from the real world, and conceiving a bitter disgust for it lived more in his imaginations than in reality. Hence the stage as the true world of imagination was his natural refuge from all his difficulties and sufferings, he felt that here alone he could breathe freely, and move in his true element.

At the same time he had a certain sense of the real objects which surrounded him in the world, and did not wish entirely to give them up, because like other men he had a sense of life and existence. This led to a perpetual struggle within him. He was too serious to give himself up entirely to the suggestions of his fancy and be content with himself: on the other hand he had not the strength of character resolutely to pursue any concrete plan which conflicted with his fanciful imagination.

In him, as in countless others, there was a conflict between truth and illusion, dream and reality, and which was to prevail was undecided: this sufficiently explains the peculiar states of mind into which he fell.

Contradiction from within and without had so far been his whole life. The question is, how these contradictions are to be resolved.

1790.

PART IV

WHEN Reiser had lost sight of the four towers of Hanover, and went quickly on, he breathed more freely, his chest expanded, the whole world lay before him and a thousand prospects opened before him.

He thought of the thread of his previous life as cut short, he was released once for all from all embarrassments; for even had he gone to the University of Göttingen his fate would have pursued him there. All the contemporaries of his youthful days would still have been a weight upon him and would have crushed his spirit. As long as he was confined to that circle he could have no self-confidence; if his courage was to recover he must lose sight of those who, perhaps unintentionally, had embittered the days of his youth.

He had now completely left this circle. The scene of his sufferings, the world in which he had lived through his young experience, lay behind him: every step took him farther from it, and in his new condition he might walk for a week without being missed. He found inexpressible pleasure in the thought that no one but Philip Reiser knew about him or where he was to be found, that even this one friend had taken very little notice of his going, and that now he was outside all relations and completely indifferent to those he came among. If any condition could foreshadow a man's complete departure from life it was this.

When the heat of the day grew less, the sun sank and the shadows of the trees lengthened he quickened his steps, and covered the twelve miles to Hildesheim the same afternoon as if he were taking a walk, as indeed he regarded it, for in Hildesheim he was as much at home as in Hanover.

When he came to the town Gate he shook the dust off his feet, put his hair in order, took a switch in his hand and played with it as he went and so sauntered slowly over the bridge, stopping now and then as though he were waiting for some one or looking out for something, and as he was wearing silk stockings, no one took him for a traveller, who was about to go a hundred and sixty miles on foot. No sentry challenged him and he strolled through the Gates with the inhabitants of the town who were returning from their walks, and he found it a very pleasant and tranquillizing thought that these people did not regard him as a stranger, that no one looked round at him, but that he was counted as one of them, though he did not really belong to them. As none among them all knew him or troubled about him he ceased to compare himself with any one, and had, so to speak, parted with himself. His individuality, which had so often vexed and oppressed him, ceased to trouble him, and he felt that he would have liked to wander thus unknown and unseen among men all his life.

When he looked for an inn near the Gate, the street seemed familiar and he remembered the time when he had come here four years before with the Rector, with whom he was then living, on Corpus Christi day, and the uncomfortable position in which he found himself then, because he was not excluded from the company with whom he went, and yet was not one of them. He felt as though a stone had been lifted from his heart, when he thought that all this was completely in the past.

When he entered the inn he was received and entertained in accordance with his dress, and he had not the courage to refuse, but let them get him some supper, assign him a bed, and give him coffee next morning. He drank his coffee quietly, over his Homer, when he suddenly awoke to the thought that his ready money, a single ducat, had not only to carry him a journey of a hundred and sixty miles, but to provide him with something over when he arrived.

He quickly paid his reckoning, which made him poorer by no less than a sixth of his whole estate, asked for the road to Seesen and left the gate of Hildesheim with anxious thoughts and a heavy heart. It was still early in the day, the road led him through a pleasant country, of mingled field and forest, and the song of the birds welcomed him as the morning sun shone on the green tops of the trees. As he walked quickly on, he felt his spirits grow lighter, cheerful thoughts, charming prospects and brave hopes gradually rose in his heart, and he formed a resolve, which at once set him above all cares and made him rich and independent on his whole expedition. He had only to limit his food to bread and beer, sleep on straw and never spend the night in a town, and he could reduce the daily cost of his living to a few pence. In this way he could take a month on the way and still have something in his purse at the end. As soon as he had made this resolve, which he carried out steadily from that day forward, he felt as free and happy as a king : this voluntary giving up of all comforts and limiting himself to the barest necessaries gave him a feeling like nothing else. He felt almost like a being removed above all earthly cares, and for this reason lived undisturbed in his world of ideas and fancies, so that this period, in spite of apparent discomfort, was one of the happiest dreams of his life.

But another thought imperceptibly passed into his mind, linking his present life with his former life and so preventing it from becoming quite a dream. He thought how fine it would be, if after some years he could come to life again in the memory of those men to whom he had as it were died, if he could appear to them in a nobler form, so that the dull days of his youth would disappear in the dawn of a better day. This idea remained with him, and lay behind all his thoughts and he could not have given it up for anything ; all his other dreams and fancies hung on it, and it gave them their chief charm. The thought that he would never again see those who had known him hitherto, would have taken all interest out of his life and robbed him of his dearest hopes.

When midday came he went into a common village inn, where money would not have bought him anything but bread and beer, and therefore there was no question of his being offered better entertainment and having to refuse it. He was immensely delighted to get for a halfpenny a piece of black bread large enough to stay his hunger for the whole day. He soaked some of it in beer and so had his first midday meal under his own strict laws, which he observed to the journey's end.

Then he made what haste he could to get out of the stuffy inn-parlour into the open, where he sat beneath a shady tree, reading Homer's *Odyssey* for his recreation. Whether this reading of Homer was suggested by *The Sorrows of Werther* or not, it was certainly no affectation with Reiser ; it gave him real and pure pleasure, for no book suited his condition so well as this, which in every line depicts the man of wanderings who has seen many men, cities, and manners, and at last after long years arrives home again and finds once more the same people he had left there, whom he never thought to see again.

The way went up and down hill ; the heat was pretty severe, and Reiser quenched his thirst whenever he came to a clear brook, where he could drink for nothing. In the village where he stayed the first night, the parlour was full of peasants, who made a great noise, so that he could not read ; he buried himself in his thoughts, and a very old woman who sat in the arm-chair nodding her head, attracted his whole attention. She had been born there, brought up there, grown old there, and had always had before her eyes the walls of the parlour, the great stove, the tables and benches. He thought himself by degrees into the thoughts and ideas of this old woman so completely that he forgot himself and fell into a kind of waking dream, as if he were bound to stay there and could not move. Such a dream was very natural in the sudden change that had come over his circumstances. When he collected his thoughts he felt the pleasure of variety, expansion, and unlimited freedom all the more: his fetters seemed to fall from him, and the old woman with the nodding head again became indifferent to him.

This way of thinking himself into the ideas of other people and so forgetting himself, stuck to him from childhood; one of his childish wishes was that he might be able for a moment to look out of the eyes of another person and know how things about him looked to him.

As he lay down on the straw for the first time his thoughts ranged far and wide; he laid his sword beside him and covered himself with his clothes. But his thoughts gave him no rest, the future grew brighter and more dazzling before his eyes. The theatre lamps were lighted, the curtain had risen, and all was full of expectation, the critical moment had come. The consequence was that no sleep visited his eyes till after midnight and when he woke in the morning, the scene was in a moment completely changed: the empty parlour, the beer-mugs and the languor of fatigue. He had to pay for his delightful visions with dreadful discontent and ill-humour, which lasted a good hour. He lay with his head on the table and tried in vain to sleep again, till the cheering beams of the sun shining through the window waked him to life, and as soon as he had started on the road and left the stuffy inn-parlour his low spirits quickly disappeared, and the delightful play of ideas began again.

He thus lived as it were two lives, one in imagination and one in reality. The real remained beautiful and in harmony with the imaginary, except the inn-parlour, the clamour of the peasants and the straw; these would not fit the tune, the evening set too close a limit on the unbounded freedom of the day-time, for till the next morning he could have no surroundings but these. Certainly outward circumstances had a continual influence on his inward thoughts; his ideas generally expanded with his horizon, and every view into a new region brought with it a new outlook on life.

One day he had climbed painfully uphill, when all at once a broad plain lay before him and he saw in the distance a little town by a lake. This view at once revived all his thoughts and hopes. He could not turn his eyes from the distant water, which inspired him with fresh courage to go far afield. His way from Hildesheim went by the Salzdethfurth, Brockenem, and Seesen to Duderstadt, from which he meant to go by Mühlhausen to Erfurt and thence to Weimar, which was the goal of his desire, for there he expected to find the Eckhof Company of actors, and there his acting career was to begin.

And so as he went walking along he played in imagination all the parts which one day were to crown him with fame and applause and so reward his manifold sufferings. He thought that he could not fail, because he felt each part deeply and knew how to represent it perfectly in his own mind.

He could not see that all this was only his own thoughts and, that he had not the faculty of representing his feelings to others. He imagined that the strength with which he felt his part, must carry everything with it, and make him forget himself. He actually did forget himself as he went on and his imagination grew more and more excited, and at last in the open country when he thought himself alone he began to storm aloud with Beaumarchais and to rage with Guelfo. This character from Klinger's *Twins* had become a favourite part of his before he left Hanover, for he found in Guelfo his own self-derision, self-hatred, self-contempt, and passion for self-destruction, but combined with force, and Reiser delighted in the scene where Guelfo, after the murder of his brother, smashes the mirror in which he sees himself. All these overstrained horrors had bemused his brain, he staggered up hill and down dale in his intoxication, and found a boundless stage wherever he went.

Clavigo, who had cost him so many tears, he now found too cold and Beaumarchais took his place: then came Hamlet, Lear, Othello, who had not then been represented on any German stage; but he had read them aloud to his friend Philip Reiser in thrilling night sessions and had himself felt and played all these parts.

Poetry came in company with drama. His verse, he felt, flowed so gently and tunefully, his Muse was so modest yet so proud, that she was bound to win him the favour of all hearts. He did not quite know what sort of poem it was to be, but it was the most beautiful and harmonious he could imagine, because it was a faithful reproduction of his deepest feelings.

While his thoughts took this lyrical flight he was walking along a path near Seesen, which led him from the road across a meadow, where target-practice was going on, and this nearly put a sudden end to all his bright visions of the future, for a musket-ball whistled close past his head, while every one called to him to keep clear. He hurried through Seesen and walked quietly on, till he put up for the night in a little village.

On the second day of his walk Reiser crossed part of the Harz mountains, and early in the day saw on the right of the highway the walls of a ruined castle on a hill. He could not refrain from going up to it and there he ate the piece of black bread he had brought with him for breakfast, in the ruins of this ancient home of chivalry, and looked down on the highway through the forest. It gave him one of his happiest moments to think that as a wanderer he was taking his morning meal within these old ruined walls, and was thinking of the times when men still lived there, who looked down, as he was doing, on the highway through the forest. In his ears rang as it were a prophecy from those times—that those walls would one day stand desolate, the wanderer would rest there and remember the days of old. Here on the height his black bread was a banquet: he came down refreshed in spirit and went on his way rejoicing, leaving the higher regions of the Harz on the left.

Walking became now so easy that he felt the ground under him like a wave on which he rose and sank, and so was borne on from one horizon to another, himself keeping passive, as each new scene rose before his vision. The noonday visit to the disagreeable inn-parlour was soon over and once more he was in the open with Nature: but the visit was distasteful and he thought of avoiding it, as he chanced to go through a cornfield and thought of the disciples of Christ, eating ears of corn on the Sabbath. He made the experiment of plucking a handful of grain out of the ears, sucking the flour and spitting out the husk. But he found this way of feeding, though it served to pass the time, was no substitute for the inn. The pleasure of it consisted chiefly in the idea of it, which increased the sense of freedom and independence.

As he had completed a second day's journey, not far from Duderstadt he went into an inn in a little village, but found no one at home. It was just before twilight; the gate to the inn-yard was open and in the yard was an arbour with a table but neither chair nor bench. Reiser lay on the table to rest, and, as he could still see to read, he read the passage in the *Odyssey* of the cannibals, who destroy the ships of Ulysses in the quiet harbour and seize and devour his companions. Suddenly the host returned, and in the gathering darkness saw a man lying on the table in the arbour in his yard, reading a book. He first spoke rather roughly to Reiser, but when he rose and the host saw that he was well-dressed, he asked him at once whether he was a lawyer, the usual name in this neighbourhood for a student, because students of theology for the most part study in monasteries and are regarded as clergy. The host's wife had died and there was no one in the house besides himself. He had plenty of talk and Reiser took his supper, which consisted as usual of bread and beer, in his company. The man told him of many lawyers who had lodged with him, and Reiser informed him that he, too, was about to go to Erfurt, to study there.

All conversations of this sort, otherwise insignificant, took a poetic colour in Reiser's mind from the picture, which was hovering before his thoughts, of the Homeric wanderer, and even the untruths in his talk had something in harmony with his poetic prototype, by whose side Minerva stands and smiles approval of his well-devised lie. Reiser thought of his host not merely as the host of a village tavern, but as a person whom he had never known or seen and now met for an hour, sat at table with him and exchanged words with him. That which had become common and insignificant, because human institutions and connexions had turned attention from it, was now by the power of poetry restored to its rights, became human again and recovered its original dignity and worth.

The man was not prepared to spread some straw for a bed, as it was seldom that any one spent the night here, and Reiser slept in the hay-loft, which gave him an agreeable couch.

Early next morning he continued his journey, and his stay in this house alone with his host was one of his pleasantest memories.

That day his inner world of thought was very active. He had now come a considerable way towards his goal, and he began to be anxious what he would do, if his prospect of immediate success and applause failed, and if his schemes for a theatrical career should entirely break down. At once two opposite extremes presented themselves, to be a peasant or a soldier, and at once the poetic and theatrical aspect came in, for his ideas of peasant and soldier became embodied in a theatrical part, which he played in imagination.

As peasant he gradually expounded his higher ideas, and so to say made himself known; the peasants listened attentively to him, their manners grew gradually refined and he educated all about him. As soldier he gradually captured the sentiments of his comrades by delightful stories; the rough soldiers began to listen to his teaching, and developed a sense of nobler humanity, the guard-room became the lecture-hall of wisdom.

While he thought then that he had prepared himself for just the opposite of the stage he had again fallen completely into theatrical dreams and visions. But it was inexpressibly pleasant to him to think of becoming a peasant or soldier because he thought that in such a position he would seem much less than he really was. While he was busy with these thoughts he went through the town of Worbis, where some Franciscans from the monastery met him and gave him a friendly greeting. As he went past the monastery he heard the singing of the monks inside, who had now left the world, lived without cares, plans, or prospect, and were all they wished to be. This made some impression on him, but not nearly such a strong one as the first sight of a Carthusian monastery did later, where the inmates were completely parted from the world by their walls and never set foot again on the scene they had once left. But the wandering Franciscan friars made the idea of retirement seem petty and flat, their quick walk did not accord with the dress of the order and the whole lacked poetic dignity.

The High-German speech of the people in these regions sounded pleasant in Reiser's ears, because it brought home to him more vividly his departure from the Low-German country. That day, too, he had had fine weather, and in the evening he entered a village called Orschla, intending to go on from there next morning to the imperial town of Mühlhausen. The village is Catholic, and, when he came to the inn, a crowd of people stood before the door, among whom was the schoolmaster, who addressed him with the words *Esne literatus?* 'Are you a scholar?' Reiser said 'yes' in Latin, and to the question whither he was going he replied 'to Erfurt, to study theology', for this seemed to him the safest answer. Meanwhile the peasants stood round, listening to their schoolmaster talking Latin to the foreign student. The schoolmaster's son too came, who had studied at Hildesheim and was now assistant to his father. Reiser then entered the inn-parlour and in further proof that he was a scholar laid his Homer on the table, which the schoolmaster at once recognized and told the peasants in German that it was Homer. But he continued to talk Latin to Reiser, as well as he could, not without amusing incidents. As he talked a good deal of his scholarly teaching Reiser asked him whether he read the Church

Fathers with his pupils. At first he was rather embarrassed but then collected himself and said *alternatim* (in their turn).

He then took leave of Reiser, who meant to go away early next morning, warning him to beware of the Imperial and Prussian recruiting-officers in those regions, and not to be intimidated by any threats if they said they would take him by force.

Reiser lay down quietly to sleep on his straw, but next morning it rained so heavily that in the clothes he wore and his shoes and silk stockings he could not go out of doors, much less continue his journey, especially as the soil is clayey here, which makes walking on the road in wet weather extraordinarily heavy. This was something that Reiser had not reckoned on; he had trusted too much to the weather at this season and was not prepared for this, being unprovided with boots or other equipment for rainy weather and he had nothing to wear beyond his ordinary dress. There was nothing to be done but wait till the sky should clear and the earth dry again; but this day and the next it rained steadily. Quite early an Imperial non-commissioned officer, who was recruiting in this place, came into the inn-parlour and sat down familiarly at the table by Reiser with his pot of beer and began to talk to him at large of the soldier's life, and presently became more pressing and finally assured him that the Prussian and Imperial recruiting-officers would not let him pass Mühlhausen, and therefore he might prefer to enlist at once and get seven gulden bounty from him. So it looked as if the soldier of Reiser's imagination might be a reality before he expected.

When the soldiers had gone the schoolmaster came in again, bade Reiser good morning, and privately warned him to beware of the recruiting-officer, though he himself did not consider the soldier's life such a bad one, as his son had been two years in the service of Mainz; he said that without a passport it would be difficult for any one to get through. Reiser assured him that he had all necessary credentials. This consisted of the Latin poster of the School speech day in Hanover, when he gave an address on the birthday of the Queen of England, and his name was printed as Reiserus, not Reiser: there was also the printed prologue to *The Deserter from Filial Love*, with his name as author, together with a poem on the induction of a teacher, where his name appeared in print with the other members of the VIth Form. He was reluctant at first to show these documents, until he was hard pressed and given to understand that he was regarded as a vagrant. Whereupon he produced his printed papers, which made a better impression than he expected at first, because he did not produce them all at once. First he unfolded the big poster in Latin and pointed to his name Reiserus. Here again the schoolmaster had the opportunity of showing his proficiency in Latin, by translating the poster into German; so Reiser had gained much in his eyes. Next he brought out the prologue, and pointed out his name printed in German to the bystanders; this was all in keeping, and the schoolmaster said he had acted in a play at the Jesuit School and his name had been printed. Finally Reiser showed the poem, where again his name appeared printed in the list of his schoolfellows. Thus all doubt of his identity completely disappeared as he could show his name repeatedly printed in different ways. Even the recruiting-officer was silenced and seemed to view Reiser with some respect.

This gave him rest: he ordered pen and paper and began to translate one of the Homeric hymns into German; in the evening the schoolmaster returned and talked to him, and so the day passed and Reiser went to sleep in peace. But when he woke next morning and saw the sky as dull as the day before and heard the rain beating on the window, his courage began to sink. He left his bed of straw and sat sadly at the table; he could not get on with the Homeric hymn, he went to the window to see if there was any chance of the sky clearing, when the soldier came in again to pay his morning visit. As Reiser dressed and plaited his hair in a cue, the man of war again began to pay him compliments on his height and the length of his hair and to say what a pity it was he would not join the Army. The schoolmaster joined in: they had reflected since the day before that the documents exhibited had no seal, and laid stress on the argument that he would not get past the recruiting-officers and therefore he had better enlist with the man who had the first claim to him. This lasted through the whole day, which was one of the saddest for Reiser, who could not go forward till towards evening it cleared and at once his courage revived. He summoned all his powers of persuasion to convince his hearers by most urgent representations that it was his fixed purpose to study at Erfurt and that nothing could deter him, so that at last they seemed to believe him. The schoolmaster told him in Latin that if he walked towards Mühlhausen early next morning he would meet the landlord of this inn, who also spoke Latin, and had gone away to fetch his people (*suos*), while the soldier, to his horror, promised to accompany him next morning and take him through a wood on to the road. Next morning the soldier was there to bear him company, and wanted to pay Reiser's reckoning, but this he stubbornly refused.

They walked from the village of Orschla towards Hähnichen and on to a rising ground: the soldier was silent, and as they went through a wood Reiser expected every moment the crisis of his fate, which he felt he could not escape. All at once the soldier halted and made quite a moving speech to Reiser, begging him to consider whether he really was confident of not falling into the hands of other recruiting-sergeants, for the one thing which would vex him would be if he heard that Reiser had after all become a soldier and so had in a way deceived him; if however he was really resolved to be a student and not a soldier, he wished him luck in his enterprise and a good journey.

With that he left him, but Reiser was not confident until he had gone a good distance without anything remarkable meeting him except a humpback driving two pigs, who addressed him in Latin as he took him for a student. This was the landlord from Orschla, who the schoolmaster had told him was fetching his folk (*suos*) and who had fetched his pigs (*sues*) whom the schoolmaster of

Orschla had declined in the second declension and so exalted them into his folk (*suos*)!

As soon as Reiser found himself in the open again and was aware that no one had lain in wait for him, he felt fortunate beyond his hopes, but the danger he had escaped made him think anxiously about the future as he went along. He reflected that it made a good impression on every one when he said that he meant to go and study at the University, and indeed the idea of it was not uncongenial, but this only lasted until the wings and the footlights once more took hold of his imagination, when every other prospect had to give way. He walked till towards midday with some discomfort, as the ground was not yet dry, and moreover to his horror his shoes began to suffer, and in his present circumstances they were an irreplaceable part of his person. He felt the loss that threatened him at every step, and about noon the sky was again overcast, and the clouds prophesied more rain; presently rain began and interrupted Reiser's journey for the second time.

Luckily he soon reached a gamekeeper's cottage, standing in a field surrounded by woodland, he went in with confidence and was politely welcomed and entertained. The people in this lonely dwelling received him in such a friendly way that it was as though they had prepared for him beforehand. It was as if they took it for granted that in such weather a wayfarer must be taken in. The rain never ceased all day and they pressed him to stay the night. When they pressed him to take supper Reiser declined, because he had not enough money to pay for it, as he had a long journey before him and had to limit himself; whereupon the keeper half angrily drew him to the table. Reiser felt it a wonderful experience to have such a welcome from unknown people. He felt quite at home; he was given a good bed at night, the first time on his journey that he was offered it. Next morning he was waked for breakfast and pressed to stay the whole day, as it was still raining. The man went into the forest, and bade Reiser occupy himself in the meantime with his library. The library consisted of a great collection of calendars, funeral discourses, the story of a Göttingen student, and an Erfurt weekly, *Townsman and Peasant*, in which the peasant spoke Thuringian, and the townsman answered him in high German. Reiser found plenty of amusement in these things, and from time to time let his thoughts range freely, for his kind host and hostess were people of few words and not in the least inquisitive; they never asked him whither he was going or whence he came, so that there was nothing to disturb his thoughts. This hospitable room with the little window, which gave a wide view over the field to the woodland, amid the pouring rain outside, remained one of the pleasantest pictures in Reiser's memory.

On the third morning the sky cleared. When Reiser took leave of his benefactors they tried to spare his thanks, by accepting a mere trifle in money for their three days' entertainment, and when he went away did not even ask his name.

The thought of these people gave Reiser many a pleasant hour on his journey, and also gave him courage and confidence in men, among whom he was now lost as in an ocean. The road at first was heavy from the rain of yesterday, but as the sun was hot, the ground soon dried and Reiser towards noon reached the imperial city of Mühlhausen, which now lay before him with its towers, a new and unfamiliar sight.

Here he had been warned was his chief danger from recruiting-sergeants. He therefore took all possible pains, before entering the Gate, to make his toilette carefully, and once more, as at Hildesheim he succeeded in playing the part he had already tried of a casual pedestrian, so that he passed happily through the Gate into the city, without being questioned by a sentry. He hurried through the town as quickly as possible, asked for the Gate from which the road to Erfurt starts and quickened his pace whenever he saw what looked like a uniform in the distance.

How gladly did he shake the dust from his feet over this city, when he had passed the last barrier and saw no Prussian recruiting-officer behind or beside him. The green spires remained the only picture that he carried with him of this collection of houses; everything else was a blank, so lightly had his imagination passed over the scene.

He was now getting nearer and nearer to the goal of his journey and contemplated the road he had traversed with great pleasure; he felt a special sense of triumph over his frugal and hard living, now that his difficulties were nearly over. At the same time he began again to feel anxious as the space narrowed between him and his uncertain prospects. For what had met no obstacle in his imagination was now to take shape in fact and to contend with hindrances which could be foreseen. Reiser now thought it much easier to wander into the wide world with fine and pleasant prospects, than to be on the spot and have to make the prospects a reality.

Reiser then would have gladly wished his goal farther off, had be been able to continue his wanderings. But as he sadly observed his shoes, the loss of which in his present circumstances would be irreparable, the sight put a stop at once to all his distant visions and made him reflect seriously on his situation. It is remarkable how the most contemptible realities can thus hinder and destroy the most brilliant creations of fancy, and how a man's fate may depend on these same contemptible things. The success Reiser hoped to make in the world at this moment literally depended on his shoes: he could part with no other piece of his dress, if he was to appear respectable, but tattered shoes, which he could not replace, made all the rest of his dress look unsightly and contemptible.

This plunged him in sad and melancholy thoughts as he went on the way towards Langensalza, until a peasant and a travelling artisan, who were going the same way, joined him and entered into talk with him. The artisan told him of his travels in the Electorate of Saxony, and the peasant had a law-suit, which he wished to bring before the Elector in Dresden. It was a little after midday and the heat was stifling. The artisan's boots were hurting him, and Reiser saw the state of his own shoes get worse at every step, and the peasant was complaining of dreadful thirst, when they came upon some working folk in the fields, who had a bucket of water standing by them and gave the three tired walkers a drink. A scene like this, where men unknown and remote from one another, meet for a moment and share necessity and comfort and encouragement with one another, as though they had never been unknown and remote, made up to Reiser for all the unpleasantness of his wanderings and he could look back on it with intense pleasure.

His companions left him outside Langensalza, where he did not stay, but tried to reach the next place, where he wanted to spend the night. He arrived late at the inn, where he spent the last night before his arrival at Erfurt. When he woke next morning his first thought was of a shoemaker, and he was greatly delighted when he found one here, who for a few pence made his shoes sound while he waited, and so he was relieved from his chief embarrassment.

He now walked on towards Erfurt: dressed as he was he could appear before any one, and therefore he once more had courage and self-confidence. In the last village before Erfurt he ordered a drink of beer. The inn was very lively, and one could see that the town was near, as many of its inhabitants were there, among others a scholar, to whom the rest were speaking of his works.

From this village Reiser at last got a view of Erfurt, with its old cathedral, its many towers, its high ramparts and St. Peter's Mount. This was the native town of his friend Philip Reiser, who had told him much about it. There were cherry-trees planted on the road towards the town. The midday heat had abated and the people were coming to walk outside the Gate, and as Reiser thought of Hanover as he walked along, he felt just as if he had taken an easy walk from there to Erfurt, so short seemed to him the interval he had travelled.

He had never seen so large a city before; the sight was new and unfamiliar. He walked up the broad and handsome street called the *Anger* (meadow), and could not refrain from walking about the town a little before he went on; he wanted to go as far as the next village on the road to Weimar. As he wandered through the streets of Erfurt he came to one of the suburbs, and as it was not late, went into an inn. The host, a fat man, was sitting at the window and Reiser asked him whether the Eckhof Company was still in Weimar. 'Not at all,' he replied, 'it is in Gotha!' Reiser then asked whether Wieland was still in Erfurt. 'Not at all,' he replied, 'he is in Weimar!' He said 'no' each time with a kind of resentment, as though it vexed him to say 'no'.

This harsh 'no' of the fat host at once upset Reiser's whole plan. His thoughts were centred on Weimar: he thought that there unexpected opportunities would occur, there he would see the admired author of *The Sorrows of Werther*. And now in a moment Gotha rang in his ears instead of Weimar.

However he would not let this put him out, but got up hastily to walk the same evening towards Gotha, and to spend the night in the next village according to his strict rules. Before sunset he had left Erfurt behind, and before it was quite night he reached the first village on the road to Gotha. The cathedral and the old towers of Erfurt made a new picture in his mind, which he carried away with him, and which seemed to invite him to return.

In the village where he stopped he had very disturbing neighbours on his straw to end up with. These were wagoners, who got up from time to time and talked to one another in a very common dialect, in which one word occurred which sounded specially repulsive in Reiser's ears and which had for him a multitude of ugly associations. The peasants said *quam* instead of *kam* (*kwame* for *came*). This word seemed to Reiser completely to express them; all their coarseness was concentrated as it were in this word, which they always pronounced with full cheeks.

Hardly had Reiser begun to fall asleep when this hated word woke him up again, so that this night was one of the wretchedest he had ever spent on a bed of straw. When day broke he saw the spongy bloated faces of his sleeping companions, which seemed quite in keeping with the *kwame*, which still rang in his ears when he had left the inn and was walking towards Gotha with long strides in the early morning.

As he had slept little in the night his thoughts on the way to Gotha were not very cheerful, and besides, with every step his prospect narrowed and his fancy had less play. It was Sunday and a shoemaker, who had gone into the country to collect debts, accompanied him to Gotha and told him among other things that living was very dear there. This news was very serious for Reiser, who had only about a gulden in his pocket, and whose fate in Gotha must therefore very soon be decided. His talk with the shoemaker, who complained to him of his poverty as an inhabitant of Gotha, was not encouraging for him and moderated his ideas, for he now realized what actual life would be in a town where nobody knew him and where it was very doubtful whether any one would sympathize with his fortunes or pay regard to his wishes.

These disagreeable reflections made the way more painful and he grew wearier with every step until the two little turrets of Gotha appeared, one of which the shoemaker told him was on the church, the other on the theatre. This pleasant contrast and lively appeal to the senses gradually cheered his spirits, and once more his quickened pace put his companion out of breath. The turret marked for him the spot where immediate loud applause was to be won and the wishes of young ambition were to be crowned. This place asserted its rights by the side of the consecrated temple, and was itself a temple, dedicated to Art and the Muses, where talent could unfold, and where all and every feeling of the heart in its inmost recesses could reveal itself to a listening public. This was the place where noble tears of pity were shed at the fall of goodness, where the genius who had skill to produce powerful illusions and to melt men's hearts, triumphed with loud applause. Here pity for the dead and honour for the living nobly untied all knots. Reiser already lived and moved in this world, where men felt the feelings of past ages, and every scene of life was lived over again in a little space. In a word it was nothing less than human life with all its vicissitudes and varied fortunes, which rose like a picture before Reiser's mind at the sight of the turret of the Gotha playhouse ; the complaints of his companion the shoemaker and his own anxieties were lost in the general sea of life.

With his one gulden in his pocket Reiser felt himself as happy as a king, so long as this wealth of pictures, hovering round the turret at Gotha, floated before his eyes and once more beguiled him with a fair dream of the future.

As they were not far from the town Reiser let his companion go on and sat down comfortably under a tree to put his dress in order and make a dignified entrance into Gotha. He succeeded so well that some work-people who were walking outside the Gate of Gotha lifted their hats in respect, to the great surprise of Reiser, who had slept with wagoners on the straw all through his journey and had cut no brilliant figure. He now went through the Old Gate of Gotha into a rather dark street, up which he walked and soon came in sight of the *Golden Cross Inn*, which he entered, as it seemed to him not a grand one.

When he entered he found in the inn-parlour a throng of travelling artisans, shouting and making a din, and he was about to turn back when the old landlord came to him, addressed him in a friendly tone, and asked him if he wished for a lodging. Reiser replied by asking whether it was not an inn for journeymen. 'No matter,' said mine host, 'you shall be content with your lodging,' and thereupon pressed Reiser to enter his own well-ordered parlour, where he found an old captain, a court valet, and other well-dressed people, to whom Reiser was introduced by the host and was received politely. They asked no rude or inquisitive questions and paid him flattering attention. There was a piano in the room, on which a young man called Liebetraut was playing. This Liebetraut had casually come to the inn a little time before and made the acquaintance of the tenants, who, as they wanted to retire, had persuaded him to lease the inn, so that he was the actual landlord, though they still gave him advice and had to help in the entertainment of visitors. Young Liebetraut soon entered into a conversation with Reiser on poetry and the fine arts, and showed himself a man of taste and education, and, what was most remarkable, appeared to hint pretty plainly that Reiser must have come here to go on the Stage.

Reiser for the present kept his own counsel, and a room was shown him where he could be alone. Here he collected his thoughts and formed a plan for visiting the actor Eckhof next day and putting his request before him. While he was thus engaged in his room, alone with his thoughts and standing at the window, the choirboys came in front and sang a motet, which Reiser as a schoolboy had often sung with the choir amid wind and rain. This recalled to him all that dismal period of his life, when discontent, self-contempt, and the pressure of circumstance robbed him of every gleam of joy, when all his wishes failed, and he had nothing left but a pale glimmer of hope. Was the dawn, he thought, at last to break from this darkness ? And a deceptive illusory hope seemed to say to him that instead of being a torment to himself as he so long had been he would one day have pleasure in himself, and that the happy change in his fortunes was not far distant.

For him the Stage was now the height of happiness, for it was the only place where his insatiable desire to live through every scene of human life could be satisfied. As he had had too little life of his own, from childhood up, the fortunes of all outside him attracted him the more; that was the secret of his passion in his schooldays for reading and seeing plays. The fortunes of strangers drew him out of himself, and it was only in others' breasts that he rediscovered the fire of life which outward pressure had almost quenched in his own.

What attracted him then was no true vocation for the Stage, no pure dramatic impulse, he was more anxious to act the scenes of life within him than without. He wanted to take for himself all that art demands as a sacrifice. He wanted to play the scenes of life for his own sake, they attracted him because he found pleasure in them, not because all his concern was to present them faithfully. He deceived himself, taking for a genuine artistic impulse what was merely the product of chance circumstances. How much anguish this deception cost him, and of how many pleasures it robbed him! If only he had felt the sure sign of the artist, and realized that he who does not forget himself for his art, is not born to be one, it would have spared him much vain effort and much wasted trouble. But his fate from a child had been to suffer the pains of imagination, for his imagination was in perpetual discord with his actual condition, and had to pay for every lovely dream by bitter torments afterwards.

After his long wanderings Reiser spent the first night in Gotha in peaceful slumber, and when he woke early next morning it was as if the closing words of an air from *Lisuart and Dariolette*, sung by the bewitched old woman, welcomed him.

> To-day perchance relieves me
> Of all the pain that grieves me
> And brings release at last.

While these lines lingered in his mind he dressed and asked his young host where Eckhof lived, whom he meant to visit that forenoon. For this purpose he had ready his printed prologue which he had composed and Iffland had declaimed in Hanover, and which he hoped would be his chief introduction here.

The young Liebetraut pressed him to breakfast with him and seemed to take special pleasure in his company, and began to confide his love-story to him, telling him that he had taken the inn, in order to be able to hasten his marriage with a young woman whom he loved.

Reiser then went to Eckhof, and on his way all the plans he had made since he started crowded once more into his mind, because he saw the end of his journey near; the music and the words from *Lisuart and Dariolette* still rang in his ears, and this time at least his hope did not deceive him. Eckhof received him surprisingly well and talked to him for nearly an hour. Reiser's youthful enthusiasm for the Stage seemed not to displease the old man; he talked freely to him on matters of art, and did not disapprove of his desire to devote himself to acting, and added that there was a want of men who go on the Stage from a genuine impulse towards art and not under the pressure of external circumstances. What could be more encouraging for Reiser than this remark ? He imagined himself already a pupil of this excellent master. He then brought out his printed prologue, which received Eckhof's entire approval ; he asked to have it, and remarked how nearly related were the talents of the actor and the poet and how the one in a measure implied the other.

Reiser at that moment felt himself happy as only a young man could feel who had walked a hundred and sixty miles on dry bread to see and speak to Eckhof and become an actor under him. As to his engagement, Eckhof said he must apply to the librarian Reichardt, to whom he would speak himself on Reiser's behalf.

Reiser did not delay a moment to follow this advice and went straight from Eckhof, who was living in a baker's house, to the house of the librarian Reichardt, who received him politely enough but was much more on guard than Eckhof. Meanwhile he held out hopes of a début which was all that Reiser could desire, for if he had that, he had no doubt of success. He went home in good spirits for he thought this was a very successful beginning of his enterprise, and in these favourable circumstances was confident that he could not be disappointed. And though he did not tell his host everything the latter seemed to have no doubt that he would stay in Gotha and enter on his theatrical career there. Full of confidence in himself and his fate Reiser spent midday very pleasantly in the company of the old captain, the court valet and his host; and full of bright prospects, in which everything confirmed him, at this meal for the first time he went beyond his means in the flush of his joy, and for that reason thought himself more closely bound to Gotha and to the most strenuous pursuit of his plan.

He now paid a visit nearly every day to Eckhof, who advised him, to begin with, to be constant in attending the rehearsals in the theatre; Reiser did so, and saw old Eckhof quite in his element there, attending to every detail, and giving many a reminder even to the foremost actors. Reiser was also given a free seat for a performance in which one Bindrim made his début with the part of the father in *Die Zaïre*. As this actor was not specially applauded and Reiser felt how different the expression should have been in certain passages, he was all the more eager to make his début on the boards, and earnestly begged Eckhof that a part might be given him in one of the forthcoming plays.

As the next performance was *Poets à la mode*, Reiser proposed to undertake the part of Dunkel, but Eckhof dissuaded him on the ground that as he played that part himself it was not advisable for a novice to make his début in a part which the audience were accustomed to see played by an old and practised actor.

Thus his début was put off from one performance to another, while his hopes were still being encouraged and his whole fate hung on the decision. When he began to be disheartened Reiser found comfort and fresh hope with Eckhof; the fact that Eckhof was glad to talk with him gave him confidence and courage. Nevertheless several remarks of Eckhof's were very depressing. When they were talking of his engagement and Reiser referred to a young man who had played the part of Reimreich in *Poets à la mode*, Eckhof said that he had been accepted mainly on account of his youth, and seemed thereby to imply that for Reiser this reason existed no longer. At that time he was only just nineteen, but every one, it seemed, took him for much older, so that he had not only lost the joys of youth but its appearance as well.

Another time, when they were talking of Goethe, Eckhof said that he was about Reiser's height, but with good features, a remark which would have utterly destroyed the actor in Reiser, had not Eckhof by chance encouraged him just afterwards, by asking him whether he had not written other poems besides the prologue. Reiser said yes, and as soon as he went back, wrote down his verses, which he knew by heart, to hand to Eckhof. He spent several days over this, and his host got the idea that Reiser was writing a dramatic work for the stage. He could not be persuaded that this was not so, and congratulated Reiser beforehand on the brilliant career he was to enter upon.

When Eckhof had read the poems, he showed Reiser his approval and said he would give them to the librarian Reichardt to read. This specially encouraged Reiser, as he remembered Eckhof's previous remark that the actor and the poet were near akin. He did not doubt that these poems would pave his way to the theatre and soon bring him nearer the goal. Besides this, the actor Grossmann, who was in Gotha and met Reiser one day in the street, gave him fresh courage, by telling him that he would not have been kept waiting so long if they had not meant to engage him, perhaps without a début, for it was now the third week that Reiser had been there. These comforting words and the friendly attitude of Grossmann were a precious balm to Reiser as he walked up and down, a solitary figure, by the Palace, where they were building, and reflected with gloomy discontent on his still uncertain fate. He now went home hopeful, and spent the day agreeably with his landlord. Next morning he went to the rehearsal; they were rehearsing the operetta of *The Deserter*, in which a stranger called Neuhaus acted the deserter and his wife, Lilla. Eckhof showed great energy, and Reiser standing in the slips watched with delight how the effort and attention of each individual actor produced the splendid work of art, which was to delight the evening audience. His lively imagination made him feel how near he was to these delightful activities: his fate would soon be decided by his acting on this very stage, and here his own career would begin.

For after his wide travel all his interests were bounded by this narrow stage; here he saw himself and found himself again. Here the future unlocked for him its rich treasures of golden visions and opened up an even fairer vista.

He had often stood behind the scenes plunged in thought like this, and so it was that day, when suddenly he saw the librarian Reichardt come towards him, whose decisive answer he had been expecting for some days. His face foreboded bad news, and he coldly told Reiser that he was sorry to have to tell him that there was no hope of an engagement for him, or even of a début. With these words he returned to Reiser the manuscript of his poems, adding by way of consolation, that his verses ran smoothly and that he should not neglect this faculty.

Reiser, wounded in body and spirit, could not answer a word, but went away to the back of the theatre, where the back-scene is close to the bare masonry, and leant with his head against the wall. For now, indeed, he was unhappy and doubly unhappy. Want, real and imaginary, combined alarmingly to fill him with fear and horror of the future. He saw no way out of the maze, into which his own folly had led him : here was indeed the bare blank wall, the illusion of the stage was gone.

He hurried outside the Gate and in despair walked up and down the avenue where he had busied himself before with the most agreeable thoughts; people went coldly past him, and no one knew at this moment he had lost the one hope of his life and was one of the most forlorn of men. And it was strange that, just as he was in this most forlorn condition, he felt an unfamiliar need of love stirring within him, because his despair turned into compassion for his own state, and he felt the want of some one to sympathize with him.

He did not venture to go home for dinner : he ate nothing and only came back in the afternoon, and in the evening he went to the theatre where the operetta *The Deserter* was performed, which marked the death of his hopes. Never in his life did he feel a stronger sympathy with another's fate than he felt that evening at the fate of the lovers, who were to be parted by the threatening stroke of death. What Homer says of the maidens who wept for the fallen Patroclus, 'they wept for their own fate', was true of him. His strongest emotion was at the scene where the deserter, who knows of his death-sentence, wants to write in prison to his beloved, and his drunken comrade gives him no rest, because he wants him to teach him to spell a word.

Reiser felt profoundly how little one human being means to his fellows, how little they are concerned with his fate, and he saw again in his mind's eye the picture of his friend and the cockade. Why did he smarten his cockade except to please his one and only love, who was then his goddess, in whom he was fain to find himself, and be loved by her again?

The play ended happily, the unhappy were consoled, weeping was turned into laughter, and mourning into joy, but Reiser went to his own lodgings sad and heavy in spirit, all was dark before him and he saw not a ray of hope left. When he arrived home he lay down on his bed, his senses were dulled, his thoughts could find no utterance, and nothing was left him but to sleep. He felt as if he would never awake from this sleep, for all his prospects in life were cut off and he had no hope left to awake to. The thoughts of dissolution, of complete self-forgetfulness, of the cessation of all memory and all consciousness were so pleasant to him, that that night he enjoyed the boon of sleep in richest measure; for no secret desire intervened to check the complete relaxation of all his faculties, no dream of illusory hope hovered before him. All was over and ended in the eternal night of the grave. Such is the beneficence with which Nature hands to the man without hope the cup from which he is to drink forgetfulness of his sorrows, and wipes out the memory of anything that he once desired or strove for.

When Reiser woke out of his deep sleep late next morning he felt wonderfully renewed in body and mind, he felt capable of anything, even of attaining the goal of his desire in spite of circumstances. An idea occurred to him that he should try and earn his living by giving lessons, and serve for nothing in the theatre. This resolve grew stronger and stronger, and as soon as he saw a glimmer of hope again he grew confident of attaining his end. As he reflected thus, he dressed and went to Eckhof, to whom he confided his resolve, assuring him that he could manage to live, without revealing how he thought of living. Eckhof praised and approved his persistence, and said he had no doubt the offer would be accepted. The librarian Reichardt, whom Reiser acquainted with this resolve, promised to give him an answer next day. So Reiser went home full of new hope; his whole enterprise now seemed to him more honourable, because he was now combining with his art, diligence in useful affairs, and earning a living, and was sacrificing all his other hours to art. This noon he once more dined with his host, full of confidence, and felt in himself irresistible courage to endure life's hardship for the sake of his art, to limit himself to the barest necessities, and not to rest day or night, in order to practise his art and at the same time to attend to his lessons properly.

With these resolves, which inspired him with a true heroic spirit, he went to Reichardt again next day and heard his final decision that they could not accept his offer, to serve in the theatre gratis, and that in any case no new engagement would take place in that theatre now. If Reiser had come a few weeks sooner something might have been done for him, but now all attempt was vain. This second unexpected refusal produced a kind of inward bitterness in Reiser; he began at this moment to hate and despise himself and asked whether he might not become prompter or copyist or candle-snuffer in the theatre. Reichardt answered that he was very sorry, as Reiser showed such zeal for the Stage, that his enterprise had failed here; meanwhile perhaps he would succeed elsewhere.

Reiser, now deep in thought, left Reichardt and walked up and down by the building near the Palace where some were wheeling stones in barrows and others arranging them. He stood and watched the work for an hour, and a strange desire rose in him to take off his good coat and to wheel stones for the building with the other workmen. It was drawing near to noon, and the sun's heat was growing stronger. The workmen were tired and took a rest and ate their midday meal on the ground. Reiser talked to one of them and asked what his day's pay was: it was more pence than Reiser possessed and could be earned in a single day. At that moment Reiser had so resolved to work for this wage, that he felt obliged to laugh to himself at the workman speaking to him bareheaded, not knowing that perhaps next day they would be comrades. This resolve, which restored his self-respect, was the only thing that could soften his bitterness and self-hatred and self-contempt. He now intended to disclose his condition to his landlord, leave his sword and coat with him in payment, and then wheel stones for the palace building.

As he made these reflections he thought he was in earnest and did not realize that he was again being cheated by his imagination, and that he was once more acting a part. He felt that as builder's labourer he had touched bottom; this voluntary degradation had an extraordinary charm for him: he would live like the rest of his class, go regularly to church on Sundays, like a quiet religious person, and in his solitary hours enjoy Shakespeare and Homer, living in his thoughts the real life which he could not have outside. In these imaginations what moved him most was the thought that he would go regularly to church on Sunday and listen attentively to the preacher. For thus he reduced himself as it were to nothing, as he would regard the words of the worst preacher as very instructive and wished to be no wiser than the most simple-minded.

He thought himself back in the position he had been in as hatter's apprentice, when he regarded the preacher of his choice as a superior being and even looked with respect on the choirboys in the street. In these circumstances he could hardly have any idea of the Stage, and yet he felt as though this condition might perhaps in some wonderful way bring him nearer again to his first desire. But before he actually applied for a place as labourer at the Palace, he could not do other than go once more to Eckhof to say farewell, and to tell him that his last hope had failed.

He could not tell his story without anguish and emotion, for his mind was filled with thoughts of his present position as a whole, and he felt much more than he said. The kind Eckhof encouraged him not to lose heart; the Barzant Company was only twelve miles off at Eisenach, and he would certainly be accepted by them. He should try to get some training with them for a time and then return to Gotha, where perhaps circumstances would then be more favourable, and he would find it easier to get admission when he had already been with a company for some time. He might easily try this and take the journey from Gotha to Eisenach by the high road as a walk.

This advice of Eckhof immediately swept away from Reiser's mind the whole plan of the stone-wheeling labourer; for he saw the goal of his desire brought near to him again, and all doubts vanished when he thought of the road from Gotha to Eisenach as a walk, for this meant no breach of faith with his landlord, whom he could repay from Eisenach as an actor easier and quicker than he could from a labourer's wages. So, as it was already midday, he started straight from Eckhof's house to Eisenach, just as he was and without turning round. The road was indeed as easy as a walk, for in a moment all his dead thoughts had revived and made an agreeable and lively contrast with the melancholy ideas which had led him that morning to want to hire himself as a labourer. He thought of himself as always near to Gotha, and imagined how he would return next day and bring good news to his landlord. The beauties of Nature once more delighted him, and he walked with intense pleasure through the romantic valleys among the mountains and when he first saw the towers of the old Wartburg, of which he had heard since childhood, everything he saw appealed to his feelings so strongly that its beauty was doubled. He felt himself in a pleasant dream, in which his earlier thoughts one after another became real before his eyes. He felt as if he could be in any place that he wished, because he saw himself transported in a few hours from Gotha to Eisenach, which had not been in his thoughts when the morning began. He had left at home his overcoat and other things which he generally carried, and walked into Eisenach in his best clothes, with his sword at his side, just as on his visits to Reichardt and Eckhof. It chanced that he still had in his coat pocket the manuscript of his poems and the Latin programme with his name, but he had left behind in his overcoat his Homer and some of his linen.

When he entered the town everything seemed gay and cheerful; the people seemed attuned to joy, so that he entered the inn where he meant to stay the night with nothing but happy anticipations, and inquired when he had sat down whether there would be a play that night.

The answer struck him like a thunderbolt:

'The Barzant Company went off to Mühlhausen this morning.' It was as if a hostile fate always pursued him, and deliberately ruined all his hopes. Besides, this was no imaginary misery, his misery was real, and doubly bitter, for the only hope of earning a living and paying his debt in Gotha depended on his being received by the Barzant Company at Eisenach, and now the Company had gone off that very day in the direction from which he had come.

His position made him nearly desperate, and for the first time he was lifted above his fate into a region where he forgot himself and seemed outwardly glad and cheerful. This unforeseen and malicious stroke of fortune seemed to have cut him loose from all ties, so that he could look on himself as a neglected and forlorn being, no longer worth considering.

He had taken no food all day, and now ordered beer and bread and a bed for the night, where he enjoyed the quietest sleep, because he no more counted on any future and no thought of the future or his own fate disturbed him, for his prospects were completely at an end.

But next morning he felt that this beneficent sleep had renewed his dormant faculties once more: instead of being crippled he felt a sort of defiance and bitterness against fate, which gave him courage to endure all and to dare all once more in order to achieve his end. He resolved to pursue the Barzant Company and to retrace the road from Eisenach to Mühlhausen by which he had come. When he had paid his reckoning at the inn he had only five or six halfpence left, with which he climbed the

Wartburg and from there looked out over the wide and beautiful prospect. The official at the Wartburg asked if he would like to see the sights, to which Reiser replied that he would be coming again with a party in the afternoon, but that now he only wanted to take a look round. As he looked about him he felt on this height lifted above his fate, for in spite of all difficulties he had reached this spot, and no one could deprive him at this moment of the enchanting view into the surrounding world of Nature. He gathered strength here to face the troublesome and anxious journey which he meant now to begin again.

The plan which he had formed was nothing less than to use the few halfpence he had left merely for his lodging and to feed by day on the roots of the country, for on the road from Gotha he had tried the experiment of pulling up a few roots in the field, which gave him a very agreeable refreshment, as he had had nothing all day. He had remembered this when he woke in the morning, and it was chiefly this which made him defiant of fate, of which he now thought himself almost wholly independent.

He began that day to carry out his resolve with the same self-confidence with which on his former journey he limited himself to beer and bread and felt twice as independent as then, for while the official at the Wartburg might be waiting for him and his company, to show them the sights, Reiser was already consuming his meal of raw turnips in the open, cutting them into slices with an old clasp-knife which he had from his friend Philip Reiser, and eating them with the greatest gusto.

But as he had stayed too long at the Wartburg he was hardly four miles from Eisenach, and when he had eaten his roots he was overcome by irresistible heaviness, so that he fell asleep in the middle of the fields and did not wake up again till sundown. In trying to get to the nearest village he missed the right way and did not reach an inn until late; there he ate nothing but next morning paid only for his straw. As he went on from this village next day he lost himself among the fields, where he looked for roots, the heaviness of the day before overcame him, the heat was stifling, and when he found a shady tree he lay down and immediately went to sleep, so that he spent nearly four days on the road from Eisenach to Gotha, which he had walked in a few hours going the other way.

His wanderings were as tortuous as his fortunes, he could not find his way out of either. Outside Gotha his road seemed to bend back, and yet he had to go on, if he wished to continue his journey to Mühlhausen, and as he was now afraid of the direct road, he was glad in a sense to lose his way.

Twice his Latin programme helped him. Once, when he was taken for a suspicious person because he could show no pass, and a second time when a pass was demanded of him, to show that he did not come from a district where the cattle-plague prevailed; he showed his Latin programme and added that he was a student and therefore carried a Latin pass. The village judge or mayor, who wished to appear in the eyes of his wife and the other peasants as understanding Latin, read the notice out with an air of importance and said it was in order.

While Reiser spent these days in a sort of stupor and walked about as if in a maze, his imagination dominated him, for as he was living in the open he felt all ties severed and gave free rein to his imagination. He did not think his fate romantic enough. That he had wanted to be an actor and had failed he thought was a dull part to play; he must have committed some crime which drove him wandering; he imagined that he had gone to the University of Göttingen with the young nobleman whom he taught in Hanover, and that the man when drunk had forced on him a duel, in which he only defended himself, but his opponent in a fury ran on his sword, whereupon he took to flight, not knowing whether the man was alive or dead. This romance of his own invention impressed itself on him as a fact while he wandered in the country, and he dreamed of it when he went to sleep; he saw his adversary lying in his blood, and declaimed aloud when he woke, and thus in the open country between Gotha and Eisenach he acted the parts which had been refused him on the stage. This was the only thing which saved him from despair, for had he thought of his condition as utterly empty and futile as it really was, he would have abandoned himself completely and sunk into contempt. But now he could bear the bitterest fate. On the second day of his return from Eisenach to Gotha it was Sunday and oppressively hot. Reiser had left the open and was passing through a village and looked for shade, which he could only find on a green planted with trees just opposite the church. He got himself a glass of water in a peasant's house and then lay down under the trees, while they were singing in the church opposite. As they sang he fell asleep and did not wake till the minister came out of church, walking with his son, who had just returned from the University. Both came up to Reiser and asked him whence he came and where he was going. He gave confused answers and finally confessed that he was running away because of a duel which he had fought at Göttingen. He felt as if the confession was very hard to make, and it hardly occurred to him to think of its falsehood, for, when once he had come to live in the world of ideas, everything that had once impressed itself on his imagination was real; he was cut off from all relations with the real world, and the barrier between dream and reality threatened to collapse.

The minister pressed him to come into his house and wanted to entertain him. But Reiser, as if pursued by terror, got away as soon as possible, for in his imaginary circumstances he was bound to avoid human society. Near to Gotha another minister pressed him to come into his house, talked with him for half a day, and told him that a year or two before a travelling scholar, well dressed, had come there on foot: he had a long conversation with him, and noted the day in the calendar and was pretty certain that it was Dr. Barth.

The minister then told Reiser his story: how he had long lived a roving life as a tutor and had finally found a resting-place in this old parsonage, where he could only look from a distance on what was going on in the world. Reiser then told the preacher his own imaginary unhappy story, whereupon the minister gave him some refreshment of preserved fruit in a coffee-cup and encouraged him by saying that he could perhaps some day atone for his crime. Then he looked at the white sheath of the sword that Reiser wore and asked him whether that sort of sheath was not the sign of the freemasons, and whether Reiser did not belong to that order. The more he denied it, the more the minister thought he was a freemason who did not wish to reveal himself on this point.

This minister looked at Reiser many times from head to foot, and seemed to form peculiar views of him. He regarded him as a man who kept back more than he said, and with whom he did not quite know where he was. Nevertheless he could not give up questioning him, until at last, as it was near sunset, Reiser took leave of him and the preacher's exhortation to him for his journey was to atone for his crime by repentance.

Reiser's imagination was still more excited by the long conversation with the minister and by his exhortation. He arrived at Gotha in the evening, and in a sort of obstinate stupor and indifference he walked past the *Golden Cross* where he had lodged and out of the Gate, through which he had first entered Gotha, and took the road for Erfurt, in order to go on from there to Mühlhausen and finally overtake the Barzant Company. For, as soon as he had passed through Gotha again, the imaginary story which had driven him wandering for three days about Gotha gradually disappeared, and his first prospect opened up again. Once more Gotha lay behind him and became the centre of his efforts; he hoped to return there from Mühlhausen, as he had done from Eisenach, but with better fortune.

But it was dark before he could reach a village and he went astray and went almost four miles round, but at last hit the right road and arrived at the same inn where he had spent one of the most disagreeable nights on his journey from Erfurt to Gotha in the company of the rough wagoners, whose 'kwame' was still fresh in his memory. The inn was still very much awake, and he found an artisan sitting on the ground among the peasants, relating his travels in Electoral Saxony. Just as Reiser came in, the landlord entered and commanded silence, as it was late at night and time to go to sleep. The artisan and the peasants lay down on the straw, which was already prepared, and Reiser joined them. The mechanic could not bear with the rudeness of the landlord and could not go to sleep, asserting over and over again that he had not met with so rude a host in all Saxony.

When Reiser had paid his halfpenny next morning for his lodging, his property was reduced to nine farthings, and he began to feel so much exhausted, from feeding only on raw roots, that the thought of having to walk four miles filled him with horror, for that morning he felt crippled, and the space between him and Mühlhausen seemed a fearsome desert, through which he had to travel without meat or drink. The mechanic who had talked late into the night the evening before of his travels in Saxony, was now starting for Erfurt, and asked Reiser whether he was going that way too. Reiser said 'yes', and they walked on together at a moderate pace. The workman, who was a journeyman bookbinder and of some age, asked Reiser what his occupation was, and he replied that he was a shoeblack, and found a kind of dignity in the name, for in that character he was at least something, while as one who pursued a mere delusion of his fancy, he was nothing.

The bookbinder according to his story seemed to have made a regular business of travelling for many years, and was unreserved in relating his experiences to his companion, explaining to him how it was possible, especially in summer and fruit-time, to make long tours for half a florin, without being hard put to it. No one would refuse fruit anywhere and scarcely refuse bread, and thus often one need not spend more than a penny a day. He had travelled several times all through Saxony in this way and had fared well: in a word he counted Reiser worthy to be initiated into his order, the advantages and delights of which he described most attractively, as it was a life full of continual variety and independence.

Reiser however felt his knees giving way and his weariness increased so much at every step, that at that moment he would have been content with the most monotonous and dependent life, if a quiet resting-place had been offered him. His companion seemed aware of his distress and tried to comfort and encourage him, when as they approached Erfurt they came to a clear and cool spring, which was known to the bookbinder, and where they both quenched their thirst in the oppressive heat. This beneficent spring, which is well known to the inhabitants of Erfurt, can never have refreshed a traveller more than it did Reiser, who in his utter exhaustion threw himself down beside it and received direct from the treasury of Nature the refreshment which he often scarcely dared to ask from men.

This incident was doubly precious to Reiser, who added the poetic touch which for him became reality, and which might be called the only compensation for the necessary consequences of his folly, a folly for which he was not to blame, because it was bound by natural laws to blend with his fortunes from childhood up.

When the old towers of Erfurt rose once more from the valley and Reiser, hopeless now, returned to the place whence he had started a short time before in the young sunshine of early hope, it seemed strange when his companion the bookbinder suddenly said to him that he did not believe that Reiser was a shoeblack, but took him for a student who wanted to study at the University of Erfurt. Reiser, who was near fainting again and ready to collapse, felt as though recalled to life by these chance words of the bookbinder.

If only he chose to study and stay in this town, which lay so near him, his painful wandering was at an end. This was the purpose and goal of his journey, which he now saw so near : here he could change his plan, with honour. The more his weariness increased the more attractive and desirable did he think it to stay in this spacious town, where as he thought, a corner might be found for him. This sad and hopeless state of wandering, in which he had been involved for several days, could no longer be outweighed by any spell of a strained and excited imagination.

The thought of utter helplessness wearied him more at every step, and the weariness again increased the thought of helplessness which arose chiefly from the failure of his courage and the exhaustion of his physique.

They now entered the town, passing a bakery where a quantity of loaves were piled in the shop. Reiser wanted to pick one out but had hardly touched the pile when nearly the whole heap of loaves shot down into the street. The people in the house began to make a great to do and Reiser and his companion had to turn a corner quickly to avoid their abuse. Thus Reiser's ill luck pursued him to the uttermost. They now entered an inn, where Reiser could not control his thirst, and ordered some beer which he paid for with the few pence he had left. For this one drink he had spent the money for three nights' lodging, and no course was left him but to live in the open air altogether. As he reflected thus he felt as though with this one drink of beer he was drinking forgetfulness of all the future and the past, and was to be freed at once from all distress. For now he gave himself up to his fate and regarded himself as a creature outside himself, for whom he could think no longer, as he was irrevocably lost. He fell asleep and slept for an hour. When he awoke it wanted an hour to noon, his companion had gone away and he was sitting with his head resting on his hand, in dumb despair, when a man who was sitting just opposite him addressed him and asked whether he was not a foreign student.

When he said 'yes', the man, just as if he had known Reiser's position, said that the present

Pro-Rector of the University, the Abbot of the Benedictine Monastery on St. Peter's Mount, was an extremely humane man, who shortly before had procured maintenance for a young man who had come there with nothing, and had befriended him most humanely. If Reiser liked to visit this prelate he need not hesitate; he would be certain to meet with a kind reception. Other people then came up, with whom the man conversed. Reiser, however, who had somewhat recovered his strength after the complete relaxation of his faculties of mind and body and the beneficent sleep which fell on him in consequence, felt at once inspired with new hope and courage when he thought of the prelate in the Benedictine monastery on St. Peter's Mount. He at once started on his way and inquired for St. Peter's Mount. A young student whom he met not only politely directed him, but went some way with him, to see that he went right; this he took as a good omen. He climbed the fortified Mount and the guards let him pass. He arrived at the Abbot's house, where the servant received him with a friendly face, and as soon as he said he was a student, promised to announce him to the Abbot.

He was led up a staircase into a great hall hung with pictures, among which was one of Peter warming himself by the fire in the house of the High Priest. While Reiser's eyes were still fixed on the picture, the Abbot in the black habit of his order, with his breviary in his hand, came out, and Reiser made a short Latin speech to him, which he had thought out as he came up the Mount; saying that driven about by adverse fortune he had come to Erfurt hoping to find a maintenance there to enable him in some way to continue the studies he had begun. The Abbot very affably answered him in Latin, asking whether he was a Catholic or belonged to the Augsburg Confession, and when Reiser said the latter, the Abbot, almost using his own words, said that he was very sorry that Reiser was driven about by adverse fortune, but that he saw no means for his finding maintenance at the University. However he did not wish to deprive him of hope. Thereupon he asked for Reiser's birthplace, and when he was told Hanover, he went on to say that he would advise him to apply to Dr. Froriep who was in some degree his countryman: he should present himself to him, and then come again. With these words he pressed a silver coin into Reiser's hand and begged him to make shift with that for his dinner. If anything could raise the courage of a broken spirit and rescue the victim of abject misery from despair, it was the tone and gesture with which Abbot Günther answered Reiser's petition and gave him his advice.

Moved almost to tears by this treatment, Reiser hurried away and thought he was dreaming when he stood again outside the door, looked at his coin and found himself suddenly in possession of half a gulden, when a moment before he had not a halfpenny for a night's lodging. This half-gulden seemed to him now priceless wealth, and so indeed it was to him, for it gave him courage again, and his whole fate hung on that. He went to an eating-house and enjoyed a warm meal again for the first time, and as soon as that was over he inquired for the Merchant's Church, near which Dr. Froriep lived. He found him just as he was about to give a lecture at two o'clock and addressed him in Latin as he had done Abbot Günther.

When Dr. Froriep heard that Reiser was from Hanover, he received him in the most friendly way and took him into his lecture-room, where the students were already seated, with their hats on, an unusual sight for Reiser, all the more as he noticed that they commented on him for not being covered too. Thus he suddenly found himself sitting among students in a professor's lecture-room at Erfurt, when that very morning he had no place to rest in except the open country through which he was wandering.

Dr. Froriep was lecturing on Church history, and told many lively anecdotes which amused his audience, who received them with peals of laughter. It was all a dream to Reiser; he remembered the days of his childhood when he regarded even the school lecture-room as sacred, and now he was in a University lecture-room, the most exalted place of all.

When the lecture was over Dr. Froriep took Reiser to his room and asked him for his history, to which he now gave a new turn, saying that he had incurred the enmity of an eminent man in Hanover by a misconstruction put on something which he had written, and had had to leave the place. As he had no prospects he had conceived the idea of going on the Stage, but after mature consideration he had abandoned this, because he saw that such a step would be fatal to his future, and his plan therefore now was to become a student again at Erfurt.

Now it was remarkable how Reiser, before he told this lie, tried to make it true in his own mind, and how sophistically he deceived himself. He tried to convince himself in his own mind that he really did now see the folly of his enterprise and that he had altered his plan of his own free will and would stick to his resolve even though the best opportunity should offer of going on the Stage. As to the first half of his lie he tried to persuade himself that in the address he gave on the Queen's birthday there were really some questionable passages, which might have been misconstrued to his disadvantage. Whether this was really so did not concern him, he was content to think it possible, because he could not help himself otherwise. For if his choice of the student life was to appear plausible he could not say that he had left Hanover from love of the Stage, and the story of the duel was unsuitable here.

Dr. Froriep seemed not quite to believe him, but he formed a higher opinion of Reiser than he could expect, taking him for a son of persons of position with whom he had quarrelled and whose name he would not tell. Reiser thought it flattering that such an opinion of him should be entertained, and welcomed it the more because it covered his lie most agreeably, as Dr. Froriep, though he did not believe the falsehood, excused it.

What followed was a great surprise. Dr. Froriep told him to be of good courage for he would provide for his bed and board to begin with.

Reiser, who that very morning found himself abandoned by every one, could scarcely believe the words of comfort that he now heard and regarded Dr. Froriep at that moment as his guardian angel. He wrote him a note which he was to take next morning to Abbot Günther, who at Froriep's request would matriculate him without fee.

Such a happy change in his fortunes put Reiser in a frame of mind which made him forget all his difficulties, so that he did not regret his aimless wanderings, as they led him to experience a moment which no one can fully appreciate who has not once in his life been destitute of all help, sick in body and spirit, without prospect and without hope. In the joy of his heart he rushed to the inn, where he meant to stay the night, asked for writing-paper and began once more to write out his poems which he knew by heart, in order to take them next day to Dr. Froriep, and so show himself in some degree worthy of his notice. He wrote on into the night and finished his task in some score pages. Early next morning he climbed St. Peter's Mount with very different thoughts from the day before, and kind Abbot Günther was much pleased to see him again, gladly granted his request and at once wrote out his matriculation paper, giving him a printed copy of the University Statutes and pledging him to observe them by clasping his hand.

This matriculation paper inscribed *Universitas perantiqua* (most ancient University), the Statutes, the hand-clasp, Reiser regarded as sacred things, and for a long time he thought they meant far more than being an actor. He was once again in the ranks, and made member of an order of men who try to distinguish themselves from all others by a higher level of education. His position was defined: in a word, when he came down from St. Peter's Mount he regarded himself as a changed being.

Towards noon he showed Dr. Froriep the document he had received and handed him his poems, which this time were much more of a success than he looked for. The fact was that at Erfurt the study of *belles-lettres* was still rather rare among the students; Dr. Froriep was pleased to have one more student, who would serve as an example to the rest in this field. The effect of the poems was that Reiser's new patron took a much greater interest in him, and would not let him stay a night longer at the inn, but at once instructed the University quartermaster, who was also fencing-master, to procure him a lodging. In the first instance he found him quarters with an old student of medicine, who lived in his house, and as he was charged with arranging free board for the students he took him, to begin with, to his own table.

In these happy circumstances Reiser became again for many an hour the unhappiest man in the world, because his bringing-up and the misery of his school years oppressed him. The thought of the free meals that he had had to eat as a boy lay like a burden on him, and he really felt far more unhappy in having to sit at the table of the fencing-master than in eating raw roots in the country between Gotha and Eisenach.

The consequence was that the students who sat at the same table regarded him as shy and timid, and as his host, who behaved to the students as one of themselves, treated him with some freedom, he felt his position less bearable; he seemed to have sunk from unlimited freedom into the most abject dependence. However, in spite of his shyness he was treated considerately, and for this he had to thank his written poems, of which Dr. Froriep had spoken to different people, and which without his knowing it had won a certain repute among the students at Erfurt, so that his peculiarities were set down to his poetic genius.

He now had no clean linen, and if he had been able to confide in people, he could very easily have supplied this want; but he found it impossible to confess this want, which weighed on him most and was the chief cause of his gloom. He always attributed it to something else, for which he pretended to reproach himself, because the want of linen seemed too petty and unpoetical a subject.

The fencing-master then assigned him permanent quarters with a student called R——, where he had to share the parlour; his host planned to edit a weekly paper with him, having formed great ideas of Reiser's talents as poet and writer. Reiser soon thought out a plan for a weekly, which was to begin with a satire on weeklies and was to be called 'The Last Weekly'; when however his new house-mate found that he brought no money with him and had no very definite prospects of getting any, he began to cool towards him, and advised him to pawn his sword, which Reiser did and was then looked upon more kindly. For Herr R——, who was a man of very regular habits, had no desire to advance money on their joint literary enterprise. They both went to a printer in Erfurt, named Gradelmüller, and produced the plan for their new weekly, but he impressed upon them how hazardous an enterprise it was, and how much safer it would be to contribute their compositions to a paper which was well-known and in favour with the public, e.g. *The Citizens' and Peasants' Weekly* published by himself and hawked by beggar-boys in the inns of Erfurt. It was in fact *The Citizen and Peasant* which Reiser had found in the keeper's cottage near Mühlhausen on his first wandering, to which he was now invited by the publisher and editor to contribute with his house-mate. They both had to sup that evening with the printer: radishes and a kind of very hard oblong little cheeses, which are common at Erfurt, were set before them, and both contributors ate away at them incessantly, while the printer's wife kept casting sour looks at them.

The first composition which R—— sent to *The Citizen and Peasant* was a prose imitation of Horace's ode *Beatus ille*, and Reiser's was his stilted poem on the world, which he had composed at school in Hanover. As however no fee was paid for these compositions and R——'s plan of earning a considerable sum by editing a weekly with Reiser had come to a standstill, he ceased to be interested in Reiser. For this he could not be blamed, as Reiser could not be anything but a gloomy companion on account of his melancholy, which arose chiefly from his want of linen and now also from the bad state of his shoes.

R—— therefore, after living with him for a week, took pains to transfer him to another lodging.

This was near the Kirschlache (Cherry-Pool) in the house of a brewer, where another student was lodging and the son of the brewer was at school. Here again Reiser had no room to himself, but like the other student had to live with the family. But the house was pleasantly situated; it stood in a row of small houses, with a narrow stream flowing in front, bordered with trees on the nearer side. It was not a confined street: the running water and the smallness of the houses contributed to give this region of the old town an open and rural appearance. Immediately behind the house was the old city wall, from which there was a view of the Carthusian monastery. The top of the wall was overgrown with grass and in different places was half ruinous, so that it was easy to climb up and overlook the great garden plots which surround Erfurt inside the walls.

Meanwhile Reiser received regular free board from the University and the idea of quiet residence there so completely took hold of him again that now at the age of nineteen he wrote to his friend in Hanover that he hoped and desired to spend the rest of his days in Erfurt. He would pass straight on from his career as a student to that of a teacher, and thus reach the goal of his wishes and hopes. He thought that he had now given up all other attractions, and all the imagined glories of the Stage seemed for a time to have vanished from his mind.

He felt suddenly transported into a new world and had made an amazing advance on his residence in Hanover. As he walked round the ramparts of the city he had a lively sense that he had rescued himself from an intolerable situation by his own efforts, and altered his position in the world by his own exertions.

When he heard the bells of Erfurt ringing, gradually all his memories of bygone days were awakened. His existence was no longer bounded by the present moment; the present included all that had vanished into the past. These were the happiest moments of his life, when his own existence began to interest him, because he looked at it as a connected whole and not as a series of single and detached events. What always caused him distress and disgust was to feel his life fragmentary and incoherent, and this feeling came whenever the pressure of circumstance kept his thoughts from rising above the present moment; then everything seemed trivial, empty, and flat, and not worth a thought. It was this which made him long for the coming of night, a deep sleep, a complete forgetting of self. Time seemed to creep at a snail's pace, and he often could not understand why he was still alive.

In the early days of his residence at Erfurt such moments were few: he contemplated life as a whole, the change of place was still fresh and his imagination was not yet fettered by a sense of the recurring round. It is the recurrence of the same sensual impressions which chiefly keeps men in check and confines them to a narrow field. A man feels gradually attracted irresistibly by the uniformity of the sphere in which he moves and comes to love the old and shun the new. It seems a sort of outrage to step outside his surroundings, which have become a sort of second body, to which his first body has adapted itself. Reiser's life by the Kirschlache seemed calculated to fetter his imagination again. The view over the gardens to the Carthusian monastery had a romantic feeling which irresistibly attracted Reiser and fixed his gaze on that peaceful home of solitude, for which he felt a secret yearning.

As the structure of his fancy was in ruins and he had been unable to enact the bustling scenes of the world either in real life or on the stage, his feelings recoiled, as generally happens, to the other extreme. The idea of living out his days in quiet solitude, forgotten by the world and withdrawn from men, had an irresistible attraction for him, and this retirement gained a richer value to his mind from the greatness of the sacrifice he offered; he was giving up his dearest desires, which seemed woven into the web of his being. The lamps and the wings, the lighted theatre, had disappeared, and the lonely cell received him. The high walls surrounding the Carthusian monastery, the turret on the church, the separate little houses ranged in a series within the wall, every one with its own garden-plot, parted from the rest by a wall—all this makes a very interesting scene; the high walls, the separate houses and the gardens between mark in a very striking and significant way the solitude and separate life of the inmates. Whenever the bell in the turret was rung, it sounded in Reiser's ears like the knell of all earthly desires and of all prospects in this life: for here a bound was set to all: the foot of the initiated could never step outside these walls, here he found his perpetual dwelling and his grave.

The Carthusian bell sounds sadder and more melancholy from its slowness and the manner in which it is rung. When the Carthusians assemble in choir each in turn rings one stroke of the bell and then takes his place, till all from the eldest to the youngest have come in.

Reiser listened to the sound of this bell, now in the stillness of noon, now at midnight or early morning, and always the impression it made was so fresh and lively that it called up in him the image of the solitude and peace of the grave. He felt as if these secluded monks survived their own death, and were moving and holding out hands to one another in their graves. This thought became so familiar and so attractive to him that many a time he would not have exchanged it for the pleasantest prospect.

He now received a letter, the first since he left him, from Philip Reiser in Hanover, which, like his conversation in old days, instead of special sympathy with his friend's fortunes, contained a long description of his love-affair of the moment, the point it had reached and the hindrances in its way. Nevertheless Reiser constantly carried the letter with him and often re-read it, because Philip Reiser was his only friend. There was a pleasant walk near the Kirschlache, where a clear stream flowed along the valley amid green undergrowth : there was no view, but it had the charm of solitude. Here Reiser spent many an hour on the green turf by the side of the stream, thinking over his fortunes, and when he was too tired to think, he read over his friend's letter, and though its contents interested him little, he at last knew it almost by heart, for he had nothing to read which could come closer to him. There was the added interest that Erfurt was Philip Reiser's birthplace, so that they had exchanged towns, and Anton Reiser was now on the very spot where his friend had spent the early days of his youth, and received his first impressions from the surrounding world. Here in imagination he lived over again Philip Reiser's years of childhood, and as he sat in the valley by the stream reading his letter, which recalled his whole personality, he felt himself doubled in his friend. That was why he made a special friend of Ockord, who had known Philip Reiser at Erfurt, and with whom he very often talked about him. Ockord was an amiable young enthusiast, for whose imagination life had still the charm of youth; inspired by a lofty sense of friendship he had a touch of affectation but was at heart a man of genuine feeling. Reiser found his mate in him and did not rest till he went with him one Sunday into the Carthusian church, for he had not dared to go in alone, because he thought it would attract attention.

They had talked on the way of the emptiness and shortness of life, though it is to be noted that Reiser was then nineteen and Ockord twenty, and they did not know what to do with the rest of their lives, when they entered the monastery and went into the church, the bare white walls and the lonely choir of which preached the silence of the grave. The church is visited by hardly any one except the Carthusians, and as there is no congregation there is no pulpit or chairs or benches, nothing but bare walls and flat pavement, which gives the church, in the glimmering light which falls through the windows from above, a very solemn and melancholy aspect.

Ockord and Reiser knelt quite alone at a desk in front of the choir, when the white-robed monks came in one after the other, and each bending his head pulled at the bell. They sat in the choir and intoned their penitential prayers in deep melancholy tones: presently they stood up and sang hymns, which echoed sadly; then they fell on their faces and prayed for mercy in deep and plaintive tones. At one end of the semicircle stood a very handsome young man with pale cheeks. Reiser could not turn away his eyes from the young man's eyes as he lifted them reverently to heaven. Ockord knew this unhappy man, who had entered the Carthusian Order because the friend of his youth had been killed by lightning at his side, and Reiser could not banish the young man's face from his mind.

He spent half-days on the old wall behind his house, longing to enter the peaceful walled enclosure, which to his mind shut out all the world with its deceptions and illusions. He would fade away to the grave there with that young man, would dig his garden in solitude, greet the soft rays of the setting sun in his cell, and released from all earthly desires and hopes, look forward to death in peace and cheerfulness. In this mood he composed the following on the old ruined walls behind his house.

Home of holy peace, foretelling the grave's last silence
Strangely thou drawest my tearful eyes to thy lonely dwelling

Moving my soul. Hail thou O grey-haired reverend tenant
Living in pious peace, far away from the crowd and its rumours,
Far from all vain illusion, from proud men's ostentation.
Here thou canst busy thy hands, thy lonely garden adorning,
While, as thy soul is striving oft with noble impatience
Out of its prison to fly, thou makest it every day nobler,
Ready for heaven. Oh hail! Be it thine that solitude holy
Still to enjoy, that thy spirit which earthly thoughts has abandoned
May at the last dissolve in pure angelic emotion,
Rising in strength to find its source eternal in heaven.
Splendid thus were thy lot. And thou, who saddened by sorrow
Lived a full life, but still hast strength, thy hair all unsprinkled
Yet with grey. And thou in the glamour of youth and its power,
Who hast exchanged the joys of life for the peace of the cloister,
Wast thou haply the victim of scorn from the arrogant worldling?
Did a false friend betray thee or didst thou come here persuaded
Men's desires are as naught and all their hopes are as nothing,
Nothing, yet full of pride? Or was it bitterness merely,
Sense of the hollow taste of the joys of living which made you
See in life's flower-decked stage but a scene of desolation?
Then it is well with you, who have found a city of refuge
Strong to meet the cunning devices of evil and save you
Far from the chatter of fools, from vice's glowing seductions,
Far from illusory joys of life. But what do I see now?
Lo from the young man's eyes a tear down trickling slowly
Silently speaks: careworn and pale he weeps the departing
Strength of his shattered life. It fades as a withering flower
Dies away in the heat. O thou who in prison most holy
Pent from the light dost faint from discipline or unkindness,
Weep, ah weep, my son! For tears thy God will forgive thee,

Sorrow which Nature prompted thy inmost being to utter.
Could I but make my tears with thy tears mingle together,
Bringing comfort and soothing calm to thy soul's deep anguish!
Softly smiling thou seest the spring sun go to its setting,
Look how its last red glow thy lonely window illumines,
Whilst thou, laid on thy bed, dost dream of days of the future,
Full of glorious visions art rapt and lost in the mazes,
Wandering joyous onward. But then from thy happy slumber
Straight thou wakest to see—the four bare walls of thy chamber.
Gone is the smiling sunshine of hope. Go, zephyrs, and whisper
Gently about his dwelling, caress him in sympathy tender,
Wipe the tears from his eyes. Ye flowers, bloom in his garden!
Nightingale, sing at his window thy song of comfort and cheer him
Till the All-loving at last from life's tormenting fetters
Looses his suffering soul; and thou in sympathy tender
Oft in the dewy night by his grave wilt go and lament him.

Reiser was indeed so completely taken up with the Carthusians that he began seriously to think how he could spend his days thus secluded from the world, so that he might be released once for all from whatever oppressed him, and from the wishes and desires which tormented him.

When he had been deep in such thoughts for some days Ockord came to him and said that the Erfurt students intended to act a play, and that some parts were still unassigned. This had such a powerful effect on Reiser's imagination that the Carthusian monastery with its high walls at once retired into the background and the lighted stage suddenly came to the fore. When Ockord went on to say that they intended to offer Reiser a part in the play they wished to act, every serious and melancholy thought vanished at once.

The play that the students meant to act was called *Medon* or *The Sage's Revenge*, and it might be called an epitome of all morality, such wonderfully virtuous sentiments were preached by all the characters. Reiser was to take the part of Clelia, the beloved of Medon, because his chin showed but the slightest trace of a beard, and also his height did not seem strange for a woman, as the actor who played Medon was almost a giant. In spite of the obvious peculiarity of the part Reiser could not resist his inclination to tread the stage somehow or other, especially as the opportunity was offered him unsought.

Meanwhile Dr. Froriep had written to Hanover and inquired about Reiser's conduct in the house of his former teacher, Rector Sextro, and the Rector to Reiser's surprise had given him a testimonial which brought him into still greater favour with Dr. Froriep. The Rector had written that the young man's abilities showed much promise. This was enough to induce Dr. Froriep to look with indulgence on the less favourable part of the testimonial, and to take up Reiser's cause with redoubled zeal, in order if possible to secure him the favour of the Prince again. The testimonial itself was indulgent in tone, except in one point, that on account of his night walks he was suspected of profligacy; this was an accusation which was wholly unfounded, as he was deterred from it by his hard lot, his self-contempt and even by his enthusiasms. His passion for the Stage was the cause to which they traced his other irregularities, a passion which had led many other young people at the Hanover school astray. And indeed just at the moment that the letter arrived Reiser was about to act with the students of Erfurt. Dr. Froriep tried to dissuade him, but when he saw how set he was on it he gave way to his folly and did not withdraw his favour.

The preparations for the play were made: Reiser learnt the part of Clelia by heart, and frequent rehearsals were held, which made Reiser acquainted with most of the students in Erfurt, who all treated him very politely and had a favourable opinion of him; he was thus transported into a world very different from that in which he had lived since childhood.

Between the rehearsals Reiser did not fail regularly to attend Dr. Froriep's Preacher's Course. This consisted of a class of students, who practised preaching in the Merchants' Church with closed doors before Dr. Froriep and the other students. It was Reiser's desire to be allowed to appear here and be heard declaiming, and the prospect of Dr. Froriep allowing him to enter the pulpit there was most attractive. He had actually thought out a subject, in handling which he would describe the beauties of Nature and the changes of the seasons in poetic colours, and would give a moving peroration by describing the bright and dazzling prospect of eternity. But hindrances intervened and this desire was never fulfilled in Erfurt.

As was natural when his wishes were so strong, he doubted whether the play would really be performed, and he would keep his part, but his wish was fulfilled. He was dressed with all care as

Clelia. The lamps were lit, the curtain rose, and he stood before a large audience and played his long part without embarrassment or thinking of his unnatural part, so completely was he absorbed in the thought that he was taking part in a theatrical performance and that his co-operation was necessary at every moment.

This absorption in his part made him forget himself and led the spectators to pay less heed to the fact of his taking a woman's part, and his acting was applauded. As he had now appeared on the stage and yet remained a student he was doubly pleased, and for a few days he felt so happy in the memory of that evening that everything which had happened to him in the few weeks that he had spent in Erfurt seemed like a dream.

Now too he inserted poems from time to time in *The Citizens' and Peasants' Weekly*, and so his name as a writer became known among the townsmen of Erfurt. He also corrected proofs for Gradelmüller the printer, and through him made acquaintance with a scholar, who, though a man with great gifts of mind and character, was pursued by adverse fortune till his death, because long and continuous sufferings had destroyed his power of making his merits felt, and crippled his ability to get his footing and hold his own in the world.

This Doctor Sauer had written a series of weekly articles for Gradelmüller the printer called *Medon or the Three Friends*, which had appeared for a year. This showed what struggle he had had with circumstances, how hard it must have been for him to write a series of trivial articles, though they showed sparks of suppressed genius. Yet he had to write and hand in his manuscript every week, in order to keep his miserable life going for a year. As the publication now ceased, he had to earn his living by correcting proofs: and though he had valuable dramatic works of his own lying in his desk, which he had not the courage to bring out, he had to copy out a tragedy with great care and correctness for a man of position in Erfurt, in order to prolong his life for a few days by the earnings of a copyist. As a doctor he earned nothing, for he felt a strong bent to help just those who need help most and who get it least; and as these are precisely those who cannot pay for their treatment, the physician was in great danger of starving, if he had not published articles, read proofs, and copied tragedies. In a word he would take nothing for his services, and even brought medicines to the poor which he made up himself, and spent on them the little he had to spare, nay even more. As he was thus in the habit so to speak of throwing himself away, the people of the great world had no confidence in him, and most people did not know his name, though he had wide experience and considerable skill.

In medicine too he had produced some excellent publications, which unfortunately were lost in the crowd and like their writer unnoticed by his contemporaries. So, while he kept his other medical writings shut up in his desk, he was obliged to translate into Latin the work of a French physician, who came to Erfurt and knew better how to attract attention than Dr. Sauer, that he might live on his earnings as translator, and provide more medicines for his helpless and poor patients. Such indignities and humiliations at the hands of fortune were bound to tell upon a man of any feeling. Dr. Sauer faced them with a smile, yet at heart they sapped his strength and crippled his courage. How could he have confidence in his own merit, when all the world failed to recognize it?

Because of his connexion with Gradelmüller the printer, for whom he read proofs, he sometimes wrote articles in the famous *Citizens' and Peasants' Weekly* of Erfurt, and there Reiser read a poem by him *To the liberated Americans*, which would have deserved a place in a collection of the best German poems; as it was it was buried in a paper which was hawked in the beer-houses of Erfurt. It was as if his repressed spirit had in this poem once more expressed all its sense of freedom, such energy and ardent sympathy dominated its ideas.

Enchanted by this poem Reiser could not rest until he had made acquaintance with such an important fellow-worker in *The Citizens' and Peasants' Weekly*. But he found it difficult to gratify his wish, as Dr. Sauer felt no great desire to associate with any one from the class which had so to speak cast him out. However, a means of approach was found, as Reiser had continued his study of English at Erfurt, and offered to teach Dr. Sauer, who had expressed the wish to learn the language. The offer was accepted, and so Reiser had the opportunity at least several times a week of meeting the man to whom he wished to attach himself as closely as possible.

On these occasions Dr. Sauer opened his heart to Reiser and told him of the many ways in which from childhood up he had suffered oppression from his relations and teachers, and then all the successive strokes of fate which had beaten him to the dust, so that Reiser with rising indignation could not help describing as malicious the chain of circumstance which seemed of set purpose to hold down and torment a being endowed with thought and feeling. While Reiser thus expressed his indignation, Sauer framed his mouth into a gentle smile, which showed that he was far above such indignation, but also that he was already freed from earthly ties, and looked forward with anticipation to his complete liberation before long. His struggle was almost ended, he needed no longer to resist or defy fate. Nevertheless, many a time the fire of life kindled again in him. Sometimes he hoped to see happy days again, and was very eager to learn English, because he promised himself much from this study, especially to make use of medical works in English and also to earn money by translating from it. There was also some little prospect of some sort of maintenance in Erfurt, and he regarded this as a very lucky change of fortune, which he ascribed to his perseverance. If a man wanted to get anything in Erfurt, he used to tell Reiser, he had only to wait long enough and not lose patience : so modest were his desires and so easily was he encouraged by even a glimmer of better fortune.

He did not realize that no outward fortune could help him any more, because the spring of happiness had dried up within him, and the flower of his life was destroyed, so that its leaves were bound to wither. Reiser felt drawn to him by a sympathy as strong as if the man's fate were his own or inextricably bound up with his own. He felt as if the man was bound to be happy, if the course of the world was to go on. Reiser was deceived then, as often afterwards, in his presentiment, and in his belief that suffering in the past was bound to have its compensation on earth. Sauer passed away a few years later, without seeing better days. When outward fortune smiled on him a little his inward strength had been crushed, and he remained unnoticed and unknown until his death, so that in the little street where he lived his nearest neighbours asked, when the coffin was carried out, whose funeral it was. A death so unnoticed is very striking in a town so sparsely populated as Erfurt. The few days which Reiser spent with Dr. Sauer in Erfurt were very important for him because they gave a new impulse to his character. He summoned all his strength to fight the repressive forces which had had such a paralysing influence on Sauer's spirit, and the indignation he felt at this inspired him with a defiant resolve not to succumb even to the hardest suffering, and to avenge his friend's suffering by resistance.

One day they had gone to a village outside Erfurt, and Ockord was of their company: as they returned home towards evening, they came to a stream bordered with thick bushes, crawling darkly along between its banks. Here Sauer stood still and tried to measure the depth of the water with his stick but could not reach the bottom. He then gazed into the water with his arms crossed, watching the black surface of the stream as it crawled along. The picture of Sauer, with pale cheeks and arms crossed, gazing down intensely at that Stygian stream, came vividly back to Reiser's mind, when he heard the news of his death some years later. For if ever a picture had the significance of symbol and fact coinciding, it was there.

But once more a cheerful prospect opened before Reiser, for the students, having tasted the pleasure of play-acting, bethought them of another performance. The plays they chose were *The Suspicious Man* and *The Treasure* by Lessing: in the former Reiser again had two women's parts, for which he had to wear women's clothes, and in the latter the part of Maskaril, and his credit as an actor was so well established among the students, that it was regarded as a kindness that he should undertake the parts, and there was no need for him to thrust himself forward.

While the preparations for this second performance were being made, Reiser began a treatise on sensibility, with which he proposed to make his first appearance as author. In this work affected sensibility was to be made ridiculous, and true sensibility put in its proper light. The intended satire on sentimentality was rather coarse, as he compared it to a plague which must be shunned: any one who came from a district where it prevailed was to be barred all entrance into city or village. Reiser's indignation was chiefly roused by the *Sentimental Journeys* which were appearing one after another in Germany and by the many affected imitations of *The Sorrows of Werther*, though in his heart he had to accuse himself too of this sin, but that only made him more anxious to cure himself by attacking it.

Just as he was engaged in writing this treatise one evening the printer Pockwitz from Hanover came in and brought him a letter from Philip Reiser. This was the printer in Hanover for whom he had written a number of New Year's poems, by which he had seen himself for the first time in print. As Reiser saw the printer out of the door, the latter pressed a small piece of gold into his hand, sufficient at once to lift out of the dust a man who for weeks had been destitute of money and yet wished to conceal his need. This unexpected gift had an added value from the way in which it was given, as the printer added that this trifle was an old debt he was repaying, because Reiser had written him new year's wishes, poems, &c., in Hanover for nothing.

In Reiser's circumstances a golden gulden was invaluable, and at once relieved him from a number of petty embarrassments which he could not have told any one of. As a result he passed some happy days at Erfurt, when he felt no oppression either from within or from without, and had no gloomy views of the future. Philip Reiser's letter too was more interesting than the last, for he was told that several of those schoolfellows who had acted with him in Hanover had followed his example, and some of them had slipped away secretly, to go on the stage. Chief among them was Iffland, who had acted Beaumarchais in *Clavigo*, the son of the Precentor Winter, the Prefect of the Choir, Ohlhorst, and a minister's son, one Timaeus, with whom Reiser had taken some romantic walks in Hanover before he left. Reiser, finding they had all copied his example, found a peculiar pride in the fact that he first had the courage to take this step.

Then Philip Reiser wrote to him in his exaggerated style that the poet Hölty had died at Hanover, and ended with the words: 'Rejoice, O poet; weep, O man!' The letter contained little about the progress of his love-story.

While Reiser was occupied with the parts in the second play he found a new friend at Erfurt, a student called Neries from Hamburg, living with Dr. Froriep, who showed him a copy of Reiser's poem 'The Carthusian Cloister', and so procured the writer a new friend. This became a friendship exactly of the sentimental kind, against which Reiser was engaged in writing. Young Neries had indeed a heart full of feeling, but he let himself be carried by the stream, and at every opportunity played the part of the man of feeling, without knowing it, for he often vied with Reiser in attacking the absurd affectations of sentimentality, but as he tried not merely to seem a man of sentiment, but really to be so, he no longer looked on it as affectation, but regarded it as a serious thing, not to be ridiculed, and gradually drew Reiser into this current of sentiment which strains the character till it falls into the most mawkish condition imaginable.

Reiser felt it an encouragement that any one who was well off should make friends with him in his poverty. Gradually he developed a strong affection for young Neries, which was increased by his genuine friendship for Reiser, so that they grew nearer to one another, even in their follies, and mutually encouraged one another in melancholy and sentimentality. This happened especially in their lonely walks, when they very often posed against a background of Nature reading Klopstock's *The Disciples of Emmaus* at sundown, or Zachariä's *Creation of Hell* on a dull day, and so on.

Their favourite resort was the slopes of the Steigerwald, from which there is a view of the town of Erfurt with its old towers and the whole circuit of its gardens. The inhabitants of Erfurt often take their walks there, and perhaps light a fire and make coffee in the patriarchal style.

Here Neries and Reiser often sat for hours at a time, reading to one another in turn from some poet. Most of the time it was hard work and involved some discomfort, but this they did not confess to one another, that they might go away with the thought 'we have sat together in friendly fashion in the Steigerwald and looked down from it into the charming valley and at the same time feasted our minds with a beautiful poem'. When you consider how many circumstances must combine to make sitting and reading in the open air agreeable it can well be imagined how many petty difficulties Neries and Reiser had to contend with in these sentimental scenes, how often the ground was damp, ants crawled up their legs, and the wind turned the pages.

Neries found a special pleasure in reading the whole of Klopstock's *Messiah* to Reiser. Both found it horribly tiresome, though they would not confess it to each other and hardly to themselves, but Neries had the advantage of reading aloud, which passed the time, while Reiser was compelled to listen and express delight. The hours so spent were the dreariest he can remember in his life, dreary enough to frighten him more than anything else from living his life over again. For nothing can well be more painful than a complete flatness of spirit, when a man is trying to emerge from it, and innocently blaming himself every moment for the dullness which prevents him from being moved and touched by the lofty poetry which is ringing incessantly in his ears.

Though Nerics and Reiser were almost inseparable, Reiser longed again for the solitary walks which had given him the purest pleasure: but he had spoilt their effect, for in general he expected too much from them, and so came home dissatisfied if he had not found what he looked for. As soon as ' There ' became ' Here ', it lost all its charm, and the spring of happiness dried up. The vexation which then took the place of eager hope was of such a coarse, common, and bare kind, that it admitted no tinge of tender melancholy: it was very much the feeling of a man wet to the skin with rain, who returns home chilled and shivering, and finds a cold room.

This was the sort of life Reiser led while he went on with his treatise on false sentiment; but once in his solitary walks he noticed an uncommon expression of sensibility in a man of the people where he would least have expected it. He was walking among the gardens of Erfurt, and as it was the season for plums, he could not resist plucking a fine ripe plum from an overhanging branch: the owner of the garden noticed it and attacked him roughly, asking whether he was aware that the plum he had plucked would cost him a ducat. Reiser tried to beat him down, but was obliged to confess that he had not a penny on him. But in order to content him he was obliged to give him his only good pocket-handkerchief, which he was very sorry to lose. As he went away sadly he saw only a few steps farther on a fine clasp-knife lying on the ground: he picked it up quickly and called to the gardener, proposing to exchange the knife he had found for the handkerchief.

What was Reiser's astonishment when the gardener, who had been so rude to him before, suddenly fell on his neck and kissed him, and offered him his friendship, for Reiser, he said, must be a friend of Providence, which had let him find the knife, which the gardener himself had lost. He gladly gave Reiser back his handkerchief, and assured him that his garden was open to him at any time, to pluck as many plums as he chose, and that he would serve him in any way he could, for such an incident had never happened to him before.

When Reiser reflected on this odd chance as he went away, he was struck by it all the more because this was the first time in his life that a really lucky event, which required a rare combination of circumstances, had befallen him.

His luck seems to have exhausted itself as it were in this trifling incident, to make him pay all the more heavily for the mere fault of his existence. He was like the Vicar of Wakefield, who threw an extraordinarily lucky throw of the dice, when he was playing for pence with his friend, just before he received the news of the merchant's bankruptcy, by which he lost all his property. Fate for a little while held back the humiliations designed for Reiser, and left him undisturbed in the pleasure secured him by the second theatrical performance, in which three parts were assigned him. His most ardent wish was now in some degree fulfilled, though he had not been able to appear in any tragic part. What was more, some confidence was felt in his theatrical views, his advice was asked and he became better known among the students by his taking part in the play as well as by the poems he had written: they addressed him with politeness, a pleasant compensation for his position in the School at Hanover.

He now diligently visited the University Library, where he took special pleasure in studying Du Halde's description of China, and wasted a good deal of time over it. Just then too appeared *Siegwart, a Story of the Cloister*, and he read the book through several times with his friend Neries, and both put the greatest pressure on themselves, in spite of the most horrible ennui, to keep up to the same pitch of emotion through all three volumes. Finally, Reiser was bold enough to plan converting the story into an historical tragedy, for which he made all sorts of rough drafts and wasted time over them. When he did not succeed as he wished, at each failure of his efforts he experienced the most miserable hours imaginable. Nature herself and his own thoughts had lost their charm, every moment was a burden and life itself was nothing but anguish.

The Pains of Poetry may therefore be regarded as constituting a special section in the history of

Reiser's sorrows, which is to represent his inner and outward condition in all their relations, defining what in many men remains hidden even from themselves, because they are reluctant to penetrate to the source and foundation of their unpleasant feelings. It was these secret sorrows with which Reiser had to contend almost from childhood. When the spell of poetry came upon him unbidden, first a sorrowful feeling arose in him: he imagined a something in which he lost himself, and in which all he had ever heard, read, or thought, lost itself, a something whose existence, if only he could represent it properly, would give the reader a hitherto unfelt indescribable pleasure. But he could not tell whether this was to be a tragedy, a romance, or an elegiac poem: enough that it must be something, which would arouse a feeling of which the poet had in some degree had a presentiment. In the moments of this blessed presentiment the tongue could only produce a few stammering sounds, something like those in Klopstock's Odes, the gaps between which are marked by dots. These single sounds always indicated general ideas such as 'great', 'exalted', 'tears of joy' and the like. This lasted until the feeling subsided, without having produced a couple of rational lines to make a definite beginning.

During this crisis then nothing beautiful had come into being which the mind could lay hold of afterwards, and everything else which was actually there was not deemed worthy of any more attention. It was as though the mind had had a dim presentiment of something which it could not be, and by which its own existence was made to look contemptible.

It is an unmistakable sign that a man has no true vocation as a poet, when he is moved to compose by some feeling in general, without having present in his mind at the same time or even earlier the definite scene which he means to create. In a word, the man who, while he feels, cannot fix his eyes on the scene in all its details, has feeling but no poetic power. And certainly nothing is more dangerous than to surrender oneself to such a delusive tendency; a young man cannot be warned too soon to test himself and see whether the wish is not taking the place of the faculty, and because it can never take its place, the forbidden pleasure is punished by a perpetual feeling of distress.

This was Reiser's fate: he darkened the best hours of his life by unsuccessful attempts, by idle striving after deceptive illusions, which constantly hovered before his mind, but vanished suddenly into smoke and mist just as he thought he was grasping them. If ever there was a man for whom the spell of poetry was in sharp contrast with his life and fortunes, it was Reiser. From childhood up he was in a sphere which depressed him to the dust; he could only rise into the poetic atmosphere by passing from one stage of culture to a higher, where he could not keep his footing. Once more he found this in his present position; he had no sitting-room to himself, and as the weather began to grow colder, had to live in the common sitting-room, the occupants of which had to go out while it was being swept. The whole family lived in this room, as well as Reiser and another student, and everybody received visits there. Conversation, children crying, singing, quarrelling, shouting, went on there: these were the immediate surroundings in which Reiser wanted to write his philosophic treatise on sentimentality and give body to his poetical ideals.

Here then the tragedy of Siegwart was to be written, which began with his stay with the hermit. This was always a favourite idea of Reiser's, and the favourite idea of almost all young people who imagine that they have a vocation for poetry. This is very natural, as the position of a hermit is in a way itself a poem, and the poet here finds his material almost ready-made. But when a writer hits on such subjects it is generally a sign that he has no genuine poetic vein, because he looks for poetry in the subjects he handles, instead of ennobling by his own poetic gift any subject which presents itself to his imagination. In the same way it is a bad sign when the supposed poetic genius chooses the horrible as his subject: for here too the poetry is in the subject, which is used to cover the emptiness and barrenness of the writer. Thus, Reiser when at school in Hanover tried to pile up perjury, incest, and parricide in one tragedy to be called *Perjury*, and while writing it imagined the performance of the piece and the effect which it would make on the spectators. This second sign should also act as a deterrent to any one who carefully examines himself on his vocation as a poet. For the true poet and artist does not hope for his reward or find it in the effect his work will produce:

he finds pleasure in the work itself, and would not consider it lost even if no one should see it. His work attracts him involuntarily, his progress depends on his own resources, and honour is only the stimulus which spurs him on. Mere ambition may inspire the wish to take a great work in hand, but it can never give creative power to one who did not possess it before he knew ambition.

A third bad sign is when young poets are inclined to take their subject-matter from the remote and unknown ; when they choose Oriental settings and the like, where everything is remote from the scenes of man's everyday life, and where too the material is therefore poetic in itself. This was Reiser's case : he had long been in travail with a poem on the Creation, where the material was the most remote that can be imagined and where instead of the detail, of which he was afraid, he found nothing but great masses to handle, which might be taken for elevated poetry, a style to which young poets without vocation always incline rather than to what lies close to men, for to everyday subjects their genius must impart the elevation, which in uncommon topics they hope to find ready-made.

Meanwhile Reiser's situation became daily more trying, because the help he hoped for from Hanover did not come, and the people of his house looked askance at him, the more they realized that he had neither money nor the prospect of it. He was no longer in a position to pay for the breakfast and supper that he had in the house, and they made it clear to him that they were not willing to advance him money any longer. As they could get nothing out of him and he was dull company as well, it was natural that they wanted to get rid of him and gave him notice. There was nothing strange in this, but Reiser took it tragically. The idea of being in the way, the idea that he was barely tolerated by the people among whom he lived, made him hate his whole existence. All the memories of his childhood and youth crowded into his mind, he poured scorn on himself and in desperation wished again to resign himself to blind fate.

He wanted to leave Erfurt again that very day, and all sorts of romantic ideas crossed his mind; the most attractive was that he would go to Weimar and become a servant on any terms to the author of *The Sorrows of Werther*. He would thus as it were incognito be close to the person of the one man of all others who had made the deepest impression on him; he went outside the Gate and looked across at the Ettenberg, which lay like a dividing wall between him and his desires. He went to Dr. Froriep to take leave, without being able to give him a good reason for leaving Erfurt again. Dr. Froriep set down his resolve to melancholy, advised him to stay and would not let him go till Reiser had promised him at least not to go away till after the next day. This sympathy with his fortunes flattered Reiser's feelings, but as soon as he was alone again the thought of being a burden to his neighbours pursued him like a tormenting spirit, and gave him no rest: he wandered about in the loneliest parts of Erfurt, near the Carthusian Monastery, for which he now seriously longed as a safe refuge, and gazed tearfully at its peaceful walls. Then he wandered farther on till evening came, and the sky was overcast with clouds and heavy rain fell, which soon drenched him to the skin. His feelings of unrest were aggravated by a feverish chill, which drove him about in storm and rain past ancient walls and along empty streets, for he could not bear the thought of returning to his lodging. He climbed the high steps to the old Cathedral, tied a handkerchief round his head and tried to shelter himself for a time from the rain under the old walls. From sheer weariness he fell into a kind of stupefying sleep, from which he was roused again by a fresh downpour and by the howling of the wind, and wandered off again through the streets. As the rain beat against his face the words from *Lear* came to him 'To shut me out, on such a night as this!' and in his despair he acted through the part of Lear and forgot himself in the fortunes of Lear, when, driven out by his daughters, he wanders through the stormy night and calls upon the elements to avenge their horrible offence. He was so absorbed in this scene that for a time he thought of his own condition with a kind of rapture, but presently this feeling was deadened, and he was left with the bare reality, which made him burst into loud scornful laughter at himself.

In this mood he returned to the old Cathedral, which was now open, and where the Chapter were assembling for early matins by candlelight. The old Gothic building, the scattered lights, the reflection of the high windows made a wonderful impression on Reiser, who had wandered all night and now sat down on a bench. He was sheltered from the rain, as in a house, and yet this was no home for the living. These dim arches seemed to invite the men who sought a refuge from life, and one who had lived through a night like that which Anton had just been through, might well be inclined to follow the call. Seated on the bench in the Cathedral Reiser felt himself transported into a kind of remoteness and tranquillity, which was inexpressibly pleasant, relieving him from every care and every pain, and making him forget the past. He had drunk of Lethe and felt himself dreaming away into the land of peace. His gaze was fixed on the pale reflection of the high windows, and it was this above all which seemed to transport him into a new world. What a stately bedchamber was this in which he opened his eyes after dreaming the whole night through!

For such moments in Reiser's life were indeed like dreams of a fevered brain, yet they were real enough and arose from his fortunes ever since he was a child. For was it not always self-contempt, repressed self-consciousness, which reduced him to this state? And was not this self-contempt caused by the constant pressure of circumstances, for which chance was more responsible than men?

When dawn came Reiser returned from the Cathedral with quieter feelings, and on his way met his friend Neries who was attending an early lecture, and was alarmed when he looked at Reiser's face and saw how the night had exhausted and distracted him. Neries would not rest till Reiser had confided his condition to him. After friendly reproaches for not trusting him more, he took him back to his old lodging, tried to set him in a better light with the people there, and settled his friend's small debt. This warm sympathy on the part of his friend restored Reiser's wounded self-confidence; he felt proud of his friend and honoured himself in him.

And now, in order to be sure of solitude, he stipulated that he should occupy a garret-room, where they gave him a bed and where, left to himself again, he passed a few weeks not unpleasantly. Here he read and studied, and would have been completely happy in his retirement, if his poem on the Creation had not tormented him, for it often drove him to despair when he tried to express things which he thought that he felt and which yet were beyond all expression.

What caused him most trouble was the description of Chaos, which occupied almost the whole first canto, and on which he best liked to dwell with his morbid imagination, and yet could never find expressions to fit his vast grotesque ideas. He imagined Chaos upheld by a false deceptive structure, which in a moment turned to dream and illusion; a structure which was far more beautiful than reality but for that reason unsubstantial and unenduring. A mock sun rose on the horizon and announced a brilliant day. Under this deceptive influence the bottomless morass became covered with a crust, on which flowers blossomed and springs murmured: suddenly the contending forces worked up from the depths, the storm roared from the abyss, darkness with all its terrors burst from its hidden ambush and swallowed up the new-born day in an awesome grave. The pent-up forces struggled angrily to expand on every side, and groaned under the resisting pressure. The waters rose in billows and roared beneath the raging winds. Deep down the pent-up fires bellowed—the earth which was about to rise, the rock which was about to settle to its foundation sank back again with thundering crash into the all-devouring abyss. With such vast images Reiser's fancy overwrought itself in the hours when his mind itself was a chaos, with no beam of tranquil thought to light it, when the faculties of his mind had lost their balance and darkness overshadowed his spirit, when the charm of the actual disappeared and dream and illusion were more prized than order, light, and truth. And all these phenomena had their source in some measure in the idealism to which he naturally inclined, and in which he was confirmed by the philosophic systems that he studied in Hanover: and on this bottomless shore he found no place for his foot to rest. Painful struggle and unrest dogged him at every step. It was this which drove him from the society of men to garrets and attics, where he often spent his pleasantest hours in fantastic dreams, and it was this too which inspired in him his irresistible bent for the romantic and theatrical.

Through his circumstances at this time, inward and outward, he was again completely lost in the ideal world, and it was not surprising that on the first opportunity his old passion took fire, and his thoughts once more centred on the Stage, which in him was a necessity of life rather than a necessity of art. The occasion soon presented itself as

Speich's Company of actors came to Erfurt and received permission to play in the Ball-room where the students had acted their play.

Reiser was already known and had got a certain reputation for his talents as an actor, so he became known at once to the Director of the little troupe, who was willing to engage him, as soon as he chose to turn actor.

What Reiser had striven for in vain while he struggled with all the miseries of life was now suddenly offered him without asking, and the temptation was too strong. He put all other considerations aside and lived and moved only in the world of the theatre, for which once more as in Hanover he cherished an enthusiastic reverence, which extended even to the programme, and he regarded all the Company down to the prompter and the copyist with a kind of envy. One of the company named Beil, who afterwards became a famous actor, specially attracted his curiosity. He was specially distinguished among the members of this Company, and Reiser's most ardent wish was to make his acquaintance, which he did without difficulty. He confided his wishes to Beil, who encouraged him in his resolve to go on the stage, and Reiser hoped at once to find a friend in him.

He now set aside all other considerations, and tried as far as possible to conceal from himself all thought of Dr. Froriep and his friend Neries, and without telling any one engaged himself to the Director of the troupe; he was bold enough to hope that he would so distinguish himself in his first part, that every one would approve his resolve. The question now was, in what part he should first appear, and it chanced that *Poets à la mode* was to be acted in a few days and he was offered a part in that.

He wished to play Dunkel and had already learnt the part by heart, but his new friend Beil dissuaded him, because he himself had always played this part with great success, and therefore, he said, Reiser had better play Reimreich, a part which was taken by a less important actor. Reiser was well content to accept this, as the applause he had won in the parts of Maskaril and of Master Blasius gave him some confidence in his capacity for comic parts. So he wrote out his part and learnt it by heart. So far as his stage career was concerned he was supremely happy, when he noticed something which filled him with anxiety and alarm in the midst of his hopes. He felt like one buffeted by a messenger of Satan : he noticed that he was threatened with the loss of his hair. Just at the moment when he had most need of a body without flaw, this misfortune befell him, and filled him with horror in anticipation. In his trouble he hastened to his faithful friend Dr. Sauer, who encouraged him to hope he would keep his hair. So on the evening when *Poets à la mode* was to be acted he found himself in the dressing-room behind the slips, and dressed so as to make Reimreich look as laughable as possible ; his name was posted up that day on the play-bills at every street corner.

When the play was about to come on his friend Neries came to the theatre and reproached him bitterly. Reiser would not be disturbed in the excitement of his stage-fever, and was completely absorbed in his part, in which his friend Neries at last sympathized so far as to laugh at his comic get up. But suddenly a messenger appeared, who informed the Director that Dr. Froriep would go at once to the Governor and make a complaint if he dared to allow the student whose name was printed on the programme to appear on the stage : in that case he would certainly lose his licence to play in Erfurt.

Reiser stood as if petrified, and the Director in his anxiety did not know where to turn, till an actor offered to play the part as well as he could with the help of the prompter, for at that moment the pit was stamping for the curtain to go up. Reiser walked up and down in a rage behind the scenes, gnawing his part which he held in his hand : then he hurried as quickly as he could from the theatre and wandered about all the streets in the storm and rain till towards midnight he flung himself down exhausted on a covered bridge which protected him from the rain, and rested for a time, and then wandered about again till daybreak.

These extreme efforts were the only thing which in the first and bitterest moment of his distress could at all make up for what he had lost. His continued state of passionate excitement had in it something which gave fresh food to his unsatisfied longings. The whole failure of his stage career was crowded into this night, in which he traversed within himself all the scenes of passion which he had been debarred from representing on the stage.

Next day Dr. Froriep sent for him and talked to him like a father. He made use of the flattering expression that Reiser's gifts were destined for something better than the Stage, that he misread his own nature and did not feel his own value.

As Reiser saw that it was impossible to satisfy his desire in Erfurt he deceived himself once more, and persuaded himself that he was voluntarily giving up the idea of the Stage, because everything as it were combined to hinder his resolve, and Dr. Froriep's warning had in it so much that was flattering. But he was scarcely alone again when his self-delusion avenged itself by a renewal of bitter vexation, irresolution, and inward struggle: then a few days later came the hardest blow of all, the blow he had hoped to avoid—he had to lose his hair.

The thought of having to appear in a wig, a thing quite unusual among Erfurt students, was intolerable. With the little money he still had left he went to the far end of the town and put up at an inn, where he only slept and was served with bread and beer in the evening, so as to make his money go farther. In the daytime he wandered in lonely places, seeking shelter in churches if it rained, and so spent nearly a fortnight, while no one knew what had become of him, until one of his friends caught sight of him and immediately he was surprised unexpectedly in the inn by Neries, W——, Ockord and some others who were interested in him and reproached him in a friendly spirit for absenting himself. By this time he was able to comb the hair on his forehead over his wig, and then if he powdered heavily he gave the impression of wearing his own hair. He resolved then to join the friends who fetched him and go into society again, but he wished as far as possible to confine his society to this group and to live a retired and solitary life.

This wish too they tried to gratify. The kind-hearted W—— at once spoke to his uncle, Professor Springer of Erfurt, describing Reiser's state and his need of solitude. Professor Springer sent for Reiser, and no one ever spoke to him with more encouragement and real sympathy than this man, for whom Reiser conceived the greatest attachment and veneration. At that time he was delivering a statistical course, several lectures of which Reiser attended, and as he was much interested in the subject, Springer urged him to take it up and promised to help him in every way. He began by providing Reiser with the retired lodging he desired, by giving up to him his own summer-house. Reiser was given the key of this, and from his window had the most beautiful view of the network of gardens which surrounded Erfurt.

Reiser again enjoyed free board, Dr. Froriep took the liveliest interest in him and tried to provide him with maintenance. He began to attend lectures on mathematics, and his kind friends let him share in all their literary meetings and read him some of their productions. All was now in the best train, when unluckily a new access of poetry spoilt everything.

To begin with, his new retired and romantic lodging contributed not a little to excite his imagination, and a letter which he wrote to Philip Reiser at Hanover hastened his relapse. This letter was written in the tone of the Letters of Werther. He had to call up 'patriarchal' ideas, but unfortunately could not do it without affectation. To enable him to write this letter Reiser first procured a teapot and borrowed a cup, and as he had no wood in the house he bought some straw, which is used for fires in Erfurt, in order to boil water for tea in the small stove in his room, and at last succeeded after being almost stifled with smoke. And as soon as he had done this he wrote in a sort of triumphal tone to Philip Reiser, 'Now, my friend, I have as charming surroundings as I could wish. I look out of my little window over the open country, and see in the distance a row of trees rising on a low hill, and think of you, . . . I have the keys of my lodging and am master of house and garden. . . . When I sit, as I often do, by my stove and make my own tea. . . .' So it ran on and grew into a long and important letter, and as Reiser could not find it in his heart not to show this fine letter to his critical friend Dr. Sauer, the kind-hearted doctor did him a mischief by the handsome compliment that, if it were not that he loved Reiser's presence too much he would like to be parted from him, so as to get such letters.

And so the impulse to poetry which had almost subsided was once more called to life. Reiser first tried to conduct his poem on the Creation safely through Chaos, and with fresh agonies began to lose himself in describing horrible contradictions and vast and involved mazes of thought, until at last he was redeemed from a very hell of ideas by two hexameters which he took out of the Bible :

Over the silent waters the voice of th' Eternal resounded
Gently, 'Let there be light', He spoke and light had arisen.

It was remarkable that the desire to continue the poem passed away, as soon as the subject ceased to be terrible. He therefore looked for a subject which was bound to remain terrible and which he could handle in several cantos, and this could be no other than death itself. He found it a flattering thought that one so young as himself chose so serious a subject, and began,

A man who, still in youth, had drunk of sorrow's cup.

But when he got to work and began to attack the first canto, the title of which he had written out fair, he found that he was bitterly disappointed in his hope of discovering a wealth of fearful images available. His wings drooped and his spirit was crippled : he saw nothing but a dark and empty desolation before him, where there was no sign even of the fermenting life that he had described in his scene of Chaos. Eternal night veiled every figure, and eternal sleep arrested every movement.

With a kind of fury he strained his imagination to introduce images into this darkness, but they grew dim and black like the green poplar leaves of Hercules' crown when he approached the house of Pluto to fetch Cerberus. Everything that he wanted to write dissolved in smoke and mist, and his paper remained blank.

At last he collapsed under these constantly repeated and vain efforts of an unreal passion for poetry, and fell into a kind of lethargy and complete disgust with life.

He threw himself one day on his bed, with his clothes on, and went on lying that night and the whole of the next day in a kind of stupor, from which he was only roused in the evening of the next day, which was Christmas, by a messenger from Councillor Springer, whose wife sent Reiser a large Christmas cake as a present.

This gift only confirmed him in his lethargic condition: he shut himself up with this big cake and lived on it for a fortnight, because he ate very little, as he spent day and night, except a few days at the end in bed, if not in a continuous sleep, at least in a perpetual doze. There was the further circumstance that he had no wood to warm the room: though he would only have had to say a word to satisfy this need, if he had not, in a way, preferred to have the want of fuel to allege as a motive for this peculiar way of life.

Reiser meanwhile was not disturbed by his friends, because he had often told them that he wanted for once in a way to be quite alone for a week or two. But his condition had a peculiar effect on Reiser; the first week he spent in a state of complete exhaustion and indifference, reproducing in his own person the condition he had in vain tried to describe in verse. He seemed to have drunk of Lethe and to have no spark of the wish to live left in him. But in the week which followed he was in a state which, when he looked at it as a separate thing, he had to regard as the happiest in his life. His dormant powers gradually recovered through his long-continued relaxation. His sleep became less disturbed, new life seemed to pervade his veins, the hopes of his youth one after another revived, he imagined himself once more honoured with fame and applause, and fair dreams gave him a prospect of a golden future. He was as it were intoxicated by this long sleep, and whenever his consciousness emerged from pleasant slumber he felt himself in an agreeable ecstasy. Even his waking life was a continued dream, and he would have given anything to remain in that state for ever. So he welcomed the sight of the frost on the windows because it forced him to stay a day longer in bed. He looked at the big loaf on his table as a sacred thing which he must spare as much as possible, because his happy condition could last only as long as the loaf.

Once more he felt equal to anything, if he had the chance. Again the Stage in all its glamour appealed to him, once more the passions of the Stage one after another stormed through his being, and he felt his acting overwhelm the emotions of the spectators.

When his loaf was finished he got up towards evening, and put his dress in order as well as he could : his first walk was to the theatre where he sat in a corner and watched first a play called *Inkle and Yarico* and then *The Sorrows of Young Werther*. The author of the latter had done little more than turn the letters of Werther into dialogues and monologues which were very long, but still interested the public and the actors profoundly because of their moving subject.

But a comical incident occurred in the tragic catastrophe of this play. They had borrowed a couple of rusty old pistols and had been careless enough not to test them beforehand. The actor who played Werther took them up and said, word for word as it is written in *Werther* : ‘ Your hands have touched them, you have wiped off the dust with your own hands, etc.' Then, in order to make the picture exact and complete, he had had a glass of wine and a loaf brought in, and the attendant had put a knife on the table. The play was so arranged that at the close Werther's friend William, when he heard the shot fired had to rush in and cry ' My God ! I heard a shot '. This was well enough, but when Werther seized the unlucky pistol, held it to his right temple, and pulled the trigger, it failed to go off. Not put out by this unlucky chance the determined actor threw away the pistol and exclaimed with pathos, ' What, wilt refuse me even this sad service ? ' Then he seized the other, pulled the trigger as before and unluckily again it missed fire. The words died in his mouth. With trembling hands he seized the bread knife which lay on the table, and to the horror of the spectators drove it through his coat and waistcoat. As he fell his friend William rushed in and cried ' My God ! I heard a shot fired ! ' A tragedy could hardly have had a more comic ending. But it did not stir Reiser from his high-soaring imagination, because he saw an imperfect production, which had to be replaced by something perfect.

He heard that the actors would leave Erfurt in a week and go to Leipzig, and that Beil, the cleverest actor of the Company, had received a call to Gotha. He had therefore, no rival to fear ; Leipzig was the place for him to distinguish himself, he could skilfully conceal his wig under his hair, which had now grown again. How many causes combined to give the passion which he had long cherished, and had only slumbered for a time, the victory over his reason !

He at once acquainted his friends with his resolve to go with the Speich Company to Leipzig. He felt, he said, an irresistible impulse, which would make him unhappy if he tried to suppress it, and yet would hinder him in all his undertakings. He put his reasons with such force and passion that even his friend Neries could say nothing against it, though he had before painted the most attractive pictures of how next spring they would read Klopstock on the Steigerwald.

Reiser now stayed with the actors and took the key of the garden-house back to Professor Springer, giving him a lively description of his misery if he should try to suppress his bent for the Stage. Professor Springer treated him again with the greatest toleration. He advised him to follow his bent, if he found it so irresistible; perhaps this impulse, which had constantly returned to him, meant a real vocation, which he ought not to renounce. But if on the contrary Reiser should find that he was deceived and was not happy in his enterprise, he might in any circumstances come boldly to him again and be sure of his help. Reiser took leave of him with such emotion that he could not utter a word, so deeply was he touched by the man's generosity and indulgence. He reproached himself most bitterly as he went away for not being able to show himself for the moment more worthy of such love and friendship.

When Reiser came to take leave of Dr. Froriep, who already knew of his determination through Neries, he was treated by him with the same indulgence as by his other benefactor, and Dr. Froriep explained that he would not only not dissuade him from his purpose but would even encourage it, if the Stage were already a school of manners as it really might be and ought to be.

But not without reason he added an ironic touch at the end by saying to his little daughter whom he was carrying: ‘ When you are big you will some day hear of the famous actor Reiser, whose name is famous in all Germany! ’ But this well-meant irony had no effect on Reiser, who notwithstanding remembered with deep feeling and bitter self-reproach all that Dr. Froriep had done for him, with a purpose which he was now frustrating. But it now seemed to him a duty of self-preservation to pay no attention to these inward reproaches, because he thought himself firmly convinced that he would be the most miserable of men if he did not follow his bent. But in recent weeks the Speich Company had fallen into extreme poverty for want of receipts. The Director Speich went on alone in advance with the properties to Leipzig, and the rest of the actors had to make provision for themselves, to reach their destination as best they could; some travelled on horseback, others by carriage, others on foot, as their means allowed, for the common purse had long been empty, but in Leipzig they hoped soon to recover ground.

Reiser then took the road on foot the same afternoon that he had said his farewells, and his friend Neries accompanied him on horseback to the first village on the road to Leipzig, where Neries intended to preach the next Sunday.

When they had entered the inn, and had recalled once more the happy scenes they firmly believed they had enjoyed together when they read Klopstock's *Messiah* on the slopes of the Steiger, Reiser went on his way again and Neries accompanied him a good way farther till it was dark. Then they embraced and took leave of one another with much emotion, calling one another 'brother' for the first time. Reiser tore himself away and hurried quickly on, calling to his friend 'Ride back!' When he had gone some distance he looked round again and cried once more 'Good night!' He had no sooner said the words than he thought them odious, and he was vexed whenever he thought of them. For they gave a jar even in memory to the whole scene, for it sounds absurd to say an ordinary 'good night!' to a man, to whom one has said farewell for a long time or it may be for ever, just as if one might pay him a visit again next morning.

It was bitterly cold. But Reiser, without any burden to carry, went forward on his way, accompanied by delightful prospects of fame and applause. Often when he came to rising ground he stood still for a while and looked across the snow-covered fields, while for a moment a strange thought flashed through his mind, as though he saw himself as a stranger walking along there, and his fortunes in the dim distance beyond. But this illusion vanished as soon as it arose, and then, as he went on, he thought how Leipzig would look and in what parts he would appear and so on.

Thus, he traversed the road from Erfurt to Leipzig very pleasantly, and as he walked he often uttered the name of Neries, whom he really loved, and wept violently at the thought until he remembered his absurd 'Good night!' which he could not reconcile with these moving recollections. In Erfurt he had been told that he must go to *The Golden Heart* where the actors always lodged, and had so to say their head-quarters. When he entered the parlour he found a fair number of the Speich Company there, whom he was about to greet as his future colleagues, when he noticed an extraordinary depression in them all, which was soon explained to him when he was given the consoling news that the worthy Director of the Company had sold the properties as soon as he arrived in Leipzig and had absconded with the money. The Speich Company was now a scattered flock.

INDEX

WITH SHORT NOTES

The dates and notes are taken chiefly from *Allgemeine Deutsche Biographie* and Gödeke, *Grundriss zur Geschichte der deutschen Dichtung*: and also from Dr. Hans Henning's edition of *Anton Reiser* and from *Anton Reiser* by Hugo Eybisch. The numbers refer to the pages. O. B. G. V. is the *Oxford Book of German Verse.*